PRAISE FOR *THE LAST GIRL*

'Fast-paced and reading like the script of a movie you really want to see.'
HERALD SUN

'Brings class to teen-lit.'
ROLLING STONE

'Doesn't skimp on smart intrigue or sharp menace ... magnificent.
Bring on the trilogy.'
EMPIRE

'A very different end-of-the-world scenario. Forget vampires and zombies,
thoughts are the refreshing Big Bad in this tense page-turner of a YA series.'
YEN

'An explosive sci-fi thriller, with an original premise and a plot
that reads like an action movie, this book is a mad –
almost literally mad – race to the end.'
THE NEW ZEALAND HERALD

'Gripping and fast-paced, with exciting action scenes.
Danby is a strong and resourceful character.'
BOOKS + PUBLISHING

'Danby is a sharp, witty narrator and the pace is fast. *The Last Girl* has the
potential to be for a new generation of readers what John Marsden's
Tomorrow series was in the 1990s.'
AUSTRALIAN BOOK REVIEW

'Full of pop-culture references, sly humour, out-of-the-blue violence,
and challenges to narrative conventions.'
Kirsten Krauth, author of JUST_A_GIRL

'Danby is Australia's answer to Katniss Everdeen, a kick-ass reluctant
heroine that you just keep rooting for.'
Evie, GOODREADS

'Everyone needs to run out and grab a copy of this
epic book as soon as possible!'
SPECULATING ON SPECFIC

Also by Michael Adams
The Last Girl
The Last Shot

MICHAEL ADAMS

the last place

ALLEN&UNWIN
SYDNEY • MELBOURNE • AUCKLAND • LONDON

This edition published in 2016

First published by Allen & Unwin in 2015

Allen & Unwin – Australia
83 Alexander Street
Crows Nest NSW 2065
Australia
Phone:(61 2) 8425 0100
Email: info@allenandunwin.com
Web: www.allenandunwin.com

Allen & Unwin – UK
Ormond House, 26–27 Boswell Street,
London WC1N 3JZ, UK
Phone: +44 (0) 20 8785 5995
Email: info@murdochbooks.co.uk
Web: www.murdochbooks.co.uk

A Cataloguing-in-Publication entry is available from the
National Library of Australia www.trove.nla.gov.au
A catalogue record for this book is available from the British Library.

ISBN (AUS) 978 1 76029 341 3
ISBN (UK) 978 1 74336 895 4

Cover and internal design by i2i Design
Cover and internal word web © Marika Järv, 2015
Cover photography: (girl) by Christopher Phillips Photography, model Alissa Dinallo; (explosion) by iStockphoto.com
Cover and internal images (flames, bush, helicopters) by iStockphoto.com
Internal images (icons, thumbprint) by Shutterstock
Set in 11.5/18.5pt Minion by Midland Typesetters, Australia
Printed in Australia by McPherson's Printing Group

10 9 8 7 6 5 4 3 2 1

For Clare and Ava

To whom it may condemn:
If you're reading this I'm dead.
But I'm not over. I'm just starting.
I used our time apart well. Was initiated by
a master whose knowledge dwarfs your own.
Acquired powers that only reach exaltation
when the soul flees the physical body.
I curse you to wander amid the bones. I curse
you to be haunted in mind and dream. I curse
you to be without light or love.
Everything evil ends.

I await.
Vade Satana

Draco maledicte adjuramus te
Terribilis Deus

1
gimme
shelter

ONE

That's me sprawled dead in the street, beneath the brown sky, amid dry bodies and dusty cars. Under mirrored sunglasses and a tangle of platinum hair my face is sour green and rippled with sludgy ridges. My jeans are dank. A rat gnaws at sausage loops that spill from the sodden sweatshirt that covers the flak jacket with my letter to Jack sewn inside it. I stink something fierce and flies buzz in and out of the sticky fluids and grey meat. In one arm I cradle a tablet with a shiny blank screen. My other arm stretches out and ends in the corn-chip bag I was raiding when I died. I'm just another corpse now. Billions like me. Nothing to see here.

A breeze lifts litter along the street. Rattles the packet against my wrist, fans wisps of hair against my cheek. That same wind carries mechanical sounds. Engines. Louder. Nearer.

The tablet screen lights up. It's 12.51 p.m. April first. Exactly three months since I set out from Shadow Valley to kill Jack. A video window shows two motorbikes following the stretched ribbon of bitumen that leads into town. Jeans and boots, flak jackets and helmets. Assault rifles on their shoulders.

I blink a fly from the corner of my eye. As far as I can see, the outriders are the same searchers I saw from my mountain yesterday. But it doesn't matter if they're not. Whoever they are, they'll do.

Their visors scan the cow paddocks—left, right, back again, robotically steady as they rumble towards town. Just as they reach the last rise, they slow their rides. Bingo: they've seen the flattened weeds and gleaming plastic in the paddock just off the road.

They stop, dismount in unison and study the drone wreckage. One rider gazes at the splayed propeller blades and crumpled nose. His offsider wades through grass to a section of white wing. They walk together to the long tube of fuselage. They must see the bullet holes. Maybe even smoke or steam from its cracked innards. By now it has to be obvious that the little aircraft didn't crash because of a malfunction, that someone shot it out of the sky not fifteen minutes ago. And it stands to reason that whoever was responsible is—or very recently was—in the town of Baroonah that's just a little farther along the road. The very same settlement where grey smoke curls from a brick chimney among the western rooftops.

That the bikers don't lift their visors to look at each other says a lot. These guys don't need to make eye contact any more than they need to reach for radios to tell their comrades farther afield what they've found. They're as much remotely controlled

as the destroyed plane they've just inspected. They're Jack's—
or Jacks—however it works now.

Back on their motorbikes, the Jacks roar down the road,
disappear off the bottom of the tablet screen. Snarling and
barking from the other side of the pub is met by the crackling
of gunfire and followed by pitiful whimpering. The bastards
keep shooting, sending surviving mongrels galloping along
the main street, bounding over bodies and thumping through
shop doorways. When the dogs are gone, the outriders appear
in my peripheral vision, straddling their bikes as they rumble
into town. Baroonah used to have a population of two hundred
and six. Now it's three. Me and these bikers. Two if you want to
get technical: me and Jack.

The tiniest twitch of my finger shows me a better tablet view
of the riders as they kill their engines and set their machines
on kickstands outside the pub. The Jacks dismount with mirror
movements, remove their helmets, reach rifles from their
shoulders. Both are men. One tall, one wide. In their previous
lives maybe an accountant and a teacher or maybe a waiter
and a truckie. No way to know. Gangly and Stocky each have
grown-out hair and thick beards now. They look like the bikies
they've been forced to play.

I need to imprint every little detail. I'm recording it but
the tablet's hard drive's just a backup and something to show
the others. Memory's better than video. Takes hold deeper.
Becomes part of you.

Gangly and Stocky have no panniers or backpacks on
their bikes. They're travelling light, eating and sleeping in the

houses of the dead, each carrying an AR-15. I'm guessing their little shoulder bags are for a few extra ammo clips and maybe some grenades. These two have been equipped to fight and kill but they're not carrying enough hardware to win against a larger enemy. They're not so much soldiers as they are human tripwires. Cannon fodder: that's what expendables like this are called in the military books that've been by bedtime—and daytime—reading these past couple of months.

Stocky stops, looks at his boot, picks off a little white ball and sniffs it. Gangly bends and examines another little clump a few feet along the road. The chewie he's found is still sticky. Hasn't had time to dry out. Stocky retrieves a torn gum packet from the gutter. It's the same brand Jack left at my bedside that first morning in Parramatta.

A plastic Santa watches Gangly and Stocky step over gnawed human remains and between derelict cars. Moving slowly, boots crunching broken glass, they peer into the shadows of the town's few shops. Nothing moves in the deli, bank, newsagency or health food store. Reefs of grass have erupted through cracked bitumen and cobwebs criss-cross verandahs. All that's missing is a tumbleweed.

I bet Stocky and Gangly have seen a lot of places like Baroonah. Every coastal and country town their kind is searching right now probably looks like this. But a drone shot out of the sky? The same place my chewing gum is found? That's got to be a strong lead. Stronger, say, than the marine flare exploding out of a burning yacht that their comrades in consciousness are investigating farther up the coast.

A tiny swipe returns the tablet screen to blank. As the outriders close in on where I lie, getting bigger through my tinted sunglasses, I lock the air in my lungs and the muscles in my limbs. Splayed here: it's the third time I've played dead since the Snap on Christmas Day, when everyone went bonkers and started reading everyone else's minds. My first two efforts didn't work out well at all. Nearly got killed by the Party Duder. Got shot by Jack. But both those times I was the hunted. Now I'm the hunter.

Stocky glances at the bodies around him. For a moment his eyes find my face and I see his lips moving as if in silent prayer. My blood cools because I don't know what this means. My finger tightens ever so slightly on the trigger of my .45. Then he turns his attention to where Gangly stares—farther down the road to the other side of the intersection. That's where businesses give way to houses. That's where smoke rises from the chimney of a mansion on a leafy corner block. That's where whatever trouble they're going to face will be.

As they get closer, I hear my prey breathing loudly in unison. In, out, in, out, like a couple of gun-toting yoga freaks. But there's something else. They're whispering. *Shit.* Jacks don't need to talk. Not with their whole hivemind thing. These two could be Specials—rare people like me whose minds can't be read and who can't be controlled by Jack. Or they could be more of my newly discovered Normals—the few who didn't experience the telepathy at all. Maybe I've screwed up here big time. But if they're not Jacks my little show with the drone's gonna bring the real deal soon enough and—

I strain to hear. Realise Stocky and Gangly aren't conversing. They're muttering in tandem. Like crazed cultists droning some weird prayer. I wonder whether they've been so freaked out by everything that this is how they cope. But my skin prickles as they get close enough for me to make out the words.

'She could've been the one bearer of make her pay can't be let her go gotta make him then we it'll just be . . .'

Rat scurries up inside my sweatshirt with a *scree-scree-scree* and her little body quivers against my gooseflesh.

They don't react to Rat's noise. Rodents feeding on bodies is commonplace. I don't take much notice of them these days and they've gotten so bold they don't even run from me. But my Rat is reacting to these guys. Like the dogs trying to defend Baroonah, like Lachie the cockatoo who warned me about Minions, like the chimpanzee who attacked more of them in the darkness of the housing estate, Rat senses their wrongness. And it's all the evidence I need.

'Die she's gotta be dead gone,' they mutter as their shadows fall across me, 'but to see and pay, Danby must know why and where she was wrong . . .'

On they go, stepping carefully, babbling quietly, closing in on the mansion. I tilt my head slightly. Gangly and Stocky have their backs to me. I don't need to take a deep steadying breath. I don't need to count to three. I just stand in a fluid movement and Rat's little claws dig into my shoulder and she squeaks more insistently.

Scree-scree-scree-scree!

Gangly stiffens, sensing movement, before his head shatters in a crimson thunderclap. Another blast sends Stocky falling forwards through a red shower. Gunshots echo as the Jacks topple. Arms and legs twitch. Then they're still. Bodies twisted together. Blood commingling on the bitumen. The corn-chip packet smoking and shrivelling in green flames beside them.

I stand over the men, .45 in one hand, tablet in the other. I don't need to feel for weak pulses or listen for struggling respiration. Their faces will be mostly exit wound. That's because I've used a knife to carve crosses in the lead points of each round in my pistol. Dum-dums: that's what the military manuals call the style of bullet. Also known as: hollow point. Goes in small. Fragments as it penetrates. Creates a helluva mess inside and then comes out huge. Using them was a war crime. That was before. This is a war but no crime. It's a public service. These guys are dead. But I didn't kill them. They died months ago. What I've done is set them free. Eliminated more Jacks from the world.

I tuck the pistol into my jeans, pull off my wig and throw it under a car. I catch my reflection in a dark shop window. I've worked out so much in the last few months that I've lost all my soft edges, all that's left is lean and hard. I'm a shadow of what I used to be. My outline's not even broken by hair. I palm a spray of sweat off my stubbled scalp, fingers tracing the hard scar along the side of my head where one of Jack's bullets nearly did to me what I just did to two of him. Shaking off the strange feeling of no longer being sure I exist, I open the car door to grab my AK-47 and backpack.

Rat pops out of my sweatshirt. I stroke her nose as I turn full circle, looking from my tablet to the town, one last chance to check before the rest of the Jacks arrive.

TWO

'I'm sorry,' I said.

What was left of my little brother had his hands raised in surrender as Jack made him cackle wildly. My rifle muzzle was pressed to the back of his skull, finger curling around the trigger. Evan, wherever he was, wouldn't feel a thing. Nathan was at the edge of my vision, hands threading at his waist, like he was trying to . . . take off his pants.

What the f—

Focus. Breathe in. Out. Squeeze the trigger. Don't pull.

'Safety's on,' Nathan whispered, close by me now.

My eyes dipped and in a speedy blur Nathan knocked the barrel away from Evan's head and used his looped belt to lasso my little brother's wrists and yank him off his feet.

Nathan spun around, Evan kicking like a snared animal, as I recovered and trained the gun on them.

'Put him down,' I shouted. 'I need to do this.'

'Danby, you don't,' Nathan snapped, dark eyes as fierce as I'd seen them. 'You don't.'

I stepped towards him, sighting down the rifle at Evan's heart. To anyone else it'd look like Nathan was hiding behind a little boy. But I knew what he was counting on—that if I fired I risked the bullet going through my little brother and into him. I'd kill them both with one shot.

'Let him go,' I said.

I looked at Evan's face, split into a leering grin, eyes wide with Jack's delight.

'Nathan,' I said. 'Now.'

He shook his head, hoisted Evan higher, taking a pummelling from his thrashing legs. 'You can't kill him.'

I didn't know what Nathan meant. That I couldn't kill my own flesh and blood? That I couldn't kill Jack? Both maybe.

'Yes, you can,' Evan said cheerfully, little face beaming. 'Do it, Danby.'

'Don't,' Nathan said, hauling Evan back with him towards the Courthouse's open door. 'You can't.'

'Stop,' I said.

Evan's expression turned in a heartbeat. His bottom lip quivered. Tears spilled down his cheeks. 'Don't hurt,' he pleaded in a watery voice. 'Scared, Danby!'

Heart shredding, blinking burning eyes, I tried to maintain my aim as I stepped after them.

'Don't do it,' Nathan yelled. 'He wants to fuck you up. Don't.'

Evan's mouth contorted into a leer. 'She kills me, she kills me not,' he said merrily. 'She kills me, she kills—'

'Shut up!' I yelled. His eyes bulged and he grinned tightly, like he was holding back a tsunami of laughter.

I tore my stare from him and saw Nathan's calm certainty. Jack was goading me to kill my little brother. But Nathan was risking his life to stop me.

I screamed at the sky. Jabbed the gun at them both like a spear. Then lowered my rifle. Followed it down to the lawn in a heap.

'You're too good to me,' Evan said, twisting on the end of Nathan's belt. 'Really, you—'

Nathan clamped a hand over his mouth. 'Like she said, shut u—aaaaah.'

His eyes widened in pain. Blood spilled from his palm and down Evan's shirt. But he didn't let my brother go as he dragged him biting and kicking into the Courthouse.

I looked across the lawn to our friend and comrade Tajik, dead where Evan had stabbed him. Slumped against the stone wall that overlooked Samsara. The blood oozing from his knife wounds would still be warm. Smoke rose from the valley where we'd blown a chopper out of the sky and killed a dozen of Jack's goons. My eyes drifted to the Rainbow Arms Hotel where I had left Jack's mangled body just minutes ago. I struggled to grasp how it'd all gone wrong so quickly. I tried to understand how it could be that death hadn't stopped Jack. How he could still be in Evan—and in the rest of the Minions. I couldn't get my head around any of it.

What I knew was they'd be on top of us soon. Evan had said so. Men and women on motorbikes and in helicopters. All of them somehow still *him*. All of them wanting to kill me and Nathan. And I'd die taking down as many of them as I could.

15

Inside the Courthouse Evan was wailing with laughter. A heavy toilet cell door shut with a *clunk* followed by the *thunk* of an exterior bolt sliding into place. The noises seemed far away, like they were cutting in from a parallel universe. Drawers rattling. Cupboards slamming. Nathan urging me to find car keys. It made no sense to me.

Click went the clip of the assault rifle as I ejected it to check how many bullets remained. Seven. Seven rounds weren't going to get me many of them. I shouldered the weapon and picked up Tajik's assault rifle from beside his body. Checked his clip. Empty. He had fired everything he had to cripple the second chopper and send it retreating down the valley. By emptying his weapon he'd saved our lives twice because if there'd been bullets left I'm sure Jack would've used my little brother to blow us away.

I wiped my eyes furiously, tried to see and think straight.

Get down to the chopper crash site. Salvage guns and bullets from the dead Minions. That's what we had to do. Except the enemy would be on top of us before we had time to stage our last stand.

'Danby?' Nathan stood in the doorway, hand wrapped in a tea towel, the backpack slung over his shoulder.

'Get it together?' he said, voice higher than usual, raised like his eyebrows. 'Let's get some guns?'

He nodded back inside the house. 'Let's get a car and—'

He cut himself short, like he'd just realised Evan could hear every word and relay it to Jack.

'Crap, sorry,' he stage whispered, still loud enough for Evan to hear inside the Courthouse. Nathan pointed to the dense bush rising behind the building, made a walking motion with two fingers.

I had seven bullets against maybe one thousand Jacks. Staying here wasn't putting up a fight. It was letting him kill me. But leaving Evan like this after everything we'd done to try to save him? It seemed worse than a final futile firefight. I couldn't move. I felt like the earth had grown up through me. Wouldn't let me leave.

'Danby?'

I shook my head, whispered, 'I can't.'

He hurried over to me, crouched on his haunches. I flinched when he went to touch my arm.

'It's okay,' he said, withdrawing his hand. 'But you can't help him. Not now. Not like this. We have to go.'

I looked at Nathan. Nodded dumbly. Managed to get to my feet. As we crept away from the Courthouse, Evan's taunting laughter rang in my ears.

We stopped and rested on a rocky ledge near the top of the ridge, hidden by trees rising steeply from the hill we'd just climbed. Between leaves and branches, Samsara was spread out beneath us. Nathan handed me a water bottle from the backpack. I took a few sips and passed it back. He showed me a rectangle of tourist map where a thin brown line twisted through an enormity of green.

'This,' he said softly, 'is the Great North Road. If we can make it there, it'll get us to the Central Coast.'

My mind wasn't with Nathan on the ridge and I wasn't skipping ahead to any escape route. I was still back on the

Courthouse lawn, face to face with Evan, his eyes not connected to his soul but to Jack's, his little hand holding the bloodied knife he'd used to stab Tajik. Our friend's death was on us. On *me*—it'd been my plan. We hadn't even buried Tajik, said a prayer, anything. We'd just left him there like a bag of rubbish. Tajik dying like that. Me leaving Evan. Our failure—my failure—was complete. The Wonder Woman bracelet—a gift from Mum, retrieved from Jack—glinted on my wrist. I didn't deserve to wear it. I slipped the bracelet off and let it drop into the trees below the outcrop.

Nathan looked at me. Didn't say anything.

'How did Evan get out,' I asked dully, 'if Tajik locked him in a room?'

'I think I know what he did.' Nathan swallowed hard, fluttered the map.

'What?'

'Every room had this map—and a pen and letterhead for guests. Tajik locked the bedroom door but he left the key in the lock. Evan spread the map under the door, poked the key out of the keyhole with the pen, caught it on the map and dragged it back under. The map was still on the floor in the doorway.' Nathan wiped a tear from his cheek. 'Poor Tajik. He—'

'Died because of me.'

Nathan wiped his eyes. 'Don't think like that.'

'Why not?'

'You—we—couldn't know. Everything we knew pointed to Jack's control ending . . . I mean, Danby, you killed him.'

Apparently not. I laughed bitterly. Angrily rubbed tears from my cheeks.

'Danby, come here,' Nathan said, opening his arms to me. But that moment we'd shared on the bed just down the hill a few hours ago seemed like it'd happened to different people in the distant past. Now I felt numb. Dead. I shook my head.

Nathan nodded, lowered his eyes and arms. Unwrapped the tea towel. Blood welled from my brother's teeth marks in his hand.

'Is it bad?' I asked.

Nathan re-wrapped his hand. 'It'll be fine.'

'You should've let me kill him.'

Nathan closed his eyes, pinched the bridge of his nose, like he was trying to concentrate before he looked at me again. 'We don't know whether Jack's in him for good. Until then there's still—'

'Hope?' I spat.

Nathan's face went slack.

Feeling was coming back in me. Rage. Burning rage.

'I could've set Evan free,' I said. 'You should've let me.'

Nathan's mouth opened but he didn't say anything more than my name.

'See?' I said, looking away from him and down into the valley. 'Now they're coming to take him.'

A handful of motorbikes were rumbling into Samsara along the road from Wisemans Ferry. They didn't slow as they passed the smouldering carcass of the black helicopter and the dozen burned and blown-up bodies. I got flashes of the bikers through the trees and buildings as they passed the antique store and hippie pub where Jack's body lay like a skin a snake had shed. They headed for the bridge. They needed to cross it to get to this side of the valley and follow the road we'd presumably taken north.

'We need to go,' Nathan said quietly.

'Not yet.'

The five Minions on motorbikes stopped behind the hatchback blocking the bridge. To get past they would have to roll the car out of the way. Syncopated little soldiers, they climbed off their bikes, four lining up along the back ready to push, while the other one walked around to the driver's side door to release the handbrake and steer.

I heard Nathan swallow. 'Danby, we have to—'

'I want to see this.'

We'd anticipated we might face motorbikes as well as choppers. So we'd used the first big barbecue cylinder we'd taken down the hill from the Courthouse to booby trap the hatchback. Wrapped it in a blanket in the cargo space. Opened the gas valve up and closed all the windows. Taped matches inside the driver's side doorframe.

The lead Minion lifted the car's door handle and pulled.

I hoped the Jack inside him heard the scratch of phosphorus and saw the spark in the moment before the centre of the bridge disappeared in a dirty orange flash. A shockwave blasted up through the gritty air as the explosive roar cracked and rumbled along the valley. Back in Samsara, the next wave of motorbikes skidded to a halt as their riders stared at the fist the smoke made as it punched up into the sky.

I smiled. The five Minions were atoms and the bridge ruined. No road vehicles would make it to this side of the valley for a while.

'We've got to go,' Nathan said urgently. 'Come on.'

Without waiting for me, he crept off between sandstone crags and gum trees. I didn't move, just watched him picking his way towards the top of the ridge. Then I turned, looked back down at the Courthouse roof far below. Pictured Evan in that cell. Waiting for others like him. Part of the hivemind. I shrugged the rifle from my shoulder. Aimed it at the corrugated iron. Wondered if I could shoot through the roof and hit him. Knew I couldn't.

Instead, I swung my gun up at a distant clump of Jacks on the other side of Samsara. There were a dozen or so moving cautiously on foot and glancing around uncertainly with their weapons. They didn't look so confident after the bridge booby trap. Like any of the cars or houses in this little town might be rigged to explode. Like they didn't want to be the next to die. I hoped that inside each of them Jack retained some instinctive fear of pain and suffering and death. Because that's what I was going to send his way every chance I had. Surely the filthy parasite had to die if he ran out of host bodies. From now on I'd make my life about that. I wanted him to know what he'd pushed me to become and what he'd forever be up against.

The Jacks advancing into Samsara were mostly men but it was one of the women who stood out. Blue-haired hippie chick in a tie-dye T-shirt. I recognised her from the NiteRite in Penrith Plaza. Back then she'd been in limbo on IVs that Tajik had tended. She looked like the sort of person who would never have picked up a gun. But Jack had raised her up and put an assault rifle in her hands so she could stalk through Samsara as part of the army sent to kill me and Nathan.

There was no breeze. Hippie chick was maybe two hundred metres away. Within the rifle's range as Oscar had explained it to me in that grandstand in Richmond. If I aimed for her face at least when gravity dropped the bullet—

'Danby?' Nathan's voice floated down from above and behind me. 'What're you—'

Crack!

Bloody mist sprayed out of hippie chick's T-shirt and she collapsed onto the road.

Not dead. *Free.*

The gunshot echoed every which way, sending Jack's muzzle monkeys scrambling for cover, faces and weapons whirling wildly at the shadowy mountains all around them.

I kept low as I crept up the hill towards Nathan. The look in his eyes—it was like he didn't recognise me.

THREE

I'm in a cellar beneath a farmhouse that was wrecked by fire long before the rest of the world went up in flames. On the outskirts of Baroonah, it's only a few blocks from where I shot the two Jacks dead in the main street. Although I'm about to be in the middle of occupied territory I feel safe. Safer at least than the last time I took refuge down a black hole.

The Jacks are about to tear Baroonah apart. But there's nothing above my head worth investigating. The farmhouse's red brickwork is charred and collapsed and the carbonised rafters lie crashed across each other like big burnt matchsticks. Sprigs of bog grevillea and spotted gum saplings push out from the muddy ashes. A scorched sheet of corrugated metal that I dragged into place behind me covers the cellar opening at the top of the stairs.

Now I've been bunkered down a few minutes, I switch on a little flashlight and quickly strip off my disgusting clothes. I use wet wipes to clean my skin of the sticky goo and pull on my camouflage gear and lace up my combat boots.

Rat sits on my backpack, a chocolate bar in her little paws.

'Good work back there,' I say.

I switch off the torch and nestle in a dusty beanbag that's tucked behind cobwebbed furniture at the far end of my underground lair. Cold brick wall at my back. All my tools within reach: .45 pistol, AK-47 assault rifle, a dozen hand grenades, three hundred rounds of assorted ammunition. What more does a girl need? Well, actually, my straight razor. And mine's in my breast pocket. If they find me I'll kill as many of them as I can before opening my throat ear to ear. From what I've read, gravity will dump the blood from my head immediately and I'll be dead in seconds.

Hiding out here is a big gamble. I could've been ten kilometres north by now, off a fire trail amid the grey acacia, quad bike covered under netting and me all but invisible in my camouflage yowie suit that makes me look like part of the bush. But then I wouldn't know whether my plan had worked.

I check my watch. It's just gone 1 p.m. I've been awake for over thirty hours. I crack a bottle of electrolytes and wash down another Dexie. It's the fourth one I've had since I woke up. At this stage the little amphetamine pills still have me as sharp as my razor. But I know by this time tonight I'll be fraying at the seams and need to sleep.

I click my tablet on and stare into its glare. The screen's gridded into dozens of smaller windows, each relaying a different 'Cameleon' view of Baroonah and the roads leading into and out of the town. Each little spy camera is no bigger than a fingernail and nanofinished so it'll mimic the colour and texture of whatever you attach it to—hence the name. I've stuck Cameleons everywhere in Baroonah. On the sign that bears the town's name and its Aboriginal meaning. On the granite war memorial in the park opposite the bank. On shops and cars. On the brick mansion's letterbox and its verandah and up in the oak tree that commands a view of its front yard. I stuck one in the darkest part of an oil portrait over the fireplace where books and papers now burn. Placed more in the main bedroom and upstairs bathroom and rambling backyard.

If any of the Jacks are using Bluetooth and my signals are intercepted I'll be screwed because it'll be obvious whoever's watching has to be nearby. But from what I saw of Gangly and Stocky just a few minutes ago, and from what I saw of the Jacks farther up the coast yesterday, I'm pretty sure they're still way beyond needing technology to share information and images.

Pinching open a video rectangle, I zoom in for a closer look at the centre of town. A dog licks at the blood and brains gleaming around Stocky and Gangly. Another one slurps up the sausage guts I left behind. Good for you, Fidos. Avenge your buddies. Get fresh meals into the deal. The rest of the town is still and quiet.

It's been eleven minutes since I shot those two Jacks. Feels like longer. But time plays tricks now. Shortening. Lengthening. Like it's become elastic because there's not enough people left to pin it down. I'm still sixteen for a few more months. But I feel twice that age. Christmas Day and the Snap seem like they happened a thousand years ago. But hanging with Mum and playing chess and listening to records could've been this morning—her and her place seem so close I could almost reach out and—

No need to think about that.

Nearly getting caught out in Baroonah by the drone was a stroke of luck. Initially I'd thought I'd need to set a big fire to bring the riders in from the coast and get them where I wanted them. After working through the night and morning to set up the mansion and cams, I concluded that torching the pub was probably my best bet at getting their attention quickly. The Empire Hotel, on the edge of town, would be my blazing beacon. I hoped the inferno would be visible from Crowdy Head or however far north they'd gone from there. If they didn't come, I'd fire a flare. It would look more suspicious but I knew they'd investigate it.

Half an hour ago I'd been in an upstairs guest room at The Empire, about to splash petrol over the antique furniture, when I nearly shat myself at the shadow rippling across the sky behind the gauzy curtains. Easing low through the French doors and crouching behind a wrought-iron balcony, I spied a drone circling over the edge of town. It was bigger than the ones Jack had been using in Clearview. They'd looked like overgrown model airplanes. This one was white, stealthy, powered by silent propellers, with a bulbous nose I assumed housed cameras to scan the landscape.

I'd been as careful as I could with my travel and setting up. Rode my quad bike on bush trails and back roads with night-vision goggles. Did my outdoor preparation and house searches in Baroonah during the darkest hours. Worked the mansion's rooms after dawn. Yet if the drone had flown over the town even a few minutes earlier it would've busted me siphoning petrol from a dusty car for my act of arson.

Now I was trapped until it left. But watching it coming closer to the centre of town, I realised the little airplane was exactly what I needed. A downed drone would work so much better than a burning pub. The Jacks at its controls would see its sudden demise and want to investigate ay-sap.

'Revise your stand, improvise a plan, pulverise the Man' wasn't advice from Mum's art journal but a motto from *Agile, Mobile, Hostile*, another literary treasure from my recently acquired survivalist library.

Crouching on the balcony, chewing gum, I watched as the drone cruised low over the street and banked east towards cow country. I popped up and fired five rounds at its retreating silhouette. Months of target practice meant I didn't waste a bullet. The aircraft shredded in a cloud of plastic and smoke and went into a fast and fatal spiral.

If my guesses were right the Jack network would alert the outriders at Crowdy Head to their spy plane's abrupt crash and they'd be revving this way in minutes. I tore down the stairs, bolted from the pub and along the street, streaked through the intersection and up the mansion's front stairs into the living room.

I scooped Rat from the mantelpiece and bent to light the brochures, books and maps I'd arranged in the fireplace. Sparking a match and fanning the flames got it going with a *whoosh*. On hands and knees, I checked to make sure the artfully crisped page from a Dubbo guidebook was still in place under the coffee table.

Outside, under the cover of the oak's remaining brown leaves, I changed into jeans and a sweatshirt and stowed my camo gear in my backpack. I lathered my face with green mud mask like that woman in Clearview who I'd thought was dead because she'd crashed out during her beauty regime. I'd mixed coffee dregs and red wine and rose fertiliser in a plastic bag and I rubbed this thick and stinky goo into my cheeks and daubed it over my jeans and sweatshirt. I tugged the platinum wig over my crew-cut and checked myself in a little compact mirror. I looked like death. Smelt like it, too.

Back in the middle of the town, I slid the backpack and AK-47 under a car. Popped open the can of sausages and smeared them around myself. Put a corn-chip bag over the .45 in my outstretched hand. Clutched the tablet in the crook of my other arm. Then I lay in wait.

'Go on, Rat,' I said. She scampered off my shoulder and sat happily feasting on my fake innards as flies descended.

I looked like just another person who'd crashed out gorging on fast food and digital distraction. Maybe a little better preserved than most but my green face and mushy body weren't completely out of the ordinary. From barely rotting to bleached skeletons, I saw people in radically different states of decay every day. At first I'd thought it was simply the varying weather conditions that caused the disparate rates of decomposition. But lately I'd wondered whether it was diet. It'd make sense that organic vegans would return to the nitrogen cycle quicker than their fast-food-loving cousins whose bodies had been filled with preservatives.

Ever since I'd seen the outriders in Crowdy Head, I'd known I'd need to do this up close and personal. Even as good as I'd gotten with my AK-47, I couldn't guarantee killing them cleanly with split-second headshots that'd ensure they didn't know who or what had hit them. It had to be a mystery. Something for Jack to piece together. Him owning it, feeling smart and superior, would be what'd sell him on the rest of the story.

It's 1.07 p.m. when I see movement via the Cameleon I ran up the flagpole attached to our fading national flag. A camouflage-patterned military chopper. Speeding low over the countryside from the south. Looks like an ARH Tiger. The ARH stands for Armed Reconnaissance Helicopter. In addition to whatever weapons its occupants carry, this predator comes loaded with powerful miniguns. The wall vibrates against my spine as the Tiger and its hateful hum bear down on Baroonah.

FOUR

'Down there,' Nathan said, panting and pointing into the valley. 'Can we rest?'

We'd picked our way down the other side of the mountain from Samsara, followed a dry creek along a shaded gully, pushed ourselves up through brush and boulders to another ridge, dashed over its peak and lost ourselves in a dizzying maze of shining gum trees growing from honeycombed sandstone.

Now we were on the last slope into another dark gulch whose shadows seemed as likely to embrace us as smother us. I locked my arm around a sapling, steadying myself against tumbling into the darkness, and looked back up to where Nathan was clinging to his own slender tree.

'Yeah,' I called. 'For a minute.'

Sweat stung my eyes and salted my lips. Walls of eucalyptus and rock towered around us under the densely smudged brown sky. No choppers yet. But that could change in a heartbeat. I reckoned we'd only put a few kilometres between us and

Samsara. At least we'd be hard to spot, at the bottom of this crack in the earth.

I adjusted the rifle on my shoulder, lowered my centre of gravity, continued the slipping and sliding of my controlled descent.

Nathan caught up to me under a rock overhang. I passed him his half of a bottle of water.

We stood, catching our breath, scanning all around, eyes wide open for any flash of movement or colour.

'See anything?' he said.

'You'd be the first person I'd tell.'

'How far do you think we've come?'

'Not far enough.' I reached for the empty water bottle. 'Turn around.'

'Why?' Nathan said it too sharply. I saw wariness flicker in his eyes. Anger sparked in me. Did he think I was going to shoot him?

'Why?' I snapped. 'Because we don't want to leave plastic lying around for them to find.'

Nathan nodded sheepishly, let me take the water bottle and turned his back to me. I yanked open his pack, crumpled the bottle in among the stuff he'd taken from the Courthouse after he'd locked Evan in the toilet cell. We had baked beans, tinned fish, a bag of sultanas and a few packets of ginger biscuits. Four more bottles of water. Flashlight and a first-aid kit. It wasn't much.

Nathan rocked on his feet as I fossicked.

'What're you doing?'

That suspicious tone again. I let out an angry sigh.

'Stocktake,' I said, zipping the backpack closed.

Nathan faced me. 'I grabbed everything I could. We've got enough food for a few days. It's maybe ten more kilometres like this to the Great North Road.'

'And then?'

His eyes limped away from mine. 'Fifty kilometres to the first town.'

Five. Fifty. Five hundred. It didn't matter. We'd never make it. Not through this terrain. Not this sore and exhausted. Besides, any second now we were going to be shot by snipers up on a ridge or by gunmen leaning out of a chopper roaring over an escarpment. Right then I wanted to just wait and make the most of the remaining six bullets. Five for them. One for me. Or four for them and two for us.

'What?' Nathan said, face weary and worried.

I'd been staring at him.

'Are you all right?' he pressed.

That snapped me out of it. 'Am I all right? You're seriously asking that?'

'It's just you . . .'

'I just what?'

'Shot that woman,' he said softly. 'For nothing.'

'She wasn't a woman and it wasn't for nothing. It was—'

What *had* it been for? To show Jack I could be as brutal with him as he'd been with me? To make up for not being able to put my little brother out of his misery?

'Was what?' he asked.

'To set her free.'

Nathan's eyes dipped for a moment to the assault rifle in my hands. His frown, the downward set of his mouth—they reminded me of how he'd looked in Parramatta just after he'd nail-gunned the Party Duder and thought I was going to reach for my attacker's dropped .45. Like he was afraid he'd made a mistake by saving me. Like he was unsure if I was going to turn on him.

'You want to carry it?' I said, holding the rifle out to him.

Nathan shook his head. 'No, it's okay, we just need to—'

'To what?'

'I was going to say "relax".'

I let out a snort. 'Relax?'

'I meant ... between us. Look, I'm sorry. About Evan. About everything.'

'None of it's your fault. But you can't fix any of it either.'

'I know but—'

'I'm done talking,' I said. 'Let's go.'

He nodded curtly and brushed past me. I'd made him angry. Good. I didn't want to be the only one whose blood was boiling.

We were halfway up the next rise when a *thwocka-thwocka* escalated from nowhere, echoing down off canyon walls and up out of the valleys. I didn't know where it was coming from, where it'd appear in the sky.

I dropped beside a log. Nathan made himself small by the base of a tree. There wasn't nearly enough cover under the canopy of straggly gums. I squiggled around in the mulch to get the assault rifle off my shoulder.

Nathan's eyes were frantic. He had a hand up telling me to freeze.

He was right. The afternoon had grown deep and dark. We'd be hard to spot if we stayed still. But some Jack with sharp eyes might see us as more than shadows. Some Jack with infrared goggles might see us as heat signatures. No way I was getting a bullet in the back. I rolled over, faced the sky, weapon across my chest.

The chopper veered into view. Off to the south. Red and yellow. The same one Jack used to fly Tregan and Gary around. They weren't up there now. We'd have been able to tune their thoughts long before we heard the chopper. Instead the bird would be bristling with spotters and snipers. All Jacks.

If it came overhead they'd be dead—or we would be.

It'd likely be the latter. I didn't think I could shoot the chopper down with six bullets. But I'd give it a red-hot go. The safety was off. My finger was on the trigger.

The chopper dipped over the other side of the mountain and its thunder receded. When it was quiet again, I sat up as Nathan crept over. He blinked at me, hand trembling as he wiped sweat from his forehead.

I wondered where the other Nathan had gone. The one who'd killed the Party Duder. The one who'd pulled a gun on Jack's Minions in that taxi and taken a bullet through the chest. The one who in the early hours of today had singlehandedly taken out a black helicopter with his assault rifle. The one who had helped me bring down another chopper and kill a dozen Minions.

'What's wrong with you?' I said.

'What?'

'You're so afraid all of a sudden.'

Nathan looked at me like I was crazy. 'There's hundreds or maybe thousands of armed people after us—'

'It's been like that for days.'

'And I've been afraid the whole time. The difference is then it felt like we had a fighting chance of getting away. Now it feels like—'

'Like?'

'We can't outrun them,' he said. 'Not now.'

I heard what he really meant. We'd had a chance to escape. If the Jacks had believed what Evan had heard about us escaping in a car then their numbers would've at least been dispersed more widely. But since I'd taken it upon myself to shoot one of them they knew we were on foot.

'We can't outrun them but you also don't want to take them on?' I asked.

'I don't want to die for nothing.'

Nathan's eyes were hard and his mouth a tight line. He wasn't afraid of fighting—he was afraid that I wanted to do it so recklessly.

'We can't run and we can't fight,' I said. 'Then what?'

'I don't know, Danby.'

I gazed at the valley we'd crawled out of and the ridge looming up ahead. I remembered what I'd seen of the map. Samsara sat as a little dot by a thread of river. All around were topological ripples of green and brown. Bush and mountains radiated in every direction for dozens and dozens of kilometres.

'There's a thousand square miles of bush,' I said. 'They won't find us.'

Nathan stared at me. 'Sooner or later, they will.'

I didn't know what the hell he wanted me to say. 'Well, we either stay or go. Simple enough.'

He shrugged and stood.

I forced myself up after him, legs aching more with every step.

It was almost dark when we dragged ourselves to the floor of the next valley. We weren't alone. Blurred people slipped off the creek path just ahead of us. Melted right into the sandstone walls.

'Did you see that?' I hissed.

'What?' Nathan said, turning around, face framed by ferns.

'Listen,' I rasped.

I couldn't see the people anymore. But I could hear them. Murmuring. Conferring. *Conspiring.* I pushed past Nathan and swung the rifle at the shadows. 'Come out, you bastards.'

Nathan stiffened at my shoulder. 'Danby, there's no one.'

I strained to see and hear. The only movement and noise was the cry of cockatoos flapping lazily through the dusk.

'I thought I—' My voice was raw, my throat thick and sore. My head felt soft but spiky. A sponge filled with needles.

'No one,' Nathan said, coming around me with a bottle of water. 'Here, I'll swap you.'

I lowered the gun. He took it gently. Handed me the drink. As soon as the water touched my tongue I started to guzzle.

'Slow down,' he whispered, pulling it free. 'Take it easy.'

I pushed away from Nathan, leaned against a boulder, head throbbing as the edges of my vision sparkled and my pulse thumped in my ears.

Then I was being pulled into the bushes off the path, a hand over my protesting mouth and arms holding me tight as I tried to fight my way free.

'Don't move.' Nathan said it right into my ear so forcefully it froze me.

I was dehydrated and delirious but I hadn't just been seeing stars and hearing my heart. A chopper searchlight was scouring the dry creek that ran the length of the valley. The brilliant beam stabbed through trees, returning pockets of brush to daylight, as we cowered and clung to our shadow. Then the chopper was moving on, blazing along the valley. Nathan's arms relaxed and I sprang up and stumbled away.

He scrambled after me, hand landing on my shoulder. I shrugged him off, spun to face him.

'Let me go!' I said.

Me-go-go-go-o-o-o: my words reverberated before tailing away to silence.

'Sssh,' Nathan said.

'Don't tell me what to do!'

To-do-to-do-o-o-o.

The world seemed to spin. Next I knew I was sitting in leaf litter on the path and watching a shadow on hands and knees wielding a shielded torch through flickering fronds. I had the bag of sultanas in one hand and a bottle of water in the other. I was chewing, releasing sweet energy, water and sugar flooding my cells.

My words had echoed. Like repeating thoughts. Was this some new manifestation of the telepathy? If Nathan and I started hearing each other's thoughts we'd be finished.

'You all right?' Nathan said.

All-right-ight-ight.

I stared at him. The echo wasn't inside my skull. Or his. Reality sharpened again. I'd spaced out. There'd been a chopper. We'd managed not to be seen.

Nathan was looking back at me from where he'd pushed apart fronds to inspect a round mouth of rocky darkness. When he released the ferns, they shushed back into place across the entrance. If it hadn't been for the echo, we'd never have known it was there.

'This is our best bet, Danby.'

Bet-Danby-anby-anby-aby-by: Nathan's words resonated from the foliage, like the voice of God in some Bible story.

'Is it a cave?' I whispered.

Nathan parted the green curtain again and stared into the black hole. It was nearly perfectly round, bored straight into the mountain, like a bullet wound in the earth.

'It's a tunnel,' Nathan said. *Tunnel-tunnel-unnel-unnel-unne-unn.* 'Could've been for mining.' *For-mining-ining-ining-ini.* 'I'm going to check it out,' he said, shining the torch in there. *Check-it-out-out-ou-ou.*

I didn't say anything as Nathan crawled into that nothingness. For a second his light glowed and then it was swallowed up by darkness. Silence and night draped themselves over me. I wondered who I was, where I was, whether all of this was a hallucination. Maybe Nathan was dead in that shed back in Samsara and I'd been talking to his ghost in my exhausted delirium. Maybe it stretched further back than that and I was still back in Beautopia Point and fighting off some awful fever while Dad and Stephanie kept a worried bedside vigil.

Nathan's light and face appeared in the tunnel mouth. He clicked off the torch, stood up and dusted himself off. I could barely see him in the twilight.

'I'm fine,' he whispered. 'Thanks for asking.'

I mumbled something. It might've been 'sorry'.

He crouched by me, spoke in a low voice.

'It goes in about fifty feet and then dog-legs and opens out a little. I don't know if it was for ventilation or an exploratory shaft or what. But we can hide in there.'

I didn't want to fight anymore. Not with Jack. Not with Nathan. Not with myself. I wanted to crawl into the earth to my rest.

'Follow me,' he said. 'It's not too far.'

Too-far-too-far-ar-ar.

By the glow of the torch, we went on hands and knees into the mountain, creeping along an avenue of soft wet dirt, hair brushing cobwebbed sandstone overhead, air warm and stale in our lungs. I wondered whether we'd perish in here. Crushed flat by a cave in. Die frothing in poison gas. I told myself Nathan got in and out okay. That this would be fine. I fought to keep my breathing steady. I couldn't lose my shit again like I had outside. It'd nearly gotten us killed.

After a while, Nathan branched left and the tunnel ended in an alcove the size of a pantry. He stood, stooped, turned around and sat down against the wall. I did the same.

'We'll be safe here,' he said. 'No one can find us unless they crawl all the way in. See?'

I didn't when he turned the flashlight off because the darkness was total. My world became my heart beating and the sound of our breathing. Nathan clicked the flashlight back on against the palm of his hand. When our eyes adjusted he shone it around the chiselled walls and low rocky ceiling. 'What do you think?'

This was like solitary confinement built for two. This was like being buried alive. But saying either of those things wouldn't help. Dimly I knew he was right. We probably wouldn't be found here.

'Can we have something to eat?'

Nathan smiled a little, looking pleased I was still capable of saying something normal. 'What do you want?'

'Doesn't matter.'

He pulled out a tin of baked beans and I popped the lid and ate them straight from the tin with my fingers.

'Don't go gassing us,' Nathan said.

'Huh?' I looked at him.

'Doesn't matter. Do you feel better?'

I didn't know if he meant physically or mentally or both.

'I'm so tired,' I said. It'd been days since I'd woken up in Clearview and since then I'd had five hours' sleep.

'I don't know how long these batteries will last,' Nathan said, holding up the torch. 'I'm going to conserve them, okay? Let's get some sleep?'

Nathan clicked off the flashlight. There was nothing but blackness. He scooched closer to me.

'I'll hold you, okay?' he said.

'Don't,' I said. 'Please.'

'Okay.'

I felt him stiffen and move away. I squashed myself into my own corner, only realising then maybe he'd wanted comfort for himself as much as he'd wanted to give it to me. Guilt stole up on me.

'Nathan?' I said.

When he didn't answer, I started to fume. He wasn't being fair. I hadn't meant to offend him. Everything was just so confusing and I didn't know—

A snore shuddered from Nathan. He wasn't pissed. He was asleep. Somehow that seemed worse.

The darkness was so complete I could've slept with my eyes open.

FIVE

Baroonah's not just about drawing the Jacks. It's about seeing how they come. What army and armour and aircraft we're up against. But now, watching the Tiger helicopter fly in on the tablet, I realise it's not just *how* but *when* they come that I need to record.

I've been assuming Jack's range of control over his Minions is the same as the limits of our telepathy: a radius of about thirty-five kilometres. But I know there are Jacks with choppers about that distance north of me so the Tiger should've gotten here sooner if it was inside a circle that size. I've made it my business to read up on all the aircraft Jack's likely to have liberated and I know the Tiger's maximum airspeed is three hundred kilometres an hour. It's been twenty minutes since I freed Gangly and Stocky from their maker. Assuming the Tiger was on the ground, and it took them five minutes to scramble a crew and get airborne, they've had fifteen minutes of flying time. Which means it could've just covered ninety kilometres from the south. There's plenty of room for error in my guesstimates but I've got a sinking feeling that the Radius works differently since Jack 1.0 died and was upgraded to whatever the hell he is now.

From cam to cam, I follow the Tiger as it swoops low over the town, nosing briefly over the dead riders before sliding down the street to circle over the mansion, big calibre guns trained on the house, buzzing rotors thinning the chimney smoke.

Another chopper comes into view at 1.20 p.m., also seemingly arriving at top speed from the south. Best I can tell, it's a Viper—just as fast and deadly as its companion. If it's been making top speed, it just covered more than a hundred kilometres. It skims the town and continues north, presumably checking the road out of Baroonah for getaway vehicles.

I wonder whether the Jacks in the Tiger hovering over the mansion have noticed that one body is missing from the bloodbath in the main street. I guess that depends on whether Gangly and Stocky actually paid any hivemind to my corpse in the first place. If they did, they might be seeing this for the staged scene that it is. They used to say it took ten thousand hours to get really good at something. I've managed nearly a quarter of that time since the Snap. But I guess I qualify as a survival expert just by virtue of not being dead. What's really freaky is trying to calculate how many hours Jack has racked up in that same time. I laugh in the cellar when I consider that his megamind might've accumulated expertise across hundreds of disciplines by now. I imagine him as this army of Einsteins, Mozarts and Picassos, rolling across the wasteland, looking for

43

me as they solve physics mysteries, compose sonatas and leave art masterpieces in their wake. But surely if the Jacks were *that* smart they would've found me and the others by now. Stocky and Gangly's brains didn't look bigger than normal as they sprayed out the front of their faces. And there's the muttering. What the hell was that gibberish about?

On the tablet, the chopper prowls over the mansion. I scroll through the screens but see no movement except the slow drift of clouds, the shining silver of leaves shifting in the breeze and a black-winged kite diving for a rodent out in the paddocks behind the pub.

At 13:26:13 there's a tremble in the wall and I hear the distant clatter of another chopper. I really have to peer hard at the screens to see it: a little bulb coming in from the south. A civilian model. Like the ones that used to monitor traffic. The chopper's too far off to know exactly which make it is. But if it's, say, a Robinson, its maximum speed's two hundred clicks an hour, meaning if it got airborne at the same time as the Tiger it has just flown a hundred and thirty kilometres to be here.

The hits just keep on coming. First to arrive on the road is another pair of motorbikes that burn into the main street from the highway. They weave around obstacles and pull up at the intersection. These riders, wearing camouflaged body armour the same as Stocky and Gangly, jump off their bikes, and, bent double with their assault rifles, hustle behind an old Ford opposite the mansion. The men take up firing positions— one over the bonnet, one by the boot—and they're still in their frozen stances when the next motorbikes arrive a few minutes later and peel off along the side street so they can cover the rear of the mansion.

I keep watching and jotting down arrival times in my notebook. It's all being recorded to the tablet's hard drive but my thoughts are always clearer after I've written them down. I feel sick at the picture that's emerging of Jacks stretched all along the coast and maybe even inland, now able to spread themselves out across thousands of square kilometres as they scour the earth for me and lay waste to whoever else they find. If they've enlarged the Radius—or freed themselves from it entirely—and can share a mind over enormous or unlimited territory then there's no place for us to run and hide. It's game over.

'Crap,' I say to Rat.

An armoured vehicle—I identify it as a LAV-25—rumbles along Baroonah's main street, shoving cars aside and grinding bodies old and new to pulp and dust under its heavy tyres. The LAV goes over the intersection, stops outside the mansion and swings its turret so its massive M242 autocannon is aimed at the front door. In the armoured vehicle's wake come other motorbikes, a fleet of four-wheel drives and a block of broad Humvees. Men and women, some in army uniforms, others in civilian clothes, pour from vehicles with weapons at the ready as they add themselves to the siege. More choppers arrive to hover around the town and its outskirts.

No one moves on the mansion. Surely they can't be that chicken shit. They must have a hundred assault rifles trained on the place. The LAV's autocannon could rip the building to pieces. Same goes for the Tiger's sixty-millimetre miniguns. Then it dawns. They're not waiting because they're afraid. They're waiting for something. Or someone.

SIX

'How did he do it?' I asked. 'Jack, I mean?'

Nathan and I had just had a tin of sardines between us, three ginger biscuits each and shared a bottle of water. Lunch or midnight snack? The watches we had from Samsara read twelve but didn't indicate whether it was night or day.

'I don't know what he did,' Nathan said. 'Let alone how he did it.'

'Do you think Evan's the boss now?'

The thought of my little brother not just controlled but possessed by Jack made me want to spew up everything I'd eaten.

'No,' Nathan said. 'Back at the Courthouse, Jack was really trying to goad you into killing Evan. He wouldn't have done that if it'd finish him and release everyone else, would he?'

'Then where's Jack now? Who's he in?'

I waited. Nathan didn't say anything but I sensed him shudder.

'You think he's all of them?' I said.

'I hope not.'

We were quiet a while.

'Tree of heaven,' I said almost to myself.

'What's that?' Nathan asked.

I told him about the warning leaflet for this species I'd read while I'd lain in ambush under the caravan. Despite its lovely official name, these rapacious pest plants had destroyed large patches of bush around Samsara and all over the state. They thrived under any conditions, specialised in taking over disturbed ground, grew quickly to a huge size and emitted chemicals that suppressed the growth of competing foliage.

'The pamphlet said they ruin the environment so badly they're nicknamed "the hell tree",' I said.

'Sounds like Jack,' Nathan replied. 'Did it say how to get rid of them?'

I shook my head in the dark.

'That's the worst thing. It's almost impossible to cut them down or dig them up because they'll reproduce from the smallest bit of twig or root.'

'Nothing is indestructible,' Nathan said softly. 'There has to be a way.'

'I'm just telling you what I read,' I said, unable to keep the irritation out of my voice.

Nathan shifted. It felt like he was farther away. 'I meant about Jack.'

•••

I was on a peak-hour commuter train, everyone clacking portable typewriters, barking into old dial phones, guffawing at sitcoms crackling from boxy televisions. Squashed into the space allotted to me, I marvelled at how it all worked, these people thigh to thigh and elbow to elbow in seats, pounding keys and adjusting ribbons, criss-crossed by power cords with silver antennae bristling in all directions. Commotion and locomotion. Industrial harmony. And then a voice burbled over the public address speakers to tell us they regretted the inconvenience but a coal train was coming for us head on and a crash of the system was imminent.

I snapped awake in the darkness. Relieved for a second and then sinking as I remembered that reality was worse than a train-wreck nightmare. Nathan snored beside me. I readjusted my arms and legs, tried to stretch, wondered what time it was, decided it didn't matter.

No matter what Nathan had said about this place being safe, I was expecting noises would eventually echo along the tunnel as they crawled in to get us. There was nothing to do to prepare. Nowhere to hide. No way to defend ourselves after I'd fired our few bullets. Hell, they wouldn't even need to come into the tunnel. They could pump in gasoline and incinerate us. Or drown us with water. Seal the entrance and let us suffocate. Wait until we starved to death. We should've stood our ground and fought and died in Samsara. The more I stewed on it the angrier I became.

'You awake?' Nathan said.

I wondered whether my bad vibes had reached into his sleep.

'Yep.'

'I was dreaming about—'

'Do you think we have the right to die?' I didn't care that I'd cut Nathan off mid-sentence. 'You must've given it some thought studying medicine.'

Nathan clicked on the torch, light cupped against his hand so it didn't blind us. Even in the faint glow, I saw how my question affected him. He thought I was talking about suicide.

'Euthanasia,' I said.

He sighed, relieved. 'Yes, I do.'

'But you wouldn't let me euthanase Evan?'

'Oh, Danby,' he said.

'Don't patronise me.'

'I'm not.'

'You would've agreed with removing life support to a—a—a—'

'Brain-dead patient?' Nathan said. 'I would. I'd also agree a terminally ill patient had the right to refuse treatment.'

'Well, what's the difference?' I said loudly enough that my voice echoed along the tunnel. If anyone was outside, I'd just given us away.

'Sssssh!' Nathan said.

'Well?' I hissed at him. 'What's the difference?'

'In the first case, there's no hope. In the second case, it's the patient's choice. Neither of those applied to Evan.'

'But it is—is—'

'Hopeless? I don't think you really believe that, do you?' Nathan's dark eyes seemed huge in our shadowy tomb. 'If you did, you would've pulled the trigger straight away. But you gave me the chance to stop you.'

I turned my head, tightened my jaw, stared at the sandstone inches from my face until Nathan switched off the torch and we sat in the darkness and silence.

· • ·

Shining the torch on the watches was to mark the time—12.47, 4.15, 1.32, 9.16, 2.43—without being sure how much of it had really passed. Whenever I lolled into sleep I didn't know if it was for minutes or hours. The clocks we really obeyed were thirst and hunger. The one time I had to crap, I got halfway along the tunnel, the entrance appearing as a dim circle of dawn or dusk, before a rumbling chopper stopped me in my tracks. I shat there and buried it in the dirt. After that, I didn't have to go again, not even to piss, as if my body was absorbing every bit of moisture and nutrition and wasting nothing. Perhaps as another defence mechanism, we kept conversation to the polite minimum needed to share food.

Mostly we slumbered in our separate corners, occasionally waking each other moaning from our nightmares before we mumbled apologies and slipped back into sleep.

Evan glowed out of the darkness, wearing oversized pants, like Dopey in Snow White, guffawing as he swung a golf club. 'Marvellous drive, old chap,' he said. I didn't know if he was parroting somebody or being controlled by someone named Jack. Jacinta wanted to know whether I was going to Mollie's next party. It was going to be a Princess Hellbanga theme and she was wondering how to make a wimple. Dad was at Luna Park, feeding novelty socks into a cotton candy machine, while

Stephanie was making big bucks as a busking Pilates instructor. Mum sat up on the roof of Coney Island, rolling a joint, telling me to check myself before I wrecked myself. They came to me collaged, bleeding into each other, all still alive in a world I didn't belong to anymore. They were all still there. I was the one who'd gotten lost. The thought was frightening but comforting. Easier for me to find my way back to all of them than—

I awoke with my face scrunched up, my chest hitching and heaving, dry crying again in the darkness. I bit my knuckle, tried to keep quiet, not wanting to wake Nathan again or have to explain myself to him. I'd lost count of how many times it'd happened, this silent sobbing that never provided any relief.

I was calming, coaxing myself back to sleep, hoping for rest without dreams, when my mind asked me how long I thought I could endure this. It already felt like I'd been in here forever. That nothing consciousness after the Snap: it'd swallowed almost everyone and I'd struggled and suffered and survived just to end up trapped in its physical equivalent. We didn't have much food or water. But that wasn't the problem. Oxygen: that was what we needed. The air was thick, getting thicker, thick-too-thick to breathe. I thrust my hand out, gripped Nathan so hard he woke up.

'How long,' I gasped, 'has—ha—have we been here?'

'No idea. Two days maybe.'

'I ca—can't—ca . . . no air.'

'It's okay,' he said gently. 'Calm down. You're just—'

It wasn't okay. I wasn't just. I had to get out. I threw myself forward and scrabbled around the corner before Nathan could stop me. My head and hands were going pins and needles as I crawled along the tunnel.

'You're hyperventilating.' Nathan was a voice in the void behind me. 'Just try to calm down.'

I scrambled through the darkness towards more darkness. There was no daylight at the end of the tunnel when I pushed aside the fern fronds. But the air was fresh and I gorged myself and then sat, head spinning with my face between my knees. I knew this feeling. I'd had it at Mum's on New Year's Day. Panic attack. I concentrated on breathing slowly and gradually came back to my senses.

I was vaguely aware of Nathan. He'd crawled out of the cave and sat near me with the torch cupped in his hand.

'Sorry,' I said.

'Feeling better?'

I nodded. 'Do you think it's safe to go?'

'I'll go get the backpack and—' was as much as he said before a chopper shook the sky somewhere nearby.

Nathan clicked off the torch and we scurried back into our hole and hibernated like bears.

•••

'We've got to go,' Nathan said, shaking me.

'What?' I lolled in my trance.

'Wake up,' Nathan said, brow furrowed in the faltering glow of the flashlight.

I was still struggling out of sleep molasses. 'What?'

'We're out of food and water.'

I nodded. This wasn't news. Despite ourselves we'd bickered over the last of the beans. We'd started to talk again about leaving then but were cut off by the rumbling of choppers. That'd been a dozen hours or a day ago or maybe more. I didn't know why food and water mattered all of a sudden. I was comfortable and safe. Didn't even feel hungry or thirsty anymore. Just tired. Always tired. 'Please, I want to sleep.'

'I've stayed awake and checked my watch,' he said. 'There hasn't been a chopper for—'

I didn't hear what he said after that.

Then Nathan was shaking my shoulder again and shining the torch in my eyes. 'Wake up.'

I had no choice now. 'All right, I'm awake, what?'

'We have to go,' Nathan said. 'Take our chances. We're just getting weaker now. Hiding this long has either worked or it hasn't.'

•••

At least it was daylight outside. Nine thirty according to our watches. We blinked the morning glare into focus and saw that the weather was on our side. A thick cotton of fog had settled over the mountains and valleys so that earth and sky merged in a beige haze. We wouldn't be spotted from the air. And any Jacks around would have a hard time seeing us. It was cooler and the air in my lungs felt fresher. It'd rained heavily enough that the creek flowed.

'Risk drinking it?' I asked.

Nathan nodded. 'It'd be better if we boil it.'

'I seem to have forgotten my billy can.'

We filled our bellies and our bottles. 'Which way?' I asked. Nathan checked the map. Nodded up the hillside.

We trudged up through the wet landscape, taking it slow so we wouldn't slip to our deaths, the mist soaking us and our conversation reduced to whispered basics of 'this way', 'over here' and 'wait up'.

Nathan and I had done nothing but talk when we'd first been together in Parramatta but now it was like we'd exhausted all the words we'd been allocated. Or maybe there just weren't words to describe what we'd seen and felt and done. I tried to think simple things—one foot after the other; fifty steps till a little rest; reward sip of water at the rock overhang—but I kept returning to the moment when I'd failed to free Evan. My eyes would burn into the back of Nathan's skull until I reprimanded myself—it wasn't his fault. Then I'd go back to counting steps until I pictured Evan stuck in limbo and it'd start over.

It was midday, the fog lifting, when we reached a rocky track no wider than a car. Skirted by an ancient gutter and buttressed by a stone wall on its low side, the road climbed steeply through thick bush before disappearing behind an outcrop.

'This is it,' Nathan said. 'The Great North Road.'

'North I can see,' I said, kicking at a piece of sandstone. 'Great and road, not so much.'

Nathan sketched a smile.

My stomach growled. I quieted it with a big mouthful from my bottle. At least the creek water hadn't made us sick. If it had we'd probably be dying now. As it was, we were slowly starving.

'The map says it's been closed to vehicles for decades,' Nathan said.

I crouched by a roadside rut brimming with brown rainwater. 'This track is from a motorbike.'

Nathan ran his hand through his hair. 'It could've been made weeks ago by someone trying to get away from the Snap.'

I took the rifle from my shoulder. 'Or they could be up ahead.'

The doubt returned to Nathan's eyes. I thought I saw calculation there—whether he had a better chance of surviving if he went alone.

'It's possible,' he said carefully. 'But I think we were in the tunnel long enough that they would've spread the search area pretty wide and maybe—'

'Maybe what?'

'They've just given up. It's not like we're any threat.'

I knew in my bones Jack would follow me to the ends of the earth to end me. 'Do you really believe that?'

Nathan shrugged and sighed and shook his head.

The road undulated beneath collars of cliffs before winding back into the cleavage of valleys. Visibility dwindled as trees closed around us. But I found the bush hypnotic and reassuring. It wasn't monotonous and motionless. It was bursting with life. Sandstone strata had eroded into intricate vertebrae and a ridge of bushfire regrowth glowed like a reef of gold against the grey sky. All around, bark hung in long strips, the ghost gum trunks perfectly smooth and white underneath, while isolated flame trees burned amid silvery eucalypts. A banksia in bloom was swarmed by so many bees that the whole tree buzzed and shook. I saw a blue-tongued lizard and a brush turkey and orange and green parrots and pink and white galahs. I was happy that they didn't take any notice of us—and worried that I wondered what they'd taste like.

A wallaby sat frozen on the road ahead. I took the rifle from my shoulder. Nathan eased to my side.

'I could shoot it,' I whispered, glancing his way. 'We could eat it.'

'The noise'll carry for miles,' he said.

He was right. And it wasn't like we could eat its meat raw. Even if we had fire the smoke would give us away. We watched the wallaby bounce off the road and into the bush, furry head bobbing through the brush until the mist enveloped it.

'Don't worry,' Nathan said. 'We'll find food somehow.'

I looked at him. 'Check your map. Bound to be a drive-thru soon.'

Nathan frowned. 'I don't like this any better than you do.'

I'd meant to be funny but I'd sounded like a sour bitch. Before I could explain, he walked ahead.

• • •

The Great North Road didn't look like it'd been an escape route during the Snap. There weren't any bodies. But people had left their marks here long ago. Arrows pointing to the sky were carved into the sandstone gutters and ramps. I puzzled over what this ancient graffiti could've meant. This way north? This way to heaven?

I got my answer an hour or so later.

'What is it?' Nathan said, an edge in his voice, when I stopped in the middle of the road.

I pointed to a plinth with a larger reproduction of the arrow. A bronze plaque explained the symbol had meant government property, which is what this road and the slaves who built it had been. Nathan and I stood side by side and read the thumbnail history of the Great North Road. Convicts had worked for a decade from 1826, cutting trees, blasting rock, laying down stone, building retaining walls and drainage tunnels and the rest of it, all while suffering dysentery and rickets and consumption and the brutality of their overseers and the threat of attack by the local Darkinjung people defending their way of life. Against the odds, at the cost of countless lives, the convicts succeeded in creating a road that linked Sydney to settlements further north. But by the time the last stone was laid their work was rendered obsolete by the invention of steamships that could transport people and cargo along the coast quicker and more comfortably. I pictured those poor bastards at their Sisyphean task, dreaming perhaps that if they worked hard enough they would be pardoned, or trying to muster up the courage to escape into the bush and walk to China, which they somehow thought they could do. As bad as they'd had it, our predicament was worse. Wordless, we walked on into the brooding gloom as a light rain began to fall.

'We need to use the torch,' I said back to Nathan's shadow, after an hour of this trudging.

His boots scuffed the wet gravel. 'I don't think that's a good idea. We should hide somewhere, wait until dawn.'

I clicked my fingers. 'You can do that if you want. I'm done with hiding.'

'Danby, the only possible way they can see us is if we—'

'Use a flashlight? That's not true. The choppers have search-lights. If they've found infrared gear they can see us as clear as day. They could be around the next bend. Lying in wait. There's plenty of ways for them to find us, Nathan. We've been stuck in a hole for however long. We have to keep moving.'

Nathan stepped closer, took the backpack from his shoulders and held it out to me. 'We're starving. The goddamned bullet hole in my chest hurts almost as much as my legs are sore from walking. My idea of a smart plan isn't wandering in the dark and waving a light so that a bunch of mind-controlled maniacs can come kill me. But the torch is in there. You might get another hour out of the battery. You go for it, Danby.'

I looked at him, at the backpack. Just as I had no idea where we were or what day it was, I couldn't work out whether he was being cowardly or I was being crazy.

'Jesus, all right,' I said with a frustrated sigh. 'Where do you suggest we hang out until dawn?'

We picked our way down off the road and nestled beside a tall retaining wall. It protected us against the wind but did nothing to stop the cold rain. It was almost enough to make me miss the tunnel. But I made a point of not huddling into

Nathan. I wasn't being petulant. I didn't have the energy for that. It was because I knew he could be gone at any minute. Get sick of my shit and go his own way. Get unlucky and get killed. I had to get used to being alone.

We slept fitfully, teeth chattering, breaths misting around us. I clamped my hand over Nathan's mouth, felt him struggle against me.

'Ssssh,' I hissed in his ear. 'Listen.'

Motorbikes. On the road. Revving closer. Right above us. Headlights glistening off wet leaves and getting soaked up by the low clouds. Then the bikes were receding, red taillights glowing, heading back the way we'd come. If we'd kept going like I'd wanted we would've run straight into them. Nathan had been right about that. But he'd been wrong about the searchers being spread thin across the landscape.

Through the night, helicopters swept up and down the Great North Road, across the hills and valleys near and far. We weren't just behind enemy lines. The whole territory belonged to the enemy.

SEVEN

In a dizzying flash I'm no longer seeing the outside world only through the Cameleons streaming video to my tablet. I'm in another helicopter, brown countryside rushing below my window. It's been months since I've been in another person's mind and being in Tregan's sucks the air from my lungs. Her thoughts and memories are like a violent invasion. Even after everything, I can still be jolted.

Hope-this-time-they-get-Danby-and-Nathan-Closure-I-need-closure-And-payback-Admit-it-But-it's-weird-Things-happen-for-a-reason-If-they-hadn't-killed-him-Might-never-have-been-with-Damon-Hope-this-time-we-can-stay-together . . .

Tregan, the woman Nathan saved, only for her to be seduced by Jack into turning against us. I must fend off fury and fear. Focus to function. More warrior wisdom from my military manuals. It takes a few moments to follow through but once I'm breathing steadily I delve into her mind.

She throbs with lust for Damon and burns with hatred for me and Nathan. My mouth goes dry as I understand how these emotions spring from the morning at Richmond Air Base when she watched Jack and his men take to helicopters and fly into the dawn to attack us.

As Tregan and Damon walked back into the base, her confusion and guilt about her fiancé, Gary, deepened. When she reached out to him with what she hoped were appeasing thoughts his anger streamed back through her mind.

Babe-we-need-to-talk—

This-is-talking?

About-Jack-I—

You-don't-think-I'm-as-strong-as-them?

It's-not-that-no—

Don't-I-make-you-feel-as-safe?

Well-you-did-fall-off-your-bike-and—

You-bloody-bi—

Gary!-We-can-work-this-out-Just-let-me—

What?-Share-you?-That's-what-you-want-I-can-feel—

Dammit-someone's-knocking—

Tregan had watched as Gary opened the door of the commander's quarters they'd been sharing. A reedy man with thinning hair stood in mechanic's overalls. Gary hadn't seen him before. Neither had Tregan.

'What do you want?' Gary demanded, thinking, *Goddamned-grease-monkey-Tregan-I—*

'Traitor,' the man said as he pulled out a silver pistol. 'This is for Danby.'

Shit-Gary-look-out-he's—

The flash, the bang, burning punch: they hit Gary as one sensation. As he staggered backwards into the room and fell his head was flooded with Tregan's anguish and her vision of being held by Damon as he urged men and women with guns past them to defend the base.

The mechanic's face loomed over Gary. The pistol's muzzle was like a black hole. Ready to suck in all life and light.

'Please,' Gary managed, bubbles of blood bursting on his lips. 'Please don't.'

I-don't-want-to-die-Tregan-where-are-you? Jesus-neck-But-they've-got-surgical-facilities-here-Tregan-you-can-save-me-Please-hurry—

Gary didn't see the muzzle flare or hear the gunshot. Tregan screamed in Damon's arms as more retorts reverberated along the corridor and into the hangar. Through her tears and yelps she'd been vaguely aware of shouts and screams and then silence. It seemed like just seconds later that she was surrounded by sad faces in the infirmary before the sedatives eased her into sleep. When she awoke, an ashen-faced Damon sat by her bed. In a dull voice he told her that not long after Gary was assassinated by one of Danby's followers, Jack and a dozen others had been slaughtered in an ambush in a tiny village called Samsara. Then it'd been Damon's turn to cry and she'd hugged him to her.

A day later, Tregan's clinical side reasserted itself. She made Damon take her to the base's morgue so she could see Gary and Jack. Their wounds weren't just ghastly. They were barbaric. Her fiancé had been shot in both eyes. Jack was similarly disfigured—he'd also been burned and mutilated before he died.

'They're trying to terrify us,' Damon said.

Tregan felt steel in her spine and acid in her veins. 'She has to be stopped.'

Damon's eyes were stormy. 'We're doing our best.'

A few hours later, Tregan stood by a big trench by a runway that was piled with the bodybags that contained Gary and Jack and the others who'd died at Samsara. There were hundreds of mourners, the crowd suffused with anger and sadness, bristling with assault rifles like some Middle Eastern street protest. But the outpouring made sense to Tregan. The dead in the ground beneath her feet were martyrs who'd died fighting a war for humanity's future.

Damon said a few words and bowed his head. Tregan's heart bled when she saw a tear glisten from the end of his nose and drop into the grave.

'We won't rest until this world is safer,' he said, finally looking up at the crowd and, through Tregan, at the Revivees spread across western Sydney. 'And those who murdered our friends are brought to account.'

After she'd released a handful of soil and the funeral service was over, Damon sat Tregan at the commander's desk and got her to write down the locations of all the Revivees her mind could find. When she was done, he took her hands in his, looked into her eyes and beyond.

'Everyone out there,' he said, 'Tregan's given us your locations and we'll start sending helicopters out this afternoon to rescue you.'

Seeing Gary's death and hearing of Jack's fate had spread a fever among the Revivees. Most everyone wanted to be picked up in choppers, offered protection from Danby and her army of murderers. They squabbled about who'd be rescued first, whose predicaments were worst, whether choppers would be able to land near the places they'd holed up.

Tregan relayed these concerns to Damon and he calmly spoke to them through her.

'The first choppers will be airborne in an hour,' he said. 'Tregan's tuning you all. We'll coordinate our pilots. We'll bring food and first aid and anything else we can see you need. We're going to take you all to secure locations far from our enemies. No one's going to be left behind. Just have patience.'

Tregan and Damon sat side-by-side in a control tower. Another five black helicopters that had been taken from the hangars were fuelled and readied and one after another they swept east.

'They're on their roof,' Tregan said into her headset to the pilot of the easternmost chopper as it zeroed in on Ravi and Wayne's suburban abode just outside Parramatta.

Ravi-Wayne-keep-calm-you-should-see-the-chopper . . .

We-can-hear-it-Oh-thank-God-there-it-is-How're-they-gonna-get-us?

Men-will-rappel-Harness-you-Winch-you-It'll-be-okay.

Tregan sipped her coffee, smiled at Damon. 'They're nervous about the lift.'

'I would be too,' he said, resting his hand on her shoulder.

Tregan watched as Ravi and Wayne were rescued. Their salvation, the relief they felt when they were safely inside the black helicopter and soaring over the ruined landscape, caused a clamour in Revivees who wanted to be next.

'Nicely done,' Damon said into his mike.

'Copy that,' the pilot replied.

Behind him, the flight-suited crew strapped Ravi and Wayne into their seats.

Honey-we're-safe-God-I'm-hungry-Where-are-we going?

'Where are we going?' Ravi asked.

'Where are you taking them?' Tregan asked Damon, curious herself.

'I can't say,' he said. 'Their minds might relay that information to Danby and the others.'

Ravi and Wayne accepted the logic of that—their main desire was to be as safe as possible—but Tregan wasn't sure how it'd work.

'Won't Danby know anyway?' she said. 'She'll be able to see.'

Damon shook his head. 'Not if we get everyone safely out of range.'

In the control tower, drinking coffee after coffee, Tregan believed she was the lynchpin who made possible the rescue of the Revivees. Anne was carried drunk and unconscious from her sister's house. Cory was picked up at Penrith Plaza and his offer to become a soldier for Damon was graciously deferred. Others were ushered across lawns or winched from rooftops. In ones and twos and small groups they were flown south until their minds dwindled and disappeared from Tregan's. Choppers flew back empty, refuelled and left again, collected more people and whisked them to safety.

All of this pouring into me from Tregan makes me sick to my stomach. I already know the horrible fate that befell at least one of those Revivees. I can only hope the others are still merely captives. But Tregan's memory also confirms that at the same time the Jacks were swarming around Samsara looking for me and Nathan, they were also back in Richmond and Penrith and flying Revivees far south out of range. All that bull he'd spun me about letting Minions go. I think he'd been mastering his abilities and insinuating himself deeper into them so he wasn't restricted to the Radius. When I'd killed Jack, I'd made him more powerful. Like some evil Obi-Fucking-Wan.

I focus on Tregan's mind. The next morning, with everyone they'd rescued safely tucked away, she'd experienced something she'd wondered if she'd ever have again: mental silence. Her mind was her own for the first time since the Snap. A weight had been lifted from her. She smiled at Damon.

'You should rest,' he said. 'We both should. It's been a huge couple of days.'

Tregan placed her hand on his.

'I've got new quarters for you,' he said. 'Not as big as before but—'

Damon didn't need to finish the thought: her new bedroom wouldn't be a reminder that she hadn't been able to save Gary, that all of them were vulnerable in the face of such a determined and devious enemy. Damon escorted her through the corridors. She turned to face him in the doorway. She hadn't noticed it before but Damon and Jack could've been related.

Tregan couldn't say exactly how. Maybe it was the eyes: green with gold in them.

'I don't want to be alone,' she said.

Damon had taken her in his arms and kissed her deeply, the two of them falling onto the bed in a mad scramble to get out of their clothes. He'd dominated her, anticipated her every desire, played her body and pleased her in ways she'd never come close to with Gary or anyone before him. The flash of her remembered rapture brings bile to the back of my throat for the violation it really was. She wouldn't have given herself to him if she'd known Damon was in her mind and that by being with him she was with Jack and all of them. Despite her hatred of me, I feel sick and sorry for this woman who's been so used. What makes me want to scream is that her fate's not too different to what Jack planned for me.

Tregan and Damon didn't leave the bedroom for a day. Subordinates brought and cleared food. Tregan thought she could've stayed there forever, safe in his arms, happy he didn't push her to talk.

'I'm going to have to get out there after her,' Damon said eventually. 'Them.'

Tregan nodded. 'I'll come with you.'

'I wish you could,' he said. 'But she'll pick up your mind long before we get near them. And I want to make sure you're safe.'

After another night of what she thought was lovemaking, Tregan let Damon lead her to a waiting chopper. They held hands on the flight back south, passing over Penrith and following the Nepean River out across vast green carpets of national park. Then the chopper landed in a cleared area with wooden cabins by a sparkling lake.

'Where are we?' Tregan asked.

'Nattai National Park,' Damon said. 'A long way from anyone and anything that could hurt you.'

A guy and a girl in camouflage fatigues and guns stood outside one of the cabins.

'These two will make sure you're okay,' Damon said.

Tregan gripped his fingers tighter. Remembered their bodies entwined just an hour ago. The campsite was surrounded by bush-covered hills. 'It's so quiet.'

Damon nodded. 'We've stocked the place. There's a generator. Think of it as a chance to heal.'

Tregan laughed. 'A spa retreat? I'd rather share it with you.'

'As soon as this is over, we'll be together all the time.' Damon offered a cheeky grin. 'But until then I'll be sure to visit with the supply chopper.'

'Supply chopper? How long do you think it's going to take?'

Damon shrugged. 'She could be anywhere by now. It'll take time. But we'll find her.'

She-she-she-Must-really-be-the-mastermind-Damon-hard-ly-mentions-Nathan-now-Poor-disturbed-creature-Probably-swept-up-in-her-craziness . . .

Tregan's guards were polite but spent most of their days and nights patrolling the perimeter. She took walks around the lake. Tried to lose herself in books and music. Did Pilates and practised meditation in a room with wind chimes. Mostly she counted the days until Damon's visits. When he came they'd spend an afternoon in her cabin. And on each visit he told her the same thing: that it wasn't yet safe to leave. Weeks became months.

Then, just an hour ago, the traffic helicopter had swooped unscheduled on the Nattai camp. Rotor blades still spinning, Damon had rushed out, wearing a flak jacket and a grim expression. He told Tregan she was needed.

'Where are we going?' she asked as the countryside blurred by beneath them.

'Little town called Baroonah.'

'What's happening? Have you—we—got them?'

'It's the best lead we've had,' Damon told her. 'I think we can end it today. I need you as observer. If we can, I'd still like to take her alive, end it peacefully.'

Tregan wondered whether the passing of the months had softened Damon. But she hadn't forgiven or forgotten. 'Why?'

'So we don't create more bad blood,' Damon said. 'I know how hard this is for you but I don't want anyone else to die. When we get closer they're going to be able to see us through you, okay? I want them to see what they're up against. But I also want them to know, through you, that surrender's an option—and they won't be harmed.'

'Is that true?'

Damon nodded. 'I'm prepared to take Danby and whoever else to somewhere like Nattai. They won't be able to leave but they won't want for anything either.'

Tregan used binoculars to look east at Sydney. There were gaps in the city skyline where buildings had collapsed. Fires had blackened more suburbs. The Central Coast and Newcastle scrolled by in the distance. From what she could see they'd been as ruined as Sydney and its suburbs. The chopper flew over wineries and farms and forests. Not a person alive amid all the greenery. Wherever Tregan looked she saw a vast lifeless landscape. She was amazed they'd managed to find anyone in all this countryside.

..•..

Finally the chopper slows. Tregan sees other helicopters hovering over the small town she presumes is Baroonah. There's a small army of men and women down there with machine guns surrounding a big house that's also in the firing line of an armoured vehicle. *Whoever's-in-there-doesn't-stand-a-chance-Not-against all-of-that.*

Tregan realises why she's been brought to this place at the same time I do. Just like I've placed cameras all over Baroonah so I can see what's about to unfold, Damon wants whoever has killed his outriders to see what they're up against and who's after them. And if that's me, he wants me scanning Tregan's memories and hearing him tell her he wants a peaceful ending. Maybe he thinks I'm tired after all these months. That I'll lower my guard and give in to hope. He has nothing to lose in trying to soften me up, lure me out, take me alive and torment me. I'm vaguely insulted he thinks I'm that stupid. That he can get to me so easily.

Their chopper settles into a paddock. Damon leads Tregan from the cabin to a waiting four-wheel drive. When he opens the back door, she sees a young boy with golden hair and sharp eyes. My heart swells and splits.

My little brother. Or what used to be Evan. He's grown so much. At least his body has.

'This is Evan,' Damon says. 'Danby's brother.'

She hates me but she feels nothing but pity for this boy.

'Hi there,' she says brightly. 'I'm Tregan.'

I scream into the beanbag.

EIGHT

'The way I see it, Jack was like a big server, right?'

Nathan said it from behind me as we trudged through afternoon mist along the stone road. At some point he'd decided that he didn't care if I wanted to talk or not and had begun to think aloud.

'So, it's like he was housing all the main operating software, administering and backing up all the slave computers, okay?'

I wondered if he was delirious with hunger. I wanted him to shut up so we could listen for motorbikes. But I didn't have the energy to shush him.

My feet stumbled on. We rattled as we walked because we'd accessorised our ever-looser clothes with gum twigs and leaves. Bits of bush were threaded into our tops and tucked into our jeans and boots. It wasn't comfortable but it was some camouflage against the choppers that'd spear over the treetops and up and down the road with only seconds' warning.

My head ached. My eyes felt big in a face that would be all cheekbones if I could see myself. My stomach had folded itself into a painful density that I pictured like a golf ball's innards. We'd managed to fill our bottles with rain the night down by the wall but that was gone. I'd taken to licking the dew off gum leaves.

The fifty kilometres of convict road defied my dull attempts at calculation. Five kilometres an hour: that was the pace my best friend Jacinta and I did on a school charity walk. That'd been a sunny ramble through flat suburbia. This was a wet slog through hilly bush. But even at half that speed we should've reached the end of the road long ago. It seemed we'd been walking forever, the gravel track curving left then right, climbing steeply to curl around ridges, dipping back randomly into valleys and doing it all over again. Maybe it was fifty kilometres straight as the crow flies but exponentially greater when all the twists and turns were taken into account. Maybe it was like the horrible measurements I remembered from biology class—that my lungs could be spread out to cover a tennis court, my intestines would unravel to the length of a football field and my blood vessels would wrap around the earth a few times over. I didn't know anything anymore. Certainly not why my mind threw up such gory trivia. Certainly not how Nathan found the energy to talk and theorise . . .

'. . . but the thing is, a server, a mainframe, usually would be huge, right? Much bigger than the computers connected to it, and faster and stronger, too. But here's the thing, Jack's brain, as far as we know at least, wasn't any different to yours or mine or Evan's or anyone's. So, with the link there, theoretically, he could download himself—all his knowledge, his capabilities, his software, if you like—into any of the slaves and make them into the server. Or make all of them the servers, independently.'

Nathan wasn't waiting for me to respond. He was talking to himself, to the trees, to the kookaburras.

When I looked up from my dusty boots, I didn't dare believe my eyes.

'How did he do it?' Nathan said behind me, as if echoing a question I'd asked. 'Well, that's something I don't know. Not any more than I know how telepathy was suddenly around us like air or how Jack could resurrect and control people. But the big question, the big question, is whether people can still be rescued—'

'Would you shut up?'

'—whether maybe it's possible for us to somehow get Evan and—'

'Nathan!'

Hearing his name snapped him from his rant.

'Shut up. Look.'

'Good heavens,' he said.

Understatement of the century.

The Great North Road had opened out ahead to connect with a stretch of blue bitumen with double lines in the middle and steel crash barriers skirting its edges. An old station wagon was parked on the far shoulder of this route to . . . somewhere.

We didn't run like desert desperados who suddenly see the oasis that'll end their thirst. But we did speed up without a second thought for whether this was a trap. Whether the bush flanking us was stacked with Jacks ready to shoot us down.

The road was empty as far as I could see in both directions. A sign said this was the Middle Way. Following it south led to Samsara, some fifty kilometres distant, while going north would see us in Killeen, just eight kilometres away.

I crunched towards the station wagon. For days now our nostrils had been free of the stench of death. My stomach clenched at the prospect of a decaying driver behind the wheel.

'Anyone in it?' Nathan whispered.

My vision swam as we edged closer. Sky glare reflected tree shadows off the tinted windows. I cupped my hands and peered inside. The car was abandoned. I pulled the driver's door open as Nathan checked the backseat. There was a bag of Minties in the console. I grabbed it, tore open the packet and twisted the wrapper off to pop a white lolly into my mouth. It was soft and gooey and sugary and possibly the best thing I've ever tasted. Moments like these.

'Yes!' Nathan said. He'd opened the back hatch, pulled out a bottle of water, was drinking it carefully.

I hustled to his side, swapped him the sweets for the bottle. We drank and chewed a while, right out in the open, unable to care about anything other than sugar and water for the moment.

'We 'ould 'ave 'ome o' 'ese,' Nathan said around a mouthful.

I nodded, tucked the rest of the lollies and what was left of the water into his backpack.

'Let's have a look around for car keys,' I said.

We'd gotten lucky once before. Not this time.

'I could try to hotwire it,' Nathan said when we'd searched the car and surrounding road.

'You don't know how.'

'Can't hurt to try.'

Nathan found a pair of pliers in the tool kit and busied himself with whatever wires he could find underneath the steering column, snipping and striking without sparking anything.

'You know,' he said, smiling across at where I watched the road with my rifle, 'I don't think I ever saw a single movie where this didn't save the bloody day.'

I shrugged. 'Won't work if the battery's dead. Even if it isn't it's probably out of petrol. Besides, wouldn't you worry about it attracting attention?'

Nathan's smile soured. 'Killeen,' he said, staring at the sign. 'There'll be something to eat, we can find a house. We can walk there by nightfall. Another eight kilometres won't kill us.'

It just might though if we ran into the enemy or if they were holed up in Killeen. Darkness shifted across Nathan's features as I adjusted my hold on the rifle.

'Danby,' he said. 'I don't want to fight. Not now. All I want to do is find some food and a place to sleep and some dry clothes. Will you give me that?'

As much as I wanted to shoot Jacks, what he'd said sounded good. I could rationalise it. Fed, watered, rested, I could find more weapons and ammo, and then I'd be able to fight harder and longer and do more damage. I nodded and we walked on.

••

Under the low dark sky, Killeen nestled close to Route 33. The village's weatherboard buildings—post office, art gallery, general store and gift shop—looked like they'd survived on the lifeblood of passing traffic. A tiny sandstone church was just big enough to accommodate the promise made by a fading billboard: 'For where two or three are gathered together in My name, I am there in the midst of them—Matthew 18.' But I guessed the Excelsior Hotel—a double-storeyed, triple-fronted grand old dame—was where the town's real action had been. And that was true again as we watched from behind gravestones in the cemetery on a hill.

Two motorbikes and a Humvee were corralled outside the pub whose windows glowed with orange lantern light. Two Jacks came out through the front door. Each carried a plate and a bottle of beer to a wooden table in the roadside garden. They could've been a couple of mates on a road trip who'd stopped for a country feed and a cold beer. Except that they both had assault rifles on their shoulders and they didn't speak or look at each other—or care about dining in the vicinity of a dozen bodies mouldering along the main street.

Nathan's stomach grumbled. 'I wonder what they're eating.'

My hunger was back too. As tasty as the lollies had been they weren't exactly a rounded meal.

Once the Jacks had finished eating, they each rolled a cigarette and puffed away. I laughed.

'What?'

'Jack's still smoking,' I said. 'Maybe all we have to do is lie low long enough for all of them to die of lung cancer.'

Three other Jacks—all male, all armed—trickled from the hotel and took places at another table with their plates and bottles. There were five of them. I had six bullets. I fantasised about taking them all out quick and clean. Getting supplies, getting ammo, getting a car and getting away. Except that wouldn't happen. Even if I could somehow become Ultimate Sniper Girl, killing these five would just bring the rest.

I pushed the idea aside, rested my head on the top of a low grave marker and watched the Jacks as the dark grew up around us.

I wondered what it was like down there. Five men with one mind. Sharing a set of thoughts as they sipped beers and smoked. I imagined it like some dudebro bonding session conducted inside a funhouse mirror maze. They certainly didn't look on guard, like they were worried about being killed like the other five Jacks we'd annihilated with our DIY car bomb back in Samsara. Maybe that was the point: here they were, for the taking, Jack tempting me to try my hand again.

Then, as one, as if a scheduled break had ended or they'd been summoned from afar, the Jacks stubbed out their smokes and went inside and put out lanterns. The pub dropped into darkness. Motorbikes rumbled and Humvee doors slammed and headlights flared as the three vehicles burned up the road towards us.

For a moment I feared they somehow knew where we were, that they'd heard the intensity of my murder plans, like a disturbance in the force in *Star Wars*. Who knew how this telepathy thing worked or how it had continued to evolve? My assumptions had been continually proved wrong. Not having Evan at my side was proof of that. Maybe Jack was now some sort of disembodied consciousness who'd just figured out how to hack into my mind so he could communicate our whereabouts to his earthbound brothers.

Slipping the safety off, I steadied the rifle against a granite crucifix. I kept my sight on the lead motorbike rider's helmet, feeling Nathan's eyes boring into me from the next grave. We both knew there was nothing he could do to stop me if I squeezed the trigger. Heart hammering, mouth dry, I mentally sketched out my plan. I'd shoot the first rider. He'd crash. Maybe take down the other one. I'd put two bullets into the Humvee's windscreen. Then we'd have to run. Keep moving. Try to get away before the rest of them arrived.

I curled my finger tighter around the trigger. The headlights played across the graveyard's iron fence and swept around the curve to head south. When they were gone, engine noises fading, I returned the rifle to safe and pointed it at the sky. Nathan let out a long relieved breath and clambered over to my grave. We looked down at Killeen.

'Let's check it out,' he said.

'I thought you were against taking risks.'

Nathan sighed. Like he was trying for patience.

'I'm willing to take risks for a *reason*,' he said. 'What I'm not willing to do is pick a fight we can't win just for the sake of it. But if we don't get some food soon we're gonna be in trouble.'

I couldn't help but laugh. After a moment Nathan joined in.

'More trouble, I mean,' he said.

•••

We crept between rows of headstones and along the narrow dirt road that led down to the highway and to Killeen. We hunched by a semitrailer that'd pulled into a rest stop and never left. I could smell the driver, festering up in his cabin. Best I could see, there wasn't any movement inside the pub or the shops. But they could be waiting behind any door or window. They might've followed our example at Samsara, and booby-trapped everything with explosives.

A plaintive *riaaaow* came from under the truck and a cat appeared, slinking between the big wheels and arching its back against my leg. I rubbed its neck. Set off an eruption of purrs. It was some sort of pedigree. Collar around its neck. Still soft and plump. Not a feral who'd lived its life in the fields before the Snap. This was a refugee who'd cleared out when the Jacks arrived.

I stood up, picked up the puss, calmed it in my arms.

'What're you doing?' Nathan said.

'Stay here,' I whispered and padded towards the black outline of Killeen.

Despite my patting and reassuring murmurs, the cat's ears flattened against its head as the fur along its spine stood up. I crouched, set it down on the road. The thing looked at me accusingly, as if it'd misjudged me terribly, and then shot back past Nathan and disappeared under the truck.

'I've never been much of a cat person,' I whispered when I returned to Nathan. 'My stepmother's cat hated me. But this? It doesn't feel right.'

My hackles were up, back of my neck prickling, telling me that if we went any closer to Killeen's pub we wouldn't even get to put up a fight.

'Let me go in,' Nathan said. 'I'll be quick and quiet. You stay and cover me. I'll just get some food.'

Now *he* was being reckless. Desperate.

'Town north-east of Samsara,' I said. 'If I was going to lay a trap, this is one of the places I'd do it.'

'But they were just here,' he whispered. 'We saw them leave.'

'We don't know if they all left,' I said. 'Could be two on bikes, one driving the Humvee and two still inside. How does it feel? Your gut?'

'Empty,' he said. 'Hungry.'

'Underneath that?'

Nathan dipped his head. 'Okay, what do you suggest we do?'

'Go around the town. Stay off the road until it's safe.'

'Safe?'

'Safer.'

NINE

'Hello,' Evan says as Tregan climbs into the car next to him. Damon goes around the vehicle and gets in the other side so my little brother is between them. Jack's showing me he's got what he wanted without me. A woman who puts out and does as she's told. And Evan makes three. It's an abomination.

The shell of my little brother leans into Tregan. 'Look,' he says, showing her the tablet. '*Snots 'N' Bots.*'

She smiles warmly. I want to throw up at how clucky she feels already. Like they're a goddamned family.

Damon grins at her—at me—and ruffles Evan's hair as the four-wheel drive bumps down a dirt road towards Baroonah.

'Where did you find him?' Tregan asks softly.

'Danby and Nathan left him behind in Samsara.'

'You're kidding.'

Damon shakes his head. 'Luckily he's not really aware of what's going on. We've been keeping him at another safe house with other kids.'

The lies pour out of Damon like honey and the single doubt Tregan has about him makes me despise her even more.

He's-too-sweet-I-hope-he'll-know-when-to-be-ruthless-Kill-her-him-avenge-Gary-Jack-Don't-think-that!-She'll-hear-If-you're-listening-Danby-Damon's-serious-wants-peaceful-surrender-Better-than-you-deserve-you-fuc—

Tregan closes her eyes, inhales deeply, pictures herself doing wind chime meditation, exhales the bad energy, clears her mind. When she opens her eyes, Evan and Damon are staring at her.

'Danby,' Damon says, 'if you're here, I want you to see we've taken good care of your brother.'

Tregan nods solemnly, but her soul flares jealously. *So-much-time-away-from-me-looking-for-that-bitch-Now-he-talks-to-her-through-me?-That's-why-I'm-here?*

'Danby, I want you to know,' Damon continues, 'that there can be a peaceful outcome to all of this. There doesn't have to be any more killing.'

Their four-wheel drive turns into Baroonah's main street. I see it on my tablet, joining another vehicle with tinted windows. The cars drive through the intersection and stop amid the vehicles and soldiers laying siege to the mansion.

'They're in there?' Tregan asks. She imagines the place riddled with bullets, me and Nathan as full of holes as Bonnie and Clyde. *Don't-think-that-Visualise-your-wind-chimes—*

'We think so,' Damon says. 'Make sure they can see it all.'

Tregan obediently pans her head like a camera so that I get a good look at their military might.

'Danby,' Damon says, 'you can see we've got you surrounded. If you and whoever else you're with put down your weapons and come out I guarantee you won't be hurt. We'll talk. We'll take you somewhere safe where you can live your way. You can see how Tregan's been kept safe. You can have that and take Evan with you. We don't want any more violence.'

Tregan nods and her heart swells at how good it feels to be with this man and on the side of righteousness.

I don't come out of the mansion with my hands up. Even if I was in there I wouldn't. I'd be in an upstairs window trying to shoot Damon, Tregan and Evan dead in their vehicle.

Minutes tick by. Damon sighs theatrically and shakes his head at Tregan and thus at me.

'Maybe her friend can talk sense into her,' he says. 'It's all we've got left.'

My blood chills. Friend?

Tregan frowns as the doors of the Humvee ahead of them swing open to release the driver and his shotgun passenger. Hulking specimens. Clad in fatigues. Clutching assault rifles across chests protected by body armour. I don't know these Jacks. Have never seen them. One of the men opens a passenger door and nods for whoever's inside to come out.

My throat knots and the spaces behind my knees go slack as a slump-shouldered man with grey dreadlocks steps onto the street. Marv. The only Special who'd been alive in Clearview when Jack and I rolled into town with his unholy army. The man who'd saved me from being shot on the bridge. The man who'd escaped with us and selflessly carried my little brother, even as it put him farther and farther from his own family. The man I'd last seen setting out on a desperate and likely doomed mission to save his wife and child from Jack's control.

'We didn't hurt him,' Damon says to Tregan and me. 'Not even when he came at us with a machine gun.'

She nods sagely. Thinks: *Bloody-hell-I-would've-blown-his-ass-to-kingdom-come.*

I want to be glad that Marv's alive. That he wasn't killed by Jack on his way back to Clearview to save his wife Jane and daughter Lottie. But seeing him like this isn't cause to celebrate. I wonder how close he got to rescuing his family. My answer comes a second later when a tween girl climbs from the back of the car. Overalls hanging from her waif's frame, she's olive-skinned like her dad. Lottie: I watched Jack raise her in Clearview, along with her mother, Jane, who's next out of the vehicle, a slender woman under a smudge of strawberry blonde hair.

Damon nods at Tregan and they climb from the back of the four-wheel drive and make their way to where Marv and his family stand together on the road.

'Marv,' Damon says with a nod. 'This is Tregan.'

Tregan sticks out her hand. Marv lets her hang but Lottie breaks from his side.

'Hey,' she says, shaking the offered hand. 'I got my dad back!'

'I'm glad,' Tregan says.

Her smile bounces from Lottie to Jane but flatlines when she meets Marv's hard stare. The look in his eyes tells me his wife and daughter are still Minions. Not that Tregan sees that.

Marv's-alive-got-his-family-back-And-he's-still-ungrateful-what-a—

'Ungrateful?' Marv spits. 'How can you be so stupid?'

Tregan stiffens. She's forgotten what it's like to be around anyone who can read her mind. If only she knew the truth. Her thoughts fill up with her wind chimes.

'You can't block me out,' Marv says with a sneer. 'You bloody bi—'

Damon steps up to him. 'Enough!'

Marv flinches. Backs away a little. Glances at Jane and Lottie. I'm guessing he still has hopes they can be freed from Jack's control.

'What do you want?' Marv says, looking past Damon at the amassed army. 'Doesn't look like you need my help.'

Through Tregan, through the video cameras, I see Marv's shock when Evan climbs from the four-wheel drive and wanders across the road to take Tregan's hand. My gut churns at the mirror image mockeries: Marv trapped with his fake family; Tregan unaware she's stuck with a man and child who share the same soul as everyone here except Marv, the man she can't stand.

I can only imagine what Marv thinks as he stares at my little brother. The boy he spent long days defending and carrying, now standing as part of the enemy and eyeing him coldly. I wish he could know I did everything I could to save Evan. Except that's not quite true.

'We think Danby's in there,' Damon says, nodding past the trees towards the brick mansion. 'She knows you. If she's in there, she can see we haven't hurt you or your family. If anyone can help her end this peacefully, it's you. Just go up, get her to come to the door, talk to her.'

I scream into the beanbag for the second time. *This* is Jack's plan to lure me from hiding.

'We'll come with you,' Jane says.

Marv shakes his head at Damon. 'I'm going alone.'

Jane touches his shoulder. 'We'll do this together.'

'Dad, it'll be okay,' Lottie adds.

'If they're with you, Danby's less likely to do anything silly that'd hurt them,' Damon says.

'We're not going to hurt anyone,' adds Tregan, proud to be part of the peace process.

Marv looks away from her in disgust and glances again at all the guns before his eyes settle on Damon. I think he senses he has to choose his words carefully. 'If we do this, that's it. You let us be. Me, Jane, Lottie—we get to go somewhere far away.'

Damon nods. 'I promise.'

Marv's eyes glisten. He's clinging to the hope that if he's no longer useful he can be free and Jane and Lottie can go back to being themselves. I wonder if Marv would want to kill them if he knew Jack was in them forever. The way I still want to end Evan.

I begin to cry as Marv gathers Jane and Lottie behind him and they walk through the mansion's gate and along its garden path. I see him via the cam by the front door, wiping sweat from his brow, arms sweeping backwards to ensure his wife and child are shielded by his broad body in case I'm inside and start spraying bullets at my enemies.

Hostage-negotiator, Tregan thinks about Marv, not seeing that the phrase is only half true. *Surely-Danby-won't-shoot-Not-him—*

Marv stops at the bottom of the steps and cups his hands and shouts my name. The cams don't have sound but I hear him through Tregan even above the choppers. Marv waits.

When there's no answer, he turns and looks past Jane and Lottie. Damon waves him forwards, mimics knocking and opening the door. Marv shakes his head and Jane begins to step around her husband. He grabs her arm and shepherds his wife back behind him so she's beside Lottie.

Marv crosses himself, mouth whispering in silent prayer, as he climbs the verandah steps like a condemned man ascending the gallows. His face looms in the camera lens by the front door. He turns to look back down at Jane and Lottie, framed by roses blooming out of season.

This is where I should run screaming from the cellar. Fire my rifle to get their attention. Surrender on my hands and knees. Kiss Damon's boots. Except none of it would serve any purpose. It wouldn't save Marv and it'd kill me.

'I'm sorry,' I whisper.

I pinch the screens, zero in on Damon's face, see him through Tregan. A smirk lingers at the edge of his mouth and there's a glimmer of anticipation in his eyes. I dig my nails into the palms of my hands so hard they bleed.

Damon has sussed I'm not in the mansion. Jack knows I'd have to be stupid to hole up there after ambushing his outriders. But whether or not he thought I was inside didn't matter until Marv was put into play as a pawn.

My friend raises a fist and knocks. He waits. Knocks again. Turns to Jane and Lottie. Through Tregan I see Marv's lips move. He's telling them he loves them. I can't watch. I bury my face in the beanbag. But I can still see everything. *This* is the reason Tregan's been brought to the siege. So *I* can't look away.

Marv turns the doorknob, opens the door a crack and leans in to shout into the house. There's no response. He pushes the door wider, calls again. Nothing. He turns to Jane and Lottie, a look of relief on his face, and I read his lips: 'I don't think there's anyo—'

Marv and Jane and Lottie disappear inside smoky orange flashes. There's a tremor in the wall behind me and then the explosions reach me as a dull *bhumpff*.

I sob into the beanbag. Two of my grenades. Just inside the hallway. Wired so the pins would be pulled when the door opened. I did it because it'd look suspicious if the house *wasn't* booby-trapped. The idea was to kill a few random Jacks. Not one of the only people I had left in this world.

Oh-my-God-oh-my-God: Tregan thinks, held tight by Damon, Evan under his other arm. *She-killed-him-Oh-my-God*.

Through her blurred eyes, I see Marv and Jane and Lottie, blown onto the lawn, brown smoke swirling from the smouldering verandah. Then Damon's dragging Tregan and Evan back to the four-wheel drive and shouting at them over her ringing ears to stay down. She huddles with my little brother on the backseat.

'I'm scared,' he whimpers.

She kisses his cheek, mouths that everything's going to be all right. Evan blinks up at her, nods and smiles just for me.

I scream again. Want to scream until I turn myself inside out. But inside the agony there's a centring force. Hatred. It burns cold and it's by that light that I gather myself enough to focus on the tablet.

My cams show clearing smoke. Marv, Jane and Lottie crumpled where they fell. Soldiers pour up the path past them, weapons sweeping every which way, as they rush through the shattered doorway and smash their way in through the windows.

After the car bomb in Samsara, Jack was wise to my moves. I couldn't have known he'd use Marv and Jane and Lottie like that. But somehow I should've. What I do know is I'll make them pay.

TEN

We retraced our steps to the cemetery, went over its back fence and cut through paddocks, only risking the flashlight on the outskirts of Killeen. Once we made it back to the highway we clung to the gravel verge, ready to dive into the trees at the first sound of a vehicle. We walked and walked. Giving in to exhaustion wasn't an option. Laying down here would mean laying down to die.

• • •

I thought about all the people who'd had to do this through history. The millions taking flight from disasters, fleeing tyrannical despots, making exodus from pogroms, escaping warring soldiers and pouring out of bombed cities. What had kept them going was the promise of safe haven, whether in some sprawling refugee camp or under the protection of a friendly army. We didn't have that. All Nathan and I had was each other. Even that felt like it was slipping away.

We came upon a clot of cars. I cupped the flashlight at a driver's side window. Knew what I'd see from the smell oozing from the sedan. Dude slumped behind the wheel. Skin shedding from his face in slimy sheets. My empty stomach tightened painfully. I lurched away, clambered onto the bonnet, quickly shone the torch north along the road. Snarled traffic receded into the darkness. I joined Nathan at the next hatchback. He was sniffing the air around it.

'Empty.'

He eased open the driver's door. The interior light came on. The battery was good. The keys were in the ignition. There was probably fuel. Nathan raised his eyebrows at me. I shrugged and shook my head.

'If you want,' I said. 'But we won't get far.'

Nathan sighed with frustration. I handed him the flashlight. 'Take a look if you don't believe me.'

He grabbed the torch, clunked up onto the roof of the hatchback, shone the weakening yellow beam ahead. Seeing his shoulders slump didn't make me feel vindicated. There were dozens of cars in our way.

'Let's at least see if there's any food,' he said, stepping back onto the bitumen.

People had to have crashed out before they managed to eat and drink whatever supplies they had.

We chewed the last of our lollies. I smeared minty saliva under my nostrils against the smell we were about to unleash. Nathan did the same.

We threw open car doors and poked into the shadows past bloating bodies as thick stench wrapped itself around us. I tried not to breathe. I tried not to hear the gurgling and hissing sounds the dead made as liquid and gas found its way out of them. In a mini, down by the swollen feet of an elderly woman, a plastic shopping bag held tins of peaches, packets of nuts and a box of pretzels. I yanked it free and stumbled away, vaguely aware of Nathan retching alongside me as he lugged a six-pack of bottled water. We staggered through the brush until we came to a fallen log where we could sit and breathe clean air again.

Every door we'd opened had sunk that stretch of road deeper into a soupy cloud. It'd been worse than Parramatta, than Shadow Valley, than Greenglen or Samsara. People had been dead for weeks now. I couldn't imagine what the cities were like. I remembered what Jack had told me: that life would be unliveable amid millions of decaying bodies.

My gut growled to remind me I'd join them if I didn't eat soon. I rustled in the plastic bag, handed Nathan a tin of peaches and popped one open for myself. I gobbled the chunks and slurped the syrup. The sweetness hit my throat and stomach and unleashed a sugary wave of wellbeing. Then I imagined the woman's smell penetrating the steel can and permeating the fruit and juice. Afterthought or aftertaste? Either way I started to retch. I clenched my fists and closed my eyes. Forced myself to hold it in. My mind and stomach started to settle.

'Are you all right?' Nathan asked.

I vomited into the grass.

When I'd finished puking he handed me a bottle of water.

I washed out my mouth, drank a little.

'Thanks,' I said. 'Can you do me a favour?'

Nathan regarded me warily.

'Unless you want to hear "no" or me lying, stop asking me if I'm all right,' I said. 'Nothing's all right, okay?'

Nathan nodded curtly. 'Okay.'

After a while, I ate some pretzels and nuts. It wasn't a lot but my stomach felt full. Maybe it'd shrunk.

'Do you want to check more cars?' Nathan said. 'There's probably more food.'

I gazed at those tombs. Imagined the horrors we'd have to endure for the chance of another tainted meal.

Whatever look I had on my face answered the question for Nathan.

'Me either,' he said.

• • •

We tramped through bush parallel to the road until the cars tapered out. The sky began to brighten. Now we couldn't risk returning to the bitumen in daylight. We kept on for hours beneath the trees, sweating and sore, cicadas screaming so loudly a chopper might've been on top of us before we heard it.

By midday I might've been walking asleep when I bumped into Nathan and nearly knocked him over. When we regained our footing, he pointed at a flat stretch of road and a red roadside mailbox with a sign for 'Harry's Enclave' that had a cartoon picture of a guy holding lemons.

'Lemons?' I said. 'You're kidding.'

'There's bound to be food at the house,' Nathan said. 'At the enclave, I mean.'

I squinted. Couldn't see any dwelling. Harry's property stretched west. A rough driveway led up a hill between paddocks with a few sheep. I guessed the enclave and lemons were over the rise.

'Well?' Nathan said.

I nodded. We came out of the bush, nipped across the road and trudged up the track as sheep eyed us and let out random bleats. We crested the rise and Nathan looked at me and summoned a grin. Fields of lemons lined our way to Harry's Enclave.

'You even like lemons?'

'Oranges would be righteous,' I croaked, kicking rocks over a drainage ditch. 'Cheeseburgers even better.'

Nathan managed a little smile. 'Not wrong there but when life gives you yada yada.' He reached over a fence, picked two lemons and handed one to me. I tore into it, squeezed juice into my mouth, screwed up my face at the bitterness.

'Yeah, not helping,' he agreed, tossing his half-sucked lemon back in the field. 'Come on.'

Harry's Enclave was a large country homestead backing on to hills of thick bush. Wordlessly, we walked on, slow when we should've been speedy, each step heavier and harder, the house not seeming to get closer.

Down a slope from the road, a body puffed out of its dungarees amid bottles of booze on the bank of a duck pond. Harry, I presumed. Like the sheep up by the road, I hoped the birds down by his corpse might be an early warning system if evil came calling. Provided, of course, they hadn't already said their piece, bleating and quacking long before we arrived, at Jacks who now lay in wait for us.

The house was cream brick, big and wide, with a garage off to the side, roller doors up to reveal the gleaming noses of a four-wheel drive and an expensive red sedan. In a side paddock, small legs stuck half out of a cubbyhouse whose roof was adorned with a deflated Santa. Across a lawn of grazing plastic reindeer and jaunty candy canes, another child-sized bundle was curled up inside a wire enclosure next to what had been the family dog. Nathan and I didn't say anything. We stuck to the centre of the driveway, not wanting to stray from our path into pockets of foul air.

The wreath-decorated front door was open. We sized each other up for a moment on the porch. Nathan's left eye fluttered and his throat bobbed. I guess my pinched shoulders and white-knuckle grip around the rifle didn't inspire confidence in him either. Neither of us wanted to step over the threshold. But this tired, hungry, exposed—it wasn't like we had a choice. I walked into the house, seeing the hallway along my rifle barrel. Nathan followed me, picked up a baseball bat that'd been left inside the door to defend against home invaders just like us.

We stood in the doorway to the lounge room. Shiny gifts were by their empty boxes, like creatures that'd crawled from cocoons. Balls of wrapping paper lay on the carpet. Spiders had added silvery webs to the Christmas tree's tinsel. We kept on in silence, checking the house. Bedrooms and bathrooms, home gym and study, laundry: there was no one, alive or dead, benign or malign. I tilted the blinds in the media room, looked out on a backyard with a pool as green as the overgrown lawn. Beyond the yard were paddocks and bush.

'Do you think they've been here?' Nathan said at my side.

The carpets and tiles didn't have dirt tracked across them. Nor did it look like anything had been searched. Not that either of those things really meant much. I didn't know whether to hope they had, which would mean we were still behind the leading edge of Jack's forces but safe for the time being, or to hope they hadn't even though that risked them rolling up on us at any moment.

'I don't know,' I said. 'Let's see what there is to eat.'

In the kitchen, I clicked open big cupboard doors and sagged in relief at shelf after shelf of tinned foods and bottles of juice.

'Oh, man,' I said. 'Mother lode.'

I popped a packet of corn chips, scooped out a handful and held the bag out to Nathan. But he seemed to have lost interest in eating and instead stared at the fridge's magnetised photo gallery.

'The mother,' he said, peering at a happy snap of a big lady beaming beside two kids laughing on quad bikes. 'Where is she?'

I swallowed chip shards, throat dry and painful, unable to answer. I wanted to say it didn't mean anything. She might be holed up in the garage. She could have taken another car or stumbled off into the bush. We'd checked all the rooms. It didn't matter. Unless she was hiding somewhere, watching us and—

'Lounge room,' Nathan said.

We'd only glanced in there as we entered the house. Stomach rolling, I crept back with him. The lounge room looked like a time capsule, unchanged since Christmas morning, when empty couches had been bunched in front of heavy curtains to create a clear patch of carpet for the kids to see what Santa had left for them. And they'd made out like bandits: a Robopony, action figures, Shades, retro Debbie dolls. Mum and dad had done all right, too: perfume and cologne, celebrity cookpad and golfpro hologram, laser lady-shaver and . . . men's socks. I turned them over with my boot. They were classy, argyle numbers, not the cheapie novelties Stephanie had given Dad with disastrous results. Seeing them made me miss him—and Mum and everyone. I couldn't believe they were all gone—and that Christmas had only been a few weeks ago. Looking around the lounge room, I wondered what secrets and lies had caused this nuclear family to explode and die scattered in the fallout of their shattered minds.

Nathan touched my arm. 'Listen.'

I heard it. Wheezing. From the far side of the room. As we crossed the soft carpet, the air became thick and sickly, a sour cloying cloud. Nathan and I dragged a sofa out from the curtains. There was the mother. Lost down behind the couch like the punchline to some bad dad joke. She'd done her best to hide from the world with a carton of eggnog that'd ended up spilling all over her.

'Is she alive?' I asked. It felt like a stupid thing to say. With the couch out of the way, we could hear air whistling in and out of her. But last night on the road had reminded me that bodies weren't always as quiet as the grave.

Nathan knelt, took her pulse, nodded up at me wide-eyed. 'She is. How, I don't know. Maybe her weight. It's let her body feed off itself.' He looked back at her. The big lady had reached her sunken end, had shrunk in her clothes, skin drooping in pouches from her bones. We had no way of saving her and there was no sense prolonging her suffering. I set my rifle down, picked up a cushion from the couch and crouched beside Nathan.

'No, Danby,' he said, frowning and shaking his head, putting himself between me and the dying woman. 'No.'

I didn't understand. Nathan was the one who told me every person like this was dead no matter what. The night we rode the horses north he'd told me about the plane that crashed in World War II and how the men who parachuted clear never had a chance because the desert was too vast and no help was ever coming. We'd had the right-to-die conversation in the tunnel. Surely *this* met his bloody criteria.

'Nathan, you wouldn't let a dog suffer like this.'

'Give it to me,' he said.

I held tight to the cushion. 'I want to do this.'

Nathan's shoulders bunched and his eyes flashed. 'That's the fucking problem,' he hissed. 'You *want* to do this. Like that woman you shot in Samsara. You didn't have to. No one should want to do this.'

I stood dumbly, felt stripped bare, didn't resist when he pulled the cushion from my grip. I stepped back, head spinning, subsided into the single seater.

Nathan knelt by the woman, gently suffocated her with one hand while the other held her wrist in a gesture that seemed half comforting and half the pragmatic task of feeling her pulse cease. She didn't drum her hands and feet. There was no appreciable difference between her being alive and being dead. I wondered what was happening inside her. Whether it was as simple as her lungs stopping and her heart and brain following. Whether she had a soul that'd been trapped all this time and was now grateful to be unmoored so it could float away. Nathan spoke softly to her. A shiver went through me. It reminded me of Jack creeping on people's minds with his 'open, you're mine' commandment.

'What are you saying?'

Nathan glanced at me annoyed, cheeks wet with tears. 'A prayer.'

'I thought you were an atheist,' I said.

'Yes, but she wasn't,' he said, stabbing a finger at the pictures of Jesus and Mary and Joseph that adorned a corner of the lounge room. 'Shit, Danby.'

Shaking his head, Nathan went and got an X-Men doona from one of the kids' rooms and covered their mother. With a grunt, he pushed the couch back into place.

'Come on,' he said. 'We need to eat.'

That he could say that after what he'd just done made me feel better. Maybe it wasn't just me who'd become callous. He just couldn't see it in himself.

I stood, shouldered the rifle and we closed the lounge room's French doors behind us to seal the woman in. It wasn't much of a burial but it was better than most got these days. At least she had someone to acknowledge her passing. Nathan's prayer might—somehow—have offered some comfort as she crossed over or whatever. I pictured how goddamned crowded the 'other side' must be now. Standing room only. Bit of a backlog. Take a number and wait. St Peter will be with you in approximately ten thousand years. I laughed at the thought and caught a sharp glance from Nathan as he stepped into the kitchen.

Without speaking, like some cranky couple, we rattled out plates and cutlery and tins and bottles and sat side by side on stools and picked at our plates of canned salmon and sundried tomatoes and buttered mushrooms and anchovy-stuffed olives. We washed everything down with lukewarm cola.

I stared at the side of Nathan's head, eyes boring into his pulsing temple as he chewed, until he couldn't ignore me any longer.

'What?'

'Sorry,' I said. 'About in there.'

He shrugged, went back to eating. 'Me, too.'

I didn't know what he had to be sorry for. I didn't know what I had to be sorry for. I tried to douse my anger and nausea with another big jolt of crappy cola.

Out of the corner of my eye, Nathan wiped his mouth on a napkin. I could almost feel the effort it took for him to look at me. 'Do you feel better?'

The way he said it: like a doctor asking a patient to self-assess. At least he didn't ask me if I was all right.

'I'm not hungry anymore.'

'Good.' Nathan nodded, picked at his plate.

'How about you?' I said.

He shrugged.

'Is your wound okay?'

Nathan touched the bandage under his shirt. I'd robotically helped him clean and dress his bullet wound once when we'd been in the tunnel. I'd seen him wash down a few pills. I'd assumed they were antibiotics and his mood stabilisers. If he'd run out of either he might be in trouble.

'Still hurts,' he said. 'I think it's okay.'

'I'll help you check it,' I said.

Nathan shook his head. 'I can do it.'

I nodded. Stared at my plate.

'I—'

I looked at Nathan.

'I think we should sleep in shifts.'

'Makes sense.'

He glanced at his watch. 'I'll take the first watch.'

Before this, back when we were simply dealing with being hunted like vermin through the apocalypse, Nathan would've acknowledged the silliness of that gesture and statement with some kind of joke. It seemed like the end of something good that we'd once had. It woke me up.

'No,' I said. 'You take care of your wound. Get some rest. I'll keep guard. Then you can take your turn.'

The old Nathan might've argued the point with good-natured chivalry. But this one just sighed and nodded, as if he thought maybe I'd burn down the house while he was asleep but there wasn't anything he could do to stop it.

I watched him come out of the bathroom with the first-aid kit and some bottles of water and disappear into the main bedroom.

We'd left the front of the house unguarded while we searched and ate, and we were still alive. I figured a few minutes more weren't going to make any difference. I grabbed a bottle of water from the pantry and went to the bathroom. I stripped off the filthy clothes I'd been wearing for over a week, washed and soaped myself in a frenzy and towelled dry. I looked at myself in the mirror. My singed eyebrows had grown back a bit but my hair was a patchwork of clumps. I grabbed some scissors from a drawer. Wrapped in a towel, I walked to the laundry, where I picked out some clothes from the dryer. Man's T-shirt that hung to my thighs and tracksuit pants whose drawstring I had to pull tight. But I didn't care. It was just good to feel clean. At least on the outside.

I hauled a six-pack of cola from the pantry and took my place on a chair on the verandah, the assault rifle by my side, and tugged on fresh socks and my red boots in case we had to make a fast getaway. I let my eyes settle on the long driveway between the lemon trees. If they came on motorbikes or in cars or in choppers I'd have a bit of warning. Enough maybe to wake Nathan and for us to melt into the bush behind the house.

I clipped my hair by touch, cutting it down to the scalp, snipped at the stitches along the side of my head, tugged them out and felt a little blood trickle free.

Night stole over the property until I couldn't see my hand in front of my face. I settled in, sighting along my assault rifle into the blackness. I drank cola after cola, the caffeine keeping me awake, pissing the by-products on the lawn so I didn't have to creep around the darkened house and risk missing something. I flicked the gun's safety off whenever I heard bleating or quacking. If the animal noises had lasted more than a few seconds, it'd mean they were out there on foot without lights. I would've had to decide between fight and flight. I knew which it'd be. But each time the sheep and ducks settled quickly and I was left in peace and flicked the rifle's safety back on. I fantasised about battle anyway, pictured me making every bullet count, the blood and blazing guns. I'd die. Nathan'd get away. It'd be over.

'Danby.' I tensed at the whisper behind me. 'It's only me.'

Nathan making sure he didn't scare me? Or scared if he surprised me I'd whirl and shoot him?

'Okay,' I said. Nathan stepped onto the porch, hand cupping a candle, face mahogany in its glow as he crouched by my seat. I saw he had some of the husband's clothes on, too—tracksuit pants, a brown flannel shirt. They fit him better.

'What's the time?' I asked, realising I'd left my watch in the bathroom.

'Just after two,' Nathan said. 'Anything going on out there?'

'No,' I said. 'Nothing.'

'Don't sound so disappointed.'

I let out a snort. But I didn't have any smart comeback. I *had* passed hours picturing myself blowing away Jacks.

'Why don't you get some sleep, Danby?'

I nodded, stood and tried not to sway, swapped rifle for candle and followed the flickering glow to the bedroom. I blew out the flame and flopped onto the bed. Hazy blue light wafted from the floor. I leaned over and saw a little cube clock on the carpet. Thing was still going on battery. As I picked it up, it projected its blue light display on the ceiling.

Time 2:04

Temp 22°C

Humidity 82%

Tuesday 13 January

January *thirteenth*. Three weeks since the end of the world and one since I'd left Evan for worse-than-dead. My throat felt as thick and heavy as my eyes. I pushed the clock under my pillow and curled myself around the baseball bat Nathan had left in the sheets along with his scent and body warmth.

ELEVEN

Payback will come later. But now I have to make sure Marv and Jane and Lottie didn't die for nothing. I refresh the tablet screen for a Cameleon view of the mansion's dining room.

• • •

The blaze in the fireplace has died down. A big guy uses a poker to haul out smouldering refuse and rakes the ashes on the floorboards before hunching over them like someone trying to read tea leaves. What I'd torched in the fireplace was stuff I'd found in the mansion's library and on a few shelves around town. Bush survival book. Leaflet about the big cats of Western Plains Zoo. New South Wales travel guide. Map of the Central Desert. Bushranger history. War hero memoir. Motorbike maintenance manual. Stacked the way they were, I knew they wouldn't burn in their entirety and what was left would be puzzle pieces for Jack to fit together. The fireplace attendant examines a burned hardback spine. No idea which one it is and it doesn't matter so long as it seems like part of research we were doing on our destination deep inland. I hoped crash-course book-learning will remind Jack of himself in Clearview. Flatter his ego just that little bit to think I've been copying him.

I can't believe I still think of him as a *him*. It's like visualising God as an old dude with a big white beard or the Devil with a red jumpsuit and horns. Right in the mansion's lounge room there are three Jacks. Is each of them one hundred per cent him? Or are they each a tiny fraction that contains the whole? *Synecdoche.* I remember that word from my dictionary reading. Never had a use for it. Wish I didn't.

Thinking about this theoretical stuff hurts my head and dilutes my focus. The why and how isn't important. What matters is that they follow my story. I peer at the screen. A Jack scans the bookshelf, fingers the empty spaces where volumes have been removed. A girl's on hands and knees, butt in the air, head tilted to look under furniture. Bingo! She's found the scorched page fragment I placed beneath the coffee table. Lifting it with the reverence you'd reserve for a holy relic, she stares at the words and uploads them into the big Jack cloud or however it works. What she's found is part of a page from an old backpacker guidebook I found in Baroonah's rancid hostel that describes the town of Dubbo as 'the gateway to the west' and 'a must-visit for wildlife lovers'.

They're broad strokes. Jack has to finish the picture himself. See me and Nathan and other fugitives holed up here. Being spooked by the drones. Needing to travel light. Hurriedly torching evidence of our plans. Killing the outriders.

Fleeing Baroonah on the back roads. Heading west on motorbikes.

I'm also counting on Jack's access to Evan's mind and knowing that one of the best times me and Evan and Dad and Stephanie had together was a couple of years ago when we did a weekend trip to the Western Plains Zoo. We stayed in luxurious safari huts, which were inside the zoo itself, and rode bicycles around and saw lions and tigers and elephants and monkeys. At sunset and sunrise, giraffes and zebras strolled right by our front porch.

'I'd like to live here,' I remember saying.

'I know, right?' Stephanie replied. 'Amazing.'

Evan grinned as if he believed it might happen.

Animals hate the Minions. The Dubbo Zoo is an open environment. It's possible some beasts have survived there. It makes sense that we'd go to a place where no Jack could tread for fear of being trampled to death by elephants or torn to pieces by lions.

On the tablet I watch Jacks checking out the mansion's main bedroom. They're seeing men's and women's clothes, tangled sheets and an unmade bed, damp towels on the floor. As I watch, a guy picks up a pair of girl's jeans, checks the size. Another Minion's in the ensuite bathroom, pulling a bin from under the sink to see it contains tissues, discarded condoms and a genuine preloved tampon. There's wet toothbrushes, toothpaste, sunblock and shampoo, his and hers deodorants—all the usual stuff. And the less usual stuff of the post-Snap world: bottles of mineral water because the taps don't work;

candles because the lights are long gone; a bucket of water to flush the toilet. Unless they're going to dust for our fingerprints or thought to carry a mobile lab to test for DNA, it's going to look like me and Nathan were sharing the bedroom and this bathroom a few hours ago.

I haven't got cameras in the other bedrooms but they'll be finding unmade beds and glasses of water on side tables and an assortment of clothes retrieved from laundry hampers along this street. Enough to suggest there were maybe five or six people living here, judging by the number of toothbrushes in the bigger bathroom. In the kitchen, plates and cutlery are stacked in the sink, still wet with beans and sauce and other slop I smeared on them. Cups stand half filled with coffee that's cold but not mouldy.

Out in the backyard a Jack is bent over bullet casings that glint in the grass. Another one picks up a tin can shot with holes by the fence. It looks like someone did a bit of target practice here. A Jack bends down to pick up a white nugget from the path and smells it. More of my gum.

On the street, all of these discoveries feeding into his mind, Damon turns in a slow circle, eyes on the neighbouring houses, as though wondering if I might be in one of them. When he stops, he's facing the cam I stuck on a fence across the road. It's like he's staring straight at me, like the Wicked Witch gazing at Dorothy in her crystal ball as she gets ready to unleash those flying monkeys. My guts twist. My basement hideout all of a sudden doesn't feel so safe. It feels like maybe I'm already in my grave.

TWELVE

Jack was flying my way, skimming over hills and trees, powered by some infernal revving engine. But there was too much land for him to scour. If I stayed hidden, if I didn't move, I'd be safe. Jack was like Santa and Satan wrapped in one: he saw everything, naughty and nice, could get into any house with black magic. And there he was, opening the door, slipping into my room, growling and grinning, rifle over his shoulder and holding out a cartoon bomb with a smoking fuse. I didn't have a gun. Only a baseball bat. But I'd been good at softball at school. I'd get a home run with his head or die trying.

'Are you awake?' he said, and his voice was the shot of adrenaline to spring me up from the bedsheets, swinging the bat.

'Jesus, Danby,' he said, a shadow stepping back out of my range and into the door's rectangle of grey light. 'It's just me. Nathan, okay?'

I blinked and his blur came into focus. I uncoiled from the bat, let it fall to the blankets, sat back on the bed. Nathan ventured into the room, rifle slung over his shoulder, holding out a steaming mug like a peace offering.

'Just coffee, okay? I found a little gas camp cooker in the garage.'

'Thanks,' I said, taking the cup.

Nathan wore a worried smile. 'You were sleeping with your eyes open.'

'Really?'

He nodded.

'Sorry,' I said, sipping the strong brew, sweaty in my filched clothes, the sheets twisted every which way. 'The coffee's good. Thanks.'

Nathan had binoculars hanging around his neck.

'Where'd you get those?'

'Study. Quite the collection of bird-watching books.'

I looked at the cube clock. Nine thirty. I stiffened against the bedhead. 'Shit, Nathan, why didn't you wake me earlier?'

'You needed to sleep. It's not like we're on a schedule.'

I wanted to argue. Except he was right. Here, there, anywhere: we didn't know where they were. And, even if my eyes had been open, I did feel better for getting seven hours' sleep in an actual bed instead of in a tunnel or on a roadside. My body wasn't as sore. My head felt clearer.

'Has there been anyone?' I asked.

'Nothing.'

My shoulders eased. 'Excellent.'

Nathan nodded. Seemed satisfied that sleep had calmed me.

'I've got something to show you,' he said.

•••

The quad bikes sat off to the side of the cars in the garage. One red, one yellow, matching helmets over the handlebars, keys in the ignition.

'They're the ones in the photo on the fridge,' Nathan said. 'Gotta be easier than riding motorbikes, right?'

If the kids had been able to handle them I was sure we could.

'They go . . . I mean, I've started them,' Nathan said. 'I'm amazed that didn't wake you.'

I flashed to the dream. Jack's engine noise. The sound of the quad bikes had seeped in. Was this what my life would be like from now on, sleeping with my eyes open, dreams offering no escape?

'Full fuel tanks,' Nathan was saying. 'Petrol cans over there are full, too. They'd have to get us a few hundred kilometres at least.'

I kicked a quad's chunky tyres. We could ride these things over just about anything. They were called all-terrain vehicles for a reason.

Nathan pulled a slender GPS unit from his back pocket. 'Detached this from the four-wheel drive's dash. Battery backup. Fully charged. Still works.'

I stood by his shoulder and peered at the colour screen's satellite image.

'That's this place,' Nathan said, pointing at a large green rectangle by the road. 'This here is a fire trail, leads into a network of them that stretch up to the mid-north coast.

Taking one of these cars means taking the road and I think that's asking for trouble.'

'Can I have a look?'

He nodded. I pinched out to show us as a tiny speck. I ran my eye back to Samsara and Wisemans Ferry and Richmond and Penrith. Used my thumb and forefinger to inch out the distance. All up it was about a hundred and twenty kilometres as straight as the crow flies. I wondered where in that landscape Evan was. Wondered if Marv had managed to get to Clearview and rescue Jane and Lottie.

'They have to move everyone inside the Radius so they'll be slower,' Nathan said.

I nodded. Didn't say what I thought: that we couldn't be sure how it worked anymore. Yes, if Damon and the rest of them were confined to the Radius, they'd have to move a thousand people or more inside that bubble to make sure they didn't revert to themselves like Oscar and Louis had.

But Jack reincarnating after I'd shot him—body-hopping like a hermit crab changing shells, downloading himself into all of his Minions—pretty much scrubbed any certainties. Even so, the quad bikes seemed our best shot at putting serious territory between us and our enemy. I zoomed the GPS screen again and scrolled along the ventricles of fire trails north. We'd be under dense tree cover but still have the benefit of speed. We wouldn't be footsore and we'd be able to carry supplies. What also sank in was that, with the distance we'd already covered, the quads would put us hundreds of kilometres away not just from harm but from Evan. This wasn't us regrouping and rearming and plotting our counter-assault. This was us fleeing. Leaving him for dead or worse. For good.

'Whatever you decide,' Nathan said, 'I'll respect your decision.'

I handed him the GPS unit. 'But you're going?'

He nodded. 'There's too many of them for just the two of us.'

I couldn't argue with that and found I didn't want to. Sleeping in a soft bed, with a full belly and a reasonable expectation of waking up alive, had acted like a circuit breaker on my anger and confusion. I wanted to be away and safe. Get my head together. 'I'll go with you. For now, okay?'

The garage's shelves yielded a couple of backpacks, sleeping bags and a tent. I found a locked cupboard and used a metal bar to bust the padlock. Inside there was a hunting rifle and a box of ammunition.

Nathan appeared at my shoulder, apprehension coming off him, as though now I had a new gun and more bullets I'd change my mind and want to ride straight south into glorious battle.

'I'll go in the house,' he said. 'Look for stuff we can use.'

I sat at a bench and familiarised myself with the rifle. Hefty wooden stock, long black barrel, magazine that clicked free and held five big bullets with .303 stamped on their brass bases. I checked the chamber, practised using the bolt action, dry fired a few times and got used to its weight. I set the gun down and straddled the nearest quad bike. Soft seat. Comfortable footrests. I gripped the handlebars, turned them this way and that, adjusted the mirrors, squeezed the brakes, twisted the throttle. I had none of the trepidation I'd experienced when I'd gotten behind the wheel of Stephanie's car to try to escape Beautopia Point or contemplated taking Mum's Jeep up Shadow Valley Road.

What did worry me was that the quads and the matching helmets hanging off the handlebars were so brightly coloured. That wouldn't do. A quick search yielded a space under the workbench that stored a motley collection of paints and brushes. I used a spray can of drab green to coat the bikes and helmets. It wouldn't win any camouflage awards but it'd make us less visible to anyone in the air.

Nathan was in the kitchen, stuffing food into the backpack. He'd laid out some more clothing. I fingered a black sweat-shirt a few sizes too big for me. It'd go over my grey tracksuit pants like a smock. I remembered doing this at the house in Riverview. Thinking it'd keep us alive. Oscar, Louis, Tajik, Alex: dead now. Marv, Evan: lost. And Nathan? Back then he'd been shocked by Louis mercy-killing a comatose woman where she lay. Yesterday he hadn't debated it for a moment. Me? I'd seen the necessity then but I wouldn't have volunteered for the job. Nathan and I had survived but it didn't feel like there was much of us left. That was how we'd changed in just three weeks. I wondered who we'd be in three months. In three years.

Nathan zipped up the backpack. 'Let's have something to eat and get going.'

Chewing muesli bars, we rolled the quad bikes onto the driveway, used bungee cords to secure our provisions to the luggage racks.

'Nice paint job,' Nathan said.

'Thanks.'

It felt good to be if not back on the same page then at least reading from the same book.

'We ought to give 'em a test run,' I said.

I tugged on my helmet, face snug in the padding, climbed on the closest quad, turned the ignition and throttled carefully. The engine noise was going to carry. There wasn't anything we could do about that. I accelerated across the driveway, practised braking and turning, returned to where Nathan stood with binoculars trained on the driveway.

'It's pretty easy,' I said.

'Don't get too cocky,' he replied. 'These things flip all the time.'

While Nathan got used to his quad, I ran back into the house, grabbed a garbage bag from a kitchen drawer and collected our empty food tins, cola cans and water bottles, our dirty plates and cutlery and discarded clothes. I swept up my hair clippings and straightened the bed we'd slept in. Then, heart sinking, I realised that if the Jacks got here soon they mustn't discover Nathan's act of mercy. The woman's emaciation and the absence of decay would pin her death as recent. It'd be obvious someone had suffocated her and shrouded her body. In the lounge room, I pulled out the couch, lifted the *X-Men* doona and cushion from her body and returned them to where they'd been when we arrived. It felt like a violation, like exhumation. On the way out of the house, I peeled the photo of the woman and her kids and the quad bikes from the fridge and added it to the rubbish.

Nathan frowned as I carried the clanking garbage bag to a big plastic bin.

'No point leaving any evidence,' I said.

'Hope you wiped it down for fingerprints?'

I pasted on a smile. He wouldn't have joked if he knew I'd disturbed the woman's resting place.

Nathan accelerated slowly off the driveway and I followed. We jostled across the back paddocks and onto a trail that ran through the trees along the base of a ridge. Galahs watched us pass under their branches. I wondered if other birds' eyes were on us. Maybe Jack's megamind had worked out how to take control of satellites and infrared cameras high up above the smoke and clouds had just detected us as a couple of heat signatures.

Nathan set a sensible pace, slowing when we came to any sort of incline or dip, stopping on high ground to scan with the binoculars, consulting the GPS when we hit any fork in the trails. At two o' clock, we stopped for lunch and topped up the petrol tanks. We'd covered seventy kilometres in three hours. It'd taken us a week to cover the same distance on foot. Now we were nearly two hundred kilometres north of Sydney.

I was about to restart the ignition when I saw them in my mind. A man and a woman. Eli and Kirsty.

I'm-scared-hon-Don't-know-if-I-can-handle-seeing-bodies-We'll-be-fine-as-long-as-we're-together-S'pose-it's-worth-it-if-we-find-chocolate-Ha-ha-as-much-as-we-can-carry-right?

Nathan had seen them too. Was frozen in the act of putting his helmet back on.

Eli had been revived on the northern outskirts of Sydney

four days after the Snap. He didn't know who his saviour had been. But he'd drunk the electrolytes left for him, read the instruction sheet, and he'd used the syringe and few tablets of Lorazepam to wake up his girlfriend, Kirsty. Their minds had reached back to Parramatta, seen what had happened to Ray and Cassie and the rest from Tregan, Gary and others. Later, as they tried to escape to the Central Coast, Revivee minds had shown them my attack on Jack on the bridge and his subsequent claims about me and Nathan at Richmond Air Base. While most of the Revivees had wanted to join Jack and then Damon, Eli and Kirsty's gut instincts told them to trust no one—but that meant they had to get as far away as possible or risk being declared allies of me and Nathan.

Around the time we'd been blowing Jack's chopper out of the sky, Eli and Kirsty had holed up in the Central Coast's hinterlands in a fancy bed and breakfast that'd been closed for renovations at Christmas. Safe, far enough away from other Revivees to have quiet, they'd had the chance to focus just on each other rather than simple second-by-second survival. The squabbling that'd become screaming during the Snap now seemed so superficial and stupid. When they could let themselves drift together, let themselves be present for each other rather than separate in the remembered past or imagined future, it was like their beings merged. Soulmateship.

This morning they'd made the tough decision to take bikes into the nearest town to resupply themselves with food. Those few kilometres had put them into our range—and into that of Tracey, one of the original Parramatta Revivees, who'd woken up dozens of people and managed to create a safe haven in the beach town of Terrigal.

Nathan set his helmet on the quad and looked at me. 'This is amazing.'

I nodded. Through Eli and Kirsty to Tracey, we were seeing almost seventy kilometres—the distance of their joined radiuses. Tuning into survivors who owed their lives to what we'd done weeks ago. Getting glimpses of minds trying to work in harmony. Nathan grinned at me and I smiled back. We'd done some good after all.

We were back on the quads, tooling slowly, just about out of Eli and Kirsty's range and thus about to lose Tracey too when Nathan and I hit the brakes. Back there, another mind, like a black cloud, even farther away but getting closer as it sped in from the south.

Dun-de-dun-da-da. Come-in-low-out-of-the-setting-sun-Something-like-that-Maybe-they'll-let-me-fire-one-of-those-machine-guns-Just-at-like-a-cow-or-something.

Cory: another original Revivee. Zeroing in on Tracey, his thoughts blasting into hers, ricocheting through her little community, reverberating along the coast and slamming into Eli and Kirsty and bouncing into our skulls. Cory: the little bastard who'd considered using the Lorazepam we'd left him to create a captive harem. Cory: the little bastard who'd been so keen to help hunt me and Nathan down.

Now he was in a chopper and I saw what'd happened to him in the past few weeks. Tregan had helped coordinate his removal from Penrith and he'd been taken to a distant farm where he couldn't hear any other minds. Cory's guards had told him that he'd join the fight when the time was right and until then he should make the most of the supply of food and beer and movies and games they'd provided. Then, just an hour ago, Damon had landed in a chopper and told Cory his time had come, that they'd found an enclave of Revivees like him and they needed to use his telepathic ability.

Flying north, sitting beside Damon, Cory was a little deflated—he'd imagined that he might be given a weapon and a mission to exterminate Danby with extreme prejudice. But, still, flying in a black helicopter, surrounded by guys with big guns and body armour, flanked by other choppers—well, it was all kinds of shit-hot cool.

'Got them?' Damon asked Cory through his headset speakers.

Cory nodded. 'Tracey—that's the leader—she can hear me loud and clear. Mate, she's not putting out the welcome mat.'

Cory-what're-you-doing?-You-don't-know-what-they'll-do. Tracey was already grabbing her stuff and shouting at her family members and thinking ahead to the car and the road out of Terrigal.

Tracey-it's-okay-You're-not-in-trouble-We-just-need-to-know-you're-not-hiding-her-that-girl-Danby. Cory nodded to Damon. 'Tracey's telling them to run.'

Damon looked at Cory and talked through him: 'Tracey, everyone—you're not going to be hurt. We just want to talk.'

'Oh crap,' said Nathan, easing back in his quad seat.

'Go,' I said. 'Please, go.'

Nathan looked at me.

'Not you,' I said. 'Them, Tracey.'

Guys-go-go-go, Tracey screamed as she scrambled down the stairs of the apartment building she and a few others had methodically cleared of bodies and cleaned as best they could. Her mother followed. Her sister didn't want to run again. Elsewhere, in neighbouring flats and houses, other Revivees were panicking and pleading innocence to Cory and Damon.

I-don't-know-anything-Nothing-to-do-with-me-Damon-I'm-sorry-about-Jack-But-it-wasn't-me-Cory-please-tell-him-I-know-we-should've-come-to-the-base-I-we-were-just-scared-Please-leave-us-alone-No-one's-seen-Danby-Nathan-anyone-please...

It was true. They'd never seen me or Nathan—not with their own eyes and not remotely since the bridge at Penrith. If I knew this, then Damon knew this and that meant... nothing good.

Tracey jumped behind the wheel of her Mazda as her mum buckled up in the shotgun seat. With a peal of rubber, the car slalomed along the street towards the coast road. In the rear-view mirror, Tracey saw a cloud of black choppers swarm up over the southern bluff. She knew she couldn't outrun them and she slowed into an intersection.

Thirty kilometres north and closer to us, Eli and Kirsty were on their bikes and pedalling furiously, aware that if they'd seen Cory he'd seen them and knew they'd been hiding in the bed and breakfast. Fleeing farther north, getting out of the Radius again, that was their only hope.

'We're not here to hurt anyone,' Damon said through Cory to Tracey and everyone else in Terrigal. 'Please come out to the football oval.'

You-heard-him-Come-to-the-park-We'll-word-you-up-on-what's-happening-yo, Cory embellished, feeling puffed up that he was right-hand man to the guy who'd inherited Jack's command. *Like-a-boss-bitches-yeah!*

'I'm telling them,' he said to Damon. 'I'm setting them straight.'

Damon nodded, face unreadable. Just like Tregan and Gary, Cory had no idea that his mind was an open book to Damon and all the other Minions.

Revivees told themselves this would be all right. Besides, there was no way to run, not with Cory in all of their minds. From houses and cars, they were converging on the football field.

At the intersection, Tracey glanced at her mum in the passenger seat.

'Mum? Do you want to go back?'

The old woman straightened in her seat and smiled at her daughter.

'Bugger that.' *No-going-back!-Don't-turn-around-Keep-going-Tracey-I-love-you-Whatever-happens.*

Tracey was grateful for the extra time they'd had to share emotions and thoughts and memories on this level. Was grateful she only had to think *I-love-you* for her mum to not just know it but to feel its truth.

'Ditto, kiddo,' her mum said. 'Go!'

Tracey planted her foot on the accelerator and the car shot forwards up the hill. A chopper broke from the pack hovering around the oval and thundered up the coast in pursuit. In her mirrors, Tracey saw the black bird swooping low and the flare of its machine guns. In her windshield, the road erupted as bullets stitched back to fill the car with blood and fire.

'Hey, what're you—' Cory said as Tracey's car exploded and flipped off a cliff into the surf.

Machine guns roared all around him, ripping into the people in the park below. Men, women and kids flew apart and Cory's head flooded with their last moments of pain and horror.

'Why?' Cory screamed in the noise and he was still yelling when the guns fell silent. Damon looked at him without a word.

'Why?' Cory croaked. He knew me and Nathan were bad news and that Tracey had been trying to get away. But the people in the park hadn't been resisting or escaping. Now they were splattered all over the soccer field. There wasn't a person left alive in Terrigal and the only thoughts Cory could pick up were Eli and Kirsty far to the north. He was glad they were almost out of range.

'You bastard,' he rasped at Damon through his tears. 'You said you just wanted to talk.'

Damon didn't seem to hear him. Stared right through him with eyes that weren't green so much as gold. *He-looks-like-Jack.*

'Danby,' Damon said. 'If you're out there. All of this? It's on you.'

This-doesn't-make-sense-I-must-be-drea— Cory's mind was so jumbled he didn't move when Damon reared back with his leg bent. The boot hit him like a wrecking ball in the centre of his chest. His hands scrabbled as he went backwards through the chopper's open doorway. Cory fell, rotors warping the sky above him, telling himself this all had to be a dream and he'd—

Our view of Terrigal died with Cory. Eli and Kirsty blinked out of sight a minute later. It was just me and Nathan and the bush again.

Except all I could see in my mind was all the blood that had just been spilled. On account of me. I launched myself off the quad, baseball bat in hand before I knew it, and smashed the thing against the nearest tree as I screamed. My noise must've carried for miles. I didn't care. I wanted them to come. It'd been wrong to run with Nathan. I wanted to fight and end it all.

THIRTEEN

Just when I'm sure Damon's spotted my cam on the tree and knows I'm hiding nearby, he turns and walks to the four-wheel drive and I let myself breathe again. In the back of the vehicle, Tregan hugs Evan to her and watches as the Tiger chopper that's been hovering over the mansion shoots up into the air, spins and roars west across the landscape. She thinks it must be a signal because Damon's men come pouring from the house, past the bodies of the little family strewn in the garden, and pile onto motorbikes and into the Humvees and armoured vehicle.

Exhaust smoke all around him, Damon watches the vehicles rumble west out of Baroonah before he opens the back door and climbs in beside Tregan.

'Danby and Nathan? They did that?' she asks.

Damon nods, looks at her, looks at me. 'She can't have gotten too far.'

I can't tell whether he's convinced by the scene I've staged or whether he's trying to fake me out. He could be staging this 'exodus' so I'll let my guard down and come crawling out.

'Do you know where?' asks Tregan.

We-can't-let-them-get-away-Not-with-what-they-did-to-Gary-To-Jack-to-Marv's-wife-and-daughter.

Damon takes her hand, squeezes it. 'You have to go with Evan and keep him safe, okay?'

'Go? I want to stay with you! I want to help.'

'This is how you help,' Damon says firmly. 'If she's still in range she'll use you to watch us.'

Tregan holds back tears. 'Back to Nattai?'

Not-so-bad-I-guess-just-lonely-At-least-I'll-have-Evan-maybe-I-can-bring-him-out-of-his-shell.

My stomach roils at the thought of her with my little brother—even though she won't and never will be with the real Evan.

Damon shakes his head. 'You're not going back there.'

'Where then?'

'I can't tell you now,' Damon says. 'Just trust me.'

On the short drive back to the chopper, Tregan makes him promise to be careful and come get her as soon as he can—and Damon tells her everything she wants to hear. At the paddock, he takes her arm and Evan's hand and leads them to the bird as the pilot does pre-flight checks.

'It's a nice place,' Damon says. 'Where you're going. This will be over soon.'

'I fly? Whirly-whirl?' Evan says brightly.

Damon nods—and is rewarded with a big hug. Tregan's heart swells as they include her in the huddle.

'You've got to be a big sister and a mother to him now,' Damon says after he lets Evan go to clamber into the cabin.

'You're all he's got. And you take care of yourself. You're all I've got, too.'

Tregan throws her arms around him. I swear on everyone I've loved and lost that once I'm sure my plan has worked, once I'm sure I've bought everyone the time they need, I'm going to kill Damon and Tregan and put Evan out of his misery.

Damon ensures she and my little brother are comfortable and then gives the twirling finger-in-the-air signal to the pilot. The rotors blur and the chopper lifts off. I watch Damon drop away through Tregan's eyes, see the aircraft ascend via the cams and then tear away to the south.

It's only a few minutes until Tregan's view of Evan beside her and the hinterland and the coast flickers and fades from my mind.

This confirms my theory that the Radius works differently now. If Tregan's out of my range then Evan and the chopper pilot should be out of Damon's too. I'm pretty sure he didn't just send them on a course that'd set them free. What I envisage is that they're all like Jack now. Have their own spheres and as long as they're within range of each other they're part of the hivemind. Like cellphone towers whose circles of coverage overlap to form a vast network. I do quick maths. If that's the way it works and they spread out they could cover half the state. Trigger any strand in that giant web and you bring the filthy big spider down on top of you. *Fuck*.

Cars, motorbikes, Humvees and choppers pour out of Baroonah's one road west. I guess I've seen a few hundred Jacks come and go. The tablet window shows evenly spaced choppers and planes on the horizon. My guess is they have to move in staggered formation with the Jacks on the ground so that no one strays off the grid and reverts to his or her original self.

I cackle in the cellar. I really have no idea how Jack works. But from what I'm seeing it does look like I've got them heading in the wrong direction. I let out a little whoop when I see black choppers with tail markings 101 and 102 fly past Baroonah from the north and head out west to rejoin Jack's army. They're the aircraft that almost got me yesterday. Drawing them away means I've accomplished my mission.

I've got Jack fooled. But once he's scoured the roads, searched the towns west to Dubbo and prowled around the zoo, all without finding a single bit of evidence that points to me, I reckon he'll see this for the con it was. That'll lead to one conclusion: that he was sent on a wild goose chase because he'd almost had me. I've bought us a few more days. A week if we're lucky. We need to be gone before Jack turns all those men and machines in the right direction.

It's just after 3 p.m. The sky's fading and the temperature's dropping. Autumn's only been here a month but it feels like the middle of winter. Maple and oak leaves are brown and falling while woodland cyclamen and lilies of the valley are already blooming. My theory is that the blanket of smoke over everything is causing rapid global cooling. I wonder if it'll clear or if fires like the ones I've seen burning will just wrap us up tighter. Live a few more years and I might see the world enter a new ice age.

I pull my sleeping bag around me, keep one eye on the tablet's streaming windows and the other on recorded footage as I trawl for any sign a cam was spotted or that Jacks went into hiding. But nothing stirs in the mansion or Baroonah or in the skies over the town. As soon as night falls, I'll get back to the quad and move out quickly. Wearing my yowie suit, all my supplies under camouflage netting, using night-vision goggles, I'll be close to invisible even if there's a drone circling. I'll be back to the others by midnight.

I'm about to heat up a chicken curry ration pack when I notice movement on the tablet's live windows.

In the mansion's front yard.

Off the path. On the lawn.

Marv.

He's not dead.

FOURTEEN

I'm not sure how long I smashed my anger out against the tree. When the baseball bat snapped, I flung it into the weeds. Heaving, I turned to Nathan, who leaned on his quad's handlebars and watched me from under a deep frown.

'Did that help?' he asked quietly.

'No.' I stormed to my quad, sank onto its seat. 'No.'

Nathan tossed me a bottle of water. I sipped and tried to calm myself. There was no rinsing away the images. Tracey shot to pieces. People put down like dogs. Cory falling to his death. I'd been in all their minds as they'd died. Just like the Snap's worst moments. Just like seeing Ray and Cassie and the others murdered all over again. I didn't know how I had a sliver of sanity left. Maybe I didn't.

'We should go,' Nathan said. 'There's nothing we can do. Or could've done.'

I looked at him.

Nathan straightened up in his seat. 'Look at it this way—at least we know they don't know where we are.'

My mouth fell open. 'How can you say that?' My shout was ugly in my ears but I didn't care. 'What happened to them happened because of us. If we hadn't run. If we had—'

'Had what, Danby?' Nathan roared, matching me for volume. 'Had what?'

He jumped off his quad, stomped across to loom over me.

'Jack—Damon—whoever—whatever—is insane. Psychotic. Don't you get it? He knew Tracey and the rest of them didn't know where we are. And he didn't care. He couldn't even know for sure we were in range to see what he was doing. He just wanted to kill them so he did.'

Veins stood out at Nathan's temples. His eyes bulged and spit flecked his lips. I shrank from him. If he noticed he was scaring me it wasn't enough to stop him.

'You-you-you,' he said, jabbing his finger, 'don't even know who he was before you met him. He could've been a . . . a . . . goddamned serial killer who just happened to latch onto this power. You don't know. I don't know. For whatever reason, he fixated on you. Not your fault. Not my fault. You and me have done everything we can to stop him. You killed him, for Chrissakes! If you'd given up, joined him, become his girlfriend or queen or whatever, then he'd still be killing people and then their blood really would be on your hands. But it's not. It's not on yours. And it's not on mine. You want another showdown? Go.' He handed me the GPS. 'Go kill them all. Get yourself killed. Just leave me out of it.'

Nathan blinked, stepped away, stalked back to his bike, slugged on a bottle of water and stared at the bush.

Shaking and stunned, I steered my quad around him so I was in the lead on the trail north. When I looked over my shoulder, he looked away and I felt like I was about to be abandoned.

'I want to stick together,' I said.

'Whatever,' he replied.

I gunned the engine, checked the GPS and rode along a track that eased through a plantation pine forest. When I checked my mirror, Nathan was following me. I slowed so he'd keep me in sight but I didn't stop until dark.

We sat by a hiker's shelter in a national park. The GPS put us two hundred kilometres from where we'd started the day. I pulled out my sleeping bag, laid it and my rifle out on a rough wooden bench. Bunched my jumper into a pillow, set out a water bottle and flashlight.

'So I guess I'm taking first watch?' Nathan asked, shaking his head, sounding wounded and angry.

I looked at my little impromptu nest and felt unfairly accused. 'I was just laying out my stuff.'

The few feet between us may as well have been miles.

'Doesn't matter,' he said with a shrug. 'I'll wake you at one.'

Before I could say anything, he turned away and busied himself with his backpack. Whatever I'd said or done, he was just being a rude asshole now.

I took off my boots, slid into the sleeping bag and stewed in the darkness. As I lay there, biting my knuckle, I remembered when my friend Madison and her first boyfriend had broken up. She'd wept as she explained that while they'd loved everything about each other just a week ago now everything they said and did rubbed each other the wrong way. I wondered if Nathan and I were like that despite our best intentions. We'd only ever kissed, but we'd also been through more together than we could comprehend. I wondered if we were only now realising that we weren't friends or would-be-lovers but just traumatised mental cases who'd been thrown together by circumstances. If we would be better off apart. A sob escaped me despite my best efforts. Nathan must've heard it. He wasn't asleep this time. But he didn't say anything.

What seemed like seconds later, Nathan was shaking my shoulder.

'Wake up,' he said. 'Your shift.'

I pulled myself free, tugged on my boots, sat blinking on the rammed dirt edge of the shelter and listened to the bush creak and shift. Above me there was only black. Like the stars had been put out. I reminded myself that the cosmos was still out there beyond our smoky atmosphere. Suns and planets and galaxies doing what they'd been doing for billions of years. Whatever force or energy kept them going didn't care what was happening down here. Nor should it. Being that small against the scale of time and space was somehow comforting. None of this could really matter in the grand scheme of things. All of human history was like a single grain of sand in the Sahara, with me and Nathan just two atoms among billons that made up that speck.

Even so it'd be nice to see our sky again. Yellow sun. Blue sky. Red sunset. White moon. I'd gotten glimpses through the smoke from Shadow Valley and Samsara. It was possible we'd find ourselves in the clear eventually. Or at least have one good day somewhere. But if we were to do it together, repairing us had to start with me.

The bush materialised as the sky eased from black to brown to beige. I glanced at Nathan's sleeping face. He looked at peace. I hadn't known him that long but I knew he'd only done what he did with Evan because he thought it was right. If he hadn't stopped me from shooting my little brother then I'd probably have become a totally guilt-consumed basket-case. Or more of one. Nathan snapped at me yesterday because I'd snapped. We were both only human. Doing the best we could under the worst conditions. I had to restart and reset. Remember it was still us against the end of the world.

I ate a tin of pears, went to the toilet down the hill, used a splash of water to wash my face and hands. On the way back, I checked the petrol cans. Both felt a quarter full. The gauge on my bike had been at half when I'd cut the engine last night. I guessed Nathan's was the same. I did some quick calculations based on how far we'd come and how much fuel I thought we'd used.

The sleeping bag rustled as Nathan woke and propped himself up on an elbow.

'Sleep well?' I asked, handing him an apple juice and some biscuits with jam.

Nathan took my offering. 'Couldn't rustle up bacon and eggs?'

I smiled. He crunched and sipped a while.

'I'm sorry,' I said.

'For what?'

'For everything. Blaming you for Evan. Being a psycho. Losing my shit.'

'You have been a tad edgy,' he said and we both laughed. 'I'm sorry too. If we weren't going a little crazy then we'd probably really be going crazy.' Nathan's eyes were big and warm. 'You and me,' he said. 'Out here?'

My breath was trapped in my lungs.

'It's . . . weird,' he said, looking away from me and into the bush all around us. 'But being in the middle of nowhere's the safest I've felt since all this started.'

I nodded, exhaled softly, glad the moment had passed—if that's what it had been. I'd wanted him to say he wanted to hold me—and it was also the last thing I wanted to hear.

'Me, too,' I said. 'But we can't stay here.'

Just like that: wariness stole into Nathan's face and irritation flared in me.

'Not because I'm looking for a fight,' I said evenly. 'But we're gonna run out of petrol today. Based on fuel consumption so far, we'll get another hundred, hundred and twenty clicks out of what we have left. I don't want to get stuck out here on foot.'

Nathan's frown eased and he smiled.

'What?'

'Clicks?'

'Kilometres,' I said, not sure whether to be pleased or pissed off he was making fun of me.

I showed Nathan the GPS.

'The nearest town's back here,' I said. 'But that's forty kilo-metres in the wrong direction. I think if we get onto this road, Comboyne, we might find a farm or a house with petrol, or be able to siphon from a motorbike. In any case, we should have enough gas to get up here, the Oxley Highway. There has to be a petrol station or cars up there.'

Nathan took the GPS, looked at the towns of Wauchope and Port Macquarie, just to the east of where we'd emerge from the boondocks. 'Do you think they've come this far north?'

I shrugged. All I knew was that we hadn't seen any evidence they'd gone past Terrigal. That was two hundred kilometres south. I didn't know if that was far enough or if any distance would ever be far enough. But Nathan and I needed to get ourselves to a safer place.

'Best get up,' Nathan said. 'Seize the day and all that. Thanks for the breakfast.'

We buried our rubbish and topped up our tanks. Then we rode again, ducking branches, leaving our little dust clouds. After another dozen fire trail tributaries, the bush thinned and abruptly spat us out onto a dirt road. A few minutes later, Nathan held up his hand as he slowed. I pulled up beside him. Our tyres were about to be on bitumen. The road was broken at the edges, its yellow centre line nearly worn away, but the going would be easier from here. Nathan pulled off his helmet, climbed off the bike, planted his feet decisively and slowly turned in a full circle, eyes scanning the hills all around us. The way he did it made me think of an explorer landing on a distant shore—or touching down on an alien planet.

I looked where he had. No people or cars, moving or otherwise, just trees bending with the easterly wind.

'Wow,' he said, eyes closed, head tilted back, inhaling deeply. 'Sea air.'

I slid my visor up, smelt the scent I'd fantasised about for weeks. I let the salty breeze blow through me. Being this close to the ocean felt like progress. Then tears tried to bubble up out of me.

'God, that smells good,' Nathan said.

I nodded, too choked to speak, forcing away the silly images I'd once had of me and him happy on some refuge island, trying to forget that those sunny scenes had included Evan and Tajik.

Nathan wandered over to a fence, the green mountains framing him, and pointed into the hazy distance.

'You want to check it for fuel?'

I joined Nathan and stared across a field at a big farmhouse that looked like it'd stood there for a century. He handed me the binoculars. Two bodies near the front door. If the wind had been blowing the other way we might've been able to smell them. Four-wheel drive and two sedans parked under palm trees. A ute halfway down the driveway. A hatchback that had tumbled down a hill and come to rest on its roof. My mind conjured a big country Christmas. Matriarch, patriarch, sons and daughters, wives and husbands, kids and cousins and grandchildren. Some would've escaped. But I'd bet most of the clan had been cooking away in that farmhouse for weeks. I didn't fancy searching through the stink. Maybe we'd get lucky and find a motorbike by the roadside. Or a country petrol station. I wanted to delay the inevitable.

'Do you?' I asked.

'Not really,' Nathan said, returning to our quads and clicking their gears. 'Now we're on sealed road we can use two-wheel drive. We'll get better mileage. The petrol we have left will last longer.'

I laughed. 'When did you become such an expert?'

Nathan allowed himself a smile. 'I read the manual last night while you were sleeping.'

That meant he'd let me talk about fuel consumption without telling me he already knew. I felt patronised even as I saw he'd simply behaved politely. I let it go. Just like the song had instructed when I was a little girl.

We stood by each other, our closeness feeling natural, and looked at the GPS screen showing the next ten kilometres of road curving between mountains to the Oxley Highway.

'We'll be visible from the air,' I said. 'We could go back in here and still get there. It'd be safer.'

My finger traced a network of unsealed back roads through thick bush. Winding and wending the way they did would probably double the distance.

'Too much risk of running out of petrol,' Nathan said. 'I'm buggered if I want to walk again. Let's live dangerously.'

I laughed and he raised his eyebrows. 'What?'

'It's just . . .' I shook my head. I didn't want to risk another fight by saying he was as all over the place as me. One minute I'd be gung-ho and he'd favour caution. Then it was the other way around. Maybe in a way we balanced out. 'We're just funny, that's all.'

'Funny ha-ha or funny peculiar?' Nathan asked with a smile.

'Both. Let's go.'

We revved off. My speedometer sat on a pleasing thirty kilometres an hour and accelerated beyond that only to hurry us through the pockets of stench coming from the few roadside bodies and glinting cars and hillside houses.

Close to the Oxley Highway, Nathan slowed to an idle in front of a cheery tourism billboard.

'Visit Port Macquarie!' a banner instructed above photos of beaches, surfers, anglers, wildlife, restaurants and resorts. Local businesses each had a little square around the outside of the billboard with logos and contact details. Pizza joint, burger franchise, drycleaner, tackle stop, surf shop, budget motel, historic pub, riverboat rides, whale watching. There was a zoo and three different theme parks offering colonial times, wacky waterslides and putt-putt golf.

'It's got it all,' I said.

'Everything but the people.' Nathan was perusing a little information box that showed this area shaded against the rest of the state.

'Port Macquarie–Hastings Shire—Population, eighty thousand,' he read. 'Maybe add another twenty thousand people for Christmas.'

'One hundred thousand,' I said sombrely. 'That's a lot of people.'

'Actually, the opposite,' Nathan said. 'It's a quarter the area of the whole of Sydney but with a tiny fraction of the population. And if most of the people were concentrated in Port Macquarie, then the rest of the coast and countryside should be almost empty.'

He was right. Compared with the cities to our south and farther north, this could be a safe haven.

'Ten people with *Situs inversus*,' I said. 'Statistically speaking.'

Nathan nodded. 'They might've had a better chance at surviving up here. More places to run. Less chaos.'

'And no Jack,' I said.

'And no Jack,' Nathan repeated, eyes closed.

I did the same, concentrating and consciously sending my mind out.

'Anything?' he looked at me.

I shook my head. We didn't know if any Revivees had lived long enough to make it this far. But if there were any in Port Macquarie we should've been able to pick them up from here.

'Maybe they came through, kept going north,' Nathan said, pointing at the beaches, rivers and countryside all around the coastal town on the map. 'It's a huge space. It says so right here—look: "Space to retire, space to live, space to play."'

The Oxley Highway was testament to that spaciousness. Despite being a major road, the bush-lined stretch of bitumen we emerged onto was free of cars and bodies. That would change when we got to Wauchope and my heart sank when

I thought about the stink. But we had no choice about going into that town. Our fuel gauges were finally in the red.

Nathan led and I followed, keeping the double lines between my front tyres, enjoying the easy riding on the smooth road and its gentle curve between the trees.

Once we'd found fuel, maybe we could bypass Port Macquarie, find a beach shack farther up the coast. Maybe it wouldn't be quite the island paradise of my dreams but it might be enough of a breather for Nathan and I to face the future together rather than fighting each other for every step forward.

The smile on my lips died when I rounded the next bend and saw Nathan's quad in a skid as he wrestled for control. I slammed on my brakes because standing ghostly in the middle of the road was a barefoot boy with big blank eyes.

Evan.

Even before my quad stopped, I was out of my seat and running along the road with my rifle sighted at my little brother's chest.

'Danby!' Nathan yelled, whirling towards me. 'What're you doing?'

What I should've done, I wanted to scream.

'It's not him!' Nathan said. 'It's not him.'

FIFTEEN

I grab my weapons and supplies, tuck Rat into the breast pocket of my camo shirt and pull on a similarly patterned flak jacket. Pushing the corrugated iron off the cellar entrance, I crawl out into the ruins, sweep a full circle with my AK-47, as if Jacks could've somehow evaded the cams and the rodent's sixth sense. But there's no one. Keeping low, rifle in hand, I run from bush to house to tree, wait and watch, repeat until I'm crouching by a shrub in a front yard across the road from the mansion.

From here I can see the sorry heap that is Marv and his family beneath the scorched and shattered verandah. I pull out the tablet, scroll through the cam windows, get a closer view of Marv. The time's 3.24. It's been over an hour since he sustained his injuries. Twenty minutes since I realised he was still alive. He might not be anymore. He's not moving.

Fighting the urge to dash to Marv's side, I cut across yards, make my way through a park and go around to the next street. I count off the houses, run up a driveway, climb over a back fence and drop onto the lawn I left scattered with bullet casings and chewing gum.

I pause at the back door, look down at Rat's furry head, her little whiskers tickling my cheek. She's chilled. But while she can sense Jacks she's not a bomb-detection rodent. I could be about to walk into a booby trap just like the one I set for him.

I ease the door open, slip inside, and make my way quietly through the kitchen into the hallway. The walls inside the front door are broken and blackened where my grenades detonated. I crawl across splintered floorboards and slither down the front steps to where my friend lies shattered in the garden.

Marv looks dead. One cheek is torn away and his dreadlocks are burned back to stumps on that side of his head. His clothes are blasted and stained where hot metal sizzled through fabric and flesh. There's so much black blood. The movements I saw must've been a trick of the light or a glitch of the spy cams or some guilty mental projection.

I let out a gasp when Marv's remaining eye rolls at me. His mouth clacks and flaps. A wheeze crackles from his throat.

'Anby,' he rasps.

'Marv,' I say, dropping to my knees, tears rolling down my cheeks. I want to take his hand but it's too mangled.

'I'm sorry,' I say, touching his shoulder gently. 'I'm so sorry.'

In my medical kit I've got needles and surgical thread and forceps and clamps and antibiotic washes and clean bandages. I've read enough to maybe stitch a wound and remove a bullet. None of that's going to help Marv. It's a miracle—and a nightmare—that he's still alive. Burns management, emergency surgery, blood transfusion, antibiotic infusion: even if all of that stuff was possible I don't know if it'd be enough to put him back together. But in my satchel, along with my uppers, I've got enough barbiturates to ease Marv's pain and usher him from this world. I think that's all I can offer.

'Do you want me to stop the pain?' I ask, blotting my eyes.

Marv blinks, tries to speak again.

'Ive.'

My heart shatters. Marv is saying he's alive. His shock is so complete he doesn't know he's dying.

'Yes,' I say. 'You're alive. You can hang on and I'll try to help. Or I can help you to let go.'

Marv's eye darkens and he frowns. It could be a surge of pain. A realisation I'm offering to kill him. I wonder if he knows I'm responsible for Jane and Lottie dying.

'uckyouanby,' he croaks.

'I'm so sorry,' I say. 'I had no idea.'

I'm sobbing.

'Ut. Up.'

I look at him. Shut up?

'Otts ive,' he spits, fresh blood flowing from his torn cheek. 'Otts. Ive.'

My gaze follows Marv's arm to his intact hand. It grips his daughter's ankle.

'Otts. Ive.'

Lottie's alive. Jesus. Marv's asking if she's alive. It's the saddest thing I've ever heard. He can't see that his daughter is face down in the dirt, her clothes drenched in blood.

I shake my head. 'No. I'm sorry.'

Marv's eye is furious under his furrowed eyebrow. 'Otts ive.'

He's not asking me. He's telling me. I look at his hand, finger tapping insistently on a vein.

'Ulse,' he says.

Pulse. She has a pulse. My skin prickles, the hairs on my neck stand on end. 'Lottie's alive.'

Marv's eye flickers with relief.

'Elper,' he wheezes. 'Elp.'

'I will,' I say. 'I will.'

Marv's eye rolls to one side and his face slackens. Air whispers from his cheek and lips and he doesn't breathe again. I slide my hand to his neck. Feel the stillness there.

Grief and guilt: they're the next emotions I should feel. But instead it's selfish fear that slices through me.

Lottie's alive. She's a Jack. Inches from me. I've given myself away.

Except maybe Marv was wrong. She's not moving. Rat's not reacting like she did to the outriders.

I crawl over to her, listen to her back, feel for her pulse. Marv wasn't wrong. She has a heartbeat, is breathing shallowly but steadily. I gently roll her over. There's swelling on her head but all the blood and gore aren't hers—they're from her mum, who's ripped open worse than Marv a few feet away. Cautiously, I check Lottie's pupils and they retract. The blast has knocked her unconscious.

Help her. Marv's last request. I owe him that.

Help her.

I take my .45 from its holster and place the muzzle at Lottie's temple. This is the only way to help her. By doing for her what I couldn't do for Evan.

I turn my face away. She needs to die. But I don't need to see her head come apart.

Marv's dead eye stares at me accusingly.

uckyouanby

When I look back at Lottie all I can see is that boy by the side of the highway.

SIXTEEN

'It's not him!' Nathan shouted again.

He wouldn't trick me this time. Eye on the sight. Finger on the trigger. The world shimmered as I blinked through the helmet's visor. The hollow-eyed boy staring through me had an ashen face with a cinnamon dusting of freckles beneath rust-coloured hair. He wore shorts and a singlet and clutched a one-armed blue teddy bear.

Not Evan. Not even close. I quickly lifted my visor. Fresh air flooded in.

'See?' Nathan said.

'Doesn't matter,' I said.

Panic swept Nathan's face. Like he thought I'd cracked.

'What?'

'He's a Jack.'

'He could be a Special,' Nathan said. 'Then it's murder.'

Murder: the word belonged to a world that wasn't mad and at war. My eyes flicked from the boy to Nathan. His rifle was shouldered and his hands were up in surrender.

'Danby, you don't want that on your conscience. Let's just go. Keep riding. Please.'

The way the kid stared. Little bastard communing with his hivemind and showing them where we were. Shoot him and at least he wouldn't be able to tell them which way we'd gone. We might be able to take the quads off road. Get lost in the forest. 'We can't let him see where we go,' I said. 'You know I'm right.'

The boy's shorts had darkened. He was standing in a puddle of piss. Jack trying to buy a few more minutes so he could get his choppers in the air.

'Please,' Nathan said. 'Let me check him. Please.'

I faltered.

'Thirty seconds,' I said, not taking my rifle sight off the kid's chest. 'Hurry.'

Nathan whipped off his helmet, pulled the stethoscope from his backpack and put it around his neck.

'What's your name?' he asked as he approached the boy.

Kid's bladder might've betrayed fear but his face remained blank.

'We're not going to hurt you,' Nathan said, kneeling by him on the road. 'I'm a doctor. I just need to listen to your heart, okay?'

The kid didn't react as Nathan slid the metal disc inside his singlet. I blinked sweat from my eyes. Steeled myself for what I'd have to do in a few seconds. Like the woman I'd shot in Samsara. A mercy killing. The right thing.

Shoulders hunched, Nathan slid the stethoscope across the kid's chest. He scooched around, listened to his back. Finally, he lifted his eyes to mine, face turning grey as his mouth moved silently.

'Move away from him,' I said. 'There's no choice.'

'There is a choice,' Nathan said, standing up behind the boy. 'Think about it. Listen to me. We can just go. Ride off.' His words came out in a rush, louder and louder, like if he didn't leave me any opportunity to speak I wouldn't be able to do what was needed. 'Us on the quads. As soon as we're around the bend he won't be able to see us. Right? We can get away. We can—'

'Nathan,' I shouted. 'Step away.'

'Danby, no, we can just leave him.'

'Move! Now!'

Everything happened at once.

The kid darted away. I tried to follow him with my rifle. A blur of blue flashed from the bush and crashed Nathan onto the road with a horrible crack. My head thudded inside my helmet and I fell backwards as a shot rang out. Hitting the road I realised it'd been me who'd pulled the trigger. I'd blasted a hole in the clouds and now blackness was rushing in to blot out my world.

don't² fear
the
reaper

SEVENTEEN

I can't shoot Lottie even though keeping her alive could mean my death. Having her here with me out cold while all the Jacks head away from us: it's an opportunity that'll never repeat itself. Lottie is a one-in-a-million chance to test my theory of Jack's Radius. Saving her might save all of us. Give me reason for real hope again. But I have to act fast. If she regains consciousness now the army I tricked into going west will storm back here and we'll both be dead.

Holstering my .45, I leave Lottie where she is, run through the house to the garden shed and grab a wheelbarrow. Back in the front yard, I roll her into its metal tray, arrange her arms and legs and haul the wheelbarrow upright with a grunt.

Sweat streaming from me, I push Lottie away from the house, along shaded footpaths, hoping these tree-lined streets will keep me hidden if Jack has left a drone circling over Baroonah. Choppers and jets don't come streaking in to strafe me and I'm soon back at the vacant lot where I hid the quad bike behind brambles and under camouflage netting.

The wheelbarrow's too heavy and awkward to push through the thick weeds so I drag Lottie the rest of the way. Her head lolls and her face is a blank. If she's injured this isn't doing her any good but it's the best I can do.

I haul her onto the quad's cargo area, curl her up amid my gear and criss-cross her securely with bungee cords under camo netting. Climbing onto the bike, I check the tablet, scroll through the cams. Nothing's moving back in Baroonah. I think we're good. But if I drive due north, I'll be heading for the others. Which will undo all the work I've just done if Lottie comes around and gives us away. But northwest— that should work. It'll take me far from everyone and everything.

'You'll let me know if she's coming around, right?' I say to Rat.

I've driven this quad for months and it feels like part of me. I know its capabilities and limitations. Even with Lottie and all my gear, I can make thirty kilometres an hour safely on the dirt roads the map shows me lead into the middle of nowhere. I also know the engine noise carries at least a kilometre in total stillness like this. If there are any Jack stragglers in earshot I'm done. But I have to chance it.

I ride. Trusting in Rat, I resist the urge to look back at Lottie's face in its cocoon of gear and netting. Passing through acre after acre of grey and green bush, I keep my eyes on the odometer as it ticks over and night descends. After a while, I relax enough that the thrumming of the quad's engine is replaced by a snatch of song.

'We love with words/We fly like the birds/My sky's made for you/Girl you know it's true.'

The music's so loud it's like I've got speakers inside my helmet. This happens at least once a day. A song appears in my brain for no reason, like an echo from the dead world on endless loop. Of course, that isn't anything new: my friends and I used to compare our earworms and I now remember a few weeks before the Snap we'd been weirded out because we'd all woken up with Hellbanga's 'Clitler Youth' in our heads. That'd led to us streaming it on the school bus—the accepted cure for an earworm was to play the earworm. But that's not an option now. Despite the thousands of tunes I inherited on the music player I looted from a paranoid survivalist called Mac, his hard rock collection has never once overlapped with the recent hits that phantom their way into my consciousness. So the only way to banish the song is to sing it, which is what I do now under my breath with 'Lovewords' by Avarava.

Eventually, the bubble-gum pop bursts and I'm returned to engine thrumming as the quad eats up the road. The odometer tells me I've done forty clicks northwest, maybe half that straight as the crow flies. I pull over, check the map and compass. If the Jacks have stayed their course, there might be enough distance between us now. But if there are some cross-country travellers closer to me, or they've already seen through my ruse and turned around, then I'll be screwed if Lottie wakes up now. More time and space: that's what I need. I take off my helmet and put on my night-vision goggles. They hum and the world turns various shades of red. With reduced visibility like this, I ease back on my speed. No sense clipping a wallaby or coming up too fast on a car wreck.

It's 9.30 when I pull into the tiny town of Callum. The few shops are all shut tight and the streets are clear of bodies. I drive the quad up onto the Star Hotel's verandah and kill the engine.

I stay very still and listen to the silence. Anyone here will have heard me approach. But the chances of life seem next to nothing. Callum looks like it was a ghost town long before ghost world happened.

I unravel Lottie. She's breathing. Has a pulse. I prise open an eyelid. Shine my penlight on her shrinking pupil. I lift Rat from my pocket and set her on the girl's shoulder. She sits on her hind legs, paws up like she's praying, and sniffs Lottie's face and the air around her. I hope if she starts to come around, my familiar will give me plenty of warning.

With my picks, I work the pub door's lock. It takes five minutes or so but then I'm in. Another skill picked up from my months of self-improvement. If anyone comes into Callum behind us at least it'll look like the Star's been undisturbed since the Snap.

This pub's dusty but peaceful. I take a few deep breaths—all I need to establish that no one has died in here. I wheel the quad bike inside and immerse us in the gloom. No curtains on the windows in the front bar. I want a room where I can use light without being seen from the street.

I drag Lottie and my gear off the quad and through swinging doors into a saloon bar that's all overstuffed chairs and wood panels. The only window looks onto a courtyard and high back fence. It'll have to do. I roll Lottie into the recovery position and sit Rat on her shoulder. Aiming the pistol at her, I back towards the bar, scoot behind the counter, grab a packet of cashews and a bottle of red wine. I sit, remove my night-vision goggles, set my .45 at my side, light a candle and take a slug of shiraz.

The wine takes the edge off the dexies. Sometimes I use alcohol to get to sleep if I've been up too long. It's dangerous, I know, being that dead to the world, but it also helps me to not dream. But I can't drink too much now. Falling asleep might mean not waking up.

Rummaging in my backpack, I pull out a dog-eared copy of *The Art of War*. I vaguely recall Dad talking about this book being helpful when he first went into business. But I've been reading it way more literally. Sometimes it's like ancient Chinese dude Sun Tzu had me in mind when he was writing it.

'Let your plans be dark and impenetrable as night, and when you move, fall like a thunderbolt.'

Right on: that's me in Baroonah.

'All warfare is based on deception. Hence, when we are able to attack, we must seem unable; when using our forces, we must appear inactive; when we are near, we must make the enemy believe we are far away; when far away, we must make him believe we are near.'

Another good one. I read on but after a while my eyes start to wander across the bite-sized warrior wisdom without taking much in. I check the tablet. It's 10.14 and I'm fading. Another pill will sharpen me up. Except I can't sit here forever, frying myself with speed until Lottie comes around. What I have to do is sort her out, one way or the other.

The idea of killing Lottie makes me feel sick. And yet the thought of her awake makes me nauseous too. If she comes around and is herself then what on earth am I going to tell her?

If Oscar and Louis's experiences are any guide, Lottie won't remember anything after the Snap and her crashing out. That was three months ago. How can I explain who I am? Where her mum and dad have gone? How she's ended up in a crappy old man pub hundreds of kilometres from her home? And how can I explain she's spent nearly one hundred days possessed by this evil guy who's actually dead but still alive in the minds and bodies and souls of thousands of people in a world where billions are rotting all around us? I take a big drink of wine and laugh to myself. Last time I tried to explain stuff like this my interrogators didn't believe a word. Not at first.

Imagining Lottie trying to cope sends a chill through me despite the wine's warmth. When she looks in the mirror, will she even recognise herself? Her hair will be longer and her face might've changed shape. She might even be a year older, might have had a—

Birthday.

I grab the tablet. It's 10.23. April *first*. Evan turns seven today. I cry and curse myself. For forgetting. For abandoning my little brother to his limbo. For thinking this stupid plan might be the key to saving him.

Lottie hasn't moved. The poor girl's probably in a coma. It's a cruel farce that I have to end now one way or the other. I can't fail her like I failed Evan. All I've been doing is prolonging the inevitable and inviting disaster. I need to 'shit or get off the pot'. It's something I heard somewhere. I can't remember now if it was an expression Mum used. Maybe it was one of my friends. Or a Hellbanga song. Shit or get off the pot. Kill Lottie now or wake her up. I can't sit here and watch her for hours or days. We haven't got that much time.

Cold water—thrown in her face. That might do the trick. Or maybe my dexies. If they can keep me awake, can they wake up Lottie? Like in that old movie where John Travolta stabs Uma Thurman in the heart with a syringe and then *bang* she's back in the land of the living. I've got syringes. I could do it.

Except I haven't got the guts. Bringing Lottie back only for Rat to go crazy: it turns my stomach worse than anything. Wake her up to shoot her dead: if I did that I'd have to kill myself. Maybe it ends for us both now. Lottie dead can't betray me to Jack. Me dead can't accidentally lead Jack to the others. I take another hit of wine and spin my .45 on the floorboards like it has the answer. It points at plastic flowers in a vase. Big help.

Rat scampers up onto my shoulder and I'm nuzzling her when I see Lottie's eyelids start to flicker.

EIGHTEEN

My eyes flickered open and I heard Nathan's voice saying he thought it was broken. I wondered if he was talking about my brain. Made sense because it was sloshing around so much that the sky over me was swirling. My helmet had been taken off. Or shattered around my skull. Neck aching, I turned my head, and saw Nathan sitting on the road, elbows on his knees, looking at an ankle blown up as red and shiny as a balloon.

A stubby guy with a ponytail and dirty denim jacket stood over Nathan with our assault rifle. A sinewy older man in beanie and overalls kept the .303 loosely aimed at me as he tapped his companion on the shoulder.

'She's awake,' he said, voice like sandpaper.

Ponytail glanced my way. 'How's your noggin?'

'Fluckyou,' I slurred.

He looked at Beanie. 'Bring Danby over here.'

Danby. They knew my name. Jacks. Had to be. I didn't know why they were bothering to speak out loud, what new pantomime he was putting his puppets through.

The older man walked a wary arc around me as I got to my feet. Wheezing somewhere over my shoulder, he pressed the rifle barrel into the small of my back and marched me over to Nathan.

'Kneel down,' Ponytail instructed.

As I did the rifle muzzle tickled up my spine until it rested at the base of my skull. So this was it. Execution style. Quick. Like I'd wanted for Evan.

'Well, Nathan,' Ponytail said. 'You gonna check her out or what?'

Nathan sucked air through clenched teeth. He had a bloody graze on his cheek from where he'd been tackled to the road by Ponytail. His dark eyes bored into mine.

'Well, how is she?' Ponytail asked. 'Concussion?'

Nathan took my chin in his hand and tilted my head towards the sky and then back to him. He looked up at Beanie.

'Given you tried to knock her for six with that cricket bat,' he said, 'she's actually okay as far as I can see.'

I looked from him to Ponytail, hoping my enemy saw defiance in my eyes.

'Just kill me, Jack,' I said. 'Get it over and done with.'

Ponytail frowned. 'My name's Johnno,' he said. 'Old mate behind you is Stannis. I don't know who you think we are but we don't just shoot people for nothing.' He spat onto the road, rubbed his whiskery chin. 'Not like you were about to with the boy.'

I blinked at Nathan. 'How do they know our names?'

'I told them,' he said.

'Why?'

'Because they asked, Danby, okay? Because my ankle's snapped and they've got our guns and because I had to tell Johnno here how to best get your helmet off and make sure you were still breathing. Because he needed to know what name to call as he tried to wake you up. That's why.'

Johnno shook his head. 'If you two have finished with your little domestic, here's what we do next. You, Danby, help Nathan. We're walking—well, he's hopping—up the road a bit. It's not far and we'll take it slow, okay?'

The look in Nathan's eyes kept me from telling Johnno to go to hell. I nodded, stood up slowly. When I reached down to help Nathan stand, he accepted my hand like it was contaminated.

Johnno went behind us with the assault rifle. Stannis puffed alongside, covering us with the .303. Nathan hobbled and winced, arm around my shoulder for support.

'We could've just kept going,' he said to me through gritted teeth. 'We could've been miles from here now. You should've listened to me.'

•••

We'd seen this place advertised on the billboard of local attractions. Smiling convict in chains. Redcoat looking just as happy. Laughing woman with parasol. All leaning out of a steam train. But we would've missed it on our quads because a big truck had overturned right out the front and hidden its entrance from the highway. Our captors prodded us past the long trailer. An archway with the words 'Colonial Town' stood over a gift shop and a ticket booth that had a 'Closed for Xmas' sign in its window. Beside the offices there was a purple panel van and what looked like a lawnmower crossed with a hang glider.

'That way,' Johnno said, pointing us to a side gate.

I glanced back at him and his friend. Johnno looked like he could handle himself all right if he had to. But a strong wind might've blown Stannis over. I had no idea if these guys knew what they were doing with the guns. The assault rifle's safety was still on. Johnno's finger was outside the trigger guard. I could rush one of them. But that'd mean letting Nathan fall to the ground.

'No silly buggers,' Johnno said, reading the look on my face. 'Just get in there.'

Inside the gate, a path zigzagged through a rose garden and emerged at a quaint railway station straight out of the age of steam. Beyond that, beneath towering trees, shingled roofs shone through a misty blue haze. We crossed narrow train tracks and walked a dirt road that sloped into a town that could've been a western movie set. Cottages and shoppes with deep verandahs were set behind little picket fences. Maybe Johnno and Stannis weren't Dumb and Dumber after all. I could see why they'd holed up here. With the truck out front, the place was hidden.

I inhaled deeply, smelled only leaves and bark, a woodfire and coffee. Closed for Christmas—the place would've been empty when the Snap started. Marching down the hill, I saw how wrong I was. There were people everywhere. Man in a suit staring from a doorway. Woman hovering with a kettle at a window. A medico in a white coat standing inside a pharmacy by a cabinet of medicine bottles. Another guy about to strike an anvil with a hammer in his blacksmith's shop.

'Jesus,' Nathan whispered.

He'd just realised what I had. They weren't frozen catatonics. This was a town of mannequins, dressed in period garb. Then one of them moved. A blonde woman in creamy designer linen stepped from a doorway, trailed by the boy I'd almost shot, still in his soiled clothes.

'It's all right, Gail,' Johnno called to her. 'Everything's fine, okay?'

She raked her bobbed hair with ringed fingers. 'Are they staying? We'll need to set extra places.'

'We'll take care of all of that,' Stannis said with a sigh. 'Why don't you take the boy inside and get him some new pants.'

Gail's slender frame seemed to flutter before her face twisted into a bright smile. She was older than I thought. Shiny with lipstick and makeup.

'Of course, you're right,' she said. 'Lucas does need to dress for dinner.' She put a hand on the boy's shoulder. He didn't react at all as she steered him back inside. 'Come on, darling, let's get you looking suitable for our visitors.'

'To the end of the street,' Johnno said and we resumed our trek along the dirt road as the population of dummies watched impassively.

We passed a pub called The Bushranger's Redoubt. A generator hummed on its front porch and through batwing doors I glimpsed stools around barrels and a fridge that was lit up and stocked with beer. Stannis waved us into Queen Vic's Tea Rooms, a wide weatherboard with polished tables and benches that looked onto a grey lake where white geese cruised against the green bush.

'Ease him down,' Johnno said, waving us to a bench.

I helped Nathan sit and swing his injured leg up on the seat. His breath seethed in and out of him. His face was slick with sweat. I looked at Johnno as if to ask what now. He waved me to the other side of the table.

'Take a load off,' he said. 'Hands where I can see them.'

The men stood at either end of the long table and covered us with their guns.

'Get some ice from the pub for this fella's foot?'

Stannis nodded at Johnno. 'You all right with these two?'

Johnno smiled. 'They're not going anywhere, are you?'

Nathan shook his head. I stared straight ahead.

'I've got morphex forte tablets,' Stannis said to Nathan. 'Will that help?'

Nathan nodded. 'Is that all you're taking for the cancer?'

Stannis shrugged. 'That obvious, is it?'

'I spent a week working in an oncology ward,' Nathan said. 'We should be able to get you something better than that if there's a pharmacy nearby.'

Stannis nodded. 'Let's get you sorted out first.'

Johnno followed the older man to the door and whispered in his ear. I made out a few words—museum, ball, safer.

'Really?' Stannis said.

'I'd breathe easier. Can you manage?'

Stannis shuffled out onto the porch.

Johnno returned to us, pulled up a chair, sat on it backwards as his gun drifted from Nathan to me and back again. 'What the hell was going on out there?'

'I can explain,' Nathan said.

'Actually,' Johnno said to him, 'from what I saw, you were trying to stop her from shooting the boy. So I don't know that you're the one who's got to do the explaining. Danby, you're the one with a lot of questions to answer.'

'Fire away,' I said. 'I don't mean that literally.'

Johnno stiffened in his chair. His finger moved to the trigger. 'You think it's a joke? Pointing a gun at a kid?'

'You think it's a joke, pointing a gun at me?'

Out of the corner of my eye I saw Nathan slap his palm against his forehead like I'd just gotten us both killed. But I didn't flinch or take my eyes off Johnno. I wasn't intimidated. I was calculating whether I could get across the table and grab the gun before he shot me.

'You better tell me what you were doing out there,' he said, matching my stare with his steeliest gaze. 'Were you really going to kill the boy?'

I nodded. Nathan stiffened.

'Jesus, Danby.'

'Well, it's the truth. You want the truth, right, Johnno?'

The man's eyes glimmered with uncertainty. I think he'd expected me to lie. He looked rattled.

'Jesus, why?' he said, softly. 'Why would you want to kill a child?'

I was glad he couldn't read my mind and see me flash to almost shooting my own brother in the head.

'It's not that I *wanted* to. I thought I needed to.'

Nathan pushed the heels of his hands into his eyes. As though he was trying to wish me away.

Johnno ignored him, unclenched his jaw. I saw how tight his finger looked on the trigger. Any angrier or tenser and he might shoot me accidentally. 'You *needed* to kill a little boy? You better tell me what the hell you're talking about.'

'Why?'

Johnno raised his eyebrows like he couldn't believe what I'd just said.

'Danby!' Nathan said. 'Are you trying to get us killed?'

I shot him a look. 'I'm sorry about your ankle and everything. But this guy's about a millimetre from shooting me whether he means to or not. His mate's off on some secret men's business that involves me. I don't know if it's digging a grave or making a noose. I'm not going to sit here explaining myself only to say something he doesn't like or doesn't believe and get shot through the face for my trouble.' I turned my attention back to my captor. 'If you're gonna shoot me, shoot me. Otherwise, point that bloody gun somewhere else.'

Johnno's face was a mask of disbelief and offence. But he aimed the rifle away from me. 'Girl, you are a piece of work,' he said. 'I haven't killed anyone and I don't want to kill anyone. I don't *need* to kill anyone.'

A light went on in Johnno's head and his mouth dropped open.

'Oh, shit,' he said, looking at Nathan. 'You were listening to the boy's heart.'

Johnno's eyes darted to me. 'You were about to shoot him because there's—' his voice dropped, '—an infection?'

Nathan shook his head. 'It's not that.'

'He was testing the boy,' I said, 'to see if he was still himself. If he wasn't—which I'm still not sure he is—I was going to kill him.'

Johnno looked at me like I was crazy. 'Not himself. What does that mean?'

'This is the part where I say "you won't believe me" and you say "try me".'

Our eyes went to Stannis as he struggled in with a shopping cart and wheeled it to where we sat. From its canvas innards he handed Nathan a packet of tablets, a bottle of water and bag of ice wrapped in a towel.

'Thank you,' Nathan said, busying himself with pain relief.

Stannis tipped the shopping buggy on its side and dragged out a rusty chain connected to two leg irons.

'What's that?' I said.

'It's from one of the displays.' Johnno looked at me with a tiny bit of satisfaction. 'Nathan here's not going anywhere on that ankle. But I'll feel a lot more comfortable if I know you're not about to run off.'

I laughed. 'You're kidding.'

Johnno shook his head as Stannis bent a creaky knee to clamp an iron around my ankle, wind the chain up around the bench and back down to secure my other leg.

'Now,' Johnno said, leaning the assault rifle against the table, 'that's better for everyone, isn't it?'

Stannis propped his gun against a wall and took a seat. 'What did I miss?'

'Danby here was saying we wouldn't believe why she needed to shoot the boy.'

I sighed. These two were clowns. I was chained up and Nathan was crippled. But they hadn't confirmed we were alone. For all they knew we were scouts for a massive army of marauders about to descend on this place and rip them to shreds. I wondered whether I should put that fear into them. What Nathan would do if I started spinning such a story. The funny-peculiar thing was that it'd sound more believable than the truth.

But it was the truth I told them. Johnno and Stannis listened and stared, eyes occasionally flitting to Nathan, who nodded absently like he was only half listening.

'The boy isn't *Situs*,' I said to finish. 'I don't know how or why he's alive and conscious. But if he was a Jack I assume you and your mate and the woman would be too and we wouldn't be having this conversation because Jack knows all of this and besides Nathan and me would be dead on the road. So there you go—the truth, the whole truth and nothing but the truth. Can I have a drink of water?'

Johnno nodded at the bottle. I took it and drank.

'You expect us to believe all of that?' he said finally.

'I said you wouldn't.'

They both looked at Nathan. His head dipped and bounced back up. 'Every word,' he said fuzzily. 'Not making it up.'

'I'm *Situs*, Johnno,' Stannis said. 'Are you?'

'Dunno,' said Johnno. 'Haven't been to a doctor since I was a kid.'

Nathan reached the stethoscope from his neck and held it out to Johnno. His eyes were glassy. 'Listen all you want,' he slurred. 'Heartbeat city.'

Johnno lifted the stethoscope and placed it on his chest— left, right, back again. 'I don't know what I'm hearing. I'm not a bloody doctor. But even if I was *Situs whatchamaface*, that doesn't mean the rest of what you said is true.'

I shrugged. 'Why would I lie?'

He shook his head. 'So I don't think you're a psycho. I don't know.'

Stannis chewed his lip. 'If what you're saying's true then you here puts us in danger. If these Jacks find you here they'll kill us.'

I nodded. 'If I hadn't told you one day they would've come up the highway and you'd've gone out to say "Hi" and then blam. Now you might live. So, you know, you're welcome.'

Johnno looked from me to Nathan, whose eyes were closing, forehead shiny with sweat. 'Mate, you don't look so good. How's the ankle?'

Nathan smacked his lips. 'Dunno, can't feel it. Feel gooood actually.'

The stuff he'd been given by Stannis had sent him into an opiate haze like I'd experienced in Old Government House.

'Stannis, why don't we get him next door?' Johnno said.

'Who?' Nathan asked dreamily. 'What?'

'Where are you taking him?' I demanded.

'Don't get your knickers in a knot,' Johnno chided. 'Just to an empty cottage with a cot. We'll get him lying down before he falls down.'

The men eased Nathan up and held him between them. His head lolled a little but his eyes found me.

'Nice going, Danby,' he slurred, giving me an exaggerated thumbs up. 'This is all really great.'

I glared at his grinning face.

'No, really,' he said thickly. 'Good to know you.'

As soon as they were out the door I tried to stand. Their guns were a dozen feet from me. May as well have been a mile away. The chains that'd made life miserable for some poor convict held me tight. I sat down. My watch ticked. A tap dripped. Outside I heard murmured voices. Creaking on the verandah. Footsteps receding.

It was an hour later when Johnno returned. He sat opposite me and put a cold six-pack of beer on the table between us.

'Want one?' he asked.

'I'm underage.'

'I don't think that matters too much now.'

He twisted the tops off two beers. Handed one to me.

'Cheers,' he said.

'Sure,' I said, clinking my bottle to his.

I took a sip. It tasted like cold metal.

'How's Nathan?' I asked.

'Asleep,' he said. 'Comfortable. When he wakes up, we'll get into the pharmacy in Wauchope and get whatever he needs to plaster that leg. How're you?'

I resisted the urge to be a smartass. 'Okay.'

'Your head?'

I nodded. 'Still sore but I'll live.'

'Okay, Danby,' Johnno said. 'I want to go over it again. Everything. From the start.'

So that's what this was. He was playing out some detective show scenario. He'd given me a beer to loosen my tongue. Tried a bit of banter to get me on side. I let out a frustrated laugh. 'Don't you need a bad cop for this routine?'

'What?'

'For an interrogation. What I told you's not gonna change. I'm not gonna slip up and make a mistake. Because it's all true.'

Johnno's smile thinned to a slit. He polished off his beer. Got started on another. I left mine alone and didn't say anything.

'The only way you're getting out of these chains,' he said eventually, 'is for me to be convinced you're telling the truth.'

So I told him again—and this time Johnno interrupted with questions I couldn't answer: how Jack raised people up; why he killed people; how he'd survived death; why his army was still after me. His eyes narrowed each time I told him I didn't know. Like he suspected these were facets of my fantastic tale I was yet to fabricate. I wondered if he kept me like this for days or weeks whether I'd crack and start making up explanations to give him the answers he wanted. Didn't a lot of police confessions happen that way?

'I'm sorry I nearly shot the boy,' I said. 'But you can see why. If he was a Jack then killing him and trying to get away was our only chance.'

Johnno finished his last beer. Some part of me respected him for treating me this way. Stannis, Gail and the boy were depending on him. I'd nearly killed the kid. Then explained it with a wild story. I wouldn't have believed me. Hell: *I* would've shot me by now.

'Well?' I said. 'Surely you experienced some of the same stuff? At least around the Snap.'

His eyes flicked away from me. Despite the beers he'd knocked back I'd hit a nerve that was a long way from numbed.

'Where were you when it happened?' I asked gently.

Johnno stood up, scooped up the guns. 'I'll be back later.'

I hung my head, lay my cheek against the table, watched my watch tick by the hours. I drank the beer and the water, had to go to the toilet and tossed up whether it was more debasing to call out or piss myself. I went with the latter. Maybe this was Johnno's intention: let me know how the boy had felt. I sat in my own wetness and stench as darkness overtook the room.

I woke to see the Comboyne Road at dawn, crows flapping lazily over a field of swaying weeds.

I-hope-this-is-the-right-way-It-is-hon-We're-doing-good-Keep-the-faith . . .

At first I thought it was a dream spilling into the day, or an earworm of some nervy spoken-word duet, but a moment later I knew I was tuning Eli and Kirsty from the edge of my mind's range. Since I saw them last they'd been hiding in a house on the outskirts of Dungog. After much hand-wringing, they'd made a pact to go north and spent yesterday scouring neighbouring places for food, siphoning petrol from cars into jerry cans, collecting spare batteries and jumper leads and sleeping bags and .22 rifles and ammunition. They found the sturdiest four-wheel drive they could and put mountain bikes in the back. If they broke down or got blocked by traffic wrecks, they'd be able to jump start another car and fill its gas tank. If worst came to worst, they'd go by pedal power. Their other dilemmas were the stuff Nathan and I had grappled with: whether it was better to travel in the daylight or darkness, take slower back roads or go faster on more open main routes. Setting out before dawn this morning, they'd settled for a bit of both. Driving the back-road route they'd mapped out slowly with their parking lights on and then opting for speed on the Comboyne Road once it got light. Now they were thirty kilometres south, but turning west away from us, following their plan to bypass Port Macquarie and go inland. They'd be out of range in minutes. But until they were I had access to all their memories: the Lorazepam revivals; our confrontation with Jack on the bridge at Penrith; his terrible attack on Terrigal; Damon calling me out by name and setting all his murders at my feet; Cory thinking Damon and Jack were the same person the moment before he was added to the death toll. And if I could see and hear and feel all of this then Johnno and the others should too. If they were awake.

I hurled the beer bottle at a window to smash the early morning silence before I screamed and rattled my chains like a prisoner in an old movie.

I was still carrying on like a crazy person when Johnno came running into the Queen Vic.

'Did you see them?' I yelled. 'Are you seeing them?'

The faraway look in his eyes told me he had.

Johnno slumped down onto the bench opposite me. 'Oh shit,' he said, face in his hands. 'Oh, shit.'

He didn't look at me until Eli and Kirsty had faded from range. 'I think I owe you an apology.'

I shook my head. 'You don't. You did what you thought you had to. But if you don't mind I'd rather not spend the rest of this summer chained to this fucking bench.'

Then Gail was wailing crazily in the Colonial Town dawn.

NINETEEN

Rat sits happily on my shoulder as I creep closer to Lottie. She moans and her eyes flutter and I press my .45 gently against her back. Maybe she just hasn't crossed far enough into Jack consciousness for the rodent to react.

'Jack,' I whisper. 'Can you hear me? It's Danby.'

'Uggh,' she groans. 'Who?'

'Jack, talk to me,' I say.

Part of me realises I want him to be in there. Just so I can tell him how much I hate him, how much he won't win, how much I will keep killing him forever, how I've found a way to continue the fight even after my death.

'Who?' Lottie says, twisting her head slightly, eyelids fluttering open. 'My head. It hurts. Where am I?'

Rat tells me she isn't a threat. So does my gut. I can't process what that means yet.

'Thirsty.'

In all my thinking about shooting Lottie full of drugs or bullets, I haven't given a second's thought to actually helping her. I holster my pistol and lean in so she can see me.

'It's going to be all right, Lottie,' I say. 'I'll get you something to drink, something for your head.'

I cross to the bar, grab a bottle of water from the dark fridge, unscrew the cap and return to crouch by Lottie. She's still in the recovery position, except now it looks more foetal. I find some Ibuprofen tablets in my first-aid kit.

'I'll help you to sit?' I say, cupping the back of her neck and easing her up.

She clasps the bottle, sips water and washes the tablets down.

'Is that better?' I ask.

'How do you know my name?' she asks in a small voice. 'Who are you? Where am I?'

Her eyes go from me to the pub's front room. I realise what she's seeing. A muddy spray-painted quad bike. Automatic rifle. Camo netting. Open bottle of wine. Girl in combat boots and military uniform with a crew cut and a brown rat on her shoulder.

'My name's Danby,' I say, sitting cross-legged across from her. 'I know your name because your dad told me. We're in a pub in a town called Callum somewhere in the northern tablelands.'

Lottie blinks at me. 'What do you want? Have you kidnapped me?'

I can't let Lottie panic. I shake my head.

'No, I haven't kidnapped you. I'm on your side, okay?'

Lottie's eyes don't believe me.

'I want to go home. I want my mum. I want my dad.'

I nod. Tell myself to be gentle with her. 'I know you do. I'm sorry.'

'Sorry, why, why are you sorry? What have you done?'

'I haven't done anything,' I say softly, even though that's not true—it was my booby trap that blew her father and mother to pieces just hours ago. It's their crusty blood on the back of her clothes and smeared across my soul. But there's no way to explain that. I need to keep her calm and on my side. Unless Jack's putting one over on me and on Rat, then I've just made an amazing breakthrough. While the area of the combined Radius is huge, Evan can still be free if I get him far enough out of it. Jack's not in him forever. I should be dancing for joy. Except my brother could be hundreds of kilometres away by now. Right in the centre of all those overlapping Jack circles.

'What happened?' Lottie asks.

'What do you remember?'

She blinks rapidly. 'Christmas—is it still Christmas?'

I shake my head. Jesus: it's like she's coming out of a coma. Worse than that: it's like she's a time traveller arriving in the future to find everyone she loved is dead. Not that she knows that yet. 'No, it's not Christmas.'

'What day is it?'

'Tuesday.'

'So it's been three days?'

I shake my head. 'Just tell me what you remember and then I'll tell you everything else, okay?'

Lottie looks at me warily.

'I'm not going to hurt you,' I say. 'And when we've finished talking you can go if you want to.'

I chill inside: what I just said to her is an echo of what Jack once said to me. And he never had any intention of letting me go. Just like I can't afford for Lottie to be out wandering the world by herself. I don't know what I'll do if she says she wants to go back to Clearview.

'Something really weird happened, on Christmas morning,' she says. 'I was with Mum and Dad and we were doing presents and then I could hear Mum's mind.'

I nod.

'And everybody in Clearview, that's where I live? Everyone except Dad. It was really horrible. Really loud. Mum's been spying on my social media. Can you believe that? I was so angry. I wanted to run away. Is that what I did? Did I run away? My head's sore—did I fall? I can't remember.'

'You didn't run away,' I say. 'But you did hit your head. I've checked it—you're all right.'

'Are you in the army?'

I forget that I don't look sixteen anymore. I look like a veteran—of something. 'No, I'm just a regular person like you.'

Lottie doesn't believe me—and why would she?

'Do you remember feeling like you were falling?' I prompt.

She thinks a moment and nods. 'Yes, that was horrible. I ran into my room. Locked myself in. Dad shouted he had to go for a run to clear his head. Mum was yelling, out loud and inside my mind, you know? Everyone in town was screaming.

And I could see other places too. Horrible things. People crying everywhere. Dying.'

She trails off and then her eyes widen.

'I think a plane crashed into the Sydney Harbour Bridge!'

I nod and tell her I saw it too.

'I don't know how I could see it,' Lottie says, lost in memory. 'It's such a long way from where we live.'

Where we live. The present tense is killing me. I try to not let it show.

'And then, like you said, I felt like I was falling down—Mum was pulling me under, into this empty place. But that was only, like, a few minutes ago—that's what it feels like.'

'That's it?'

She nods. 'Will you tell me now?'

So I did. I told her. My story. How it started for me. How I watched my dad and Stephanie die. How I tried to rescue Evan and get him to my mum's place. About finding Nathan and reviving people. Jack gunning us down and then taking me to Clearview. Meeting Marv and watching Jack revive her and her mum. Lottie asked how she couldn't remember that. She gasped and cried and I held her to quieten her as I told her the rest. Me finding my mother dead and realising Jack was responsible. Nearly killing Jack and escaping with her dad and how heroic he'd been defending us and going back to rescue her and Jane. Me and Nathan and Tajik taking the fight to Jack and winning—only to lose and for Damon to take my brother. I tell her about Nathan's and my long hard escape and how we've found a place and how it's now threatened. While I omit specifics about Colonial Town and who else is there, it's only when I come to the end that I straight out lie. If I tell Lottie the truth about her parents' deaths I'll lose her. Instead I tell her that she and Marv and Jane were left for dead after a car they were in rolled. When the Jacks had gone I checked for survivors and found she was alive and knew she could be saved.

'And here we are. I'm sorry.'

Lottie shakes and sobs in my arms and I remember how I felt after I saw Dad die and when I found Mum dead.

'I'm sorry, Lottie, I really am,' I whisper. 'It's a lot to take in. And I know what it's like to lose everyone.'

When she won't stop crying, I give her an apple juice with a sedative crushed in it and soon after she settles on the sleeping bag. It's just after midnight and I'm starting to fade. I need to get some sleep to function. I set the tablet alarm for four. That'll give us a few hours of darkness to get to Colonial Town. Should be more than enough. I drink the rest of the wine and curl up beside Lottie on the sleeping bag, my guns and grenades in arm's reach. Just before sleep claims me, I wonder why Rat isn't snuggling with me.

TWENTY

'Gail heard everything from their minds,' Johnno said when he returned to the restaurant. 'Stannis has her in his cottage. He's trying to get her to take a sleeping pill. She keeps saying she could've saved them. If she'd known about the Lorazepam. Poor woman.'

Tears slid from the corners of his eyes and he reached for a beer even though it was barely daylight. I couldn't begrudge him that. I was taking hits of an energy drink I'd filched from the fridge. Breakfast of champions for both of us.

'You've heard my story,' I said. 'What about you?'

This time it came out of Johnno in a torrent. He'd spent the summer driving up and down the coast. Surfing and doing a bit of work here and there. Living in his panel van. He was in Port Macquarie when the Snap hit. Found himself in minds crashing into each other up and down the coast and all the way inland to the mountains. Although they couldn't hear him it was still like the weight and force of them was pushing him into the earth. He went the one place he thought there might be more peace: jumped on his board and paddled for the horizon. But he couldn't get far enough from shore to escape the mental noise. Then he felt like he was being sucked beneath the surface and trapped in a bleak place that somehow wasn't air or sea or light or darkness. When he came back to himself, he was coughing water and half drowned but still connected to his board with a leg rope. He scrambled onto it and stared back at Port Macquarie across the waves. Parts of the city were burning. Boats were stuck on the sandbar where the Hastings River met the sea between twin breakwalls. Other cruisers and speedboats and yachts had made it out but now seemed adrift in the churning ocean. Like testing a radio, Johnno had realised he could tune the people back there in and out. It made it easier to bear the voices that'd devolved into an insane babble. What was harder to bear than their noise was the silence as people toppled into the nothing place from which he'd somehow surfaced. But none of them returned the way he had.

'I floated out there all day and all night,' he said. 'Thought I was gonna fall asleep and get taken by a shark. Then, at dawn, Boxing Day, there was like this . . .'

'Scream?'

'A scream. A boom. Like the earth splitting open. I don't know how to put it. But after that—nothing. Quiet.' He tapped his head. 'Quiet up here, I mean. I guess like what you said happened to you.'

Close to dehydrating, Johnno paddled back to Port Macquarie, landed on the Town Beach. Saw what we'd all seen: catatonic people and corpses. He spent days wandering and trying to find other conscious people. In an office in an arcade he stumbled upon the city's emergency public address system.

'Power was off but it had battery backup,' he said. 'Hooked to speakers all over the joint.'

For hours Johnno blared out who he was and where he was.

'If anyone heard, they didn't come,' he said.

The next morning he climbed the communications tower. Flashed a mirror at ships at sea and at inland suburbs. No one signalled back.

Johnno cracked another beer. 'Can't believe I used to fantasise about it. You know, zombie apocalypse? Be the survivor. Everything I want finally mine? But all I wanted was for people to wake up.'

He tried everything he could think of. Water in faces. Ammonia under nostrils. Electrical jolts from car batteries. Nothing could revive anyone.

'Wish I'd known about the Lorazepam,' he said. 'Jesus, if I had . . .'

I nodded. He wiped his eyes, was quiet for a while.

The Goners had started to die and Johnno couldn't take looking at them all—or the guilt he felt for being so uselessly alive.

'I figured I'd head south in the van,' he said. 'Had to be other people. And if there wasn't I'd find some nice place no one had died in and I'd drink myself to death. I was just outside Port Macquarie when she—Gail—came running out of her holiday house. She'd heard my engine.'

Gail begged Johnno to help her save her husband, Lee, and her son, Lucas. She'd returned to them a day after fleeing on a surf ski on the river to find them crashed out. Hearing this, my heart brightened and my respect for Johnno shot into the stratosphere. This bloke had somehow managed to revive the boy *and* reverse the telepathy. It was a feat that would've made Jack's reign impossible if Nathan and I had been able to achieve it.

'How'd you wake up Lucas?'

'I didn't. He died. The husband too.'

'The boy's not her son?'

Johnno shook his head and stared out at the geese through glassy eyes a long while before continuing. When he did he told me that all he'd been able to do was sit with Gail while her loved ones died slowly. He tried to get her to leave with him. She wouldn't budge. Just wept as the death smell started to fill the humid apartment.

'I thought maybe if I buried 'em, that'd help, y'know? Closure and all that. I nicked next door to find a shovel. Was only gone a few minutes but when I come back Gail is out the front, all dressed up, suitcase packed, calling me Lee and saying we really have to go and get Lucas.'

'Shit,' I said.

Johnno took a big gulp of beer, wiped his mouth. 'She'd totally lost the plot. I thought I should leave her. But I didn't want to be alone and she would've died without me.'

They took the panel van, drove on the verge, along median strips, Johnno pushing cars out of the way when needed. He'd gotten out to do that again when he saw the boy on the side of the road, clutching his amputee teddy bear. At first Johnno thought the kid was one of the catatonics who'd crashed out standing and staring. But then Gail had spied him and streaked from the car to scoop him up and tell him it was okay because Mummy was here.

Johnno shook his head. 'I went behind the truck to have a piss. Saw this place and checked it out. There's food, drink, generators, shelter. Only a few bodies to bury. People who broke in, I guess.' Johnno looked sombre a moment then smiled and tapped his bottle. 'Plenty of amber ale, too. Makes things go a little easier.'

He'd brought Gail and the boy inside. They'd set up in cottages. She kept calling him Lee. If he was out of her sight for too long she'd start losing it. The boy didn't say a word. Just stared and clutched his bear and wandered back to the side of the highway whenever he got the chance.

'We all ended up sitting out by the road a lot, waiting to see if anyone would come past,' Johnno continued. 'You know? Like rescue or something. About a week ago, there's this buzz and that little ultralight's flying up the road with wheezer-geezer old mate Stannis at the controls.'

It took me a moment to understand Johnno was talking about the lawnmower-hang-glider contraption out the front by the purple panel van.

'Wait, Stannis is a pilot?' I asked, imagination fired by a vision of us finding an airfield with a bigger plane that he could—

Johnno shook his head. 'That's what I thought, too. You don't need a pilot's licence to fly one of those things, he said. You just need to be crazy.'

I smiled despite the disappointment.

'Anyway,' Johnno went on, 'we waved him down and he landed right on the road.'

Stannis had been on his inland property for Christmas. Pretty sure his cancer meant it'd be the last one he had with his wife. But the Snap took her and spared him. When he emerged from his grief he'd taken to the air in his ultralight to see if there was anyone else left. Stannis had flown for a hundred kilometres without spying any signs of life before he saw the trio outside Colonial Town.

'That was a week ago,' Johnno said.

He burped into his hand. 'Better out than in. Reckon they— the Jacks or whatever—will come this far looking for you?'

'Sooner or later.'

Johnno nodded grimly. 'They might not find us here.'

I tilted my head. 'Maybe.'

'In any case, we'd have a hard time going anywhere with Gail or the boy or Stannis and . . .'

I nodded guiltily. 'And it's not like Nathan's going anywhere on that ankle for a while. Why don't we talk it over with him and Stannis? See what we can work out.'

Johnno stood. 'Good enough.' He stuck his hand out to me. 'No hard feelings?'

We shook and I followed him to Nathan's cottage. Was Nathan still my friend? I hoped his seeming hatred for me was at least partly due to the shock of his injury and the narcotic painkillers. Maybe he'd be calm enough to at least discuss the boy. Despite his mute trauma, the kid appeared . . . *normal*. He didn't fit into anything we knew. We had to find out why. And I'd have to see if Johnno could help me test Gail and see if she was *Situs*.

'Knock-knock,' Johnno said as he stepped up to the open door. 'Shit.'

I rushed to the side of Nathan's cot. My friend didn't look much more alive than the mannequins bunched in one corner of the room. His eyelids fluttered in sunken sockets. He held fistfuls of blanket up to his chin as his body shuddered beneath the covers.

'Nathan?' I said, kneeling by him. 'It's Danby.'

He flinched, head twitching away, as if my words hurt his ears.

'I need to take a look at you.'

His forehead was slimy with sweat under my palms. His cheeks had gone the colour of milky tea.

I turned to Johnno. 'Have you given him anything other than the painkillers last night?'

He shook his head.

'Swollen,' Nathan murmured. 'Swollen.'

He shivered as I lifted the blanket off his legs. His broken ankle was strapped and wrapped in pillows. Stannis and Johnno had done the best they could to keep him comfortable.

'I'll find you a cast,' I said. 'But I think the medication's had a reaction.'

Nathan gave a little shake of his head. 'Swollen here,' he croaked, a finger uncurling from the blanket to point at his neck.

I ran my fingers under his chin. His neck felt hard and thick on one side.

Johnno leaned in at my shoulder with a bottle of water and a towel.

Nathan let out a little moan as I dried his brow. Perspiration beaded his forehead again in seconds. He puffed out a stale breath and pushed at the blankets.

'Hot,' he said. 'Too hot.'

I pulled back the covers. His clothes and sheets were soaked.

'I need to look at your wound,' I said.

'Later, okay?' Nathan slurred, pushing himself up from the bed. 'Shit. I've got a shit.'

'We'll get you a bedpan.' I looked at Johnno. 'If anywhere's gonna have one, it's this place.'

Nathan laughed. 'Not shit, *shift*. I'm on overnight. Slurpees don't sell themselves. Even at Christmas.'

He wasn't with me. He was back at the McJob he'd taken after he'd had his breakdown and bombed out of medical school.

'Okay,' I said, 'but just rest a minute first.'

I eased him back onto the mattress. He closed his eyes and sighed. I carefully unbuttoned his shirt and prised up the tape that held his dressing in place. Beneath the gauze, the smell was medicinal and sour, and the skin around the stitches was puffy and red with crimson streaks pointing towards the swelling in his neck.

'Nathan,' I said up close to his ear. 'Wake up. Focus.'

'Focus. What, both of us?' He looked at me for a moment and laughed. 'Jesus, you're a bitch.'

I flinched. The fever was stripping the shackles of what he could and couldn't say. Almost like the Snap.

'Give me that,' I said to Johnno, pointing at a silver hand mirror on a dresser that some Victorian lady had used while brushing her hair one hundred strokes a night.

'Nathan,' I barked. 'Wake up!'

His eyes popped open. 'What?'

'What's my name?'

'Danby.'

'Good—okay what do you think of this?'

'What?'

I angled the mirror so Nathan would be able to see his infection. His brow furrowed as he saw his chest. It seemed to bring him back to reality. 'Not good.'

'Is it blood poisoning?'

He shook his head. 'Not yet. Strep infection.'

'Can you tell me what to do?'

Nathan nodded and held on, staying lucid as he rasped out the instructions. IV antibiotic Magnicillin. Oral antibiotic Baxtacin. Electrolyte to rehydrate. More painkillers. Wet towels and Ibuprofen to bring down fever. Elastic cast for ankle. Every syllable seemed to drain Nathan of energy. His eyes closed and he started snoring.

'Have you got Ibuprofen?' I asked Johnno.

'Yep.'

'All right. You get it, wake Nathan up, make him take some and another one of Stannis's tablets with as much sports drink as possible. Keep him cool as you can. Ice the foot, okay?'

He nodded that he could do all of that. 'What about you?'

'I need my gun and some gas. Wauchope's got a pharmacy?'

Johnno got my rifle from his cottage next door and led me to a supply shed stocked with fuel cans that'd been used for ride-on mowers.

'Take care of him,' I said.

'Take these,' he said, handing me a pair of boltcutters. 'Always handy.'

I sprinted up Colonial Town's main street, watched by mannequins and by Stannis, Gail and the boy, who stood hugging each other in a doorway. I topped up the quad, retrieved my dented helmet from the road and revved off. Even under the circumstances it felt good to be moving again and to have my fate in my hands.

But all that could change in Wauchope. The engine's thrumming was going to carry. If anyone unfriendly was alive there they'd hear me before I arrived and have plenty of time to line up their own guns. A bicycle would've been stealthier. But it'd be slower and I didn't know how long Nathan had. I guessed if it got to blood poisoning he'd die and that'd be my fault. If we'd kept going like he'd said we'd be far away and safe. Nathan wouldn't have broken his ankle. Wouldn't have been too doped up to realise infection was setting in. All of this was on me. Not just the imminent threat to his life. But that even if he survived the infection he wouldn't be able to travel for weeks. That could be a death sentence in our world. I had to set all of this right. Had to keep him safe until he was whole again. Then if he wanted me to leave him alone I would.

Weaving between cars, barely noticing the bodies and trees blurring past, I reached Wauchope's shops in just a few minutes. I parked the quad up on the footpath. On Christmas Day, when people in this little town had freaked out, they'd had plenty of places to go where other people weren't—bush, mountains, beaches, lakes. The chemist was closed up, windows intact, interior dark. I was briefly absurdly grateful for the Snap. In any other apocalyptic scenario, this place would've been looted—as it was about to be.

The pharmacy's doors were deadlocked. No security grille with padlocks to cut. No time for a quiet entrance like Nathan and I had made in Parramatta. I looked away as I swung the boltcutters into the plate glass. The crash shattered the silence, reverberated in my bones. It would've been heard all over Wauchope. But I couldn't worry about who it might bring. In and out and go.

I smashed jagged glass from the doorframe. Inside, I found everything Nathan had told me to get and was on my way out when I stopped and went back to the pharmacist's shelves. I grabbed a few boxes of the medication Nathan had been prescribed for his mental illness and added them to my stash. Which led me to think Gail might need some chill pills. I snatched up a few brands I remember Stephanie taking for her anxiety. Better living through chemistry.

Nathan was still asleep when I got back to Colonial Town.

Johnno had cleaned his wound and applied a new dressing. He told me he'd managed to get him to wash down the tablets with a bottle of electrolyte drink.

I worked quickly to set up an IV and ran a tube of antibiotics into Nathan's arm. Then I hit him with a bag of saline to help replace what he was sweating out. Johnno watched with something like awe. I explained that Nathan had taught me how to do this.

'How long before he's better?' he asked.

'I don't know.'

I knelt by Nathan's side and held his hand. Tried to will him to be well. Wished we could share thoughts so he could see past my stupid anger and fear and confusion and know and feel what was in my heart. I'd only wanted the best. For him. For me. For Evan. For us to be together and safe. I heard the floorboards creak as Johnno left the cottage.

'Please don't die,' I whispered to Nathan. 'Please. Hate me if you want but please don't die.'

I stayed by him all day and into the night. Checking him with a thermometer. Mopping him with cool water. Forcing him to drink fluids whenever he came around. By the early hours of the next morning his fever had dropped enough that I felt okay about snatching a few hours' sleep on the floor by his cot.

When I woke up, someone had covered me with a blanket. Nathan slept on, red streaks receding and my relief increasing as his temperature came down closer to normal.

'Try to eat,' I said, handing him a bowl of vegetable soup later that afternoon. 'You need your strength.'

Nathan was sitting up. He'd lost more weight. Between our trek and his fever, he looked gaunt and weak. He took the bowl with a nod and spooned the soup without enthusiasm.

'I'm sorry,' I said. 'Really, if I'd—'

'Don't,' he said. 'Just don't, okay?'

I nodded. My wish had been for him to live. Forgiving me wasn't something I expected. But I still had to take care of him.

'At least tell me what to do with your leg,' I said.

Nathan set the soup aside and regarded me with hard eyes. 'How long has it been?'

'Two days.'

'Show me.'

I carefully unwrapped his ankle.

'It's been kept straight,' he said. 'Shouldn't need to re-break it.'

In a clinical tone, like I was a barely tolerable colleague deserving of professional respect only, Nathan talked me through injecting anaesthetic, slipping on the elastic cast and tightening it so that the bone was aligned and would set straight.

'Yeah, that's good,' he said when I was done.

'How long?'

'Before I'm walking again?' he said bitterly. 'It'll be weeks before I get over the infection. Longer till I can walk. If they come, I'm gonna be fucked.'

'I'll keep you safe,' I said. 'I promise.'

Nathan sniffed. 'You've done enough for me.'

I pretended not to hear the sarcasm. 'Do you need anything else to eat? Something to drink?'

Nathan shook his head. 'Just close the door on your way out.'

Out on the verandah, I slumped into a rocking chair. Across the road, through the drizzle settling over Colonial Town, the others were eating breakfast in the restaurant.

I didn't want to be with them. Nathan didn't want me with him. But I couldn't just sit there doing nothing.

TWENTY-ONE

'Lottie, how are you feeling?'

She's awake and eating crackers spread with jam. The juice I've given her is spiked with a quarter of a dexie and half a sedative. I'm hoping the combined effect is that she'll be awake but calm. I've already washed down my pick-me-up pill and can feel its dull electricity charging me up. They work less now and leave me feeling dirty inside.

'It's like it's a nightmare,' Lottie says. 'Like I'm still asleep.'

'I know,' I say. 'I still feel that way every day.'

It's a lie. I used to feel that way constantly. Like I should change my name to Dorothy. Have a little dog named Toto instead of a rat named Rat. Now I accept that it's no dream. It's simply what is. But I can't say that to Lottie. I have to tell her what she wants to hear to keep her manageable enough to travel. I can't take her with me if she's panicking. And I can't leave her alive to be found by Jack because he'd make her tell him everything she knew and then kill her anyway. Lies and drugs: they're for her own safety.

'Are you sad all the time?' she asks.

I have to lie about this too. 'It gets easier.'

'Why do you keep on?'

'Keep on what?'

'Living.'

I don't want to have this conversation. Not at four in the morning.

'To look after my friends,' I say. 'To maybe get my brother back one day.' Although I stop myself before adding 'killing Jacks' to the list, what I've already said is enough to set Lottie weeping.

'I haven't got anyone,' she says.

'You've got me.' Another lie. I might die any moment. I might still have to kill her. 'I'm here.'

Lottie sniffles. 'But I don't know you.'

So I tell her about myself. Teen stuff. What I used to do with Jacinta and Emma and Madison. The music and movies and books I liked. These are precious minutes we could be using to get closer to Colonial Town. But it distracts her from her sadness.

'Don't you miss them?'

'Every day.' Not a lie.

Lottie dreamily talks about her best friends. 'Did you see any of them in Clearview?'

'Who?'

Lottie rattles off names, descriptions. School friends, a couple of cousins, an aunty.

'I don't know,' I say when she runs out of people.

'We could save them,' she says. 'I mean, when we save your brother.'

I'm thinking Jack's presence is like that of Jesus according to the church sign Nathan and I saw back in Killeen: 'For where two or three are gathered together in My name, I am there in the midst of them.' I only saved Lottie because she was unconscious until I isolated her outside the Radius. Doing that again—finding and freeing Evan—seems like a million-to-one shot. I can't see how I could also rescue Lottie's loved ones. But I don't say any of that to her.

'Let's see what we can come up with,' I offer, 'when we get where we're going.'

She nods like this is something to hold onto. 'It's nice, right? The place you're taking me?'

I nod that it is.

'How far is it?'

'From here, maybe three hours.'

I check the tablet. Four forty-five a.m. Damnit. We'll be doing at least an hour's riding in daylight. Travelling in darkness would've not only been safer but would've protected Lottie from seeing roadsides strewn with bodies. 'We have to get going.'

She sits calmly on the quad's cargo area as I pack my stuff around her and make sure she's securely strapped in.

'Where are you, Rat?' I say.

'Who's Rat?' Lottie says.

'Rat's a rat,' I say, eyes flicking over the couches. 'She was on my shoulder when you woke up. She's been helping me work out who's a Jack and who's not. When she didn't freak out, I knew you were okay.'

I look at Lottie. She's frowning in the candlelight. A shard of terror cuts into me. Maybe Rat has belatedly realised this girl is a Jack and has cleared out.

Except if that was true then surely they'd have us surrounded. Unless this is just some game. Jack toying with me. Raising my hopes. Getting me to lead him to the others. Maybe we *are* surrounded. In the four hours I was asleep Jack could've filled the town with his selves. In this back room it's not like I even have a view of the street. I curse myself for that security lapse.

I stare at Lottie, only just manage to stay my hand from reaching for the .45 in my holster.

'What?' she says, blinking at me. 'What's wrong?'

Trust. I have to trust my gut. It's telling me she's okay.

'Nothing,' I say. 'I just don't know where Rat could've got to.'

'I must've been still half unconscious,' Lottie says. 'I didn't even notice her.'

I spend a few minutes calling for Rat, looking up the chimney, under couches and behind the bar, fearing I'll find her stuck in a trap.

The only trace of Rat is a little pile of cashews I'd set out for her. They're untouched.

'Is it time to go?' Lottie sways a little on the quad. The drugs are kicking in. I'm glad I've strapped her on tightly.

I swallow silly sadness. Rat's done a runner. Good for her. Being my pet pal didn't work out so well for Lachie.

'Yep,' I say, 'we're outta here.'

TWENTY-TWO

I took a slow walk through Colonial Town. Beyond the restaurant, quaint shops offered boiled lollies and beef jerky and handmade furniture and landscape art. I kicked gravel on the railway and followed the tracks past a vegetable garden and chicken coop, through thick forest and by steel sheds that housed a steam train and carriages. Farther along, mannequins hunched over pans in a mocked-up miners' camp and a dock jutted out into a lake on which floated a scaled-down tall ship crewed by yet more dummies.

As bad as it was being stuck here, Colonial Town had a lot going for it. The property was almost completely hidden from the air by its towering hardwood forest. A chopper would have to fly directly above the dozen or so buildings to even see them. Between the rain tanks and drinks fridges, restaurant and shop shelves and vegie gardens and chooks, it could sustain six people for quite a long time. Maybe even long enough for Nathan to heal and stop hating me.

But Colonial Town wasn't completely safe. It'd be a cinch

for the Jacks to get over the cyclone fence that separated it from the road and surrounding bush. There weren't enough of us to patrol and we wouldn't know they were on us until it was too late. Even if we had warning, we didn't have the means to get away or weapons to put up a fight. A crappy panel van, a couple of quads and an ultralight plane—they were about as much use as two guns, thirty rounds of ammunition and whatever random supplies we could grab off the shelves as we ran. That is to say, none. But I could do something about that. Even if Nathan hated me I'd still fulfil my promise. I'd protect him—and that meant protecting this place.

I walked back to Nathan's cottage. He was asleep or pretending to be. I entered quietly. There was a slate and chalk, another part of the historical display, and I scratched a message onto it and propped it up where he could see.

I'll make this right. Gone for supplies. Back tomorrow. D.

Through the restaurant window, I saw Johnno holding his head over a coffee while Gail rocked the boy in her arms and stared at the fireplace. Chin cupped in his hand, Stannis appeared to be asleep at the table.

I rapped on the glass, waved Johnno to the door.

'I'm going into Port Macquarie,' I said.

Johnno smelt of stale beer. It looked like it hurt for him to squint his eyes at me. 'Are you . . . leaving?'

The noise I made was between a laugh and a sigh. 'You want me to stay now?'

He shook his head. 'No, I mean, yes.'

'I'll be back. I need to get supplies. Can you do a few things while I'm gone?'

Johnno nodded warily, unsure what he was getting into.

'Just keep an eye on Nathan. Make sure he takes his antibiotics. Try to get him to eat.'

Johnno looked relieved. 'Sure.'

'And smash up that front office a bit. Graffiti the brickwork. Cut down the sign and drag it off into the weeds.'

He looked at me like I was crazy.

'The truck's good cover but they're less likely to come in here if this place looks like it's been abandoned for ages.'

Johnno cracked a smile. 'You're something.'

••

Every kilometre closer to Port Macquarie meant more cars and chaos on the road. Before I'd left Colonial Town, I'd visited the gift shop and lined my helmet with a souvenir tea towel I doused in locally made eucalyptus oil. But I didn't know if that'd stand up to the full city of the dead that lay up ahead. I tried to distract myself by making a mental checklist of everything we needed.

1. Ammo.

2. Guns.

I couldn't get past those two. It was like I was stuck in a loop. Problem was they'd probably be the hardest things to find. If I was riding a quad through anywhere in America finding heavy-duty weaponry wouldn't be an issue. Every second home would have pistols or rifles as their God-given and constitutionally protected right. I shuddered to think what the Snap had been like there with an average of one gun available to each of its 300 million crazy people. It would've been a bloodbath. Those who'd survived the catatonia might still be killing each other except now there'd be something like ten thousand guns left for each person with *Situs inversus*. What a psychotic symmetry. Maybe we had gotten off easy after all.

Gun shops would have hunting rifles. Better than nothing but not much good against Jacks tooled up with assault weapons. Maybe a police station or army base would have machine guns. I paused as I crested a hill that looked out over a suburban development. A sign showed I was five kilometres out of Port Macquarie.

I took the binoculars from a pannier. Nobody stirred. Dozens of houses were spread out below me. Some of them might have housed criminals. Drug dealers or bank robbers. People who needed illegal firearms. Or maybe the opposite. Cops or soldiers who brought their work home. Checking those places would be random, but if I did get lucky, I might not have to go all the way into Port Macquarie, where there'd be a hundred times more rotting corpses and a greater risk of encountering Jacks or other survivors who might be unfriendly.

I steered down an avenue and eased the quad up a driveway into an empty garage. At least if anyone drove past on the highway, they wouldn't see a crudely camouflaged all-terrain vehicle and get ideas that someone was in here looting. Standing under the eaves of the house, gazing across the rooftops, I felt like an alien in my helmet with its medicinal atmosphere, having conquered a planet of brick veneer and satellite dishes and lain waste to a race of suburbanites whose bodies now fed flies in cul-de-sacs and driveways.

'Don't be a shit,' I said aloud to myself. I couldn't distance myself from this by pretending it was sci-fi. These weren't a different species. They were my people. Most of them had been decent folk who'd lived modestly ambitious lives and wanted to improve themselves and do well by their families and friends.

I wondered whether humanity's fatal flaw had been our proud focus on the few quirks that made us individuals rather than on the almost identical DNA that made us a species. The suddenness of the Snap's shared consciousness meant we'd been made crazy by what we thought set us apart rather than united by the revelation of everything we shared. I thought if it'd been more gradual—evolving over weeks or months or years—we might've not just survived but thrived with a new empathy. Forgiven each other trespasses as we would want to be forgiven—all of that stuff. Except ... except in that brave new world it would've been people like me and Nathan who became suspect because we wouldn't have been able to join the hivemind. How long would it have been before we were hunted down, rounded up and killed off? Even in an alternate reality where the Snap had ushered in utopia, I'd probably still have been running for my life.

I went into the house, walked from room to room, scanned bookshelves and desks, drawers and cupboards. Only the bathroom yielded anything of interest. The man of the house had been old school when it came to shaving. I opened his pearl-handled straight razor. The blade gleamed as I ran it across the back of my middle finger to produce a white line that welled with blood. I wiped the razor on a towel, snapped it shut and put it in the pocket of my jeans. That little cut didn't hurt. It actually felt good. I had a fast means to my end if it came to that. Meaning one more bullet I could use on Jacks.

I returned to the garage, looked back out at the suburban vista. Nothing had changed, nothing had moved. The blanket of smoke was so uniform that the clouds and shadows seemed to have curdled. Time felt like it'd stopped.

Bandana pressed to my face against the fumes, I went from house to house, wandered through lounges and sunrooms, fingers trailing over photos in frames and stuck to fridges, seeing the people as they'd been, not as they'd become on their stained carpets and overgrown lawns. It was a connection to the world of yesterday, piecing these people together as living and breathing and meaning something to each other.

I lost count of how many places I searched. A dozen, maybe, but I didn't find any gun cabinet, militia arsenal or even a cop's service revolver. I'd have to go into Port Macquarie. I checked the GPS and found a route that meant I didn't have to go through its most populated parts to reach the business district.

Back on the quad on the Oxley Highway, I thought I was hallucinating when I crossed the bridge over King Creek. There, among the mangroves, was a Chinese junk. Wooden sides, squat canopy, jutting prow, painted dark green with red trim. I slowed and stopped. I didn't know how it was possible that it could've sailed halfway around the world in just a few weeks. I pulled out my binoculars. If the *Fu Hao* had floated here from China, whoever had come with it was long gone.

'Inscrutable,' I said in a fake Chinese accent, smiling before my heart perforated. That'd been Jacinta's 'exclusive' joke. She claimed only she could get away with it thanks to her heritage. It was the first time I'd thought about my friend today. She and everyone else were never far from my mind. I rode on so I wouldn't break down.

I tooled along the now aptly named Ruins Way, flanked by suburban mausoleums, to where it bordered the Lake Innes nature reserve. Compared with the terrain Nathan and I had negotiated, the bumpy bush paths of this little 'green corridor' were a ride in the park. Ten minutes later, I was on Pacific Drive, catching glimpses of the ocean through rainforest.

As soon as there was a break in the trees, I pulled over so I could stare out to sea. Climbing off the bike, I took off my helmet and walked on shaky legs to the edge of the road, where a carpet of vines dropped steeply to a rocky shore. My heart sank and I followed it down until I was sitting cross-legged in the gravel. I didn't know what I'd secretly hoped to see out there. Maybe my refuge island. Maybe a rescue boat. But all I saw were bronze clouds above a barren seascape and all I felt was the weight of a million square miles of dead continent behind me.

I sat there, eyes closed, barely breathing, seeing no reason to keep breathing. Then it was like I was off the cliff, in the water, part of the ocean. My *home. Our* home. Happiness shot through me. Grey shades and shapes bubbled and blurred and flashed. Me. I *was* those shapes. One. All. Exuberant. Light above. Dark below. Fluid existence in and out of both worlds. I couldn't see much. Even with so many eyes. But it didn't matter because my mind was everywhere at once. Out to the welcoming deeper water where food waited. In to the frothing shallows and shore where danger swarmed. But I was here. Safe. One of many. Many in one. Spearing up into that other world of light and air and spray before slicing back into the wetness and warmth beneath the waves. Joyful. Powerful. Peaceful.

Then it slipped away. My eyes sprang open. I'd been somewhere pure and serene. Better even than the feeling I'd had inside Evan's mind at the start of the Snap. I spun around, wondering where it'd come from. I raised my binoculars, scanned from the shore out to the horizon, saw a smattering of yachts and cruisers. They all looked dead in the water. But someone on them had to be—

Then I saw them. Far to the south and heading out to sea. Dolphins arcing up from the water, disappearing back beneath the surface. I closed my eyes. Tried to get that feeling again. Couldn't.

TWENTY-THREE

We're almost on top of the tiny town of Prestige when I see the lights and hear Frank Sinatra. At first I think this is amphetamine sparkle and another earworm. I have my doubts about myself. Since Lottie and I left Callum an hour ago I've been wondering whether Rat was real. The idea of being a bit crazy doesn't bother me the way it did before the Snap. It might be the only sane way to handle an insane world. But if I'm capable of conjuring an imaginary friend to tell me who to kill then I also might've hallucinated those dolphins a few months ago. I hate to think one of the most beautiful moments I've ever had was nothing more than me being 'Danbay-cray-cray' as Jacinta used to say.

But the glow of flames and the strains of karaoke are real. I know because Lottie leans forward to wrap her arms around my waist and asks who's up ahead on the street.

I brake the quad. Quickly tug her and my backpacks from the cargo area. Bundle them into bushes by the side of the road. Shield Lottie with my body and tell her to be quiet. The fire ahead's too bright for my night-vision goggles. I ease them off and zoom in with my binoculars. A few blocks from me dark figures cluster around a burning barrel in the middle of the street. I make out three guys. Two sit on stools at a table and sing along as their mate belts out 'My Way' with a microphone hooked up to a speaker. If they weren't making so much light and noise they would've seen us coming.

'Who is it?' Lottie whispers. 'Is it them? Jacks?'

'Stay down,' I say. 'Let me check it out.'

Confident my yowie suit makes me invisible, I melt along the edge of the road with my AK-47 trained on the men. I scan with my binoculars. What I see makes my head spin. The guy who's singing is wearing a sharp suit with a white shirt, tie and shiny shoes. His buddies are dressed identically and smoking cigars. On the table are wine bottles and glasses and plates of cheese and crackers. Their motorbikes—all fancy chrome and soft leather—gleam where they're parked in a row on the other side of the road. They're not like working-class mates in an improvised beer garden. They're like corporate executives celebrating the end of the week in some wanker wine bar.

Unless this is Jack treating his selves to a party, these guys are Specials. Or more of the Normals I'm still getting my head around.

I hold ninja still. My rifle's aimed at the singer's head as he does it his way. I reckon I can shoot them all before they get their guns. Assuming they have guns. But I can't see any weapons. Not slung over their shoulders. Not leaning against their stools. I should back away, leave them to their fun, find another way around.

Then I see the woman.

She sits at the base of a Stop sign, head slumped forwards, face under a cascade of silver hair, hands flat on the gutter beside her and legs stretched out on the road. At first I think she's a wife or girlfriend or moll who has peaked a little early on the vino. Then I see the glint at her wrist. I zoom. Handcuffs. Chain looped behind the sign's steel pole.

I fight back bile and take a better look at the men's big bikes. Rolled sleeping bags. Designer backpacks. I'm assuming they're taking whatever else they need—booze, food, women, fashion—when and where they find it. Now I see their guns. Hunting rifles. Semi-automatic. Strapped to their rides. Maybe these guys use them to shoot cows for fresh meat. Maybe they use them to blast anyone who gets in their way. That they're not slinging them, that they're content to get off their faces out in the open, tells me that they've not encountered much resistance in their travels. If they ever had discipline, they've gotten sloppy.

Anger burns. I remember Parramatta. The Party Duder doing his worst to that poor woman. How I froze and how she died before I ran like a rabbit and nearly suffered the same fate. Hunched over, I creep back to Lottie.

'There's three bad guys up ahead,' I say.

There's enough light that I can see her eyes widen. 'Can't we go around them?'

With a GPS we *might* find our way. But that tech died two months ago, not long after I established my lookout. I was up there, about to call it a night, when I saw a glow behind the sky's dense haze. Jacks in a jet? A nuclear missile? Before I could move, a fireball punched through the clouds and flared into the sea on the horizon. When the sound reached my mountain base a few seconds later it was like a whip cracking across the world. I stood still, senses on high alert, wondering if I should expect a radiation cloud or a racing tsunami, but darkness and silence reclaimed the world like nothing had happened. Gradually, I calmed. It was only when I awoke to resume my coast watch and found the GPS was dead that I realised what I'd seen was likely a key part of the global communications network crashing back to Earth.

Where that'd left me since was with my paper maps. Using them now with my night-vision goggles, I might be able to navigate Lottie and me safely around these men. But it would use up valuable time. And it would leave that woman to the mercy—or its opposite—of those three suited bastards.

'They've got a lady,' I say. 'They're hurting her.'

'All right, New York!' the guy shouts as his mates applaud and whistle. 'Now you're in for a real treat. Please make him welcome.'

'Thank you, thank you very much,' comes a voice mimicking Elvis. 'What I'd like to do for you all is a little song called "Suspicious Minds".'

With him singing and Lottie looking at me terrified, I wonder whether I'm paranoid. Maybe I should give these men the benefit of the doubt. Ask questions first and shoot later. I don't know for sure what the situation is with that woman. She might be crazy. She might be dangerous. She might be—

Me.

If Nathan had worried about me somehow 'deserving' to be in that situation in Parramatta I would've died at the hands of the Party Duder.

'There's no way around them,' I say to Lottie. 'I need you to stay here.'

I rummage for the music player and earbuds. It's loaded up with plenty of loud tunes its original owner thought would sustain his mind and soul through the End Times. I select 'Don't Fear the Reaper' and pump the volume.

'Listen to this,' I said, handing it to Lottie. 'Close your eyes. Stay in the bushes. Don't move.'

'Okay,' she whispers, 'but what are you going to do?'

'I'm going to talk to them.'

I'm not going to talk to them.

I crabwalk back along the road and lean across a car bonnet. I'm a block away from the karaoke party. I'm engulfed in darkness as I steady the rifle, flick off the safety and aim at Elvis's chest.

This isn't a Jack. This is a person. Either his *Situs* saved him as a Special or he was far enough away from big populations to survive as one of the Normals. Either way, we're all members of a critically endangered species. But he and his friends have forfeited their rights by denying the woman hers.

My gunshot cracks loudly over the music. Elvis drops the mike, clutches his chest and staggers back. His drunken buddies laugh until their mate crashes into the barrel and spreads flames everywhere. Reality cuts through the booze and they realise their friend hasn't fallen down drunk.

'Shit!' one of them shouts. 'He's—'

That guy dies in a burst of gunfire as the third one scrambles away. I open up at him but he zigzags and throws himself over the motorbikes. Goddamnit.

He's got a wall of rubber and chrome to hide behind now. Rifles in easy reach. If he saw my muzzle flash he knows where I am. Breaking cover's a risk but I need to regain the element of surprise. I duck and scurry to the other side of the road and inside the fence of a little cottage. I use my binoculars to check the woman. She's flat against the gutter. I hope I haven't hit her with a stray round. Neither of the two men I've shot are moving.

Gunfire erupts from the motorbikes and there's the *clang-whirr-thunk* of bullets tearing through metal and shattering glass as the last suit riddles the car I'd been hiding behind and sprays the road for good measure. I chew gum. Clear my mind. Aim my rifle where his muzzle flares. I'm about to let him have it when he ceases fire. I hear shuffling and whispering and the familiar squelch of a walkie talkie.

Asshole. He's calling in reinforcements.

I need this to be over. I check the distance from me to the row of bikes. About ten metres. From where the man hides to where the woman lies face down is about half that.

'Lady,' I shout. 'Stay down. Don't move.'

'My colleagues are on the way,' the suit calls out in a plummy accent, trying to sound tough and calm. 'I suggest you get out of here while you can.'

His friends may be coming but he won't be alive to see it. This guy has no clue who he's up against. I've spent a lot of time reacquiring my softball skills in the past few months. Eight times out of ten I can land a rock the size of my fist in a bin from this range. I put my rifle down, pull an F1 from my pocket and pitch it through the night. I hit the dirt as my fragmentation grenade clatters on the other side of the road.

'Aw, hell, no,' the suit says.

His shadow jumps up. Tries to run.

There's a flash and boom and the suit is blown across the footpath as the motorbikes heave and topple, chrome twisted and rubber burning.

The woman's still down. She doesn't look hurt. I hear her whimpering.

'Don't move,' I shout above the crackling flames. 'Don't move.'

My command is for her and for any of the suits who might be alive. I scan the carnage I've created. Body in the flames. Body in the middle of the road. Body visible beyond the tangle of motorbikes. No one's moving. But if I was wounded I wouldn't be stupid enough to wriggle around. I'd play dead until my attacker left—or got close enough for me to kill with a knife or pistol. I flick my AK-47 to single shot and carefully put three bullets into each of the bodies. No one screams.

I edge forward, sweeping the few shops and houses. The woman's twisted around so she's face down, chained hands over her head.

'It's okay,' I say. 'They're dead.'

She rolls over and struggles up. Maybe in her early fifties. Eyes violet and white. Nose ring glints as her nostrils flare around the red ball gag stuffed in her mouth. She has tattoos on her shoulders, red boots like the ones I used to wear. Her eyes widen when she sees me. Scarred. Crew cut. AK-47. Yowie suit that makes me look like a walking bush. If she's scared, she doesn't show it. Her eyes flick to the slumped and bleeding men around her and then we stare at each other again.

'I'm going to take out the gag, okay?'

She nods. I lean in. Loosen the straps. She spits the ball out.

'That bastard,' she says, voice thick, nodding at the guy in the middle of the road. 'Keys to the cuffs are with that one. Hurry.'

I rummage in his pockets. Can't help but notice how well put together this guy was. Cool hair. Bright teeth. Manicured fingernails. The smell of sandalwood soap mixes with the coppery tang of blood leaking from the bullet holes in his expensive suit. Even after he became a marauder, he took care of himself. I wonder how he'd lived his life before the Snap. Was he a sales executive during the week and a wannabe biker bad-ass at the weekends? When the world ended had both sides of his personality run to their extremes in the lawless world he'd inherited?

I unlock the woman's cuffs. She rubs her wrists, blinks and nods, looks like she's fighting to surface through the shock. 'Thank you.'

'We need to get out of here,' I say.

'That's mine,' she replies, stabbing a finger at a four-wheel drive. 'We can go to my place. It's in the bush. They won't find us.'

'They found you.'

'Only because I was in town,' she says. 'My mistake. I won't make it again.'

She's on her feet. 'I'm going—are you coming?'

I turn and point back up the road. 'I've got a—'

Except I haven't. Even from here I can see the quad's leaning at an angle. It's taken at least one of the suit's bullets.

'Get the engine started!' I say as I break into a run. 'Lottie! Lottie!'

I picture her bleeding out from a stray round. But she's in the bush where I left her, shaking uncontrollably, holding the music player tight like a talisman, the Blue Oyster Cult still cowbelling tinnily from the earbuds. I crouch beside her and press stop on the music player.

'What happened, Danby? What was all that—'

'There's more bad guys coming,' I say. 'Lottie—run that way, towards that car. See, with the light on inside? There's a lady waiting for you.'

'What about you?'

'I'll catch up.'

'Danby, I'm—'

'If you don't go, you're going to die,' I say harshly.

That gets through to her and she scrambles away.

I check the quad. Both tyres on its right side have been ripped apart. Cursing a streak that we have to depend on a stranger, I scoop up my gear and run after Lottie.

I dive into the four-wheel drive beside her and the woman rattles the gearstick and hits the accelerator. We speed around the corner past a couple of shitbox houses and caravans. I'm aware of how far the headlights' glow will be visible against the low clouds if the suit's friends are close by. Our engine noise will carry, too.

We sweep up a darkened road and into thicker bush. I turn and through the rear window see the flames from the toppled barrel and burning bikes. If one of Jack's drones sees a whole town burning, I might just have undone all my hard work.

'I'm scared,' Lottie says.

I put my arm around her. Tell her I am too. It's a white lie. I'm buzzing.

'Thanks for back there,' the woman says as she turns off bitumen, angles us up a dirt road.

I don't like that I don't know this woman or where she's taking us. 'Can you stop?'

'Why?'

'Stop,' I blurt. 'Lights and engine off.'

She skids, pulls up the handbrake, kills the headlights. The darkness is total. I pull away from Lottie and put on my night-vision goggles. I can see the woman looking around into the blackness. Her hands are still on the steering wheel. I ease the .45 from my holster and aim it at the back of her head. I'm glad Lottie can't see this. Doesn't know this is what I did to her just hours ago.

'What're we doing?' the woman asks.

'Getting the lay of the land,' I say. 'We'll go again in a second.'

I roll the window down. No motorbike rumbling yet. No lights glowing over the hills.

'Who are you?' I say.

She tells me and for a second I think she's said my name. My stomach plummets because I've blundered into a trap. She's a Jack or a disciple, or—

'So that's capital H, capital B,' she's saying. 'Aitch-Bee. Initials for Henrietta Bemis. Thanks, Mum and Dad, for that one.'

Her laugh relaxes me a little but not so much that I lower the .45.

'And you are?' she asks.

'Danby,' I say. 'This is Lottie.'

'Pleased to know you both,' HB says. 'Shouldn't we get going? We're too close to town here. And that last one was talking to his mates when you, when you—'

'I know,' I say. 'Who were they?'

HB shakes her head in disbelief. 'From what I heard, they called themselves the Board.'

'What?'

'Christ, I don't know. It's what they said. From what I got, they were a bunch of corporate douchebags who used to ride together for fun.'

'Did they—'

'Rape me? No.'

Lottie whimpers. I can't protect her from hearing about the world she's woken up in.

'They ... they were saving me for the ... Chairman,' HB says.

'You're kidding.'

HB shakes her head. 'That's what they called him. He was going to have first dibs.'

I put my .45 back in its holster. You can't make this up. I should be warier and test this woman for *Situs*, but I can't see how she could be a Jack and part of some elaborate trap.

'Tell me exactly what happened.'

HB sighs. 'I came into town this afternoon. Was in the bed and breakfast. Looking for books because I'd read everything I had. That's when they rolled in. I should've known better. But they were the first walking and talking people I've seen since it happened. They didn't look like outlaws. They looked, y'know, like decent guys. I came out and they're nice as pie. We talk. They ask me if I'm by myself. I tell 'em I am. When they ask me again I know I've made a mistake. I try to run inside and they rough me up a bit catching me.'

Tinny music starts next to me. Lottie has the earbuds in and her eyes shut. I don't blame her.

'Then I'm where you saw me,' HB continues, 'chained up like an animal, and they're on their walkie-talkies telling the Chairman the town's got a good selection of reds, a nice little pub and that they've found an "older one" to "diversify the Portfolio". He tells 'em to sit tight and that he and the others will be along in a while. So they're all bolshie, saying they've earned a right to have some wine. One of them brings out a bag of cocaine. That gets 'em going. They're talking about not getting the right rewards, saying there's got to be a change in management.'

HB wipes her cheeks and laughs bitterly. 'Shit, then it's karaoke time. As if I hadn't been subjected to enough horror already.'

My head's still spinning around one word. 'Portfolio?'

'That's what they said. I'm assuming it's—' Her voice trails off.

I know what it is. My stomach clenches. 'Did you hear how many more of them there are?'

HB shifts, shakes her head. 'Hang on—kinda. They said if all three of them voted and they could get Price and Bateman on side they'd have a majority.'

'Nine,' I say. Three down. Six to go. 'I need to go back.'

'You're not serious?' HB says.

'Stay here,' I say. 'There's gonna be a lot of noise. Keep Lottie calm. Give me ten minutes after it goes quiet. If I'm not back then go.'

HB turns in her seat, trying to make me out in the darkness. 'We should just go now.'

'Would you think that way if you were in the "Portfolio"?' I ask.

Then I'm gone.

TWENTY-FOUR

The view from Pacific Drive above Rocky Beach made it hard to breathe. It looked like a skyscraper had fallen from Flynns Point into the sea. Windows, balconies and walls, white steel and black glass, all tipped the wrong way and defying my mind's attempts to piece them together. Only a curve of bulbous red hull defined that I was seeing an ocean liner on its side. It was like some beached whale that had got halfway back into the ocean before it died. I tilted my head to read the name painted across the stern. *Queen Artemisia*.

I trained the binoculars over the passenger decks. Peered through horizontal doorways. Into private balconies. Bodies in Bermuda shorts and Hawaiian shirts, floral sarongs and bathing suits, hung over bulkheads and railings. The liner had stood a dozen storeys above the waterline and stretched the length of three football fields. It must've had thousands of holidaymakers aboard at Christmas. Wherever they'd been—coming into a harbour, far out to sea—they hadn't been safe from the Snap or each other.

I pictured the chaos. A floating city of strangers. As trapped mentally as they were physically. I wondered how many had flung themselves into the sea. Whether it was more or less than the number who'd locked themselves in cabins and become catatonic. Some of the lifeboat bays were empty. I hoped that meant some people had gotten away. Not that I knew if physical escape would've been enough to save anyone. I dipped the binoculars to the hull. Saw where it'd been ripped open on the sea floor.

My heart tightened. A flash of colour was moving amid the shadows and surging waves. A curly-haired man. Blue wetsuit. Trying to swim free from the hole. I was about to shout to him when I saw the fin and tail. Not a survivor but a corpse being carried off by a shark. As I watched, more of the predators swam in and out of the wreck, collecting bodies and heading out to deeper water. The beach below me was strewn with luggage and umbrellas and deckchairs and tables. But no dead people. The sharks had seen to that.

I rode on. The concentration of houses and motels became denser. I stopped about a kilometre short of Port Macquarie and took off my helmet and bandana to sniff the fresh air coming in straight off the ocean. It'd be different down the hill, across the town, all the way to mountains lying murky in the western haze. I gazed at the puzzle pieces of the nearest property. White fence. Yellow flowers. Silver car. Grey shrubs. Brown lawn. Blue jeans. Green face. Black arms. Cream brick. Red tiles. The shimmering air shuffled everything like a kalei-doscope. I tightened my grip on the handlebars. Made myself breathe slowly and be glad for the sea breeze. Told myself that nothing I saw could hurt me. Knew that didn't make me safe. I had to worry about what I couldn't see. Screened sleepouts. Shuttered windows. Verandah recesses. The shadows could conceal anyone watching me. This street would have hundreds of dark spaces. There'd be thousands more in the apartment towers of Port Macquarie I saw above the spires of pines on the next rise.

The noise of the quad could bring anyone. Smarter to go in slow and stealthy. Nathan was getting better. Johnno and the others weren't going anywhere. There was no hurry. Walking into Port Macquarie proper would be safer. But it'd also mean I wouldn't be able to get away in a hurry.

I wheeled the quad into a little park and stashed it in a tangle of banksia. Something crackled overhead and as I reached for my rifle I tripped backwards and landed on my ass in the grass. A thick goanna slid from the branches and swaggered away across the overgrown lawn. I bit my knuckle. Laughed so hard I cried.

A sign read Windmill Hill. I liked the way that rolled off my tongue. I checked the GPS. A sea path hugged the coast and would take me to Town Beach right where the city began. Holding my breath when I approached bodies, I followed a fenced track beneath a tree canopy that was sometimes so thick I couldn't see the sky above me or the sea below.

Further along, I stopped at a sign that had helped ramblers identify the bright birds they might see flitting through the trees. Rufous songlark, spectacled monarch, shining bronze cuckoo, rose-crowned fruit dove, satin bowerbird. I said the words aloud, the names as beautiful as their colourful photos.

The sea walk wound down to another beach. Here there was a high tideline of bodies and more scattered on the grass embankment. But the sand at the water's edge looked beautiful and clean. Turning my back on land could be the death of me. I'd risk it to have a few moments where it was just me and the sea.

I took off my boots, let the waves wash my feet and kept my eyes on the horizon. Coming up on the far end of the beach, crabs danced away sideways, holding up their claws in annoyance. I picked up an oval stone, enjoyed the centuries of smoothness between my fingers and smiled as I skipped it out across the surf.

From where I stopped in the bushes on the headland, I saw bodies lying along the curve of Town Beach in a horrible parody of sunbaking. I crept down to the shadow of the Surf Rescue station, by a ramp with a car whose rotting driver had been trying to get his jet ski trailer into the water. I put my boots on as I peered up at the hotel and apartment buildings overlooking the beach.

Counting storeys and multiplying by balconies, there were at least five hundred units right above me. There had to be thousands more in the towers standing side by side all the way up the hill and down into town. I scanned balconies and windows with my binoculars. Nothing moved. As soon as I stepped out, I'd be seen by anyone alive looking my way. But those rooms and apartments were an opportunity as well as a risk. If I could find one high up that wasn't a sweltering crypt then I'd have a view that'd give me the lay of the land.

Keeping low, I ran up the grassy verge. I felt like a silly kid playing storm the fort as I skidded into the shattered foyer of Sandpiper Apartments. My amusement soured when I saw the woman half out of her bikini. She was dead where she'd fallen with her shoulder bag. I reeled in disbelief because somehow jellyfish had come from the sea to feed where her skin had slipped and split. Retching, I ran past her to the fire exit, letting the door slam behind me, grateful that the air was cold and smelled only of concrete.

I climbed to the top floor and emerged into a carpeted corridor. A row of closed apartment doors stretched away. I tried the nearest one. Locked. The next one, too. These heavy doors had been designed to close tight when they swung shut. At least they'd hermetically sealed their occupants inside. I went down to the next floor. More locked doors. I could find an axe and hack my way inside. But I wouldn't know if I was breaking into an apartment that was unliveable due to the stench. Then an idea occurred that made sense even as it turned my stomach.

Tea towel around my face, I stepped into the lobby. Now I saw that I'd been wrong about the jellyfish. The glassy blobs were breast implants that'd slid out of the woman. I got my gut under control and used my rifle barrel to lift her beach bag. I went back to the stairwell and tipped out its contents. Sunblock, lip balm, water bottle, Stephen King novel—keys.

I'd start on the top floor and work my way down. Hope she hadn't lived in a ground floor apartment. Or just stumbled in here in a panic. It took just five tries for her brass key to slide into a lock and turn with a smooth click.

I pushed the door open an inch. One sniff told me the apartment had been sealed since the Snap. The place was tasteful, spacious and spotless. Open plan with polished floorboards and leather couches. Sleek screen on one wall and framed whale photos on the other. Camera and nature magazines on the coffee table. Glass sliding doors led to a deep balcony with dining setting, banana lounges and telescope on a tripod aimed out at the ocean. It must've been a great place for a barbecue, with its panoramic view of the beach, breakwalls and river. I scouted the rest of the apartment. Main bedroom with a similar view and a big dressing room and ensuite bathroom. Two smaller back rooms, one seemingly reserved for guests, the other used as a study, shared a balcony that wrapped around the corner of the building and offered a view across some of the rooftops of Port Macquarie's commercial district.

I set my rifle on the marble kitchen island. Knew better than to open the fridge and spoil the clean air. Grabbed a bottle of mineral water from the walk-in pantry and drank it as I stood by the bedroom window. With the binoculars, I scanned the coast north, where long beaches curved away into distant blurs. Like dots to be joined, bodies receded into the distance just beneath where sand met scrub. Here and there, forlorn cruisers and yachts were tossed around in the surf and swell. Closer to me, near the northern breakwall, an orange tent breathed in and out with the wind. But nothing moved of its own volition apart from a sea eagle riding the warm currents as she looked for dinner.

The river was littered with broken boats and among the wrecks was a seaplane with a snapped wing. The breakwall closest to me was a mosaic of colours. I focused the binoculars. Saw that visitors had painted their names, dates and cheery holiday sentiments on every available rock. I assumed some of those people had died in the burned caravans and charred cabins of the riverside resort park.

I scanned further west. Apartments with names like Pacific Breeze and Sea View rose from gardens of palms and pines. Some bodies on balconies already looked like mummies. I guessed weeks of dry heat and salty air did that.

Port Macquarie had looked smaller on the map. Up close it was daunting. I remembered entering Parramatta from the river and being terrified that the catatonics would spring back to life. But this city belonged to the dead.

I kept watch. The day drained of colour. As darkness crept from the mountains and rolled down the river, the dusk erupted in noise and movement. Below the Sandpiper, in the school grounds on the hill, and in every street in Port Macquarie, thousands of parrots flitted and squawked and screeched as they roosted in palm trees. There were thousands more swirling as shadows over the southern fringe of the city. I refocused my binoculars, saw that this immense cloud wasn't parrots settling in to sleep but big bats spiralling out to hunt in the night.

When the commotion subsided and full darkness descended, I figured I had my best chance of seeing if anyone human was around. Feeling safer out on the back balcony, I scanned with my binoculars: window to window, floor to floor, tower to tower. No lights to say anyone was holed up anywhere. But as soon as I crept onto the front balcony I saw what looked like the glow of a city on the northern horizon. The binoculars could only bring that part of the coast and the mountain hinterland close enough to see they were outlined in volcanic rivers of red. I turned the telescope and through its lens I saw flames twisting together into tornadoes against a wall of smoke that pulsed with purple lightning.

Bushfire. The inferno stretched from the sea and as far as I could see inland. No fire crews, no water bombing, no backburning. It'd blaze whichever way the wind fanned the flames for as long as there was fuel. Checking the GPS, my best guess was that it was about thirty kilometres north, and that hundreds of thousands of hectares of national forest were at risk. I hated to think what'd happen if it blew south. At least the Hastings River might stop the worst of it from reaching Port Macquarie and marching on Colonial Town. But it was blocking any escape route towards Queensland until it burned itself out.

A tongue of flame hit my vision, seemingly close to me. I startled, moved away from the telescope and saw a bonfire on the beach past the northern breakwall. The fire lit up the orange tent I'd seen and a shadowy figure on the sand who looked to be . . . dancing.

My heart thudded. At least one person was still alive in Port Macquarie. Long hair. Curvy body. Doing something like scary yoga. I relaxed a little as I watched her shimmy around. She wasn't a Jack: at least, I didn't think so. If he was close enough to have someone here, I didn't see why it'd be a woman doing a crazy beach dance by night. She struck me as someone who'd gotten away from the smell and carnage on this side of the river.

I wondered if I should try to make contact. Wave my torch to get her attention. But it'd be a stupid move. Asking for trouble. I didn't know if she'd survived with sanity intact. The wild gyrations didn't exactly tick that box.

I left her to it. In the ensuite bathroom, away from windows, I lit a candle and made a meal from tinned salmon, corn and asparagus. As I ate, I flicked through an old local magazine picked from a reading rack beside the deep bath. The headline was about the Winter Festival. There were stories about last year's whale-watching season, a Hollywood action film shooting in the area, the opening of an art gallery, the local soccer team's win over the Wauchope Warriors. Just life going on. No hint mass extinction was just around the corner.

I flicked absently through the motoring section, gardening pages and entertainment listings and into the restaurant guide. Indonesian, Spanish, Thai, Italian, Nepalese, African: this tourist town had it all. I would've given anything to be able to take a table in one of those places, be among people, hear laughter and the clink of glasses, smell and taste wonders coming out of the kitchen made with fresh ingredients.

I'd taken all of that for granted and now I had to be grateful for cans of fish and soggy vegetables. I was about to close the magazine when a glossy advertisement caught my eye. 'Best Junk Food in Australia!' There it was—the Chinese boat I'd seen in the river. It hadn't drifted from Hong Kong or Taiwan. It'd been a floating restaurant that served Asian fusion cuisine six nights a week at sunset. Not so inscrutable after all.

I replaced the magazine, fossicked through gossip rags, couldn't cope with the idea of reading stale lies about celebrities who were now almost certainly dead. But I did find a little booklet about Port Macquarie. By the flickering glow of the candle I read a potted history of its growth from penal hellhole to holiday mecca. There were horrific details of the punishments given to convicts and the cruelties inflicted on the Indigenous people. I closed the booklet, slipped it back into the rack. I wondered if every town everywhere was like Port Macquarie, that if you dug deep enough you'd hit violence as its bedrock. Sitting there on the bathroom floor, I figured that while Jack had a very new power, the uses he was putting it to were as old as our species.

I crept back to the front balcony. The bonfire had died down and I couldn't see the shadow woman. The only light was the bushfire's glow and the only sound was waves pounding the beach. I checked my watch: 12.08. Checked it what seemed like an hour later. 12.15.

I wondered how cops had managed to do long stakeouts. Where were my goddamned coffee and donuts? By three I could barely keep my eyes open. I imagined falling asleep and the Jacks pouring into this coastal city and swarming through lobbies and up fire stairs and along corridors. Even with all their man- and mind-power, searching Port Macquarie would be a huge job. All these locked apartments? If they couldn't find keys, they'd have to bash down doors. It'd make a lot of noise. But I'd have a better chance of getting away if I heard them sooner rather than later. I eased myself onto a banana chair and went to sleep with clean sea air in my lungs and the ocean roaring in my ears. Things had been worse.

TWENTY-FIVE

I run, a steady jog, ten clicks an hour. I could keep it up all night if I needed to, even carrying my weapons and backpack. Red night-vision landscape jostling by, I reach Prestige and quickly head for its highest vantage point. St Michael's: a little sandstone church on the hill over the road into town. A bus is parked beside this place of worship. A mummified parishioner lies sprawled face down in weeds near the tailpipe. The bus's destination sign reads 'Heaven'.

A line from *The Art of War* rings in my head: 'He who is skilled in attack flashes forth from the topmost heights of heaven.'

Hearing bikes thrumming in the distance, I monkey up the side of the bus, haul myself onto the church's roof and clamber up its corrugated iron slope to the base of its steeple. The road runs right beneath me and is hemmed in on the other side by a weedy bluff. The Board members aren't using headlights but I see the bikes as night-vision blurs farther along the valley road. Five, arranged in a flying V, trailed by a panel van that's towing a horse float. The riders wear night-vision goggles and aim their assault rifles out like lances. They think they're knights charging into battle.

If these corporate raiders read Sun Tzu to hone their business acumen, they clearly don't remember the bit where a dude says some roads shouldn't be taken to war—to which his mate adds: 'Especially those leading through narrow defiles, where an ambush is to be feared.'

At the rate they're riding they'll pass beneath me in less than a minute.

It's more than enough time. I pull out what I need and count down the seconds. When they're on the final rise, I pull pins and pitch grenades one after the other. Three are in flight when I close my eyes and fire my flare gun at the lead rider. As the rocket shrieks I duck behind the steeple.

I don't see what happens next but the world trembles with the *whumpa-whumpa-whumpa* of the grenades exploding. Screams and screeching fill the air, telling me the Board have been blinded and blasted by my rain of fire and metal—and that some of them are still alive. I pop around the steeple and fire a burst into the windshield of the skidding panel van. The vehicle spins out and the horse float slides around crazily in its wake before it snaps free and flips to slide along the road on its side in a shower of sparks.

Amid the smoke, a staggering rider spots my muzzle flare and raises his rifle. I put three rounds into his white shirt and he falls with his shiny shoes pointed at the sky. All the bikes are down. Three suits dead on the road. I assume I've got the driver in the van. Two left. I see flashes from the roadside. Sandstone chips explode from the steeple beside my head and I hear the *crack-crack* of more gunfire as I duck behind the roofline. 'Oh Jesus!' I yell. 'Aaaagh. Aaaaaagh.'

I send my backpack sliding and follow it down the slippery roof. Thumping off the bus, I bounce onto the ground with a scream that I hope sounds like I've broken every bone in my body. Crouching, I lay my AK-47 and backpack by the fossilised Christian. A few seconds later, I nestle in thick weeds between tombstones in the little cemetery, night-vision goggles on and my .45 trained on the corpse.

'The general who is skilled in defence,' I say under my breath, 'hides in the most secret recesses of the earth.'

They're on the other side of the church, talking in low voices, working up the guts to make their move. A gun-toting suit creeps to the front of the bus while his colleague covers him with a rifle. The guy peeks around the panel quickly and then hides himself. He whistles and his mate scuttles across to join him. They take turns peering along the bus with their night-vision goggles.

'Push the gun away from you,' one of them calls out.

Of course, I don't. A rifle lines up on the body. I duck my head to preserve my night vision as they riddle the corpse with bullets.

'She's done,' one of them says. 'Bitch.'

The suits edge along the bus, guns still trained on the body.

'Boss, are you sure there was only her?' says the front guy.

'Denton called it as just one chick before the radio went dead.' Boss—I assume he's the Chairman—loud and confident. 'Plus, we only took fire from here.'

As sure of himself as he sounds, Boss lets his offsider reach the body first. The subordinate kicks the backpack and AK-47 out of the way and gets ready to put his brogue into me. 'This is for our dead homies, you little—'

He stumbles back, realising the body at his feet's been dead for months. 'Oh, shit. Boss, it's not—'

I shoot him, in the neck and side, and he shouts and spins heavily against the bus. I duck as Boss turns, blasting from the hip in my direction, his bullets ricocheting off tombstones three graves from me. I aim my .45 between grave markers and fire three times. There's a shriek and the thud of him hitting the gravel. In my night vision, the guy by the bus isn't moving or making any noise while Boss's legs drum against the ground as he groans.

I crawl through rows of graves, creep along a fence, come around until he can't see my approach. Appearing over Boss, I slide his rifle out of reach, turn off my night vision and shine my flashlight on him. He has hair the colour of a storm cloud. It's sharply cut and spiky with product. He reminds me of that Hollywood silver fox even my mum couldn't help swooning over. But Boss's tanned skin and sleek threads are now all bloody.

'Help me,' he gasps.

I go to his offsider. He's dead with his chin slumped into a beard of gore that's escaped his neck. I grab my backpack, shoulder my AK-47 and go back to Boss.

I kneel, take out my first-aid kit and pull out the stethoscope. His blue eyes watch me. Pink blood froths at his lips. I've put a tight grouping of three bullets into his gut but I'm guessing I've also nicked a lung. Boss nods slightly as I slide the cold metal disc inside his soaked shirt. 'Thank you,' he rasps. 'It hurts.'

His heartbeat is strong but frantic—and on the left side of his body. He's not *Situs*. He's another Normal and he might live with medical assistance.

'Where were you at Christmas?' I ask.

I can't tell whether he's grimacing in pain or smiling at the memory. 'Nullarbor,' he says. 'Road trip. Made up a charity ride. Paid donations ourselves. Wanted it to be all about the boys. Please help me.'

I shake my head. Boss and his mates ditched their families at Christmas to go bro-bonding. His eyes slip focus and his head starts to slide. I grip his jaw and twist his face back to me. 'Who's in the horse float?'

Boss's eyes find me. I'm glad for the fear I see there. 'The girls? Not what you think. We saved them. It's not like we hurt them. Without us they would've—'

I shoot him in the mouth to shut him up.

Back on the church roof, I look down at the road. Women climb from the horse float, whose bolted doors have busted open and scattered pillows and stilettos across the road. A harem. What that asshole Cory had envisaged minutes after me reviving him, these corporate wankers had actually made a reality. I count five women, making their way between their dead captors and toppled bikes. Their sizes and ages vary but they're all in little dresses like backing dancers in some bad video clip. Specials or Normals—captured and enslaved by evil assholes.

One girl peers into the panel van. An older woman joins her with a rifle she's picked up off the road. There's movement through the bullet-cracked windscreen. I've only wounded the driver. Together they drag him from the vehicle onto the road. He pleads and cries with his hands up and the older woman fires a shot into his chest and he goes still. That's not good enough for the younger woman and she uses a piece of motorbike debris to bash the guy's head until her companion drags her off and consoles her as she sobs. My weight shifts and the roof creaks under me. By the horse float, a woman shoulders the rifle and fires before I can say anything. I drop as wild bullets whizz over my head.

What did my mum used to say about no good deed going unpunished?

'They're all dead up here,' I shout when the firing stops. 'You're safe, okay?'

I hear them scrambling and taking cover. I can't blame them after what they've been through. I should stand up, put my hands in the air, go down there, explain myself, tell them what to do. But they might shoot me in panic. Even if they don't, revealing myself means they'd be able to identify me if they run into Jack.

'Another Boss,' I shout. 'Called Damon. Much worse. Southwest of here. Coming this way. Big fires directly north. So go inland. Northwest. Don't stop.'

It's the best I can do. I've freed them but I can't save them. They have to find their own way now and fight if they have to. With that, I slide off the roof, run through the cemetery, head back to the bush road, a woman's calls of 'Who are you?' echoing in my ears.

An ember of a cigarette dances in the darkness ahead. I check my watch. It's been nine minutes.

'HB,' I hiss as I crunch up the road. 'It's me.'

'Thank God,' she says, inside a cloud of smoke. 'Are you okay?'

I take off the night-vision goggles and switch on my flashlight.

'Is that safe?' she says, shielding her eyes. 'What happened?'

'You know you can smell that cigarette halfway down the hill?' I say.

'Sorry.' She drops the smoke and grinds it out. 'What happened?'

I round the four-wheel drive and climb into the passenger seat. Lottie's curled up in the back with her eyes closed and headphones on. I don't know if she's asleep or just terrified. HB gets behind the wheel, goes to turn the ignition and then looks at me.

'Is it okay? I mean, the engine noise, headlights?'

I nod.

The world reduces to an orange dirt road in a tunnel of green bush.

'What happened back there?' HB asks again.

'A horse float,' I say.

'What?'

'That's where they had the women. Five, I think. It's where you would've ended up.'

'My God. Those sons of—' HB cuts herself off. 'Had? You said they "had" the women. Did you kill all of—'

HB trails off but I feel her eyes on me. By the glow of the instrument panel, I see my face reflected in the darkened window.

'Jesus,' she says. 'Who are you?'

It's what the woman asked. I don't know the answer.

TWENTY-SIX

I splashed my face with mineral water and looked out at Port Macquarie. Five thirty in the morning. I'd slept for two hours. It was still dark but I needed to take advantage of first light and the early morning. I figured if anyone was out there this would be when they were at their least alert. Just the way I was.

In the bathroom I mixed a few tablespoons of instant coffee with mineral water but couldn't drink more than a mouthful. Smacking my lips as I tried to get the taste out of my mouth, I searched the drawers for toothpaste. I found a tube and a new toothbrush and brushed while I snooped through the medicine cabinets. Cleansers, moisturisers, balms on the top shelf. Vitamins, fish oils, homeopathic concoctions on the next. Antidepressants, diet pills and sleeping tablets on the bottom. I picked out the Slimdex. A full bottle of tiny white tablets. I knew the brand and what they did. Mollie and her friends used to take 'dexies' to get skinny and to party. I picked one out and washed it down with mineral water.

I checked the GPS map of Port Macquarie. I was on Stewart Street on the Point. It was six blocks into the centre of the business district. That's where I'd have the best chance of finding what I needed. But wandering out in the open, even in the murky light of dawn, seemed as foolish as flashing a message to the crazy beach dancer. Jack's army might be far south but he could have drones looking for me anywhere.

A light went on in my head. My thoughts sharpened and my skin tingled pleasantly. Just like that I knew what to do.

Yesterday, from the back windows, I'd been worried by the places I couldn't see properly—narrow laneways that ran behind towers, the shadowy recesses of the public school on the hill, the dark mouths of shopping arcades down in the town. But they were what could hide me now.

I left the Sandpiper building by the underground car park, hugged the backs of buildings in the gloom, dashed across a road and into more shadows. Crouching by the roadside, I waited and listened and then sprinted to the school fence, using the boltcutters to bust the gate's padlock. Got to the next block under the school's covered walkways. Breaking another lock, I followed a tropical garden down a hill between holiday apartments until I was opposite a multilevel car park attached to a shopping centre. I crept across the road between vehicles, pulled myself over a wall and disappeared into the dark spaces of the concrete monolith.

Head buzzing, I felt like an Olympian or a ninja—maybe an Olympic ninja. Breathing deeply through my eucalyptus bandana, I crossed the car park's emptiness and entered Port Mall through broken glass doors. Pretty sure its light wouldn't be seen from outside, I used my torch to see what was in store. Ted's Tobacco, Vision City, Spec Takers, Surf N Stuff, Man Cave, GameZone. Nothing worth breaking into. I made a beeline for a help kiosk. It'd had an interactive screen for shoppers but the desk was still stacked with little maps of the mall.

My eyes flew over the list of shop names as I calculated the chances of them holding anything of use. I was thinking so fast. Like my mind had been upgraded. If I could be this way all the time Jack wouldn't stand a chance. While he might have a few thousand brains at his disposal, this was as though my processing speed had been boosted by a million times and—

I was *high*. Speeding off my face. What a bad girl. Taking drugs. After what Mum had been through I'd always thought they were stupid and dangerous. Now it seemed like they could be a survival tool. Denying myself the edge they offered—*that's* what would be stupid and dangerous.

'Just say yes,' I said aloud and then burst out laughing. The echo of me cackling around the mall gave me the creeps. I got myself under control. Focused the energy.

I was off, zipping through the mall, slipping from an exit, staying under awnings and slinking into an arcade that connected to the next street. Cafes flashed by uselessly until I was at the next exit. Hovering, scanning, left, right, dozens of shops in sight: Siam Sunset restaurant, Coastal Credit Building Society, I'm Gonna Git You Sucka Vacuum Cleaners, Vibrations Adult Store, Mobifone dealership. On and on they went on both sides of a wide street divided by parking bays and palm trees draped in red and silver tinsel.

A car near me contained a driver so swollen and black that he or she looked like overripe fruit ready to burst. But a woman in the window of the bakery to my left was so emaciated it seemed likely she'd defied the survival odds for a long time before dying. There were many more bodies. But not as many as I'd expected.

I kept on, heart racing, mind flying, through a maze of cars and into the next galleria and past a boutique and cafe and pet supply store whose inventory of plastic toys was scattered across the linoleum. When I got to the exit, I stood panting, taking a moment to see what was right in front of my nose.

The window of Top Travel featured a giant poster. Green mountains towered over white beaches. Aquamarine sea all around. Barely a building to be seen. 'Visit Lord Howe Island!' was scrawled across the bottom in big letters. My brain buzzed. *This*, this was my refuge island. I remembered the exact moment I'd first imagined it. On the highway, going back to confront Jack, I'd seen a stupid sign that'd named a grassy median strip a 'Refuge Island'. It'd gotten me thinking about a place exactly like this. I took a brochure from a plastic holder. 'Home to just 400 permanent residents, Lord Howe Island is one of Australia's secret treasures,' the blurb began. I read about how tourist numbers were limited by available accommodation but those who visited would enjoy fine restaurants and unspoiled beaches and coral reefs and rainforest walks to dizzying volcanic peaks. 'Leave only footprints,' it said, proudly boasting that the island's facilities were powered by a mixture of solar, wind and wave energy. It sounded perfect. An inset map showed that everything Lord Howe had to offer was just six hundred kilometres due east of where I stood. A month ago there had been a regular air service and a photo showed a little plane sweeping low over a beach after its one-hour flight from Port Macquarie. *One hour.* God, it was so close—and so impossibly far.

I turned the brochure over and scanned a few boxes of fun facts. Did I know that the giant stick insect had been thought extinct until it'd been rediscovered on Lord Howe Island? I had not, but any place that could resurrect endangered creatures sounded awesome to me. Did I know that the entire world's supply of Kentia palms came from this tiny island in the middle of nowhere? My heart stuttered because Mum's front yard had been filled with them and now that seemed like a sign. If we could get to Lord Howe Island, Jack would never find us. And with such a small population, it was unlikely anyone would've survived. Even with just the few of us, we could deal with the bodies. We'd be safe and free.

I turned back to the photo of the plane. If only Stannis was an actual pilot. If only that seaplane could be fixed. Maybe I could find another aircraft and learn to fly. I had to quit daydreaming and get on with the task at hand. I pocketed the brochure anyway.

Walking along the street under a wide awning, I stepped around a dead kid. Under his body was a tablet box in a pool of dried blood. Poor little looter had bled out before he crashed out. Following his trail of droplets and dropped swag led me to the smashed and spattered window of a Gizmos outlet.

I climbed in carefully and played my flashlight over phones, tablets, televisions and projectors. I walked along an aisle of printers and laptops, another of stereos and turn-tables, one more of consoles, monitors and wearables. All this *stuff* we'd 'needed'. All of it right there for the taking. None of it now worth the energy it'd take to pick from its shelf or rack. But as I turned to leave, my eyes strayed into the home security section's display of motion sensors and spy cameras and house alarms. I gravitated to a stack of Peace of Mind boxes and read the offering inside these all-in-one DIY packages. Eight programmable motion detectors attached to a 140-decibel alarm. Four video cameras feeding footage to any phone or tablet anywhere in the world over the internet or short-range via Bluetooth connection. A set-up time of just an hour for your average-sized property and an ion-lithium battery guaranteed to last a decade. All of that for the low, low price of $199.99.

This tech could make Colonial Town a little bit safer. Thing was, speedy me could easily have walked out of Gizmos without even noticing this stuff. For the next hour, I shopped slowly, using my torch like a crime-scene investigator to spotlight just one product at a time. Sitting on the floor, I unpacked devices from their packaging and preserved their instruction manuals. I got phones, tablets and plenty of extra batteries. Dozens of Cameleon spy cams that'd change colour depending on what you stuck them to. Night-vision goggles that could turn darkness into daylight. Waterproof walkie-talkies powerful enough to broadcast over twenty kilometres. By the time I'd finished shopping and filled my backpack, it'd gone ten and the day was glaring outside.

A stash of surveillance and security and communications equipment was a good start. But I needed stuff that could keep us alive and that could kill Jacks. From inside the Gizmos doorway, I scanned adjacent businesses. Newsagency, thrift store, craft shop and a dozen more whose inventories probably wouldn't be useful. Multiply that by the number of streets in Port Macquarie and its surrounding suburbs and I might wander for ages without finding what I was after. My kingdom for Google search.

Or a telephone book. I'd never used one but it seemed like a smart time to start, if I could find one. I checked the Gizmos register area. It was paperless, all scanners and tap-and-pay, but the back office was filled with out-of-date catalogues, piled uniforms, dirty coffee cups and bent store displays. Under a desk, beside someone's old socks, I found a stack of musty Yellow Pages. The most recent was three years old but it was the best lead I'd get.

I found a listing for guns—Shooter City—and another for Army Surplus—Davo's Disposals—and checked the addresses against my GPS.

Keeping under awnings and low between cars, I found another mall and sliced through it to the next block. Right there, between Chicken Licken and Golf Buddies, was Shooter City. But while other shopfronts had yielded, the metal shutters of the gun store hadn't given way to the efforts of looters, one of whom had crashed and died beside his own pair of boltcutters.

Through the slits in the gate were iron bars over plate-glass windows. Locking a gun shop up tight made sense.

I made my way another three blocks to Davo's Disposals. That it wasn't like a fortress told me Davo didn't sell firearms. Someone had got in here. Splintered the windows before sledgehammering the door. Halfway up the block I saw the likely culprits. A couple of rival survivalists lay dead among packs bulging with stuff. It looked like they'd fought to the death to stay alive.

Rifle at the ready, I went into Davo's, set my backpack down and grabbed a camouflaged army bag from a hook. Where Gizmos had seemed useless at first, it was immediately obvious this was an Aladdin's Cave of cool shit. Shirts, trousers, sleeping bags, tents and netting—all of it in bush camouflage. Knives and tools and compasses and cookers. Water purification tablets and freeze-dried meals and wind-up torches and solar radios. Everything lightweight and compact. I rolled and folded and stuffed as much as I could into the army bag. Behind the counter, I peeled off my dirty old clothes and slipped into camouflage pants and shirt, pulled off the red boots I'd taken from Mum's and laced up a pair of steel-capped combat asskickers.

Still, none of this stuff would kill Jacks. I wondered whether Davo had a secret stash of bayonets and bazookas. I climbed a staircase out back and forced my way into his office. I peered out through venetian blinds at the street below. Trained my binoculars on the park by the river and then up past where Pelican Island split the river to a marina cluttered with cruisers and yachts whose white hulls and cabins had been blackened by smoke. Davo's desk was cluttered with paperwork. A big corkboard festooned with order forms. One wall was stacked with boxes. Scrawled on most of them was 'Mac 4 p/u'. I was puzzled for a moment until it clicked. These were for someone named Mac to pick up.

The boxes didn't hold weapons. But whoever Mac was, he'd been buying up big. Five ration pack cartons for a total of three hundred dinners of dehydrated chicken curry and beef stew. Maybe he was a slob who hated cooking or a soldier addicted to meals from bags. But there were also a thousand water purification tablets, a Geiger counter, two pairs of Kevlar gloves, thermal imaging camera, hydration backpack adaptor, magnesium fire starter and solar charger. I wondered why he didn't just get all this stuff on the internet. It had to be far cheaper than getting Davo to import it and slapping on a mark-up. *Unless* . . . Mac was paranoid and wanted to stay off the grid.

I opened the laptop on the desk, battery unused since the Snap, and did a search of the customer database. From Macally and Mackintosh to McCredie and McFarlane, there were two dozen possible 'Macs'. But only one had spent fifty grand in the past year. G. Macarthur: Elders Way, Camden Haven. I tapped at the GPS. Mac's place was about twenty kilometres south of Colonial Town, in the bush near North Brother Mountain. I'd be paying a visit as soon as I could. I dragged the customer file to the trash and pressed empty before closing the laptop. No sense leaving tracks.

Walking back into the store, I spied another must-have on Davo's racks. A yowie suit—that was what the packaging called it. There was a photo of a guy wearing what looked like a poncho covered with camouflage streamers. 'Be the bush!' the marketing blurb promised.

'Don't mind if I do,' I said.

I unpacked the yowie suit, pulled it over my clothes, pictured myself staging an ambush. My grin widened when I saw another shelf stacked with even weirder stuff that I had to assume was stocked for customers going to fancy dress parties. There were spiky helmets, crazy Afro wigs, neon hardhats and Native American headdresses. I pulled down a gas mask. The tag said it was ex-French army and in working condition with a new filter. I stretched its tan latex straps around the back of my head and fitted my face with its glass goggles and a porcine grilled muzzle. It made my breathing sound like Darth Vader but it might actually be useful as the stench got worse. I giggled when I saw the gnarly black Viking helmet on a mannequin. Really, I couldn't go past that. I reached it down, pulled it on and rustled back to the mirror.

I laughed. Yowie suit, gas mask, horned helmet—I looked like a monster in a Z-grade horror film. I waved my hands and growled at myself. Being silly let off steam but my amusement faded when I pictured myself trying to share this funny moment with Nathan and him freezing me out.

Then I saw who I *was* sharing this moment with and *I* froze. Caught behind me in the mirror's reflection was a wild-haired woman staring at me through Davo's doorway. Her eyes widened as I whirled and she screamed and ran. I stumbled towards the entrance.

'Wait!' I yelled.

She didn't. Like a spooked gazelle she sprang over bodies and shot across palm gardens.

'Wait!'

Wuurrtt!

Crap. Through the gas mask my voice was a bestial roar. God knows what she thought I was. I threw off the Viking helmet, tore off the mask. Dashed the way she'd gone, yowie suit rustling and combat boots thumping on the pavement. By the time I'd reached the town's park, she was bolting past the pub towards the jetty that jutted into the river.

Panting, I slowed, not wanting to panic her further. Without even meaning to I'd cornered her against the water. I felt guilty that I was the Party Duder in this scenario. Bellowing and giving chase. Terrifying a frightened survivor. But while she might've been scared, she didn't slow as she slapped barefoot across the pier's boards.

'Wait!' I called.

Without looking back she shot off the jetty and dived into the water. I ran to the edge of the pier. The woman swam furiously for the low green shore at the back of the northern beach. Now it twigged. She was the shadow I'd seen dancing by the bonfire. But I'd just proven that *I* was the crazy one. Running after her when I should've been running the other way. Coming out into the open without my rifle. Making all sorts of noise. At least she hadn't seen my face. She couldn't tell anyone who she'd seen. But she could be attracting Jacks. Or anyone else around. And she could lead them to where she'd seen me. It was my turn to run. I sprinted back to the surplus store.

I struggled under my load back the way I'd come, through arcade and mall and laneway and underground car park and up the fire stairs. Inside the Sandpiper apartment, I felt like I was melting. Sweating crazily, heart hammering, I dumped the bag and backpack and my gun and stripped out of my sweaty camo clothes. Giddy and exhilarated, adrenaline surging with the amphetamine, I focused my binoculars on the northern beach. The Wild Woman was back home, too. She walked in circles around her tent, huffing a bong and gesticulating wildly as though arguing with herself. She didn't have a gun that I could see. Or any companion. After I while I felt nothing but sorry for her.

When I'd relaxed a little, I sat on the floor in my underwear and set out all the stuff I'd procured. My mission had been productive. Gadgets that could help secure Colonial Town. Meals enough for a week if we had to flee into the bush. Purification tablets that'd make it safe to drink from creeks. Space blankets to keep us warm and dry. A tent and hoochies for shelter and camo netting that'd make us hard to spot from the air. I closed the bathroom door, tried on the night-vision goggles, saw myself in the mirror, blurred like an alien apparition.

A little rattled by my close call in town, I decided to take the quad back to Colonial Town under cover of darkness. It'd give me a chance to see if I could ride with the night-vision goggles instead of headlights. It was only mid-afternoon and what I needed was more sleep. But my mind tumbled and my body tossed and turned in the big soft bed.

Giving up on sleep, I sat by the window with the binoculars and watched the Wild Woman up on her beach. She was using driftwood to carve patterns in a circle around her camp and had used charcoal to cover her tent with scratchy symbols and words. The binoculars weren't powerful enough to make out detail so I crept out to the telescope. Even on that hot balcony the temperature seemed to drop when I brought her work into focus.

Vade Satana Draco maledicte adjuramus te Terribilis Deus

··

There was much more—stars, pentacles, arrows and daggers and reams and reams of Latin. I had no idea what it all meant but it spooked me back inside. With everything that'd happened it was ridiculous to be afraid of some wacko who thought *Harry Potter* was a documentary. But I couldn't help it. Her witchy ways chilled me. What scared me most was that her supernatural mumbo-jumbo was meant as protection against *me*.

There was no way I'd sleep now. Not unless I dipped into the medicine cabinet's bottle of sleeping pills. Being that unconscious seemed like a mistake. Instead, with the afternoon light dwindling, I went the other way by taking another dexie to blow out the cobwebs.

When it was dark, the Wild Woman was reduced to a writhing shadow by her fire. Beyond her, the sky north glowed like the gates of Hell. But I felt good again. Couldn't let either worry me. I was heading south. I gathered my gun and backpacks, donned my goggles and found my way back along the coastal path to my quad. When I revved and rode off, I felt indestructible, like I owned the night.

TWENTY-SEVEN

'Here we are,' HB says as she swings the Jeep into a clearing in the middle of the black bush. 'It's not much but it's nothing.'

Through swirling road dust, headlights illuminate a little wooden hut that has a narrow front door with a window either side. It's as basic as a child's drawing. Arranged outside this tiny dwelling are approximations of the rooms that won't fit inside. Mismatched armchairs circle a wagon wheel table beneath a tarpaulin: lounge room. Plates and pans are stacked on a bench beside a gas camp cooker: kitchen. A porcelain throne sits under a beach umbrella: toilet. Chickens peck at the dirt around steel tubs of fruits and vegetables growing inside nets. Her hideout's pretty simple but I'm impressed.

'You did all this in three months?' I say.

'Uh, no.' HB stops the four-wheel drive and laughs at the look on my face. 'This was where I lived *before* everything went bad.'

Wow: even my mum would've thought this was extreme.

'Got it for the rent of nothing when they cut funding to

parks and wildlife,' HB says. 'They paid *me* one dollar a year to be a semi-official caretaker-type person.'

'How long have you been here?'

'Coming on three years, I guess,' she says. 'Hang here a sec while I get the generator going.'

HB throws open her door and stomps around the back of the cottage. Lottie rustles on the backseat and sits up groggily.

'Where are we?' she asks. 'I'm still so tired.'

Guilt stirs in me. The sedatives have made her more manageable. Without them she might never have stopped crying about losing her parents and her family and friends. Without them she might not have stayed quiet and hidden when I took on the suits in Prestige. But I can't keep dosing her forever. Sooner or later I'll have to let her face her emotions and the world.

'We're at HB's place,' I say. 'Safe. Far away from everyone, okay?'

Lottie sits back, frowning, seeming to look inwards.

The engine ticks as it cools. A creek trickling reaches me through the open windows. Then there's a sputter and a hum and an electric yellow glow from inside the cabin.

'Look,' says Lottie. 'Wow.'

Fairy lights dot the night all around us—twisted along tarp ropes, strung between branches, wrapped around tree trunks. HB crunches back to the vehicle.

'Come on, I'll give you the grand tour.'

I grab my AK-47 and my backpacks and we follow her into a ranger's office that she's turned into her bedroom–library–pantry.

'Put your things anywhere,' HB says.

I set my stuff beside a foldout cot but leave my rifle over my shoulder where it belongs. The walls are stacked floor to ceiling with plastic crates filled with tins and books. There's a typewriter and a thick ream of paper on a card table. Through an open door an even smaller room's filled with junk that appears to have been cleared for access to what looks like an amp attached to a microphone.

'What's that?' I ask.

'A radio,' HB says. 'For reporting fires. Calling help for lost bushwalkers.'

'Can you get Biggie and Banger?' Lottie says. 'I love those guys. Mornings on Bam FM?'

'I don't think I know that show,' HB says, arching an eyebrow at me to ask how Lottie can think that's even still possible.

I give a quick shake of my head that now's not the time to explain. 'I don't think it's that sort of radio, is it, HB?'

'This is shortwave,' HB says. 'You switch it on and press the button on the microphone and whoever's tuned to your frequency can hear you.'

'Anywhere?' Lottie asks.

'That's how it's supposed to work,' HB nods.

I stare at the thing's dials and switches. 'But you're not getting anyone, right?'

HB smiles at me. 'Actually, I have. When I said I hadn't seen anyone in months, it doesn't mean I haven't spoken to people. Or listened to them.'

'You know them but you've never met them?' Lottie says with a dreamy nod. 'I know people like that. On social media. I'll show you.' She pats herself down for her phone instinctively and then her face is stricken for a moment before it slackens. 'I—I—I—'

I catch Lottie as she sags and HB helps me get her into the cot. We sit by her as she sobs and HB says soothing things until she slips back into sleep.

'Poor kid,' HB says. 'She's not dealing?'

I shake my head. Too tired to explain.

'I'll make us a cup of tea,' HB says. 'Let's sit outside.'

I perch on the arm of a couch. Set my assault rifle within arm's reach against a footrest.

'You don't need that here,' HB says. 'We're a long way from anywhere.'

I don't know what to tell her. That the people who're after me make the Boss and his Board look like choirboys? That there's not nine suits with hunting rifles but maybe thousands of heavily armed dudes whose telepathically linked brains are like a vast military encyclopaedia? That they've got Humvees and armoured vehicles and choppers and jet planes? That the glow from her cabin and the fairy lights will be all too easy to spot from the air? That I hope they're all still pouring west away from us but I can't be sure?

I don't say any of that as she fills a kettle from a plastic keg of water and lights the gas stove.

'Who've you been talking to,' I ask, 'on the radio?'

'Family in the Northern Territory for a while there,' HB says. 'Out on a cattle station. Middle of nowhere. They're all fine. All the jackaroos and jillaroos, too. And the Aboriginal families on the next property. Weren't affected.'

'No telepathy?' I say.

'None at all.'

'How many people?'

HB fusses with crackers from a plastic container. 'About eighty.'

It's the biggest bunch of Normals yet. If eighty people in isolation could escape the Snap, could ten times that number have made it unscathed? Maybe everyone on Lord Howe Island has survived. That would be a good thing if we ever made it there. Wouldn't it?

'What're they doing at the cattle station?' I ask as HB hands me a plate.

'Doing? One thing they're not doing is talking on the radio anymore. Last thing they said before signing off was they didn't want to be swamped with refugees from the big smoke. Big smoke—takes on a whole new meaning now, doesn't it?'

HB sits opposite me and sips her tea. 'There was a bunch of guys on an oil rig in the South China Sea. Could've been two hundred of them. They were trying to put out a fire. Asking if I could get them assistance because I was the only person they could raise.' She snaps her fingers and looks at me sadly. 'I lost them like that. I figure it blew up. There's a fella I can get some of the time who's in Korea—or, at least, he is Korean. He doesn't speak much English except brand names. There was a woman in the Philippines who wanted me to accept Jesus as my personal saviour. I haven't been able to get her for a few weeks. I've heard snippets of people. Canada, Barbados, Spain.'

HB shakes her head sadly. 'The bits I've been able to piece together—it's bad all over. But a lot of the time the signals don't last long. Atmospheric interference. I think there's a lot of—'

She doesn't want to say it so I will.

'Radioactivity.'

I've been told recently by someone in a position to know that the northern hemisphere's in deep shit for the next ten thousand years or so. Regardless of whether politicians went crazy and launched nuclear missiles, in the United States alone there were five hundred reactors, each of which held decades' worth of spent fuel rods in cooling tanks. Even though the reactors would've likely gone into safety shutdown when their power grids failed, all those cooling tanks would've since boiled over and spewed radiation into the air for the wind to spread. But I have no intention of going to the northern hemisphere.

'Have you picked up anyone on Lord Howe Island?' I blurt before I've thought about what I'm saying.

'No,' HB replies. 'Why?'

I'm not sure how much I should tell her. If Jacks arrive right now I don't want her to be able to tell them anything that'd endanger Nathan and the others. 'I went there once with my family,' I lie, trying to sound casual. 'I just thought if people might've survived, that's where they'd be, y'know, because it's so far away.'

HB considers. 'Well, just because I didn't raise anyone there doesn't mean they're not okay, right?'

I nod, eager to change the subject. 'So it's just been you here the whole time?'

HB smiles. 'Me and my chooks and my books.'

'Three years,' I say. 'Are you—were you—a fugitive?'

'Economic and cultural refugee,' she says. 'Fugitive from finance and fakery, I guess.'

HB explains she'd been the deputy editor of *Hers*—having risen through the ranks on magazines like *Gossip*, *Chick* and *Femme*.

'Miracle diets, cake recipes, pet psychics, reality show romances and celebrity scandals,' she says with a laugh. 'Almost thirty years of it. I'm surprised my brain didn't melt out of my ears. But I was paying the mortgage and my husband and I got to travel a lot.'

In the space of a week, it'd all ended when HB was made redundant and hubby confessed he was in love with another woman.

'So I'm a few years shy of fifty, with no relationship, no house, no job and no kids. Know what? I felt great. The last thing I wanted to do was hook up with another bloke, get another mortgage or re-train to be a "multiplatform digital content producer", whatever the hell that is. After the payout and the house sold, I had enough to never work again if I lived modestly. And I'd have enough time at last to do three things I'd been talking about forever: read the classics, learn how to grow food and . . .'

'And?'

She smiles sheepishly. 'And write the great Australian novel.'

HB tells me how she went on a road trip, found out about this place and made her 'tree change'. The few times her city girlfriends came to visit hadn't gone so well.

'My getting nose rings and tattoos were one thing,' she says. 'But not knowing the latest about B-Lo and George? Or what was so good about *Instant Celebrity*? Sacrilege! My friends thought I'd gone feral at best and crazy at worst. Maybe they were right. I'm not sure if it was a breakdown or a breakthrough.'

I laugh. HB is a crack-up. She and Mum would've gotten along fine. Even Dad would've liked her. He'd always wanted to be an author.

'Did you write your book?' I ask.

'Wrote hundreds of pages but used them all as kindling,' she says. 'I was still writing for other people, worrying whether it sounded smart, who'd publish it, if anyone would read it.'

HB laughs, lights a cigarette, uncorks a bottle of wine and splashes out two glasses. 'But when everything went wrong and I knew none of that mattered? *That's* when the words came rushing out. Five hundred pages so far. Not even close to finishing.'

I smile. 'What's it about?'

'A cat on a space station.'

'Sounds—'

'Terrible.'

We laugh and sip our drinks.

'How'd it happen for you at Christmas?' I ask.

HB recounts how she experienced the Snap, saw Prestige and other towns go crazy, and picked up radio broadcasts that confirmed it was everywhere. She'd crashed out right where I sat, woken up and watched, horrified, until the world screamed and went silent. It was weeks before she worked up the courage to go into town. HB had hoped she'd find life going on as normal even though that would've meant her friends had been right and she really had gone crazy out here. Instead what she found in Prestige was a few dozen scattered bodies. Cars and corpses dotted the road in both directions out of town.

'I hightailed it back here. After a while I started to wonder. Were there cameras in the trees? Had the government dusted my veggies with some kind of hallucinogen? Was it all part of some experiment to observe what some person would do faced with my predicament? Real *Twilight Zone* stuff, y'know?'

I don't but I nod anyway.

'I lost a few shortwave contacts when I accused them of being in on the conspiracy,' HB says. 'But when I got the guts to go back into Prestige it confirmed I wasn't nuts. Everyone was dead where I'd left them. Since then I've tried to be Zen. Here I am with my books. I do yoga, go for walks, grow my fruit and vegetables. Life actually hasn't changed that much. Except that I ran out of stuff to read. That's what I was doing in town when those bastards found me. Thank God you came along.' HB casts an eye over me. 'Why did you come along?'

I tell my story in broad strokes. HB sits, smokes, confirms she's *Situs*, winces whenever I describe killing anyone. After I explain how many aircraft Jack has, she asks me to hold that thought while she gets up and turns off all the electrical lights and lights a few candles.

'I've got to get back to the others by tonight,' I say. 'Or my friends will probably be gone for good.'

'They'd really leave?'

'I told them if I wasn't back in forty-eight hours it'd mean I'd been killed or worse.'

'Worse?'

'Made to talk. It's why I haven't told you specifics.'

HB's eyes are white in the candlelight.

Problem is I don't know how I'll get back to Colonial Town. Me and Lottie are stuck here and completely reliant on HB. I pull out my map and trace where I think we are in the state forest west of Prestige. 'Is this us?'

HB nods. The road we drove in on continues winding through bush for maybe thirty kilometres. After that there's a highway, a few back country roads and then we'll come out near Colonial Town.

'How far away are your friends?' HB asks, guessing what I'm looking at.

'Two hours,' I say. 'Can you take us back to the highway? So we can find another ride?'

HB blows out the guttering candle. Daylight's rising around us.

'If you like,' she says, stifling a yawn. 'But I could go you one better and you could do me a solid—another one, I mean, after the whole saving-my-life thing.'

I nod for her to go on.

'I could take you to your friends and . . . maybe join you? After today, and what you've told me, I don't feel so safe here alone.'

I'm not sure what's going on at Colonial Town. I don't know how I'll be received on my return—especially if I'm bringing more people to take care of. But the truth is it's not a choice: without HB we won't make it. Even if she does drop us at the highway, I'd still have to find a car or motorbike to get me and Lottie the rest of the way. Anyway, I can't leave HB here alone and defenceless. Could I?

'I can grow food,' HB says. 'Turns out I've got a green thumb.'

I feel bad that my prolonged silence has made her think she has to sell herself. That I'm like Jack and only save people based on their skills.

'You can stay with us,' I say.

HB beams. 'Great. To be honest, a life of chooks and books can get a bit lonely.'

I smile sympathetically. I know what it's like to be alone for days and weeks. Talking to HB's made me realise how lonely I've been in my self-imposed exile.

'Well,' I say, rubbing my hands, 'we should probably go now.'

Even though it's getting light, we should be on the road.

HB shakes her head. 'I need some sleep. You look like you need a week's rest. A few hours won't matter if it's that close and you've got until tonight. I'll get some blankets.'

There's no sense arguing. HB returns with some bedding and we settle on our couches. My eyes are all over the bush. I wish I was high up and had a better view. Maybe I could climb a tree while HB sleeps. Her eyes are closed and she has a faint smile as her head rests on a cushion.

'Can I ask you a question?' she murmurs.

'Sure.'

'Did you think about giving the guys who had me a chance to surrender?'

Some pillow talk.

'Not really.'

HB's eyes flick open. Her smile's gone. 'Shoot first, ask questions later?'

I nod at her. 'It has to be that way now.'

'Maybe.' She sighs and closes her eyes. 'Maybe that means we're really done for.'

HB settles and sleeps. But I'm too hyped to go down like that. I grope along the table for the wine bottle.

What she said. It sounded disapproving. I don't think that's fair. The suits wouldn't have surrendered and I would've lost the element of surprise and HB would've ended up a slave whore in the Board's horse float. If I'd tried to talk to the Jacks in Samsara or Baroonah they would've killed me. Hesitation is death. Except I can't help but think about the times I *didn't* shoot. If I had, Evan would be dead and Lottie and the boy, too. One hand on my AK-47, the other on the bottle, I think about where I'd be then, far from Colonial Town, far from anything to hang onto, until the wine makes it so I don't think about anything.

TWENTY-EIGHT

My watch read 10 p.m. when I arrived back at Colonial Town from that first excursion into Port Macquarie. The day I'd been away felt like it had flashed by in minutes and somehow stretched to weeks. Since I'd been gone Johnno had taken my advice and chopped down the wooden sign, pegged rocks through a couple of office windows and sprayed the brickwork with nonsensical graffiti. At least now if someone did look past the overturned truck Colonial Town might appear derelict.

I wheeled the quad through the gate and hauled my stuff from the cargo area. At the top of the street, I stopped to look and listen. No lanterns in windows. No generator humming. That was good, too, but what I *couldn't* believe was that I could get this far into the place without being challenged. A cold wave went through me when I considered how loudly I'd come on the quad without thinking about the possible scenarios. The Jacks could've raided and killed everyone and be lying in wait. With my rifle in the patrol carry, I crept across the creaking verandah of Johnno's hut.

Through a window, my night-vision goggles showed him snoring in his bed, surrounded by beer cans. One cottage along, Stannis was on his porch in a rocking chair, sleeping the sleep of the drunk and medicated. Gail and the boy were curled up in their cot. I slunk into Nathan's room. He was snoring, pill bottles on the bedside table, forehead cool to the touch. Someone had wiped the slate clean and drawn a little chart to keep track of his medications.

I went into The Bushranger's Redoubt and lit a candle. Felt wired and angry. Wanted them all to wake up to themselves. Tell them how much there was to do. That I could've slit all their throats. I looked at my watch. Counted back. I'd been awake for nearly two days.

They were being reckless but I was also being paranoid. Was it the effect of the uppers I'd taken? Maybe they'd been a mistake. Except Nathan was sleeping on his painkillers and antipsychotics. Johnno had knocked himself out with beer and Stannis had added morphine tablets to the boozy mix. Gail had been calmed by the sedatives I'd gotten for her. The Wild Woman had taken hits from the bong. Maybe the only way to cope in this new world was to be out of it as much as possible. I opened a bottle of wine and chased it all the way to the bottom.

I awoke on the floor. Light outside. My watch read 6.15. It felt like my mind had been running all night despite the wine. All I could think about was how much I had to do. I got up, splashed my face from a bottle of water, cracked a soft drink and washed down a dexie. I needed clarity and speed. Couldn't afford to feel sludgy and slow. The verandah creaked and I spun around as I reached for my rifle.

'Whoa, steady!' Johnno. In the doorway. Hands up to show he wasn't armed. 'Just me.'

I eased my fingers from the gun and straightened up.

Johnno walked in, looked from me to my gear. 'Camo the new black, is it?'

I nodded at a backpack. 'More in there for you. Should fit.'

Johnno glanced at his singlet and shorts and thongs. 'Be right like this, I reckon.'

He stepped inside. 'What was it like in PMQ?'

As he used a gas cooker to boil water for coffee, I told him about the ocean liner and the Sandpiper apartment and the Wild Woman and hitting Gizmos and Davo's Disposals. 'Worst thing is there's a massive bushfire north.'

'Won't be heading that way anytime soon?' he said.

I shook my head and started spreading out the contents of the backpacks.

Johnno whistled. 'Retail therapy?'

'You want to give me a hand setting up some of this stuff?'

After we'd had coffee, he and I walked the perimeter, sticking surveillance cameras and motion detectors and alarms to trees just inside the fence. I was putting a camera near the front gate when I froze. Dead frogs and geckos and sparrows had been crucified along a section of barbed wire.

'Jesus,' I said, backing into Johnno. 'Look.' My skin pimpled. I pictured the Wild Woman following me back here and doing this.

Johnno stepped around me and let out a little laugh. 'Butcherbird. What? Did you think your witchy chick had been here doing voodoo?'

Feeling silly, I got myself together as he explained that butcherbirds killed their prey and strung them up like this as a larder.

'Don't reckon it'll scare your Jacks off though, so good thing you got all these alarms, eh?' He looked at me, nodded with what could've been respect. 'This is a clever setup, Danby.'

When we'd installed the last cam, Johnno and I went back to the restaurant, synced the tablet and scrolled through its windows. We had coverage of every part of Colonial Town. And if anything taller than a wallaby moved between the trees near the fence, the air would be filled with screeching sirens and flashing lights.

•●•

'You didn't think to tell me you were back?' Nathan said, putting down his book when I walked into his cottage that afternoon. 'I was worried.'

Just not so worried he'd stayed awake for me last night. I held my tongue. He still had more right to be pissed with me than I did with him. At least now he was worrying about me: maybe that was progress.

'My note?' I offered. 'Back tomorrow?'

'What note?'

'On the blackboard. Someone's rubbed it out.'

Nathan pushed himself up on his pillows, looked over my camouflage. I pulled up a chair and sat by him. 'How're you feeling?'

'Better.'

I handed him a new tablet and showed him the video windows streaming Colonial Town's surveillance cameras.

'You can keep watch in the day. Any motion will show with a red border and it'll beep,' I said. 'I mean, if you feel up to it?'

'So we'll know they're almost on top of us?' Nathan said. 'Then what?'

I told him the rest of what Johnno and I had done. Down by the miners' camp, we'd snipped the bottom of the fence. A dozen yards beyond that was a dirt road where we'd hidden Nathan's quad and Johnno's panel van loaded with the camping supplies I'd gotten from Davo's.

Nathan's eyes bored into mine. 'How fast do you think I can go? I don't s'pose you brought me back some crutches?'

Shit.

'I'll—'

'And if we did make it to the vehicles—two drunks, a delu-sional woman, a mute boy and a cripple—how far do you think we'll get with choppers and whatever else after us?'

I dug my fingernails into my thighs to stop myself from snapping at him. 'I'm doing my best. To make things right. To keep you safe.'

Nathan went to say something. Thought better of it. Set the tablet on the bedside table.

'And I got this for you,' I said, pulling a walkie-talkie from my backpack and handing it to him with the instruction book.

'So we can stay in communication. Wow, sorry, I'm really being Captain Obvious, right?'

Nathan didn't smile. He flicked through the manual. To avoid looking at me.

'We shouldn't use our names,' I said. 'Or say where we are, okay? Don't know who could be listening.'

Strategies cascaded in my mind, poured out of my mouth to fill the silence. 'And—and—we should ask each other a question with an answer only we know. For security. If you're under duress, add the word "red" to the answer so I know. And I'll do the same. When I'm out, you'll be able to get me—'

'Out?' Nathan said, looking at me accusingly. 'Where exactly are you going to be?'

'Well, we need more weapons,' I say. 'I've got a lead. Need to follow it.'

'Now?'

I nodded.

Nathan's mouth tightened. 'It's nearly dark.'

'Best time to travel,' I said, and made binoculars with my hands around my eyes. 'I scored some night goggles. Gotta get back out there. We really do need more guns.'

'You said that.'

Nathan set the walkie-talkie and the manual on top of the tablet. I wiped dry saliva from the corner of my mouth. He looked at me strangely. I wondered if his medical training had helped him spot I was flying on speed.

'Are you all right?'

'I told you not to ask me that,' I said too sharply. 'And anyway I'm fine.'

Nathan shrugged, eyes flitting to the paperback he'd been reading when I came in. 'Look, I'm still feeling pretty tired.'

He wanted me to go. I wanted to go.

'Yeah,' I said. 'You rest.'

TWENTY-NINE

I awake with my heartbeat in my ears, my eyes in the gum trees, checking for threats, reaching for my rifle before I recall who and where I am. I ease back into the couch when I see HB cutting fruit at her kitchen bench and it all comes back to me.

'I'm making coffee,' she says, seeing me awake. 'You want some?'

I look at my watch. Almost eleven. Feels like I slept four minutes rather than four hours. I want to shake out a dexie but doing that in front of HB would feel wrong. She brings a cup and a plate of sliced apple and pear.

'Did you sleep off whatever you've been taking?'

I blow steam off my coffee.

'Speaking fast. Grinding your jaw,' HB says, looking at the empty wine bottle. 'Drinking to get to sleep. My brother was a meth-head.'

My mood darkens. I'd learned from Mac's military books that soldiers are issued uppers to keep them going. Why should

I be any different? And it's not like there are any laws left for it to be against and she's not my mum and—

HB spreads her hands. 'No judgment. I just know that trying to stay sharp that way ends up making you dull.'

Despite myself I feel a flush of shame. I sip the coffee. Eat the fruit. Desperately want to change the subject. 'Where's Lottie?'

'Inside, still sleeping.'

I feel a twinge. Has HB worked out that I haven't only been dosing myself? If she has, she doesn't let on.

'We need to go,' I say. 'I don't know how long it'll be before the Jacks are heading this way.'

HB nods. 'I've already packed what I want to take in the Jeep.'

I feel hopeless because I didn't so much as stir while she did that. If they'd come for us I wouldn't have heard them. Would've gone to my death drunk and drugged.

'Do you wanna wash?' HB asks. 'I've got soaps, shampoos and cosmetics inside. They're all organic so you won't bugger up the creek. I can get Lottie organised while you do it. It'll do you good, I promise.'

I calm myself. While the sleep and coffee and fruit have made me feel better, washing the past few days off me would be good. 'I will. Thanks.'

'Fresh towel inside,' she says. 'Clean socks too. Sorry, don't wear undies.'

I step inside the cabin. My heart thumps. Lottie's not on the bed. She's run off in the night. But she can't have. HB just said she saw her asleep in here. I notice three things at once: my backpack's open by her cot; my tablet is on her pillow; the door to the storeroom is shut.

I click the tablet and the screen shows video of Jacks milling around the Baroonah mansion and smoke billowing from the front steps. Marv and Jane and Lottie lie crumpled on the front lawn. *Crap.* If Lottie's watched this far then she's seen everything. Me killing those two Jacks in cold blood. Her father and mother getting blown up. Me talking to Marv as he died. Me holding a gun to her head before carting her off. She knows I've lied about how her parents died. She knows that I let them walk into a house I'd rigged to explode.

There's muffled noise. Sobbing behind the storeroom door. Lottie's hiding from me in there. Guilt floods through me. She has to understand. How much it tore me up. That I couldn't do anything. She wouldn't have been saved if it'd gone any other way. I inch across the floor, stand by the door, try to work out how I can say any of that. But Lottie speaks first.

'Can anyone hear me?' she says. 'Please come and help. I'm at a ranger cabin. In the bush. Near a town called Prestige. East I think. Hello? Can anyone hear me?'

Oh *shit*. She's on the radio.

I pull the .45 from my hip. 'Lottie, stop,' I yell. 'Turn it off!'

'This girl Danby's got me,' she shrieks. 'Can anyone hear me? She killed my mum and dad. Come in. Over? Hello? Help me, please!'

I kick the door and it flies open. Lottie turns, tear-streaked, mike clutched in one hand, the other one twisting the dial.

275

I aim the pistol at her. 'Put it down.'

Lottie shakes her head, stares at me with red eyes, cheeks glistening, snot dripping from her nose. 'I saw it. You killed them,' she says, making sure the mike's near her quivering lips. 'Help me. Help me please is anyone—'

Her eyes dip to my finger as it slips inside the trigger guard.

'Put it down.' The voice is a whisper. At first I think it's some sort of delayed echo. Then I realise it's HB behind me in the office. I got sloppy and left the AK-47 outside. Now I bet it's aimed at my skull.

'She's just a child,' she says.

No one's a child anymore. And even if they are it doesn't allow or excuse anything. If the Jacks are out there listening they know where we are—or at least that I'm nowhere near Dubbo.

'She gave us up,' I say.

'Go on, kill me, like you kill everyone!' Lottie lets the mike slip with a clunk to the desk. She closes her eyes and lifts her chin at me defiantly. 'I don't care. I'd rather be dead.'

'The radio's not on,' HB says softly, at my shoulder now. 'No harm's been done.'

My eyes go from Lottie to the set. I can't tell if it's on or not.

'You're lying—to save her. She's—'

Got to die so we can live: that's what I stop myself from saying. Every part of me starts to shake, top to toe inside and out, and it feels like I'm going to fly apart. The .45 jitters. My eyes are hot. Lottie's face blurs. I see Evan. And the boy. *Liam.* I nearly shot them. Just like I'm—

The .45 weighs a tonne and it's like I'm tethered to it as my body follows it down to the floor. The room spins, HB and Lottie part of the swirl, and I'm lost inside the howling heap of myself.

THIRTY

Riding along Elder Way, world tinged red by night-vision and amphetamine, I tried not to get my hopes up. If Mac had a hidden fortress out here, there was every chance he'd come under attack from desperadoes once his mind spilled his secrets. Maybe he'd fended them off before he'd crashed out. Maybe they'd overrun him before they'd crashed out. There were a dozen bodies on this remote road, some locked together with violent injuries, suggesting that people had fought each other to get to him.

I left the quad a few hundred metres from the fringe of his property and covered the last of the road slowly on foot. Crouching in the brush in my yowie suit, I expected to see more carnage—a burned-out bunker and bodies everywhere. But Mac's place was dark and quiet. A modest kit home with a silver garage amid trees, nestled against one of North Brother Mountain's foothills. His driveway wasn't protected by big gates and his land wasn't enclosed by barbed wire. If he had a guard dog that was still alive it wasn't troubled by the kangaroos grazing around his lawn.

As I advanced from tree to tree, I was betting Mac wasn't a Special lining up his sniper rifle on my bushy silhouette. If he was a crazy paranoid before the Snap I hated to imagine what he'd be like now if he'd survived. Unless I was incredibly unlucky, he was dead. What I did have to worry about was that the danger he posed in life hadn't necessarily died with him. If he was living out here and prepping for the apocalypse then I could be walking into a house rigged to explode.

Thinking like a paranoid survivalist: it was getting easier all the time.

Forcing the front door seemed like walking into a trap. So I crept around the back. Peered through a window and saw a neatly made bed and clothes rack. No women's outfits. Mac had been a bachelor. No surprises there. What was surprising was how utterly normal the rest of the house looked through other windows. A kitchen and study and lounge. Walls decorated with pictures of racing cars and football teams. No bars on the windows. Not a rifle rack or samurai sword or fascist flag to be seen.

The garage. That had to be his HQ. But when I looked through its window I saw Mac had driven an ordinary sedan rather than an armoured tank. His work spaces held tools and hardware, not guns and ammo. This didn't make sense. There was no sign that Mac had been Davo's number one customer. Standing there in the dark, I got it. Normality: *that* was the point. When the shit hit the fan, the safest refuge would be a place of no interest. Nathan had thought that when he took us to Law of Small Numbers, the crappy little accountant's office in Parramatta. And if it hadn't been for bad luck we'd probably *still* be safe there.

I smashed the window with the butt of my rifle. Sniffed the garage's air. It was clean. I cleared the glass so I could climb inside safely without suffering the same fate as the Gizmos kid. That's when my nostrils tickled. No cloying stench of decay but a definite whiff of death. I took off my night-vision goggles and clicked on my flashlight. Shining it through the car windows didn't light up a corpse. There was no one swinging from the rafters. I got on my hands and knees. Looked under the vehicle. Nothing. But as I walked to the back of the garage the smell got stronger. I stood by a low table stacked with paint-tins and inhaled. Had someone cut Mac up into little pieces and stuck him in the cans? Or was I just mistaking their chemical fumes for the taint of decomposition? I picked up a four-litre tin, surprised to lift it without trouble—along with the two others beneath it. The next three cans the same. All empty—and all stuck together. This table looked heavily laden with paint but really held only a pile of tinned air. I pulled at its edge and the table slid smoothly out from the wall and a cloud of decay oozed into the garage from the open hatch beneath. I'd found Mac and his bunker.

Bandana over my nose and mouth, I climbed down a ladder into a room. Its ceiling was the garage's concrete slab. Mac lay on his back in the middle of the floor inside a Hazmat suit with hood and respirator. He'd been struggling to tug a glove on when he'd crashed out. That hand was purple and swollen. I guessed the rest of him was also ripe inside the suit.

But his cocoon and the cool conditions down here meant the smell was nowhere near as gross as it could've been.

I shone my torch across shelves of stuff Mac had collected to see him through any apocalypse—except the one that had actually happened. Enough ration packs and tinned food and tubs of nuts and rice and pasta to last for years. Big kegs of water. Camouflage outfits for forest and desert and snow. Two flak jackets. A compound bow and quivers of arrows. Hunting knives and fishing rods. Folding shovels and axes and binoculars and a little telescope that'd be handy. Night-vision goggles the same make and model as mine. A neatly arranged library of books about guerrilla warfare and types of aircraft and warrior philosophy and military history and bush tucker and celestial navigation. Other weirder titles like *Agile, Mobile, Hostile: Man against Oppression*, *The Smiling Totalitarian* and *Say No to Illuminati Internment!*

But Mac hadn't been all paranoid work and no play. His bunker came with a little generator hooked up to a bar fridge and entertainment unit and wall screen. I picked up a music player. The screen showed he'd actually downloaded the 1001 hard rock classics you were supposed to hear before you died and that he had a massive selection of literary and philosophical classics as audiobooks. Had made playlists of music called 'Fighting' and 'Training' and collected chapters in folders called 'On Endurance' and 'On Wisdom'.

Mac hadn't lived long enough to listen to them or use any of his stuff. There was no evidence he'd even managed to make himself a meal of dehydrated beef stroganoff before it'd all been over for him. His double bed still had sleeping bags rolled up where pillows would've been. But it was what was under the bed that confirmed what I'd suspected: Mac hadn't done *all* his shopping through Davo. I hauled out the metal lockers and opened them up.

'Far out,' I said, sitting on the floor. 'Man.'

According to the manuals, I was looking at four AK-47 machine guns, each with three banana-shaped clips loaded with thirty 7.62 millimetre rounds, and a sawn-off 30-30 shotgun, complete with two cartons of shells. I recognised the pistol inside the wooden box as a .45. There were three cartons of bullets and a leather holster for that. I counted another thirty loaded clips for the machine guns, two dozen hand grenades, an assortment of smoke bombs and tear-gas canisters. Johnno might've fantasised about surviving the zombie wasteland or whatever but Mac had been prepping to emerge as its lord and master.

'Where did you get all of this stuff?' I asked him, delighted and horrified and impressed all at once. I pictured him doing shady deals, forking over extravagant amounts of money to criminals, spending his nights and weekends down here reading up and preparing for the big day. Then a stranger shelf caught my eye: bottles of liqueur, boxes of chocolates, romantic novels. This poor deranged bloke had hoped to share the space with someone special. Some otherwise unobtainable woman probably—a high school crush, a work colleague, the wife of a friend—he'd envisaged himself rescuing and wooing. My smile went south when I thought about what might've happened the longer Mac's fantasies went unfulfilled. The crazy bastard might've shot up a school or office.

I shook off my spiral of speedy thoughts. Centred on what I had to do.

I wanted Mac's best stuff. I didn't want to keep coming back here as his body rotted.

It took me hours to lug what I needed and stack it in the garage. Then I laid down some plastic to seal Mac's smell in and slid the paint table back into place.

I hiked back to the quad, senses tingling on another pill, flak jacket on and pockets filled with grenades, slinging an AK-47, feeling I could take on all the Jacks if they were stupid enough to come at me. I rode back to the garage and loaded the guns and ammo. I'd have to come back for the rest. But now at least we'd be able to put up a fight at Colonial Town.

It was mid-morning before Johnno and Stannis were awake enough for me to run through the arsenal I'd laid out on the restaurant tables. Neither had fired more than a .22 at rabbits before so I showed them what I'd learned about the AK-47s.

'Child soldiers all over the world use them,' I said, the words sounding familiar to me for a reason I couldn't place. 'Now, these grenades?'

'Danby, can we close the curtains and door?' Stannis said. 'Gail and the boy are down by the lake but I'd hate them to see all this.'

I nodded and kept on, mouth going a mile a minute, holding up a grenade. 'From what I read, you just pull this pin here, throw it as far as you can and get the hell down.'

Pale and fidgety, Johnno and Stannis watched me with big eyes. I didn't know if it was because they were only now realising the trouble we were in. Or whether they didn't like having a teenage girl tell them how to use these weapons.

I left them gingerly dry-firing their assault rifles while I took Nathan's AK-47 to him along with camo gear in his size. He watched me open-mouthed as I raced through how if they came he could use covering fire and explosive grenades and smoke bombs to cover their retreat and—

'Danby?' he said.

I forced myself to stop talking. 'What?'

'Have you slept? I'm sure I can figure this out.'

I wasn't tired. But I probably needed to recharge.

'There's a cottage down near the lake,' he said. 'Johnno's made it up for you to get some rest. It's nearest to the fence so if anything happens, you know, you can respond first.'

That was more like it. Tactical thinking. 'Okay, but you're sure you're okay?'

Nathan nodded.

It wasn't until I was in that cottage that I realised why they'd put me here. It wasn't so I'd be the first to detect any intruders. It was so I'd be farthest from them. Fuming, I paced the room, furious they couldn't see that what I was doing was essential, that I was doing all of it for them. I marched up to The Bushranger's Redoubt, glad I didn't encounter anyone, and grabbed a bottle of wine to bring me down.

•••

On my way back from Mac's the next night, quad loaded with tools and books and rations, my night-vision goggles flashed the word 'Zoo' at me from out of the trees. I slowed, turned back and followed the sign that pointed at a little side road.

I heard Midcoast Sanctuary long before I came up on it. The squawks and snarls, whinnies and snorts, growls and howls of starving trapped animals behind its high walls stripped my soul. Not caring about the noise it'd make, I used a sledge-hammer to smash my way through the entrance. Inside cages and enclosures, alive and dead, were an ark's worth of creatures. I went to work with boltcutters, .45 in the back of my trousers in case I needed to save myself from something I was trying to save. I opened doors and gates for roos and wallabies, quolls and dingos, donkeys and camels, emus and eagles, koalas and crocodiles, meerkats and mountain lions, spider monkeys and orangutans. I found Midcoast Sanctuary's big side gate, busted its lock and left it wide open to a bush track beyond. I didn't know if the animals would escape or if they could even survive in the wild. None of them seemed inclined to make a getaway. I broke into a shed. Found huge sacks of pellets that visiting kids had fed to the animals for a dollar a cup. Dumped them out for the marsupials, who shuffled over. At least it'd rained enough for their water troughs to be full. I grabbed a recently deceased wallaby and hefted it into the crocs' enclosure. I wondered what the snow leopards had been fed and if there was any of it left. A quick search inside the zoo's buildings revealed a cool room gone to rot. I found my way into a veterinary clinic. Saw a cabinet of tranquiliser guns, a drawer of big syringes, a fridge of vials. The humane thing would be to figure out how to put these animals down. But it wasn't the human thing. Stepping back outside, I saw the snow leopards were gone. So was the dead wallaby—and the crocs. I hoped they found a river and a way to survive. Maybe they'd even pay my kindness forward by eating a Jack or two. But I wasn't going to hang around and see if they fancied today's Special.

·•·

I awoke on the floor of my cottage tangled in the earbuds of Mac's music player with an empty bottle of wine and the Lord Howe brochure at my side. I remembered drinking and thinking as I listened to the survivalist's best stuff. Rolling Stones, Blue Oyster Cult, MC5—they were bands Mum had introduced me to. I peered at the notes I'd penned in the brochure's margins. 'Light plane? Fishing trawler? Poss pop'n incl. tourists = 800. Chance of 1 x *Situs* survivor: approx 1/12. Find info re LHI food supplies/what need to take. Talk to Nathan.' *Talk to Nathan.* I might've been drunk and high when I'd decided that but it still made sense. I washed down some Ibuprofen, pounded a whole bottle of water, used another to splash my face and brush my teeth. Brochure in hand, I stepped out of the cottage.

Stannis and Johnno were recalling classic football games as they drank beers and fished from the tall ship. Gail skimmed stones across the lake while the boy watched with his amputee blue bear clutched to his chest.

I wandered up the main street towards Nathan's cottage, brochure and pad in hand. First I'd apologise for being a bit extreme. Not that I felt I needed to but it might soften things between us. Then I'd ask him to hear me out about Lord Howe Island as a possible refuge. Yes, it was a long shot, but if we could get there he'd never have to fight another Jack in his life.

Nathan was on his porch with his cast propped on a bench. He wasn't wearing the camo I'd left him. I glanced at the stuff around him: blanket, pillow, bag of boiled lollies, bottle of soft drink. No tablet. No walkie-talkie. No AK-47. Nothing I'd done had made any difference to him.

He knew I was standing there but he didn't look up from a paperback copy of *Gone Girl*. I'm sure it wasn't deliberate but he adjusted his hold on the book so the N and E in the title were covered by a finger. Message received.

I stuffed the brochure and pad into my pocket, went back to my cottage, and read about the Vietnam War. When night came, I ate a turkey curry ration pack by the lake as I listened to the forest and imagined what'd happen if the alarms went off because Jacks were inside the wire. I had my AK-47, my .45 and shotgun and grenades. I'd lay down covering fire, blast at any chopper, hope the others got to the fence and—

My shoulders slumped. It was hopeless. I didn't trust Johnno and Stannis to be much use. Nathan maybe even less now he'd given up not just on me but on himself. Sadness spread through me. Everyone here would probably feel safer without me around to protect them. The truth was I couldn't anyway. It didn't matter how many alarms or guns or rations we had. If the Jacks got to Colonial Town without warning we were finished. To survive we'd need to escape before they got this far.

·•·

Quad loaded with supplies, I wound up North Brother's steep road in the darkness and pulled into a parking bay by a picnic hut. The mountain was the highest peak around. From a wooden lookout, I could just make out the lake and beach towns east of the mountain with my night-vision goggles. There were no lights anywhere down there. From a similar point on the southern side of the peak I had a view south and west of coast, farmland and highways. No lights shone anywhere there either. When dawn came, I found another lookout, tucked in rainforest, accessible by a loop path that was half smooth footpath and half jungle track. Between the three spots I had a panoramic view of the sea, coast and hinterlands. Bronze plaques named the landmarks I was looking at and how far away they were. The farthest should've been a mountain nearly a hundred kilometres north but it was lost in a wall of purple bushfire haze. It didn't matter so much. The Jacks would be coming from the south and I could see up to fifty kilometres that way, to beaches past Crowdy Head and inland to the Pacific Highway as it ran through bush and paddocks and to a town in the distance that my GPS identified as Baroonah.

I set up my tent in a patch of rainforest and covered it with camo netting. Rolled out my sleeping bag, set out books and rations and equipment. I'd left Nathan a blunt note—'On watch—W/T = Ch#4'. I hoped he might at least give enough of a damn about us to keep the walkie-talkie with him.

I patrolled the lookouts with my telescope and binoculars. Ghost ships out to sea. Dead beaches, inlets, rivers and towns all around. Horizon free of choppers and planes. I did the loop all day, pausing on each circuit to read a few of the engraved padlocks that'd been affixed to the safety fences.

Bella & Sherrin, Here from Brussels, 2018.

Ahira + Yoshi 4 Ever!!!

Life's A Ride—Bill.

Like the painted rocks on the breakwall, they were stabs at permanence, boiled down to 'I was here'. I kept patrolling until a few hours after dark before creeping back to my tent and sleeping fitfully. I awoke an hour before dawn, took the first dexie of the day and started over.

I stuck to my schedule, scanning through all points on the hour. The rest of the time I gave myself a crash course in everything I thought I should know. I did push ups and chin ups and sprinted and jogged around the rainforest loop. I devoured Mac's books. *Fighting Skills of the Special Forces* had chapters on 'Staying Hidden' and 'Silent Killing' and I guessed one day I'd find out how much I'd retained. *Urban Warrior* set out the principles of distressing a bigger and stronger enemy by sowing chaos and confusion. While I waited for the chance to put that into effect I practised simpler stuff. Learning to pick locks was something that occupied a rainy afternoon. By the end of it I could open all the rusting relics on the lookout fences. I clipped them all back in place as a mark of respect for those who'd passed through and passed on.

Mac's books taught me about Kokoda and Z Force and the Coastwatchers whose work was similar to what I was doing on North Brother. The 'Russian Guerilla Girls' chapter of *The Assymetric Battlespace* was particularly fascinating. I read about a woman named Yevdokia Bershanskaya whose *'Night Witches'*, a squadron of female aviators, had used flimsy aircraft to bomb the Nazis. And I was stunned by the story of seventeen-year-old sniper Klavdiya Kalugina, who'd shot enemy soldiers from a kilometre away and always carried two grenades on her belt, 'one for the fascists, one for me'.

Mac's books on bush survival helped me identify the birds and lizards and flowers and trees so that the landscape around me made more sense. I could tell a casuarina from a pine and knew that the rough-scaled snake that lived down by the toilet block wouldn't hurt me if I left it alone. The red–brown rodent that had started to appear at dusk I was able to identify as an Australian bush rat rather than one of its introduced European cousins. Each night I tossed it scraps and over the blurring weeks Rat came closer until it was comfortable letting me pat it and discover she was a she. By then the name had stuck. Eventually, Rat was happy to make my tent her own and sleep there during the day.

The AK-47 became an extension of my body. I spent hours stripping it, cleaning it, putting it back together fast. I could switch clips in a few seconds and in pitch darkness. After much deliberation I decided to risk a hundred rounds on target practice, figuring actually getting good with the gun would make the remaining ammunition that much more valuable. My first few shots showed me how lucky I'd got when I'd hit that woman in Samsara. But by the time I'd finished I could put successive bullets through the centre of both O's in the rainforest loop sign from a hundred metres away. I spent hours throwing grenade-size rocks until I had range, speed and accuracy.

Every second or third night I'd return to Colonial Town, clicking the security system off so I didn't set it off as I entered, and sleep a few hours in my cottage while my devices recharged at The Bushman's Redoubt. Before dawn, I'd stock up on anything I needed, make sure everyone was alive and then head back.

Creeping in one night, I saw Nathan out on his porch, reading by candlelight. He waved me over. I was glad to see he had his walkie-talkie and AK-47 within arm's reach.

'Hello, stranger,' he said.

'Hey,' I said.

'Where've you been going?'

'A mountain down south,' I said, tapping the walkie-talkie on my belt. 'Keeping watch so I can warn you if they're coming.'

Nathan nodded and I stepped closer. Since I'd seen him last his stubble had become a beard.

'Look at you,' I said, running my hands over my chin. 'Very, uh, distinguished?'

He shrugged, managed a little smile. 'Want to sit?'

My stomach clenched. I'd convinced myself he never

wanted to talk to me again.

'Just for a minute.' I perched with my AK-47 on the edge of a chair. 'So, um, how's it going?'

Nathan laughed, shook his head.

'What?' I said.

He lifted one leg and then the other. Jeans. Legs. Boots. I slapped my forehead. 'The cast's off.'

I felt like a goose for not noticing. 'How is it?'

'A bit of a limp. I'm doing exercises but if you happen to run into any physiotherapists . . .'

I relaxed enough to smile.

'How are you?' he asked.

It was better than asking me if I was all right.

'I'm good. Teaching myself a lot.'

Nathan nodded. 'Keeping busy's good.'

The silence stretched. Maybe I should bring up Lord Howe Island.

Before I could raise it Nathan cleared his throat. 'Danby,' he said, 'I need to apologise.'

I looked at him. 'You do?'

'I did see your note on the blackboard. About making things right? That you'd be back tomorrow.'

I seethed, balled my fists by my sides. 'Why'd you lie?'

Nathan sighed, rubbed his beard. 'What happened with my ankle, the way you blamed me for Evan, how we've been with each other—everything. I was . . . angry. Like . . .'

'Like?'

'Like you . . . are.'

'Me?'

Nathan nodded. 'Angry.'

'I'm not—'

'Danby, it's okay. You wouldn't be human if you weren't traumatised. We've seen so much awful stuff it's bound to mess with us.'

'Are you saying I'm crazy?'

'I'm saying I'm worried about you out there, worried about—'

'What?'

Nathan took a deep breath. 'What you're doing to yourself with the drugs.'

I sputtered. 'You buttered me up for an intervention? Is that what this is?'

'No, it's just—'

'It's just nothing. I know what I'm doing,' I said. And I did. I was making sure I took vitamins, ate well and got some sleep every day. 'Soldiers throughout history have used amphetamines. I was reading—'

'Is that what you are? A soldier?'

'Don't make fun of me.'

'I'm not. It's a serious question.'

'I don't know. Maybe. Someone's got to keep us safe instead of just sitting around.'

'I had a broken leg, Danby.'

'You know what I mean.'

'Okay, okay,' Nathan said, hands up to placate me. 'Look, I'm not telling you what to do but let's just talk about what you're taking? Make sure you're not overdoing it.'

His tone—medical, professional—had my blood running hot.

'I'm fine,' I said, getting up, shouldering my AK-47. 'What I need is to get some sleep before I get back out there.'

Nathan nodded. Knew better than to push me. 'Okay.'

'I'll see you later,' I said and walked down the pathway.

'Danby?' he called.

I turned. He held up the walkie-talkie. 'I'm here, okay?'

·•·

I woke after dawn and berated myself for oversleeping because I'd have to risk travelling in daylight. Not going to North Brother wasn't an option. The one day I ducked my duty would be the one day the Jacks came from the south. Riding the Bago Road to the Pacific Highway in the morning, it was harder to ignore how many people had perished. Taking this route with night-vision goggles had let me distance myself, the carnage rendered in varying shades of digital red and black, like a video game. But even pushing the quad up to fifty kilometres an hour, state forest a blur of green on either side of me, I couldn't help seeing people blackened and shrunken inside matted clothes, bones and teeth white where skin had shrivelled. Then I realised what was beside a vehicle up ahead and I slowed the quad.

Next to a car that'd rolled into a tree was a plump blue arm that ended in a stubby paw. The weather had muddied the fur but I had no doubt that this was the limb the boy's teddy bear was missing. I picked it up and tucked it among my supplies.

I could wash it and maybe even use what I'd learned about stitching wounds to make the soft toy whole again. I peered at the driver, who'd died of his injuries crumpled upside down against the roof with a wallaby through his windshield. The man was too damaged and decayed for me to be able to make out any sort of resemblance to the boy. But the car was still filled with the stuff of their lives.

The man's wallet was in the glove compartment. He was Kurt Harwell and he'd lived in Canberra. Inside a leather satchel were personal papers and court documents and newspaper clippings about a mother's worry for the welfare of her five-year-old son Liam because he'd gone missing with his father during a scheduled custody visit. A photo showed heartbroken mother Sasha holding a framed portrait of the boy whose pale face was haunting Colonial Town. I opened envelopes and read angry letters Kurt had written to her but not had the guts to post. Long rants about his rights and what was best for his bloody son. Boasts that he'd taken them deep into the bush and that they wouldn't be found. Justifications that he'd teach him to be a man better than Sasha's 'poofta' new boyfriend would. The last of these semiliterate biro scrawls was dated 27 December. By then Kurt had obviously had a rethink and declared he was willing to return the boy in exchange for a guarantee Sasha wouldn't press charges because after all who would that help in the long run?

December 27—and Kurt had given no indication he had any idea the Snap had happened. I tugged a map of Barrington Tops National Park from the satchel. A glance around the station wagon showed scattered camping gear: pots, tarps, sleeping rolls, plastic containers of rice and cereal and tins of beans and soup. Kurt and Liam hadn't been fleeing the Snap. They'd already been hiding from the world. They'd been trying to go back when Kurt had hit the wallaby and lost control. At least he'd strapped his kid into a car seat. I wondered how long the poor kid had stayed with his dead dad before he wandered off.

I rode on to the North Brother turn-off. Took out my tablet and scrolled through the cams I'd put in place to see if anyone had been there in my absence. A dozen hours of fast-forwarded footage showed no one had gone to the lookouts.

Up in my tent, Rat on my shoulder, I compared Kurt's maps to my own, using my thumb and finger to measure distances. If they'd been in a remote part of a national park on Christmas Day, there was every chance they were thirty-five or more kilometres from the nearest living people. At the very least, they would've been removed from large populations. That *had* to be it. How the boy had been protected from the Snap. When everyone else was being affected, he and his dad had been far away enough to remain Normal.

It was what I'd hoped for my mum. But Shadow Valley hadn't been distant enough from the main towns of the Blue Mountains. She'd been within range of tens of thousands of people, who'd all been mentally connected with millions of others in Sydney. I wondered about the ocean liner I'd seen washed up. Had it been close enough to a big port to be infected by the insanity erupting on the mainland? Or had it been on the open seas but fallen victim because a floating population of thousands was enough to manifest the Snap? I didn't have the answers but I was getting an inkling and it gave me hope. Across the world, in its most remote and least populated places, there really could be pockets of survivors untouched by the madness.

I pulled out the tablet and spent hours pinching and zooming the world map as I searched for places that were a long way from anywhere. There were island dots off Madagascar, coastal specks with unpronounceable names in Greenland, villages in the wild mountain terrains of Tibet. Without the internet, I couldn't know definitive populations and distances, but it was possible that Normals were alive in *thousands* of these places. While I'd calculated less than a million people with *Situs inversus* had survived worldwide, there might be ten, twenty or even fifty times that number when you added in Normals. People that Jacks would never find or hurt.

As the sun faded behind the clouds, I let out a little whoop and danced around the mountain's lookout, not caring that to anyone watching I'd have seemed as crazy as the Wild Woman. When I settled down, I went back to my tablet and stared at Lord Howe Island's crescent of green in the vast blue emptiness of the Tasman Sea.

THIRTY-ONE

Even with my eyes shut, all I see are the dead. Mum, Dad, Stephanie, Tajik, Oscar, Louis, hundreds and thousands of others, in Beautopia Point, Parramatta, Clearview, Penrith, Samsara, Baroonah—everywhere. Not just the dead. People I've *killed*. Shot, burned, blown apart. A few more seconds and Lottie would've been among them.

'Go,' I hear HB say to her. 'Outside now. It'll be all right.'

I'm vaguely aware of the crying girl edging around me and then her footfalls across the office floor.

'All those people,' I croak. 'In the choppers. On the bikes. The hippie girl. They didn't have to die. The boy. Jesus. I nearly killed him. Evan, I was, was, was . . . going to shoot him.'

HB crouches beside me as I sob. She doesn't take the .45 from my hand. She doesn't touch me. She doesn't say anything. She's just there. Eventually I'm bled dry and that's when HB gently lifts the gun from my fingers and cradles me in her arms.

'Mum, I'm sorry,' I say. 'So sorry.'

'It's all right,' HB says. 'Let it out.'

I start all over again. Eyes clenched. Chest heaving. Blubbing tears and snot until a tide of exhaustion sweeps over me. HB eases me flat on the floor and returns from the office with a pillow and blanket.

'You need to sleep,' she says, making me comfortable, using a wet wipe to clean my face. It's cool and soothing. 'Just rest a while. Let your mind and body reset.'

'But the Jacks,' I say, looking up at her, barely able to keep my eyes open. 'They could be coming.'

HB smiles. 'I'll keep watch. Get some rest. We'll go in a while, okay?'

I snuffle. HB closes the door behind her softly. I try to count how many hours it's been since Baroonah and how much time I've got before Nathan decides I'm dead. I can't make the sums work in my head. I know it's not long. I should get up and tell HB we have to go now. But I'm so tired.

• •

When I wake up, I feel purged. Clean. For the first time in a long time, there's no booze or drugs in my system. I stare at the ceiling a while, listen to the sounds of birds. Make out the chortling gurgles of currawongs and prehistoric screeches of black cockatoos. Footsteps approach through the office and I sit up and resist the instinctive urge to grab the .45 that HB has left on the radio table.

'Okay,' I say to the knock on the door.

'It's me.' Lottie enters with a tray she sets on the crate beside me. She's brought a bowl of soup and a glass of apple juice. Hot shame floods through me. HB's sent her in here after telling her God knows what about me.

I pull the blanket around my shoulders. 'I'm sorry,' I say. 'About pointing the gun at you. About what happened to your mum and dad. About everything.'

Tears stream down Lottie's cheeks. She sets the tray down and sits sniffling across from me.

'HB told me what happened—' Lottie's voice hitches. 'Mum and Dad, it wasn't your fault.'

'It wasn't supposed to be like that.'

Lottie nods. 'I know. Eat your soup.'

I spoon a mouthful.

'HB used her best chicken,' Lottie says, forcing a smile. 'She let the others run free. Says in like a hundred years they'll rule this valley.'

I grin. 'It's delicious.'

'I helped make it. It's got garlic, onions, carrots, mushrooms, broccoli and spinach. HB grew everything right here.'

'She's pretty clever,' I say.

This is small talk but it's the sort of chat we need for things to start to feel normal again. I don't know if there is anything scientific behind the theory that chicken soup has medicinal properties but I feel better and stronger straight away.

When I'm finished, I look at Lottie. She still looks twelve. Except in the eyes. In just a day they've aged. I can only imagine how I look to her. I hold out my hand and she takes it.

'Sorry about the radio,' Lottie says.

'Don't be,' I say. 'I'm sorry I didn't tell you the truth. I didn't know how. Given what you thought, what you did with the radio was . . . well, it was smart and brave.'

Lottie looks pleased. 'Really?'

I nod. Her eyes go to the .45 on the radio desk. 'Can you teach me how to shoot? I need to know, right? I mean, if they come—the Jacks or like the others who had HB?'

'I reckon you might be better off getting HB to teach you how to grow food,' I say. 'I hope where we're going we're not gonna need guns.'

But for the moment we do, and I slide the .45 into the holster and follow Lottie from the back room. In the glare of the grey afternoon, HB nurses a cup of tea in an armchair under the tarp.

'You feeling better?'

'I am, thanks,' I say. 'Really. Sorry I kind of lost it.'

'Don't mention it,' HB says. 'Nothing compared to how some of the girls on the magazine used to carry on when they broke up with a guy or didn't get invited to some party.'

I doubt that but I smile anyway. Lottie taps me on the shoulder. She has a basket with a towel, soaps, shampoos and conditioners.

'Go on,' HB says. 'The creek's still there.'

I frown. 'Thanks but we should really—'

HB holds up a hand. 'It's only three. Another twenty minutes isn't going to make the world of difference. Cry, sleep, eat, pamper—the four phases of being reborn. Well, I must've written twenty articles that said something like that, so it must be true. Off you go.'

I take the basket from Lottie and make my way along the path through the bush. I set the .45 on a tuft of grass, undress quickly and wade into the creek. Its water is fast and cold and bracing. I scoop sand from the bottom, rub handfuls of it across myself, feel like I'm scraping off an old skin. Sinking beneath the surface, I tingle as the current swirls across my stubbled scalp. Bobbing up, I gaze around at the acacias and banksias and eucalypts and up into the granite outcrops and roiling sky. I don't have that feeling of being watched like I did in Shadow Valley—or the feeling of being scrutinised by the others that I've had in Colonial Town.

I look at the basket on the bank. While I appreciate HB's intentions I can't help but flash to another bit of my reading. In the Vietnam War the Viet Cong could smell the scents American soldiers used long before they spotted them. If I'd been wearing perfume when I was splayed out in Baroonah, it could've been the difference between my life and the death of the Jacks. I hate to have to keep thinking this way, but the war's not over yet.

THIRTY-TWO

I resisted the urge to ride back to Colonial Town, carrying the bear arm as a peace offering, trying to excite Nathan with my theory that there were a lot more people alive than we'd thought. As though he'd believe there was hope for the world because I'd found a stinky piece of soft toy and some letters and a map. If anyone else was delivering the news, Nathan might've considered it but as things were he'd doubt me if I said gravity was what held us to the Earth.

I stayed on North Brother Mountain. I did my watches, rotated through lookouts, exercised and studied and trained at intervals, starting an hour before dawn and finishing close to midnight. With Rat watching on and chewing dried rations, I used tweezers to extract hundreds of specks of gravel from the fur on the bear's arm and then washed and dried and brushed the limb till it was as good as new. With the arm back on the teddy, the boy—Liam—might smile and maybe even speak. That seemed more important than theorising about what his soft toy meant for the fate of the world.

Below me to the east, in the towns of Camden Haven and Laurieton, gardens and parks planted with oaks and maples and myrtles had erupted gold and orange and red in response to the early winter. The days were getting shorter and colder. It wouldn't be long before I had to go back to Davo's and loot some warmer clothing. I didn't think it should be this cold at the end of March.

As daylight dwindled on the fifth day, I prepared to head back to Colonial Town. Debating what, if anything, I'd say to Nathan about the bear arm, I did a final check of the lookouts.

People were coming.

Lights far to the south in the murk where the land met the sea. This was it. What I'd feared. What I'd been working for.

I pulled out my telescope and trained it on the headlights and tail-lights climbing the hill from the national park into the little coastal town of Crowdy Head. It was hard to tell for sure but best I could make out there were two motorbikes. I lost them in the darkness, briefly saw what I thought were flash-lights and then everything returned to black.

All night Rat and I sat on the lookout, wind whipping around us, and kept watch on Crowdy Head and the roads leading in and out. Hours dragged but I didn't see lights again. I calmly turned the possibilities. What I knew. What I didn't.

They weren't Revivees. I'd have been able to tune them at this distance. They could be Specials who'd found each other. Or maybe more Normals like Liam. But if they were Jacks then what I hadn't seen was as important as what I had. There was no evidence of any others. No headlights on the Pacific

Highway. No chopper searchlights on the horizon. What that would mean was the lights I'd seen were at the leading edge of the search. More than twenty kilometres stood between me and them—and another twenty kilometres between me and Colonial Town. There was time to confirm what I'd seen and time to inform the others. Then we could make our decision about what to do. Not that we had a lot of options. Go bush, go west or go north if the firestorms had burned themselves out.

Not long after the sky brightened enough to see, I spotted dark figures with assault rifles entering and leaving houses on a street in Crowdy Head. They'd take a property each, spend a few minutes searching, come out empty handed and then move to the next location. They weren't looting. They were looking. There was still no other activity I could see along the coast or on the highway or in the hinterland. Now I had no doubt. They were Jacks. Coming for us.

I went to the eastern lookout. Focused my telescope north. So much smoke hung there I couldn't see what the fires were doing. But I had to know before I went back to Colonial Town. I could get to the Sandpiper in an hour and be back to Nathan and the others an hour after that. The two Jacks couldn't cover all of Crowdy Head by then, let alone the hundreds of houses and apartments in Camden Haven and Laurieton. But this would be my last morning on North Brother. Its next visitors would be Jacks who'd scour for any sign of me. I hastily collected the Cameleons from their trees and packed up my books and supplies and tent. Rat sat on a branch, watching my every move, whiskers twitching as if she thought this was goodbye. She'd gotten fat on what I'd fed her and I felt guilty that I may have ruined her ability to take care of herself in the wild.

'No woman left behind,' I said. It was my version of the motto of one of the special forces units I'd read about. Rat scampered up my arm and into the pocket of my shirt. 'Let's go.'

••

I knew I was closing in on Port Macquarie when I reached Station Wagon Guy on Pacific Drive. I remembered him from my other time here. His car was still ready to go but the hand holding the car keys was mummified like the rest of him. The heat and wind had dried a lot of people along the coast road but at least now they didn't smell as bad. The cruise ship *Queen Artemisia* was still stuck where I'd seen it, streaked with rust, but the sharks had moved on.

With Jacks closing in it was more crucial than ever that I not be seen in Port Macquarie. Not by the Wild Woman or anyone else who'd made it their home. With no wind to cover my engine noise, I pulled off the road a few hundred metres south of where I had last time. I rolled the quad into kangaroo grass and coastal ti-tree and set Rat in a nest of socks in a pannier before covering everything with the camo netting.

After months jogging North Brother's loop a dozen times a day, I barely broke a sweat running the sea path, even with my weapons and supplies. Pausing in banksias over Town Beach, I scanned with my binoculars, saw clothed skeletons on the sand and up on the breakwall. The spooky tent was gone from North Beach and I thought maybe the ocean winds had blown the Wild Woman away. Up above me, hotel and apartment glass glinted in the glare. My Sandpiper balcony looked unchanged.

I kept to the bush on the headland as I passed the Maritime Museum. When I had to break cover, it took me just a few seconds to cut across the street and disappear into the shadows of the lane behind the Sandpiper. Letting myself into the apartment, I did a quick check of the rooms. Everything was how I'd left it, save for a coating of dust. Shrugging off my backpack, I crept out onto the balcony to the telescope. Aiming it up the coast, scanning east to west, I saw that the fires still had plenty of countryside left to consume.

I spread my map, peered through the eyepiece, looking for any gaps in the conflagration. I couldn't see any. Going north and hoping for a road through the fires would be suicide.

A ghost yacht drifted out past the North Beach's breakers. That's what we should do—commandeer that boat, sail up the coast, put the fires between us and the Jacks. Find a safe port. Learn all the ins and outs of sails and riggings and navigations and take it to Lord Howe Island. I focused the telescope on the yacht. *Felix* was painted on its hull. Even if we could reach it, it'd be no good to us. The mast was snapped and it was sitting low in the water with waves crashing across its bow. But something was off. I peered intently. For its troubles, the *Felix* wasn't lolling. And it was heading straight for Port Macquarie. Like it was under power and being steered. Water jetted from its hull. As though under pressure. Then

I saw him—a dark head pop up from the cabin and take the wheel.

My mind churned. The Jacks had us surrounded, were coming in from the sea—

Except they couldn't be Jacks. They were coming from outside the Radius and from the wrong direction. Surely if they were Jacks they'd be getting support from other boats or choppers. I saw the skipper yell into the cabin. He wasn't alone.

I grabbed my stuff, slammed the door behind me, took the concrete stairs four at a time and bolted along the lane. By the time I was in the trees on the headland, the *Felix* was foundering off the entrance to the Hastings River, being pushed by waves towards the southern breakwall. Through my binoculars, the skipper shouted at people below decks. I thought he'd lost control. Maybe they'd run out of fuel. Maybe the engine had gotten swamped. People staggered from the cabin in yellow life jackets. A weathered blonde woman with her arm around a curly-haired girl, followed by a younger woman and a bronze-skinned boy. The skipper urged them overboard as a wave swept the yacht closer to the rocks. The older woman held the girl as they jumped into the water and towed her clear through the swell. The other woman followed and waved for the boy to jump.

It looked like they were going to make it. Except they'd eventually fall victim to the Jacks.

I couldn't help them. Not without risking everyone. The time it took to explain the danger to them would add to the danger of the others being found in Colonial Town. And if the people from the *Felix* didn't want to come with me, they'd be able to betray me if they got caught. I was trying to decide what to do when I heard the man yelling 'No!' and saw him waving his hands frantically at the boy, who'd pulled out an orange gun.

There was a puff of smoke and a screech as the flare shot into the sky and erupted as a pink star. I was transfixed and terrified as it began its slow bright descent to the sea surface under its parachute. Ten nautical miles—that's how far it'd be visible in daylight. Forty at night. I knew because I had a flare gun in one of the quad's panniers. With the world in perpetual twilight, the distress signal the boy had just sent up would easily have been seen from Crowdy Head—or however far north the Jacks had gotten by now.

When I looked back at the people from the *Felix*, they were all in the water, five yellow-jacketed figures swimming slowly for shore together as their sinking yacht swirled towards the breakwalls. I wanted to shout they had to go faster. They had to get out of the water before the sharks arrived. Then they had to hide because worse monsters lived on land.

I leapt up and ran down the sea path towards a coastal rock platform. I ditched my rifle and backpack and raced into the surf, waving and shouting for them to hurry, to come my way rather than go onto the main beach. When they were close enough, I helped the older woman and the girl get to their feet in the cold surf.

'Thank you,' the woman spluttered. 'Help me get her to shore. But be careful—we think she has appendicitis.'

The girl's eyes were glazed and she was shivering badly.

'Up here,' I said, draping one of the girl's arms over my shoulder. 'Quickly.'

The woman and I carried her onto the wet sand in a little cove between rocks. The others waded ashore and dropped dripping and panting beside us.

'Thank you,' the man said, the boy under one arm and the younger woman under the other.

There was a splintering crunch as the *Felix* smashed into the southern breakwall's tip.

'Shit,' the man said. 'We—'

His eyes went to me and my .45.

'Come with me,' I said.

He nodded, let his people go, got to his feet and followed me. His eyes widened as I retrieved my AK-47 and backpack and I heard the women and children whimper when they saw me with the weapon.

'Please, don't hurt my family,' he said and now I heard his American accent. 'Whatever you want with me—'

'It's okay,' I said loudly, eyes going to his family, making sure they could see I had the muzzle of my gun pointed at the sand. 'I'm not going to hurt anyone.'

I lowered my voice, stepped closer to the man. 'What's your name?'

'Willard. Will. Will Jackson.'

'Okay, Will,' I said. 'I'm Danby. If I wanted to hurt you, you'd all be dead in the water. You get that, right?'

He nodded but gulped like I might change my mind. I didn't blame the guy. After months of whatever they'd been through, he'd just managed to escape a sinking yacht and make it ashore with his family only to wind up at the mercy of a crazed teenager in camouflage gear wielding an assault rifle.

'Take these,' I said, thrusting the keys to the apartment at him. He looked at my hand like I was offering him poison. I pointed up at the building. 'The Sandpiper. Enter by fire stairs at the back. All the way to the top. Apartment six-oh-five.'

'But we need to get help for my daughter,' he protested. 'We thought there might be a doctor, someone here who—'

'Do you love your daughter?'

'Do I what?'

'Will, do you love your daughter? And your family?'

He looked at me like I was crazy but nodded.

'Then get them off this beach and into that apartment as fast as you can,' I said. 'Stay down and stay away from the windows. The people who're coming? They'll kill you all if they see you.'

THIRTY-THREE

HB wipes tears from her cheeks as her cottage and camp recede in the rear-vision mirror. Lottie's in the back listening to the music player. I sit in the passenger seat with my assault rifle at my side and .45 down on the floor by my feet. The dirt road dips and twists and curves through bush. Despite the cold, I keep my window down, listening for choppers over the engine noise and the crunch of the road beneath our tyres.

'Lottie being free means you can get your brother back, doesn't it?' HB says.

'That's the idea,' I say. 'Not that it's going to be possible. He's hundreds of kilometres away and in the middle of a thousand of them.'

HB looks at me and lets out a little laugh.

'What?' I say.

'You singlehandedly killed nine armed bastards last night,' she says. 'If you get a chance to get your brother, I wouldn't want to be standing in your way.'

I'm not sure whether to take it as a high compliment or harsh criticism so I say nothing and concentrate on the sky and hills.

When we reach the highway, HB keeps a steady pace so she can weave around stalled vehicles and sprawled bodies. Roos grazing at the side of the road bound away into the clutches of the gum trees. As it gets darker, I use my flashlight to study the map, look for landmarks, give directions to the unsealed route that cuts across the countryside and comes out just a little north of Colonial Town.

In the cargo area, my backpack shares space with the six plastic crates HB packed. Five of them hold jars and jars of heirloom seeds she says could eventually feed an entire country. The sixth contains her typewriter and a manuscript. Its title page reads *The Feline Frontier.*

'So,' I say. 'How'd it get up there? The cat, I mean.'

HB glances at me with mock offence. 'What, you mean you're not going to read my book?'

She knows almost everything now. Where we're driving. Who I hope we find there. What my escape plan is. Why it's probably the only chance for freedom. How many things could go wrong.

'In case I don't make it,' I say. 'I'd hate to die not knowing.'

'It's told in the first person,' she says. 'Well, first cat.'

HB laughs and launches into the story of how a kitten is smuggled onto a tourist moon flight and transferred to the international space station where she's adopted as a pet. Fed enhanced NASA food by her keepers, her cat mind gets boosted so much that she's able to subtly help the astronauts with their mission. Then a burst of alien radiation hits the ship and she gains the ability to see through time and . . .

'I told you it was stupid,' HB says. 'I can *hear* your eyes rolling.'

I can't help but guffaw.

'I was listening,' Lottie pipes up from the back. 'I'll read it.'

'Here,' I say. 'Pull in here.'

We're at the service station a kilometre up the highway from Colonial Town. Bowsers and shopfront glass appear as HB parks under the roof canopy and kills the engine and headlights.

'It's not far from here,' I say, checking my watch in the flashlight. 'Eight fifty-five.'

I'd asked Nathan to listen to his walkie-talkie on the hour after dark and that I'd let him know when I was ready to come in. That way they wouldn't mistake me for a hostile—and I'd be less likely to wander into a trap.

'What happens if you can't get him on that thing?' Lottie asks.

I don't answer. It'll mean something has gone wrong. That the Jacks descended on Colonial Town before I drew them off to Baroonah. That the people from the *Felix* turned out to be marauders. That Johnno lost his nerve waiting and convinced the others to go bush. If I don't get a response from Colonial Town, I have to assume one or more of these nightmares has become reality. Then HB, Lottie and I take our chances driving west or north.

'I'll be back in a minute.' I get out of the car and walk across the bitumen to the verge. I don't want HB and Lottie to listen when I try to raise Nathan. There's a chance I'll get a Jack on the other end of the walkie-talkie. There's a chance I'll get Nathan but be told we're not welcome. What I've done in the past two days wasn't exactly decided on by democratic process. Drawing the Jacks away from Port Macquarie put everyone at risk if I was caught and made to talk. And promising the people from the *Felix* that they'd find safe refuge at Colonial Town might not have gone down too well with Johnno, Stannis and Gail. Returning with more people to take care of could see them lose it with me once and for all.

I check the walkie-talkie's display. Eight fifty-eight. The thing throws just enough light that I can see a fuzzy trilobite at my feet. I gasp and stumble away from a little ribcage with grass growing through it. For a minute, I fight away thoughts of dead children, focus on those I can save.

'Me,' I say precisely at 9 p.m. 'Come back. Over.'

I release the talk button and there's an immediate return crackle. 'I've got you. Over.'

Nathan. I want it to really be him. I want to say I was worried. Tell him how sorry I am for the way I've been. Say I want to be the way we were before we left Evan behind in Samsara. Say he was right about there being hope for Evan and that I'm so thankful he stopped me from shooting him. But I can't say any of it. No names. No locations. Nothing to give us away. My rules. Nathan could have a gun to his head. Or it could be a Jack imitating him.

Turn that scenario around and he's thinking the same could be true of me.

'Name the most boring place in the universe,' I say.

'Law of Small Numbers,' he says. 'Over.'

I want to dance for joy like I did on the peak. It's the name of the bland accountant's office in Parramatta. Jack couldn't know that and Nathan didn't add 'red' to his answer to indicate he was in trouble. It's him. He's safe. Colonial Town hasn't been found.

It's his turn to ask me something. 'Horse we shared? Over.'

My turn. I can't keep the laugh out of my voice as I remember us bum to bum in the saddle on that big beast. 'Prince. Over.'

It's his turn to ask me something. 'Over.'

'Two friendlies with me,' I say. 'Are we good with that? Over.'

'Hang on. Over.'

There's a long minute of radio silence. I kick at bits of crumbly bitumen. My best guess is that Nathan's conferring with Johnno and whoever else. While I'm not sure any of them really trust me, they know I'm the last girl to trust anyone I'm not sure of.

'Come in,' Nathan says. 'Over.'

'I'm here,' I say. 'Over.'

'No, I mean you're good to come in,' he replies. 'Over.'

'Be there in ten, over.'

I click off the walkie-talkie and stand there in the darkness with tears streaming down my face. I feel like I'm going home.

THIRTY-FOUR

When I got to the breakwall, I looked back to see Will and his family climbing the hill beneath the Sandpiper. Right ahead of me, the *Felix* was out in the river, listing to one side, hull cracked where it'd hit the rocks. The boat had sunk lower but it wouldn't go to the bottom soon enough. When the Jacks arrived, they'd find an abandoned yacht but not a survivor who could've fired the flare. It'd look wrong.

I pulled my AK-47 from my shoulder and took aim at the fibreglass hull. Emptying a thirty-round magazine into the boat might sink it faster but there'd still be the mystery of how a flare got fired. I set my rifle down and pulled a grenade from my backpack. My practice up on North Brother meant I could pitch twice as far as I had as a junior softballer. The cabin was home base. I pulled the pin and hurled the grenade across the water.

Stu-rike! I thought as it vanished into the open doorway and I ducked behind the breakwall's painted rocks. A roar and blast of heat rolled over me. Sticking my head up, I saw the yacht burning under a pall of oily black smoke. Gas cylinder. Fuel tanks. Something in there had gone up.

Heart hammering, I ran for the Sandpiper, and got halfway there when the atmosphere rippled with the horrible pulsing I hadn't heard for months. Diving into windbreak bushes at the top of the beach, I flattened myself in the sand and garbage just as two black choppers speared up over the headland. I tugged my yowie suit from my backpack and spread it over me. Peering through camo streamers, I watched the choppers sweep over the sea and surf, open doors showing men with guns and binoculars looking and aiming in every direction.

I had my AK-47, ten full clips, another eleven grenades, the sawn-off and the .45. But even if I could summon the luck Nathan and I had on the Bull Run Road and in Samsara, I couldn't destroy both helicopters in a stand-up fight. Even with my yowie suit on properly, the second I started firing, their bullets would strip every leaf from the trees and shred me into the deal. And even if by some miracle I prevailed, that'd only bring the rest of the Jacks swarming over Port Macquarie.

Downdrafts flattening the swell beneath them, the choppers crept towards the burning yacht, turning and tilting and giving Jack and the hivemind the best all-angles view. While the thousand-eyed monster's attention was there, I scrambled through the scrub to the coastal path. Safer beneath the canopy of banksias and vines, I watched the choppers waltz around the burning yacht. After a moment, they broke their dance—one sliding up the river while the other hovered over the burned caravan park. They were looking for any sign anyone had escaped the yacht. Finding nothing, I hoped they'd conclude there'd been a fire aboard an empty vessel and that'd been what set off a flare. That there was no one to find.

Fear spiked my veins when I thought Will and his family might be up on the balcony, waving the choppers over to rescue them from the crazy girl with the machine gun. But a glance up at the Sandpiper balcony showed it was as still and empty as hundreds of others. Maybe the family from the *Felix* had split the difference and gone somewhere they could hide from me *and* whoever had just flown in.

As soon as I'd lost both choppers behind riverside pines and hotels, I bolted across the road and followed the wet footprints into the lane behind the Sandpiper. The yacht guys had trusted me enough to do what I'd said and I hoped the wind would dry our tracks if the choppers came back this way.

• • •

'It's me,' I said, knocking on the apartment door. 'Danby.'

The younger woman opened the door and ushered me inside.

'What's going on?' she whispered.

'Where are the others?'

'Front bedroom.'

Will and his wife stood by the window, carefully peering out through the blinds at the choppers thundering over the town. The kids sat in the bath of the ensuite, the boy patting the girl's head and trying to comfort her.

Will glanced at me. 'You blew up the yacht?'

'Who's in those helicopters?' his wife added. 'What the hell's going on?'

'One thing at a time,' I said. 'You're all related?'

Will looked at me like this was hardly important. But I had the gun so he answered. 'This is my wife, Amber. Her sister, Rachel. The boy's Hal. The girl's Milly.'

I nodded. Will was tall and muscular, a better-looking version of Barack Obama before he got old. Amber was genetically blessed: wide green eyes, buttery skin. Rachel was a younger, less lined version of her sister. The kids had golden complexions and ochre curls. Half Will's genes, half Amber's. I didn't know anything about *Situs inversus* and heredity except that no one we'd encountered had a parent or sibling or kid who'd also survived. I thought if I got the stethoscope out I'd find five normal hearts—just like the boy Liam.

'Can you please,' Amber said, 'tell us what's going on? We need to get Milly some help. Is there anyone you know of? Could those people in the helicopters—'

I shook my head. 'I've got a friend who can help her. But we've got to make sure we stay safe. I'll explain everything, okay?'

The building started to vibrate as a chopper came closer.

'Down,' I said. 'Everyone.'

We dropped to the carpet as the shadow of the aircraft darkened the windows. I hoped the Jacks looking at the blinds and the balcony didn't see anything that gave us away. And I prayed they didn't look straight down and see the wet and sandy footprints we'd left on the road.

Rachel clamped her hands on her ears as the roar of the rotors increased and the chopper rose above the Sandpiper and flew low over the roof. I looked through a sliver of blind down at the road beneath the Sandpiper. The tracks that'd been there seconds ago had been dried and dispersed by the rotor's downdraft.

'Stay here and stay down,' I said. 'Keep the kids in the bathroom.'

I crawled with my AK-47 to the back study and peeked through the blinds.

'Damnit,' I said.

Chopper 101 had already landed on the green expanse of Oxley Oval behind the yellow Maritime Museum. Chopper 102, which'd just buzzed our building, was coming in to touch down beside it. A dozen Jacks climbed out. Khaki uniforms, combat boots, some wearing flak jackets, all carrying AR-15s and belts with grenades. These guys were serious. Even from here, I could see they didn't speak, just moved as though synchronised. Two stayed behind, guarding the choppers, as the others fanned out, weapons sweeping in front of them, moving steadily in lockstep towards the river.

I crept back to the front room, carefully cracked a window an inch so we could better hear what was going on. I handed my binoculars to Amber and took out my little telescope. We stood at the edges of the windows, peering through the blinds as the Jacks swept along the beach and footpath towards the breakwall. My gut heaved every time one of them paused to stare at something. I hoped the footprints I'd left there had evaporated.

'Who's that?' Will said, pointing west.

I ducked beneath the window line and uttered a long mournful *fuuuck* as I saw who he meant.

The Wild Woman was skipping along the river path, waving her spidery hands at the Jacks and singing something to them.

'Yoo-hoo'—was the sound that floated up to us. Wherever she'd been hiding, she'd decided *these* were the good guys.

'Yoo-hoo'—like she was calling a neighbour over for a cup of tea, dear.

'Does she know we're here?' Will asked urgently.

I didn't know where the Wild Woman had been or what she'd seen.

As one, the Jacks stiffened and went for their weapons. The Wild Woman shot her hands into the air and froze. A Jack slung his gun over a shoulder and beckoned her forwards. She came, lowering her hands, smiling and nodding at him and grinning at the other Jacks as they pointed their weapons at the ground or sky. The lead Jack spoke to her softly. Rolled a cigarette. Offered and lit it. She smoked. He rolled one for himself. They talked. Shooting the breeze. I tried to lip read. Not a chance even with the telescope.

The Jack pulled out a photo. The dull sky glinted off lamination. But I saw it well enough: my face. It was the last selfie I'd taken a few days before Christmas with Jacinta. It'd been on the phone I'd had to leave behind in Penrith. I'd had long dark hair then. They'd cropped her out and photoshopped my hair very short to recreate the me Evan had seen with singed hair in the wake of the chopper explosion. I wondered how many other Specials had been shown this image and interrogated.

The Wild Woman dragged on her cigarette and picked tobacco from her teeth as she stared at the picture before shaking her head. The Jack insisted she look again. She was more adamant. He pointed at the smouldering yacht. Wild Woman shook her head about that. Where she nodded—where she stabbed a bony finger—was back towards town. The Jack watched her smoking imitation of a creature with bulging eyes and long horns and waving tentacles and claw hands. She threw her arms high and wide to show them how tall and wide I was. Mimicked clawing and chewing as she pointed at the blackened bodies all around us. The poor thing had spent months living in terror of the thing she'd seen running after her. *Me.*

Wild Woman stepped back, as if to say, well, come on, let's go hunt the creature down. A red halo appeared around her head and she dropped as the gunshot reached us. We fell to the carpet, looking at each other.

'Oh my God,' said Amber. 'Did they just shoot her?'

I hadn't seen anyone die for months. It was like the first time. I fought to keep from pissing myself. Tried to remember all the books I'd read about how to control fear and focus. When I nodded at them it felt like a palsy.

'Oh my God, oh my God,' Rachel said, voice getting louder.

Will clamped a hand over her mouth.

'That photo,' he whispered. 'Is it . . . you?'

The look in my eyes gave him his answer.

'They're after you?'

'They're after anybody,' I said, getting myself together. 'Believe me, if you go out there, you're all as dead as she is.'

When we looked again, the Jacks were spreading out in a line that stretched from the road beneath us to the river. Then they started walking towards town, heads bowed, methodically scanning, like members of a search party looking for any trace of a missing person.

The poor Wild Woman's craziness had made the town the focus of their investigation. When they got to Gizmos they'd see empty boxes of surveillance and security equipment. That might be okay. But in the wake of the fright the Wild Woman had given me, I hadn't disposed of the clothes that I'd shed in Davo's. My red boots were sitting right where I'd left them on the carpet. Jack wouldn't forget those in a hurry because they were where I'd concealed the skewer I'd used to stab him.

Sooner or later—hours, days—they'd find them and know I'd been here. Then they'd all storm into Port Macquarie and rip through the apartments and houses. Eventually they'd find Colonial Town.

When the Jacks were out of sight, I told Will and Amber and Rachel my story as best I could and they believed everything I said. Unlike Johnno, they'd had the benefit of seeing the Jacks first—how they didn't talk, how they moved as one, how they murdered without a second thought.

Then it was their turn.

Will was an electrical engineer from San Diego. Amber had lived in Brisbane before moving to California to study physics. They'd met at a sailing club, married and had the kids. Mid-December they'd holidayed with Rachel in Noumea, where she taught, with the plan to sail a friend's yacht back west for a Christmas with the Aussie side of the family. But delays getting away were compounded by bad weather so they were still two hundred nautical miles east of Brisbane when December 25th dawned. They'd made a sat-phone call to Amber's parents and everyone had agreed it was no big deal, that the ham and turkey would keep and the presents could still be given on Boxing Day.

Will and Amber and Rachel had just been happy that the sun was out and the swell had died down. They cooked up a brunch of bacon and eggs and gave the kids the presents they'd been saving and spent the afternoon playing board games. That evening Amber put them another hundred miles closer to their destination before deploying the sea anchor and settling in for the night. Will woke at three and took the wheel so they'd be at Amber's folks' place by lunchtime.

A few hours later he thought he'd royally screwed up when he saw the glow of sunrise *ahead* instead of behind the boat. But the compass still said they were heading west and the GPS reckoned the yacht was within sight of the Queensland coast.

Will could raise no one on the sat-phone. Got static when he tried the radio. He tried to convince himself he was seeing a bushfire. That the yacht had drifted off course to somewhere remote and the compass and GPS were being thrown by the same interference that was screwing with the communications. But by the time he woke Amber and the sun had risen behind them, it was clear that the part of Australia they'd been trying to reach was lost inside a wall of fire filling the sky with smoke.

'We thought ...' he said, 'We thought—well, we didn't know what to think.'

Rachel joined us on the carpet. 'Hal's asleep. Milly's almost there.'

'Thanks, Rach,' said Amber, hugging her sister.

'Her temperature's down a bit,' Rachel said, nodding at me, 'Now she's had some painkillers.'

I nodded. 'We'll get Milly some proper help. As soon as we can get out of here. You were saying you didn't know what'd happened.'

Will and Amber's expressions darkened at the memory.

'A war or a comet strike,' she said. 'They were our first thoughts.'

They'd resisted the instinct to try to get to her parents and turned the boat north to where the fires on the coast seemed less intense. What they saw of the unburned shore through binoculars was even scarier: hundreds of people seemed to have died on jetties and beaches, lawns and balconies. The decks of boats drifting closer to shore were scattered with bodies.

'That's when we thought it'd been some sort of viral outbreak,' Will continued. 'We took the boat out to sea before the kids woke up.'

Rather than lie, Will and Amber told Hal and Milly and Rachel there'd been a terrible calamity and it wasn't safe to go to Australia. When Rachel had helped calm the kids, she tried to convince Will and Amber that they'd made a mistake or suffered a joint hallucination.

'It was only when we heard bits and pieces on the shortwave band that I believed,' Rachel said.

Amber touched her shoulder. 'We talked to someone in Papua New Guinea, a guy in Malaysia, some dude in New Zealand. They all said what you'd said—that everyone could hear everyone's thoughts and it'd sent them crazy and into comas.'

After that, Will and Amber concluded ghost boats didn't pose a contamination risk and, with Rachel keeping the kids from seeing bodies on decks, they'd raided drifting vessels for food, water and fuel. Two weeks ago, one hundred miles off the coast of Toowoomba and worried their luck with the weather would run out, they'd decided to try to get to Sydney.

'The guy in New Zealand said he'd heard patchy radio transmissions there at one stage,' Amber said. 'Coming out of Richmond Air Base. Choppers doing rescue missions. Was that them? The Jacks?'

I nodded, though I had no idea why the Jacks would be radioing or rescuing anyone.

'A storm snapped the mast a few days ago,' Will said. 'Then Milly started getting sick yesterday and I lost my cool. I ran us straight into a submerged boat. Put a hole in the hull and started taking on water. You know the rest.'

What I also knew was that everything they'd told me was evidence for what the teddy bear arm had suggested.

'You haven't experienced telepathy?' I asked.

They shook their heads.

'Jesus, you're so lucky.'

What I'd thought about the boy—Liam—was right. He had been far enough away. But these five people had been together.

I explained about Liam and my theory and told them about the ocean liner just a little down the coast. That there must've been thousands aboard and they'd all suffered the same fate as those on land.

They took it all in with wide eyes.

'What's the critical mass of people?' I wondered aloud.

'Chances are that liner would've been coming into a port for Christmas,' Will said. 'Been close to shore. Within the Radius you talk about. Or within the radius of other people who'd been afflicted and were trying to flee. After it all went to hell, it could've drifted for weeks.'

I nodded. It was making sense. But we hadn't answered the question of how many people it took for the Snap to occur. Liam and his dad had been safe out in the remote mountains. The five on board the yacht hadn't triggered a spontaneous Snap.

'With your family in Australia—' I stopped myself from finishing the thought. 'What I mean is, you didn't think about trying to get back to your people in California?'

Amber shook her head, told me what she feared had happened to her adopted nation's nuclear reactors—and those across the rest of the northern hemisphere. 'We're safer here than anywhere,' she said. 'Well, that's what we thought until you told us about those Jacks or whatever out there.'

Will took her hand and looked at me. 'What do we do?'

I told them the truth: that I didn't think the Jacks would leave now they were in Port Macquarie. There'd be more of them and they'd search until they found me. From what I'd seen they'd kill anyone else they came across. Fear came off Will, Amber and Rachel as a sweaty stink.

But I felt calm. It was like everything was clicking into place. I didn't need to fear this. I needed to *embrace* it. *This* was what I'd been preparing for. What I had to do was suddenly clear in outline if not detail. I was ready for whatever waited down the road. The worst that could happen was it'd be the end of me. And then nothing would matter anymore.

Pulling out a map, I told them my plan. I'd make my way back along the coastal path. My quad was parked far enough away that the engine noise shouldn't carry into Port Macquarie. I'd go south into the hinterland and stage a diversion to draw the search in that direction. They had to keep watch. Be ready to go when they saw the Jacks come back to the choppers in a rush and take off. That's when it'd be safer to go quickly and quietly to the station wagon on the coast road. I told them about the guy with the keys in his hand.

'It'll be gross,' I said.

If the station wagon didn't start, they had to find another vehicle. I showed them Wauchope. Once they got there, I told them to hide in Wauchope's pharmacy. A guy would come and make a *cooee*. He was a medical student who'd fix Milly and take them to safety. At least if they were caught and forced to talk, they wouldn't be able to name Nathan or spill about Colonial Town. It wasn't foolproof but it was the best I could do.

'What do we do till then?' Rachel asked, looking around like Jacks might be about to burst from the walk-in robes.

I told them to keep away from the windows, only use candles in the bathroom, make no unnecessary noise. I pulled the sawn-off shotgun from my backpack along with a box of shells.

'You know how to use this?' I asked.

Will nodded. 'But what you said, about their minds being linked, it won't do much good, right?'

I nodded. 'Better to have options.'

Amber put her hand over her mouth and tears spilled from her eyes. Rachel hugged her and glared at me. Will's gaze glimmered as what I said sank in. His fingers tightened around the shotgun barrel. I guessed he was tossing up another option: blow me away and surrender to the Jacks. I didn't blink and I saw the idea pass from his eyes.

'I won't let it come to that,' Will said. 'Never.'

'Good,' I said. 'Neither will I.'

'How long do we give you?' Amber asked.

'If the helicopters aren't gone by tomorrow night, you should assume I didn't make it.'

Will swallowed hard. 'Jesus.'

'And if that happens?' Amber said.

If there were still just a dozen Jacks in town these guys could conceivably elude them. I traced my finger along the patches of green that extended almost all the way from Port Macquarie back to Wauchope.

'Wait until dark. Try to get out there anyway. Once you're clear you could find a car. Or you could walk it in one night.'

They looked at me like I was out of my mind. I remembered Oscar telling us the same thing about the bush between

Riverview and Richmond. He'd been right. We could and we did walk it. But most of the people who'd started that journey were now dead.

'It's possible,' I said, tapping the map emphatically. 'It's only twenty—'

I saw where my finger was resting—on King Creek where I'd seen the *Fu Hao*.

'You guys can sail any type of boat?' I asked.

Will and Amber traded a look.

'Sure,' he said. 'Well, not ocean liners or warships.'

Ducking into the bathroom, I retrieved the local magazine and flicked to the ad that showed the *Fu Hao* in all her glory. I set it on the carpet beside the Lord Howe Island brochure.

'Can you take that from here to there?'

Will and Amber hunched over the photos.

'Why there?' Amber asked.

'Isolated location with sustainable energy and a tiny population,' I said. 'If they're all dead we can deal with the bodies.'

'And if they're alive?' Will asked.

'Let's hope the welcome mat's out for refugees,' I said. 'But if we don't take the chance then we're stuck here with Jacks and bushfires.'

'Getting there is completely feasible,' Will said.

'Really?' I let myself smile.

He nodded. 'Chinese junks are built strong to withstand big seas. So long as we had enough fuel and a bit of luck with the weather, I reckon we'd be there in a few days.'

·•·

Three hours later, I was under the cover of the petrol station near Colonial Town. I pulled out the walkie-talkie. If the Jacks were listening, they'd be in range. It was a risk I had to take and so I tapped out the Morse code for 'K' and waited. Just when I started to fume that Nathan wasn't monitoring, I heard a crackle and got a 'K' back.

'What was I carrying when I met you?' he asked.

'Nail gun,' I said. 'Over.'

'Copy that. Your turn. Over.'

What did I know about Nathan that no one else did? I thought back to what we'd talked about that first morning we were together in Parramatta—and the last time we'd traded any sort of banter while we waited to stage our ambush in Samsara.

'What star sign are you? Over.'

The walkie-talkie crackled. 'Not that I believe in it but Gemini.'

I could hear Nathan's smile. He had no idea what was going on. The past five days—the teddy bear arm, the outriders at Crowdy Head, the *Felix* and the black choppers, the Wild Woman's murder and the ride I'd just done—so much had happened.

'You're good to proceed,' he said. 'Over.'

Nathan met me at the gate with his AK-47. He couldn't hide what he was thinking when he saw me in the yowie suit. His expression was like Dad's had been when he'd visited me in hospital after my supposed psychiatric episode. Equal parts compassion and concern.

'What're you wearing?' Nathan said, hand out to me. 'Jesus, you need to come inside. We really need to talk, okay? I've been hard on you.'

'Nathan.'

'I'm sorry. You saved my life—'

'Nathan!'

'—fixed my leg, really made this place safe but—'

'Nathan!' I shouted. 'Please. None of that matters, okay? Not now. They're here.'

He flinched. 'Jacks?'

I nodded.

'Stannis said he thought he'd heard choppers in the distance. I thought he was having a morphine hallucination.'

I shook my head. 'They landed at Port Macquarie earlier today. Twelve Jacks.'

'Fuck.'

'A couple down at Crowdy Head. It's a safe bet there's a lot more farther south.'

'Are you saying we're trapped?' he asked.

'Not for long,' I said. 'I'm going to create a diversion. Draw 'em off. Buy us some time.'

'I'm coming with you,' he said.

I shook my head. Told him about Will and his family. How sick Milly was. That the diversion was also to give them a chance to escape—and that they'd be waiting for him at the pharmacy.

'Let me get this straight,' Nathan said. 'You just decided all of that? For me—and for us? We need to talk to Johnno and Stannis. They've got a right to decide if—'

'There's no time,' I said. 'If the Jacks find them in Port Macquarie, they're all dead.'

'And so are we.'

'No,' I said. 'They only know to be at Wauchope pharmacy. They don't know your name or where this place is.'

Nathan stared at me. 'It's what, a kilometre from here? And you don't think the Jacks could be waiting for me there if they get the whole *cooee* thing out of them?'

He was right.

'You've put us all at risk.'

'I'm sorry,' I said.

All I'd wanted to do this morning was make the boy smile. I pulled the blue bear arm from my backpack and showed it to Nathan. He looked from me to it and back again. I saw recognition in his eyes.

'Where'd that come from?'

I turned the bear arm in my hands as I explained where I'd found it, what I'd thought it meant and how Will and his family proved there was more hope than we'd thought. That Lord Howe Island might be a safe place. That Will and Amber could get us there. That only Nathan could save Milly's life. That I was the one who'd put them all in danger from the start and that it was me who had to try to draw it away.

'I'm sorry,' I said, blinking up at Nathan. 'I'm sorry I've put you at risk—more risk—but I couldn't just leave them. I didn't have a choice.'

Nathan studied me a moment. 'Yes, you did. You could've left them and you didn't. You made the right choice.'

'Really?'

He nodded. 'Really.'

I handed him the bear arm. 'If I'm not back—'

Nathan shook his head but he had to hear this.

'If I'm not back in forty-eight hours it means I'm not coming back. You guys make whatever plans you need to and go.' I tapped my walkie-talkie. 'If I get back, I'll be on the same channel that I was tonight. Listen for me on the hour.'

Nathan's eyes glimmered. My throat was tight. We'd gone months barely speaking to each other. Now there was so much to say and no time. I couldn't drag this out or I wouldn't go and then we'd all die.

'Sew that on for the boy,' I said. 'Liam—that's his name.'

I turned and got back on my quad. Rode off without looking back.

·•·

As I raced south on back roads, I hoped the quad noise didn't reach the Jacks I knew were out there. I had my plan by the time I pulled into the burned-out farmhouse on the back blocks of Baroonah. After I watched a while to make sure I was the only one there, I started searching houses and assembling what I needed in the mansion 'base' the Jacks would discover. By mid-morning I'd set it up the way I wanted and it was almost time to set fire to the hotel.

Exhausted from my efforts, waiting for the next pill to kick in, I sat by the window in the upstairs bedroom and looked out over the rose garden at Baroonah's intersection and main street beyond. Not long from now I'd be out there playing dead and waiting for the Jacks to come this way from Crowdy Head. There was every chance my ambush would backfire and get me killed. That'd be it. All she wrote. The end. I'd leave nothing behind. I thought about Mum's paintings in her studio in Shadow Valley. They might be found one day as testament to her time on this planet. Same went for the messages left in the guestbook at Samsara and the engraved padlocks on North Brother and the painted breakwall rocks at Port Macquarie. Individuals who'd left their mark. But there'd be no trace of me. I'd rot on the street for real. Then I'd be dust in the breeze.

I looked at an antique desk in a corner of the room and wondered whether I had time to use the quill pen and fancy paper to set down everything that'd happened to me. 'I always knew I'd see the end of the world'—that's how I'd start it. What I'd write after that—well, I didn't have a clue. Who'd want to read it anyway? Anyone who stumbled on my memoir would've seen their share of atrocities and endured their own struggles. The last thing they'd need would be to learn how it'd gone down for some random teenage girl.

But Jack. *He* would read whatever I wrote. If he was about to kill me, I wanted to have the last word. I remembered the Wild Woman's symbols and phrases and the butcherbird's victims strung up on the wire in Colonial Town. How spooked I'd been by that. That was how I wanted Jack to feel. Forever haunted. By me.

It made sense he'd believe in ghosts because he kinda was one. His very existence proved transcendence after death. If him, why not me? For all his knowledge he wasn't close to coldly rational. If he had been he wouldn't be after me.

Jack had written me a letter once to screw with my head. It was time to return the favour. I sat at the desk, got creative, added phrases and a symbol borrowed from the Wild Woman. The quill and ink made it look spiky and spooky. For a finishing touch, I took my straight razor from my breast pocket and made a little slice into myself so I could sign with a bloody thumbprint. I sealed the letter inside a plastic bag and stapled it inside my flak jacket. Right near my breast where I'd kept Jack's letter. I had nothing to lose. Just hoped that when he read it he wouldn't be able to shake it. Would feel and fear me for the rest of his days.

3

Kick out the Jams

THIRTY-FIVE

I sit at one of the big tables in the Queen Vic Tea Rooms with Nathan, Will, Amber and Stannis and we talk about the *Fu Hao*'s likely maintenance issues and how much fuel and food we'll need to load. Dressed in her best clothes, Gail fusses happily at the next table, setting napkins and glasses for the dinner party she thinks we're having. Through an open door, HB organises Rachel and Johnno in the kitchen as they baste chickens and roast vegetables from Colonial Town's coop and garden. On a mattress in a corner, Hal plays *Snots 'N' Bots* while Milly reads a tablet quietly and recuperates from the emergency appendectomy Nathan performed by torchlight in Wauchope's pharmacy. Close by, Lottie flicks the pages of a Dr Seuss book for Liam who hugs his surgically restored blue bear. All of them like this make me happy. Even though I'm sad I won't be with them much longer.

I've shown the adults the video of Jack's forces arriving in Baroonah and all the aircraft that streaked along the horizon. Explained how the Radius now works so that our enemies can cover a huge amount of territory. They know what we're up against and that even if we could escape on land we'll always be looking over our shoulders—and at the mercy of marauders like the Board or the chaos of bushfires.

We keep the conversation lighter during dinner and put the kids to bed. Then we debate my suggestion that we should camp near King Creek while we prepare the *Fu Hao* for her journey. While no one wants to eat rations and sleep in tents in the bush, especially not when we've just had fresh food and are about to head to warm beds in cosy cottages, they come around to seeing it's the safest course of action. Us all being there together means we can set sail for Lord Howe Island the moment the boat's ready. *If* the *Fu Hao* is seaworthy.

'So, everyone will be ready an hour before dawn tomorrow,' Nathan says, holding up his wine glass. 'As soon as it's light enough to drive, we roll out of here.'

'Cheers,' says Johnno, raising his stein of beer. 'I always wanted to go overseas.'

'You'll love it,' Gail says. 'I've heard this is the best time to go.'

We erupt into laughter and clink our glasses. I'm drinking mineral water. I need to stay clear.

'What?' Gail says as Johnno hugs her to him and she beams and blushes. I'm not sure who she thinks she's with or what she's about to do but I'm glad she's happy for the moment.

'What will the Lord Howe people think?' Rachel says quietly. 'Like the people HB talked to on the cattle station— they might not want visitors.'

It's a good point. We don't know what to expect. If they're not all dead, they might not want more people using their resources.

'We could radio ahead?' HB says.

I shake my head. 'If the Jacks heard, they'd know where we're going.'

'I thought the whole Radius thing meant they couldn't follow?' Amber says.

'All of them on a boat or in a flotilla, they could come after us. We'll only be safe if they don't have a clue where we've gone.'

Johnno grins in the lantern light. 'So we just land on Lord Howe Island and hope for the best, eh?'

All eyes are on me. I guess that's fair. It is my plan.

'Chances are everyone will be dead,' I say. 'But if they're not we've got a lot to offer. HB can grow food and has enough seeds for a Garden of Eden. Stannis has worked the land. Nathan's medically trained. Will's an engineer, Amber's a scientist, Rachel's a teacher. Johnno, you're a jack-of-all-trades, if you'll pardon the pun.'

'I'm a violinist,' Gail blurts, mimicking playing the instrument. 'Sydney Symphony Orchestra.'

There are smiles all around the table.

'And your skills will come in handy,' HB says to me with a cheeky grin, 'if we get there and find a *Lord of the Flies* kinda deal.'

I laugh, shake my head, glad none of them know the truth.

'Truth is we can't be sure what we'll find or if we'll even make it,' I say, looking at them all before my eyes rest on Nathan. 'But the alternative is taking on a fight we can't win.'

None of them want that. Will takes Amber's hand and HB holds mine and Nathan's.

'If anyone starts singing *Kumbaya*,' Johnno growls, 'I'll get on the walkie-talkie so Jack can come kill the lot of you.'

Back in my cottage, I unroll my sleeping bag.

When I arrived last night, I introduced HB and Lottie, explained what'd happened and what I'd learned. While I was pleased they'd started seriously discussing Lord Howe Island, I was overcome with exhaustion. I left them talking, crashed on my cot in my clothes and slept straight through until just before dinner.

I still feel bone tired. Like I have to pay back all those hours I stole with the dexies. But I can't have another marathon slumber. It's ten now and I need to be up at five. At least tonight I can sleep in the cocoon to which I've been accustomed.

Scree-scree-scree.

I shiver at the memory of Rat. Or at the memory of my hallucination of Rat. Whichever it is—was. I laugh as I picture her serving beers to other critters as the new rodent publican of the Star Hotel. Why not? She was my delusion after all.

Scree-scree-scree.

Now she's back. At least in my head. Like an earworm. Except I've been clean of the drugs for a few days. So I shouldn't be tripping like this. Unless it's some sort of withdrawal symptoms. But if I'm going to hallucinate I'd at the very least like to see my familiar. I can't conjure her except for—

Scree-scree-scree. This time it's louder and followed by a series of little *pips*. Not in my mind. Behind me. I jump up, spin around and see movement at the base of the sleeping bag. I grab my flashlight and peer into its dark folds. Rat's laying against a seam, legs splayed and six pink babies attached to her white belly. She blinks into the glare and I click the light off. I burst out laughing and then cry my heart out.

I awake on the floor an hour before my alarm. I check on Rat and family. They're all sleeping. In a few hours, Colonial Town will be theirs. I tear open a dozen ration packs and make a pile of dehydrated meat and vegetables and rice under the cot. I pour water into a bedpan and set it alongside the larder. I hope I'm giving Rat a few easy weeks or months and that she will forage happily after that. But setting out the supplies—it makes me remember doing the same for the kangaroos and snow leopards and—

I slap my forehead. Realise what I saw that night and might need one day. While Colonial Town sleeps, I pull on my night-vision goggles and gather my weapons, crawl under the section of escape fence and take Nathan's quad off into the night.

THIRTY-SIX

I'm back and making coffee in the kitchen before anyone else is awake. But by 5.30 we're all eating breakfast and the restaurant walls are lined with backpacks, sleeping bags, boxes of rations and crates of water. HB has her typewriter and manuscript. I don't mention the clink of booze in Stannis's backpack. It's like we're about to go on camp. Except for our small arsenal.

'If it's all the same to you,' Stannis says with a wheeze, 'I'll go out the same way I came in.'

Will looks from him to me with a frown. 'The little plane?'

'Ultralight,' Stannis corrects.

'Is that a good idea?' Amber asks. 'I mean, you could be seen.'

'Not in the dark I won't,' Stannis says, tapping a walkie-talkie. 'I'll go ahead, be there in a few minutes, get the lay of the land and call you lot if there's any trouble between here and there.'

There are nods around the table. Everyone wants to know we're not driving straight into Jacks out there on the highway.

I explain how to do a Morse code K and Stannis nods and coughs into his handkerchief.

HB takes his arm. 'Are you up to this?'

'Right as rain,' he says.

•●•

Nathan and Johnno and I wheel the ultralight out on the highway. Stannis climbs into the seat and stows a rifle and walkie-talkie within reach. I hand him my night-vision goggles and he straps them on.

'All you need's a scarf there, Biggles,' Johnno says, giving his shoulder a squeeze. 'Take care, you old fart.'

'Roger that,' Stannis says before he bumps along the highway and lifts off over the cars and trees.

I sit with the walkie-talkie on the quad between the station wagon and panel van. Johnno listens from his driver's seat, HB and Nathan beside him, Gail, Lottie and Liam in the back with a stack of supplies. Will pushes the last pack into the back of the station wagon as Amber, Rachel, Hal and Milly listen eagerly for Stannis's message. The radio crackles in my hand. Long beep. Short beep. Long beep.

'K,' I say.

I smile. Nod at the others. Start my engine and lead off. I volunteered to be the point person. If we encounter enemies I'm the best equipped to hold them off while the others try to get away. But I'm under no illusions that we'll survive and escape if it comes to that.

Against the dawn's brown haze, Stannis leans against his ultralight in a paddock as we bump off the highway and along a dirt track. With the day brightening above us, we stand on the banks of the creek and look at the Chinese junk.

'She's a beaut,' Will says. 'So long as we can get her going.'

'Full house,' says Johnno.

'*Fu Hao*,' corrects Stannis.

'I meant it's gonna be a full house,' Johnno says. 'All of us and all our gear.'

I have to agree. It's going to be a tight fit. Even without me on board.

••

'Don't set up here,' Will calls from the bow of the boat, apologetic smile on his face, grease all over his clothes. 'There's no need.'

My heart bottoms and Nathan and I exchange a glance over the AK-47s we've got trained on the highway. The others pause carrying stuff from cars draped in camouflage netting to the spot in the trees we'd planned to put up the tents.

'It's no good?' HB asks.

Will grins and nods below at Amber. 'Fire her up!'

With that the *Fu Hao*'s engine roars to life.

Leaving Nathan to keep watch, I creep over to the boat.

'Engine's fine,' Amber says. 'Workhorse. She'll make good speed, too. But we need to replace a few hoses and get a new alternator before we go. Wouldn't be a bad idea to get spare spark plugs and a backup battery. And we need a lot of fuel.'

'Navigational charts, too,' says Will. 'Barometer so we've got an idea of what the weather's doing.'

I tell them about the marina I saw from Davo's but that it looked like a fire had gone through a few of the boats there.

'Most of the place is still fine,' Johnno pipes up. 'Well, at least when I drove by there it was.'

We crowd around my map and I point out the marina's location. There's a quick discussion and it's decided.

Stannis's ultralight bobs across the paddock, thrusts into the air and turns towards Port Macquarie. He'll be at the marina in five minutes and let us know if there's any trouble. Will, Rachel, Johnno, HB and Gail will keep loading the *Fu Hao* and take it downriver, where Amber, Nathan and I are to meet them with the fuel and parts and charts.

·•·

'I'm glad the kids are on the river with Will,' Amber says as she steers the station wagon around desiccated bodies on the street that leads down to the marina. 'I don't know how you guys've coped seeing this all the time. I hope Lord Howe's not like this.'

I like how confident she sounds. Nathan catches my eye and smiles. I force myself to return it. But I'm going to have to tell him soon that I'm not going. That I'm staying behind to finish what I started with Evan. I realise that finding my little brother and spiriting him away will be next to impossible. But I have to try.

'There's Stannis,' I say, seeing the ultralight under a Morton Bay fig tree in the riverside park by a dry dock compound with big boats up on scaffolding.

We pull up near him and pile out.

'You good to wait here and keep watch?' I ask, handing Stannis the binoculars.

He nods, leans back against the tree, walkie-talkie in his lap. I drape camo netting over the ultralight's wings.

Port Marina looks like the maritime version of what I've seen on so many roads. Cruisers and yachts, names like *Nimrod*, *Omega Man* and *Myth Right*, jammed tight behind a houseboat that burned and sank in the exit to the river. Bodies fester on decks and boardwalks. There are skeletons in the shallow water beneath the cafes along the shore. The only sounds are ropes clanging against masts and water lapping against hulls.

'It's a miracle this place didn't blow sky high,' Amber says.

'Do we use that?' I ask, pointing along a jetty to a petrol bowser.

Amber shakes her head. 'Will can pull the boat in there. But the bowser won't work without electricity.' She points to the sheds off to one side of the boatyard. 'Let's check in those.'

It takes all of us to carry each of the three 44-gallon drums of diesel we find outside.

'Is this going to be enough?' I ask when we've rolled the last one to the end of the jetty.

Amber nods. 'Plenty.' Again I'm loving her confidence. She angles her head towards the shop. 'I need charts and the barometer.'

I hand her a menthol tube. 'Under the nostrils,' I say. 'It helps a bit.'

Amber smears liniment under her nose and walks up the

boardwalk and around the bodies that lie in the open doorway of the marina shop.

Nathan and I stand on the end of the jetty and look at the river.

'Everything got screwed up,' he says.

'The world, you mean.'

'That, too,' he says with a grin.

'Between us?'

He nods. 'Everything's been so . . . so . . .'

'I know. It's okay, okay?'

I hold out my hand. He takes it. We step closer to each other and stare across the water at the thick greenery of Pelican Island. The big birds that give it its name glide and circle and splash on the white fringe of beach.

'Nathan, I—'

I'm about to tell him what I have to tell him when we hear a *chugga-chugga* and see the *Fu Hao* slicing up the channel towards us, white waters carving off its bow. Will's at the wheel, Johnno covers starboard with an AK-47 and HB points her weapon out over a portside railing. At the back of the boat, under the low green and black roof, Rachel and Gail huddle with the kids among the boxes and backpacks.

Amber runs down the jetty and waves Will in as he reduces the throttle. As the *Fu Hao* slows, Johnno shoulders his rifle and tosses Amber a rope that she expertly ties around a jetty pylon.

I see Rachel's expression as she spies the marina's bodies.

'Let's go inside,' she says, quickly shepherding Gail and the children into the small cabin below deck.

'You've done well.' Will says, looking at the drums and parts and maps.

'How's she running?' Amber asks.

He nods. 'Bit of engine clatter I'm not too keen on but otherwise—'

My walkie-talkie crackles in my hand. Poor Stannis: we've left him out the front.

I'm about to say I'll go get him when thunder tears the sky all around us.

We whirl, eyes everywhere in the heavens, trying to find the source of the sound. Nathan points and I see them: three fighter jets streaking towards us from the south. We duck down behind the junk's low wooden walls as the planes roar closer.

'Did they see us?' Nathan mouths.

I shake my head as they scream overhead. If they had I'm sure the *Fu Hao* would be riddled with bullets or blown to pieces. Instead, they're out over the northern beaches. Risking a look, I see the jets circle and turn back south, come in low over the river and descend one after the other behind trees that look like they're just a few blocks from us.

There's movement inside the marina office. I raise my rifle as Stannis emerges from the doorway. He's been smart enough not to use the walkie-talkie. We wave him along the jetty to the *Fu Hao*.

Below decks, in the cabin, we crowd around the map while Rachel keeps the kids calm and quiet.

'This is where they landed,' I say, pointing at Port Macquarie's airfield.

'Less than two kilometres from here,' says Amber.

'If it's just three planes,' Will says, 'it could be reconnaissance or something.'

I shake my head. 'I wish. But if my theory's right, for them to get here there have to be others on the ground within thirty-five kilometres. That means—'

'They're coming,' Nathan says.

'We have to go now,' HB says. 'Before they get here.'

Johnno nods. 'If they're on the ground at the airport they can't see us. It's too far away to hear the boat's engine, right?'

Will nods. He has his charts. Amber's got her fuel and spare parts. It's only a kilometre to the breakwalls and the sea. But it'll take a long time to get over the horizon. If the jets take to the air again, the *Fu Hao* will be dead in the water. I peer out the porthole window at a circle of Port Macquarie's shops and towers.

'Danby?' Nathan says. 'What do you think?'

I'm about to answer when my mind's sucked into a chopper surging towards us from the south, one of five that've spread out like the formation that attacked Terrigal.

This-is-it, Tregan thinks. *A-new-beginning.*

Through her eyes I see Evan beside her and Damon next to the pilot. It's the best and worst thing that could've happened.

Flashing to her mind, I see that Tregan and my brother spent the first night after Baroonah under guard at a luxury suite at a Hunter Valley winery. The next morning they were choppered farther west and kept in a historic hotel. The day after that they were taken still deeper inland and put up in a roadside motel. Then yesterday Damon woke her up with a smile and said it was over.

'Did you get them?' Tregan asked groggily. 'Are they dead?'

Damon shook his head. Told her he was calling quits on the search. That the area out west was just too big.

'It's time for us to get on with our lives,' he said. 'Go somewhere they can't find us. Somewhere big enough for *us*. Not so big we can't defend it and clear it of bodies. A place we can breathe fresh air and maybe feel the sun on our faces.'

'Is there anywhere like that left?' Tregan asked.

Damon nodded. 'Have you ever been to Port Macquarie?'

There was none of the urgency of Tregan's evacuation from the Nattai cabins. Damon made her and Evan breakfast in the motel's kitchenette while choppers clattered over the countryside and cars, trucks, Humvees and armoured vehicles rumbled by on the highway.

When they left, just an hour ago, Tregan had been amazed at how evenly spaced the convoy was beneath the chopper, like stepping stones that stretched all the way from the western plains through the northern mountains and down to the eastern sea. She saw a lot of bodies and destruction on the flight but the strangest sight were the six dead men in suits just outside a town that'd burned to the ground. It looked . . . recent.

'What happened there?' she said. 'Was it her?'

Damon looked over his shoulder at Tregan—at me—and shook his head. 'It was our guys,' he said. 'They attacked us.'

Fair-enough-Glad-he's-not-afraid-to-be-tough—

'Sounds like you had no choice,' she said.

He nodded. The look in his eyes. He'd deliberately flown over Prestige so I'd see how I'd come undone.

Now, surging waves and rugged coastline rush beneath her as what I recognise as North Brother Mountain slides by to her left. They're thirty kilometres south. They'll be in Port Macquarie in minutes. I'm guessing ground troops are almost on top of the city or the jets wouldn't have been able to get this far.

'Not long now,' Damon says to Tregan—to me.

••

'Shit, that's them, isn't it?' Johnno says.

'That's the lady who was in the video,' Lottie says in a trance-like voice. 'And your brother.'

'What?' Will asks. 'What's happening?'

He, Amber, Rachel, Hal and Milly are looking at the rest of us like we're ghosts. Without telepathy, they're not seeing through Tregan.

'You explain,' I say to Johnno. 'Nathan, quick!'

I race up onto the deck and leap onto the jetty.

'What do we do?' Nathan asks. 'We can't fight them. Not that many.'

I bend to a man on the boardwalk who has been dried to leather. 'Help me get him up on the boat.'

Nathan gets my idea and grabs the guy's stiff legs.

It takes a few minutes to lug three corpses onto the *Fu Hao's* deck. I hope it's enough to make it look like just another dead boat in the devastated marina. We hustle back into the cabin and pull the doors closed behind us as the sound of the choppers fills the air over Port Macquarie.

THIRTY-SEVEN

This-is-spectacular, Tregan thinks, taking in the sea and beach and breakwall and river and towers. *I've-always-wanted-an-ocean-view-penthouse.*

'Uh, Damon?' she asks, nodding towards the bushfires in the north. 'Is that a problem?'

He shakes his head. 'Remember those big choppers that used to scoop water from the sea and drop it on bushfires? Well, we've found a couple of them.'

Tregan squeezes his hand. Hugs Evan closer to her. Below her the green lawn and white fence of Oxley Oval grows bigger as their helicopter comes in to land beside others already disgorging men and women with weapons.

'Those men,' Gail whispers to me, like she's keeping it from the others. 'They're not good guys, are they?'

Reality's finally sinking in for the poor woman. I'm about to lie that we're safe when a chopper thumps low overhead. Every atom in my body shakes until it passes. Down against the wooden hull, Will hugs Amber, who holds Hal and Milly.

Rachel whimpers on a bench seat and on the opposite side Lottie cries quietly in HB's arms. Beneath the porthole, Johnno is pale and Nathan's losing colour. Stannis sits against the cabin door, eyes closed and breathing so slowly I can't tell whether he's calm or dying.

'What're we going to do?' says Rachel, voice rising. 'What are we going to do?'

'Ssssh,' Will hisses. 'We don't know who's out there. They could be anywhere.'

He's actually not helping. They need to believe they'll make it.

'We're okay for now,' I say softly to Rachel and all of them. 'We just need to keep cool and stay quiet.'

She shakes her head but the look in my eyes keeps her silent.

'Trust me,' I say to all of them. 'They can't search everywhere at once. This boat looks as deserted as all the others and there's thousands of houses and apartments.'

What I say soothes them just enough. And that's good because Will *is* right. Any raised panicky voice might be heard by Jacks scoping out the marina.

'What's that?' HB says.

'Outboards,' Amber says. 'Boats.'

We all rock gently with the *Fu Hao* as wake waves roll under us. The buzz of engines peaks and recedes.

'I counted five,' Will says.

Amber nods.

Five boats headed upriver on this smaller waterway. There'll be more going up towards Limeburners National Park.

Checking out the canal communities. Heading inland towards Wauchope. Air, sea, land: Jacks are everywhere already. And there's more coming.

'So, Danby,' Johnno whispers, 'we just hang out and hide here until when exactly?'

'Sunset,' I reply, looking at all of them. 'Just give me till sunset.'

Not-exactly-what-I-was-hoping-for, Tregan thinks as Damon leads her into a quaint weatherboard cottage on a grassy hill between Oxley Oval and the bush bluff that overlooks Town Beach. *We-can-do-better.*

'Just temporary,' Damon says, showing her darkened bedrooms and a lounge room that might've belonged to a sea captain. 'It's a bit dusty but no one, y'know, passed away in here.'

'It'll do for now,' Tregan says. They leave Evan bouncing on a bed in perfect mockery of a boy in a new bedroom and head out onto the front verandah, with its view of the bush, beach and breakwalls on the other side of the road.

'That sea air,' she says. 'So fresh.'

Damon says something but is drowned out by Humvees chugging past and another chopper coming in to land behind the house.

'What?' Tregan says as the noise dies down.

'I said, "Should be nice and peaceful". Eventually, I guess.'

Tregan laughs.

Damon nods at the apartment towers that start on the next block and extend as far as the eye can see. 'Clearing it's going to be a big job. Still, when it's done all this—'

'Will be mine?'

Damon laughs. 'Something like that.'

A four-wheel drive pulls up and a guy and girl with friendly smiles get out. Tregan says 'Hi' and waves back. They're the couple who've shadowed her and Evan since Baroonah and now they lug suitcases and supplies up the front path. *Personal-assistants*: that's how Tregan thinks of them, liking the celebrity feel of it. But every time these two arrive it means Damon departs.

'You're not going, are you?' she asks.

'Not far and not for long,' he says with a reluctant nod. 'Just into town. I have to supervise. Allocate jobs as the rest of them arrive. Make sure we've all got enough to eat and drink and places to sleep and go to the toilet.'

Goddamnit-I-thought-now-Danby-was-out-of-the-picture-we'd-be-together, Tregan thinks. 'How long will you be gone?' she says evenly.

'Back tonight,' Damon says, kissing her cheek. 'You and Evan just sit tight, okay?'

Sit-tight-with-Evan, Tregan thinks as she watches Damon walk out the front gate and climb into a four-wheel drive that arrives with perfect timing. *That's-what-I've-been-doing-for-days*.

'It's a trap,' Nathan says. 'Evan and Tregan, left alone like that.'

We're in the *Fu Hao*'s tiny bathroom—the only place we can talk alone.

'Maybe.' I take a deep breath. 'But I'm going to try to get him. Me doing that, it'll be the distraction you guys need to get away.'

'I'm going with you,' Nathan says, not missing a beat.

I can't hide my surprise. My revelation hasn't shocked him at all.

'C'mon, Danby,' he says with a grin. 'You thought I didn't know you weren't planning to go? Once you knew Evan might be saved? Especially now he's so close.'

I shake my head. 'You don't have to come with me.'

'I know,' Nathan says. 'So, what's the plan?'

His eyes say he's not going to give me a choice about this. I've seen that calm strength before. When he was willing to die to save Evan from me in Samsara. But I can't let him throw away his chance of a new life.

'No, really,' I say, 'you're better off—'

'With you,' he says. 'Like it or not—and don't get me wrong: I do like it—we're in this together. And besides, I get horribly seasick anyway.'

I laugh and throw my arms around him. We hug so tight I feel like we're becoming one being. I look up at him. He at me. We kiss. Affectionate. Soft. Not hard like we did in Samsara.

'Well,' Nathan says when we come up for air, looking around at the mouldy bathroom, 'who says romance is dead?'

THIRTY-EIGHT

'I—we—are going to get my brother,' I say, all eyes on me and Nathan in the *Fu Hao*'s cabin. 'While I'm—while we're—doing that is when you'll have your chance.'

'But this boat,' Will says, 'it makes a lot of noise. It'll be five minutes from here to the mouth of the river.'

'And they've got choppers,' says HB. 'And there's a ton of them out there.'

In the past hour, through Tregan, we've seen dozens more vehicles arrive, seen Jacks go into apartment buildings in what she thinks are clearance missions.

'Dusk here's crazy,' I say. 'A million parrots squawking in the palm trees and as many bats flying around before they head out for the night.'

'She's right,' Johnno says. 'It's loud.'

Will and Amber nod. 'We saw that when we were leaving town the other day.'

Nathan grins. 'We're gonna make it louder.'

'When dusk comes,' I say, 'we'll make sure their focus is

away from the river. You guys be ready to go. As soon as you're out on the ocean just head east as hard as you can. No lights: you should be impossible to spot.'

'What about the helicopters?' Will says. 'They've got radar, they can—'

'We'll try to take care of them.' I nod at the AK-47s that HB and Johnno have made their own. 'But be prepared to shoot at whatever tries to stop you.'

'Do you really think this can work?' Rachel says.

'I do,' I say.

HB shakes her head. 'What about you, Danby? And Nathan? If you get Evan and knock him out, how're you gonna get away with hundreds of them? You can't. It's suicide.'

There are nods from the others. But in the bathroom Nathan and I anticipated their doubts.

'Down on the Town Beach,' I say, 'there's a trailer with a jet ski. Once we've got Evan we'll come out after you.'

Like it's that simple. What I'm not saying is that we'll never get that far. And even if we do the *Fu Hao* will be impossible for us to find on the darkened ocean. If they think it through they'll see that. But I'm counting on them not wanting to. They want to not feel guilty about us. And I want that too so they'll go.

'Sorry to be a bummer,' Will says, 'but those fighter jets are gonna be another problem.'

Damnit. He's right. I think I can take out airborne choppers. But there's no way I can be doing that in town *and* be attacking the airfield, because it's in the other direction.

Stannis emits a whistle. At first I think it's a death rattle. Then I see his eyes are open. 'You leave the jets to me, all right?'

．•．

While Will and Amber check the charts and barometer and Gail, HB and Rachel keep the kids calm and distracted, Nathan and I hunker by the door with Stannis and Johnno.

'Mate, you're sure about this?' Johnno says in a low voice.

'You're not deaf, are you?' Stannis wheezes. 'How many breaths have I got left in me? Better to burn out blah blah.'

My plan is simple. It'll be almost dark at 6.45 p.m. Three hours from now the birds screech and the bats swirl. By then Nathan and I will be at the outskirts of Port Macquarie. Stannis will take his ultralight over the airfield where he'll unload grenades on the fighter jets. Those explosions will be our signal to unleash as much havoc as we can in Port Macquarie's shopping area as we make our way up the hill towards Evan. As soon as that starts Will's to go up on deck and get the *Fu Hao* going with Johnno and HB providing cover. Amber's to stay below with the others and make sure the engine's going strong.

I open my flak jacket, pull free the letter in plastic, and stuff it in the pocket of my camo pants.

'Take this, put it on,' I say to Rachel, giving her the body armour. 'There's another one over there for Gail. These crates, backpacks, get them all around these benches for extra protection. Stay in this area with the kids.'

'Like a fort?' Hal says.

'Exactly,' I say with a smile.

As the women and kids go about making their fortress, Nathan gets changed into his camo fatigues and I load clips with ammo and stuff their banana shapes into every available pocket.

'Suits you,' I say when he's dressed.

He glances at the yowie suit I've left balled on a bench. 'You're not going to wear your finery tonight?'

I shake my head. 'If I'm gonna die it's gotta be with some dignity.'

His smile fades.

I hand him eight clips, same as me. 'Put 'em where you can reach 'em. Try to count your rounds so you can plan your reloads. I'm ready. Are you?'

Nathan shakes his head. 'Not in the way you are.'

'Just stick with me,' I say. 'Everything will be okay.'

'You reckon?' he says with a grin.

We put on our backpacks and pick up our rifles.

'We good to go?' Stannis asks.

Nathan and I nod at each other and him.

Rachel buries her head in Amber's arms. Johnno comes in to murmur something in Stannis's ear that makes the old fella chuckle. HB hugs me tight and grabs Nathan into her embrace.

'Guys,' Will says. 'I just want to say on behalf of—'

I raise my hand over HB's shoulder. 'Why don't you finish that thought when we're back on this boat?'

Will nods. His eyes glitter.

'Okay, HB,' I say, pushing free gently as Lottie latches onto her. 'You take care of each other, all right?'

THIRTY-NINE

Nathan eases open the cabin door and we crawl up to the deck. No Jacks in sight around the marina. We hustle along the jetties, through the office. Covered by my AK-47, Nathan hustles forward and lies prone behind a tree. Then he covers the road by the marina with his gun while I get Stannis to his ultralight beneath the tree.

'Hope I can do you proud,' he says.

In the dusk light, I see fear on his face. Can't blame him for that. We both know this is a one-way flight for him. But the same goes for me and Nathan.

'You don't have to do this,' I say. 'You can go back to the boat.'

Stannis lets out a wheezy laugh. 'Just me and this lawn-mower up against fighter jets? Hardly seems fair on them.'

I grin and help him into his seat. As I string six grenades in easy reach on a wing support, I tell him about Yevdokia Beshanskaya blowing the hell out of the Nazis.

'The Night Witches used planes not much sturdier than this,' I say, tapping the ultralight's wings. 'They'd cut the engines, glide in and drop their bombs and be out of there before the Germans knew what was what.'

'Let me guess,' Stannis says with a smile. 'This Yevdokia lass died in glorious battle?'

'Heart attack,' I say. 'Lived to be an old lady.'

'Well, that's not for me,' Stannis says. 'Being an old lady, I mean.'

I laugh and glance at my watch. 'Twenty minutes?'

'You even know how to ride a jet ski?' he asks.

I smile and shake my head.

'Just in case you're not fulla shit about that plan,' he says, 'there's a few things you need to know.'

After he's explained what I need to know, we shake hands, wish each other luck and say our goodbyes. Then I run crouching to join Nathan.

Parrots scream in the trees we use as cover creeping south and then east through parks and backyards. We freeze as Humvees rumble past us and over the bridge that crosses the creek just outside Port Macquarie's main grid of streets and shops. We go along the banks and around a bend and wade through low-tide waters to get into Glebe Park. Bats circle over our heads in a cyclonic cloud as we splash along an inlet, come up through mangroves and follow a track that leads past a cemetery until we're in bushes opposite a dusty bus station and a pub that's like a mausoleum. There are no Jacks here. But beyond these buildings is Port Macquarie's maze of streets and malls and, even over the shrieking parrots and chittering bats, there's the sound of Jacks smashing doors and the glow of flashlights inside darkened shops.

There's no sign of Stannis among the palms and roofs of the western sky.

'It's been twenty-five minutes,' Nathan says, angling his watch to catch the fading light.

I don't know whether us not seeing or hearing Stannis is a good thing. If he's airborne then it might mean the Jacks can't hear or see him either. Or it could mean he's still on the ground and surrounded by them. But if it was the latter I think we would've heard gunshots and him blowing himself up with a grenade.

A roar rises from nowhere all around us as a black helicopter thunders overhead and carves a swathe through the bats, their black bodies raining down in all directions. For a moment I fear the Jacks are zeroing in on the *Fu Hao*. But the chopper doesn't round towards the river. We look up through the bushes as another three choppers fly in. They're all heading for the airport.

Then hell erupts. The lead helicopter's guns blaze. An orange fireball unfurls in the sky over the airport. White machine gun fire streaks through the dusk and there's another flash out there. A chopper over us lurches, spins and spits sparks and smoke from an engine before it slams down into the mangroves in a shuddering blast. The ground shaking beneath us, Nathan and I sprint across the road as more explosions and gunfire light up the western sky.

'Stannis?' Nathan says in the shadows of the pub's beer garden.

'I hope so.'

'What the hell happened to that chopper?'

'Bats,' I say. 'Sucked into the engine.'

'Sucked in all right,' Nathan says.

Jesus-it-can't-be-her-Not-here, Tregan thinks on the verandah of the weatherboard cottage. She's just seen the choppers scramble from the oval and now she's hearing what sounds like warfare in what's supposed to be her peaceful oasis with Damon and Evan.

'Scared,' my little brother says, hugging himself to her. 'Scary.'

'It's going to be all right,' Tregan tells him as her two assistants come through the front gate with machine guns.

'Get inside,' the woman says.

Only two-guards?-At-least-I've-got-the-gun, Tregan thinks in the lounge room, pulling the .38 revolver Damon gave her from a zip pocket in her suitcase. She checks the chamber like Damon showed her. Six bullets. Fully loaded. Brass shells. Red plastic loads. I know this gun and this sort of ammunition. *Anyone-tries-to-get-in-here's-dead-You-hear-that-Danby?*

I peer from the doorway of the pub towards the river. Shadows run west a few blocks from us. I glimpse the armoured vehicle shunting cars out of its path at the end of the street. The Jacks are focused where Stannis has attacked the airfield. Time to cause more chaos.

'Follow me,' I say to Nathan and we hustle under dark shop awnings for a block and then duck between cars and gardens until we hit a mall. Before we enter, I hurl a grenade as hard as I can back along the street while Nathan does the same with a canister of tear gas.

We're inside the arcade when we hear the explosion. From here I know we can go three blocks east without breaking cover. Our best bet, our only bet, is to keep moving and leave carnage and confusion in our wake.

Agile. Mobile. *Hostile.*

'This is it,' I say when we're nearly at the end of the arcade. 'Cover me for a minute.'

Nathan crouches, sweeping his AK-47 back and forth, as I run along a corridor to the place Johnno told me about. Flashlight between my teeth, I hustle through admin offices and into a back room where there's a desk set up a bit like HB's radio. Johnno's empty beer bottles are still lined up next to the microphone he used in his futile call-out to survivors in the days after the Snap. For a moment I fear he might've run down the battery on the emergency broadcast system. But when I switch it on there's a low hum. I turn up the volume to maximum, plug Mac's music player in and select the 'Fighting' playlist. Speakers around the city's streets crackle and crowd noise swells. Then there's the fuzz of electric guitar feedback before MC5's lead singer tells everyone to kick out the jams.

Fuck, yeah.

MC5 blasts at ear-splitting levels and I hope Jacks everywhere are skidding in their boots and vehicles and wondering what the hell's happening. What I hope more is that the *Fu Hao*'s engines are rumbling unheard as the boat heads upriver. Nathan grins at me and we run to the end of the arcade, where I quickly grab what I need from the pet shop's spilled inventory and tuck it into my backpack.

We scramble into Port Mall and up its travelators to the first floor. I roll a road flare into a dress shop whose synthetics go up with a whoosh as Nathan drops a grenade over the railing into the information booth. We leave the mall floor burning as we run for the exit. Spilling into the car park, we see through its concrete balustrades that chopper searchlights are all over Port Macquarie's streets.

So long as they're not on the river, this is what we planned.

We hurry down fire stairs. We're about to open the door to the street when there's muttering outside.

'Find the music too loud goddamn they're not at the airfield jets destroyed she can't do this down this way saw movement.'

The voices are like the outriders at Baroonah. But the chorus sounds as desperate as it does insane. I wonder if Jack was already losing the plot—megamind collapsing under its own weight—and we're now tipping him over the edge. I hope so.

The babble continues. Nathan raises his eyebrows when he's mentioned and gives a cheesy thumbs up. I have to clamp a hand over my mouth so I don't laugh. The gibberish fades as they move away. I heard three distinct voices and I flash that many fingers to Nathan and then count those fingers to zero. I throw the door open, crouch and fire three quick bursts that dissolve Jack heads into pink mist while Nathan stands over me and aims back the way they came.

'Clear?' I shout.

'Clear!'

Not for long. In seconds all of them will converge on this spot. But that's what I want.

'Let your plans be dark and impenetrable as night,' I say under my breath, quoting my man Sun Tzu, 'and when you move, fall like a thunderbolt.'

I pull a tear gas grenade. Fling it at the next block. Throw another the other direction.

'Come on,' I say, bolting across the street.

Nathan and I dive into a tropical garden next to an apartment block as a chopper swoops in over where we've just been. It's fifteen metres in the air. Searchlight in smoke that its rotors are only spreading. From the garden shadows, we see Jacks coughing their way through the haze, coming from both ends of the street. Just to our left more hustle down a laneway.

Nathan sights along his rifle. I touch his shoulder and tilt my head to say he needs to climb the hill through this garden. When he's safely away, I pull the plastic throwing claw from the pet store out of my backpack. Dog owners could fling tennis balls a long way with these things. Let's see what I can do with a fragmentation grenade. I stand up, pull the pin and catapult it hard and high.

My face is down in the dirt when the explosion turns the air hot at my neck and the earth shudders beneath my body. It's only when I've crawled up the hill to Nathan that I risk a look. Below us, through the trees, the street's scattered with bodies and pieces of burning chopper as the Jacks who're left alive and still arriving pour gunfire into the upper floors of the concrete car park.

All around the city, through the gaps in the gunfire, the Minutemen bellow 'This Ain't No Picnic' from the street speakers. By the time they're done and Ministry are blasting 'Jesus Built My Hotrod', Nathan and I are in the darkness of the high school on the hill.

FORTY

Over the dark outline of the school roofs, the searchlights of three helicopters scour the streets a few blocks west. Flames and smoke rise volcanically from the mall.

'You can seriously do this?' Nathan asks.

I grin up from where I've just picked the lock to the chemistry lab.

Inside, he opens gas valves on the benches while I work the locks on the storage area to make sure the fire we're about to create reaches all the flasks and beakers of flammables back there.

'Was this on your bucket list?' Nathan asks. 'Burning down a school?'

I shake my head but laugh anyway.

'You ready to run?' I ask when we're on the breezeway outside, chemistry lab door closed behind us and my hand raised to lob a grenade through its window.

Nathan holds what looks like a string that trails back under the door. 'Let's go for a more elegant approach. Magnesium coil.'

'How long?' I ask.

'Two minutes.'

'Works for me. There's somewhere down the road we need to visit.'

Nathan bends and strikes a match to ignite the brilliant white fire of his fuse. When we're at the other side of the school, I use the claw-thrower to lob a grenade onto a playing field.

'What did you do that for?' Nathan pants as we pour down the hill and my grenade explodes behind us with a harmless thump.

'Bait,' I say. 'Wait.'

We pause in the shadows behind a car and watch as choppers swarm over the school and flashlights appear inside the fences.

'Jesus,' Nathan says, looking at me. 'They're about to—'

The chemistry lab explodes. Windscreens and windows crack all around us. The chopper directly over the school building is blown into a pine tree and crumples through its branches in a fiery tangle. Shouts and screams filter to us over the roaring flames. There are Jacks up there who're feeling this and they can't keep a lid on the anger and pain and crazy anymore.

I reach into my backpack, pull my last two grenades free, pocket one and hold up the other. 'You got any?'

Nathan holds his in a tight fist. 'Last one.'

'Over the road,' I say.

He clocks where I've brought him and nods. We pull the pins, throw the grenades and run as the petrol station behind us becomes another burning beacon in the night.

FORTY-ONE

She's-coming-I-know-it-Jesus, Tregan thinks. *Damon-where are you?*

Nathan and I don't have to rely on her mind to know she's pacing the lounge room of the weatherboard house. We can see her from the shadows of the Maritime Museum next door because she's got the curtains open and a lantern blazing. What I really wish I could see is the *Fu Hao.* So I could know that it's made it. That this has been worth it, no matter what happens in the next few minutes.

Then, like storm waves hitting the shore, my mind's buffeted by something rolling in from the ocean.

Jesus-what's-that? Tregan thinks as the same force sweeps through her mind.

On the couch, Evan looks up at her like he's been stung, eyebrows knotted fiercely and eyes burning black.

'What is it?' Nathan whispers to me.

'I don't know,' is all I can say.

It's like pressure's building. As though the very atmosphere is becoming deep and brooding. Outside us. Inside us. Unknowable but powerful. Louder and stronger as it gets closer. It feels like I'm about to be . . . judged. Like this—*force*—has the power to strike me down, smite me for my sins past, present and future. There's no time to repent, much less rationalise it, not with choppers coming up the hill behind us. I force myself to concentrate, centre myself and cut through this wall of mental noise like I did during the Snap.

'I'm going to take out those two,' I whisper, nodding at the guards out by the fence. They're looking around, guns pointing every which way, as though searching for the source of the bewildering atmospheric vibration. 'Then I'm going in to get Evan.'

Nathan nods. 'What do you want me to do?'

Live: that's what I want him to do. Jack doesn't even know he's here. With this much confusion he could escape. Maybe even make it to that jet ski.

'Go,' I say. 'Get away.'

'Not a chance,' he says.

I smile even as my heart breaks. Staying with me's a death sentence. We both know it.

'We've done all right,' he says. 'Haven't we?'

I don't know if he means just now or surviving since the Snap. But before I can say 'Yes' to both a stronger pulse ripples our souls. It's like a shockwave. An elevation. Terrible and wonderful. My mind fills with flashes. Depths. Darkness. Decades. For a moment I don't feel like it's coming to judge me anymore. I feel like I'm one with the force. All knowing. All seeing.

'This thing,' I say, terrified, awed. 'Is it—?'

'God?' Nathan gasps. 'I don't know.'

Maybe it's Death. We huddle closer together.

Nathan turns to me. I lean into him. Our lips brush. He pulls back. Tears on his cheeks. I wipe my eyes. I think this is it. But I'm not going to say goodbye.

'When this is over,' he says, 'I hope we live on somehow.'

I kiss him. 'Me too. Stay here and cover me?'

I break free of our embrace and scurry along the side of the Maritime Museum. The mental storm around me seems to intensify. I imagine myself strapped to a ship's mast in a typhoon. Focus. Whatever this thing is, I can use it. Inside the house Tregan's terrified, not least because Evan is shaking his head furiously and saying 'No!' over and over like a crazy person.

In the darkness, the guards are still distracted. I aim my AK-47 at the first one and put three rounds into his head. His partner spins in my direction and I stitch bullets up her flak jacket and into her face before she can get off a shot. Her body's still falling when I burst from the shadows, firing into the side door of the weatherboard house. I kick it open and dive into a laundry space. Eject my empty clip and slam a new one home.

My assault has snapped Tregan out of her immersion in the mental noise. *Jesus-she's-inside-Are-they-dead?-They're-dead-Please-don't-hurt-me.*

'I've got a gun,' Tregan shouts.

I stalk out of the hallway with my AK-47 and aim it at her.

'I'll shoot you,' she says, thinking *Oh-Jesus-Oh-Jesus* as she sees I'm not scared in the slightest by the .38 she's pointing at me with shaking hands. 'I swear I will.'

As much as I've hated Tregan, I'm not here for vengeance. And she's no threat to me: her hands are trembling so violently I doubt she could hit me even if the .38 wasn't loaded with blanks.

I-will-shoot-you-For-Gary-For-Jack-You-you-I-will-shoot.

I look at my little brother. Evan sits on a couch, legs crossed, elbows on his knees, hands steepled under his chin as he grins at me like a gargoyle.

'I'll kill you,' Tregan yells.

I-can-do-this-I'll-shoot—

'You *can't* kill me.' I say it to Evan. To *Jack*. His own voodoo mantra. I'm wrong about that, of course, but I hope my confidence in this moment will give the letter in my pocket all the supernatural hoodoo it needs. 'You *won't* kill me, Jack.'

Jack?-She's-crazy-Insane-Her-brother-I-should-kill-her-Do-what-Damon-can't—

My smile reminds Tregan I can hear her. She thinks she's been living in mental solitude all these months. Has no idea Damon's been mind-raping her the entire time. That every moment they spent together in bed she was spread out for all the Jacks.

'I feel sorry for you,' I say.

'For me?' she spits.

'Sooner or later, you'll see—and when you do you'll wish you'd never been born.'

What's-she-talking-about-Why's-she-like-This-isn't-how-I . . .

I let myself momentarily get lost in the mental hurricane surging towards us all. I stare at Evan. I know it's enveloping Jack, too. Revise your stand, improvise a plan, pulverise the Man: the best line from *Agile, Mobile, Hostile*.

'Feel that?' I say with a gloating grin. 'We're more powerful than you.'

I can't believe how calm and controlled I sound. Uncertainty flickers in Evan's eyes. He has no idea what the cerebral storm around us is and it scares him to think that I do. I hope this moment haunts Jack for the rest of his days. That he reads my letter and fears what I became after death. That he lives in terror of me striking him down from beyond the grave.

Steady-just-do-it-Shoot-but-No-it's-cold-blood-Last-chance.

'Last chance,' Tregan says, finally keeping the .38 level and aimed at me. 'Put. The gun. Down.'

'Do what she says,' Damon says as he steps from the shadows with an AR-15 aimed at my face.

FORTY-TWO

I keep my gun aimed at Tregan. Not that I'm going to shoot her. But every second I stall them is another second for the *Fu Hao* to get farther out to sea. Best case scenario.

A smile spreads across Tregan's face, like I've fallen into some trap she masterminded. 'Put your gun down, bitch,' she says.

For a moment, I do want to blow her away. But it'd get me killed and wouldn't help Evan. Instead, I nod and lower the AK-47, bending slightly so the strap falls from my shoulder as I ease the rifle to the floor.

'Forty-five and backpack too,' Damon says.

'Don't want any nasty little surprises,' Evan adds.

Tregan's eyes flick to him and she frowns before straightening her gun back at me.

I unholster my pistol and set it down. Take the backpack off slowly and let it fall onto a sofa. They haven't noticed the razor in my pocket. Or the grenade. If I get a chance I'll pull the pin and take us all out.

'Step away from the guns,' Evan commands.

Confusion pierces Tregan's relief.

Where'd-Damon-come-from?-Why's-Evan-sound-so-different?

'It's because he doesn't need to hide the truth from you anymore,' I say.

'You shut your mouth,' she snaps at me, before turning to Damon: 'Were you in there hiding?'

He nods. 'Came inside while you were in the bathroom. If you'd known, she would've known.'

I hear the chatter of choppers outside. Wonder when Nathan's going to start shooting. Whether he'll aim in here or at the aircraft. I hope he's changed his mind and is down on the beach trying to figure out a jet ski. I hope he hasn't been stabbed quietly like Tajik.

'Whoever else you're with, we'll find them too,' Damon says. 'This is where it ends.'

'This is where I begin.' I close my eyes, breathing in the presence all around us, let it surge through me and channel a contented expression like I'm controlling it rather than completely in its awe. I open my eyes to stare from Evan to Damon. 'This is where I begin, Jack.'

There's doubt in their eyes even as they smile the same arrogant smile.

'I would've given you the world,' they say as one. 'We could've ruled it together.'

A chill tingles through me. Speaking like that: it's more coherent than the murmuring I've heard but it doesn't sound any less crazy.

Tregan's jaw hangs open. Her mind says what she can't. *Why're-they-talking-speaking-like-that?*

'We could've remade humanity in our image,' Jack says through Damon and Evan. 'Our children would've been gods.'

'Children?' I snarl. 'You're insane, Jack.'

Damon laughs, echoed by Evan, and Tregan's mind swirls.

She's-crazy-He's-not-Jack, Tregan thinks. *Why-doesn't-Damon-say-she's-crazy?*

Damon and Evan look at her. Gold eyes glittering coldly above reptilian smirks. In that instant Tregan knows.

You-can-hear-me-You've-always-been—

'They're all one,' I say, drawing her gaze. 'They're all Jack.'

Tregan shakes her head, tightens her grip on the gun, like she wants to shoot the messenger. 'No.'

You-bastards-I'm-gonna-No-don't-think. Her repulsion and hatred dissolves into a peaceful vision of her Nattai meditation room's wind chimes.

'Tregan, what—?' Damon manages before she swings the .38 to his head and pulls the trigger. There's a flash, bang, the smell of gunpowder and singed hair and burned flesh as he staggers back, his AR-15 straying from me as Tregan fires at him again, this time from farther away and with no effect.

'You bitch,' he says, laughing, hand going to where his temple's bleeding and scorched. 'Ouch.'

Damon rights himself, raises his AR-15 at her.

In that second, I'm across the room, howling as I leap onto him like a wild animal. We go down together. His finger squeezes the assault rifle trigger. Plaster rains from the ceiling as I open Damon's throat with the straight razor. The rifle stops roaring as his finger goes slack around the trigger.

Tregan's screams fill my ears.

Beneath me, Damon's eyes are empty. His blood's all over me. I've carved a horrific smile through his airway and jugular. I push myself up off his body. Wipe my razor on my camo pants.

Evan slow claps me. I look at him. A mocking grin like we had in Samsara.

'Another one bites the dust,' he says. 'Plenty more where he came from.'

I scoop up my AK-47 and .45. Tregan staggers, back to a wall, the .38 falling from her hand. *Blanks-loaded-with-whole-time-Jack-Damon-this-thing-killed-Gary-all-of-them-screwed-me-used-me . . .*

I can't feel anything but pity for how much she's suffered. All of what she was put through by Jack in all his guises, simply to consolidate his power and get me.

'Was he—is he—are they—' she says.

I nod and she unleashes a cry of despair.

'Sucks to be you,' Evan says. 'Both of you. As soon as you step outside that door you're dead.'

'You're . . . you're dead,' says Tregan as she ducks and yanks the AR-15 from Damon's dead hand.

'Don't!' I yell from where I'm down by the backpack and Tregan stiffens. 'It's not his fault.'

But-he's-in-there.

'Sure I am, Tregan,' Evan says. 'Man, we had fun, didn't we? And I mean we. Fucking you was . . . team building.'

Jack knows I won't kill Evan. But he's trying to make Tregan do it to get at me. Nauseous anger floods her. *Gotta-kill-the-little-Has-this-thing-got-a-safety?*

Tregan's really going to fire this time.

'It's not his fault,' I yell, stepping between her and Evan. 'Like it's not yours.'

Tregan blinks, like she's deciding whether to just kill us both, then her face goes slack.

It's the strongest wave yet. Evan starts screaming.

'No! No! No!' he yells, hands clamped to his head, like he's being deafened. 'No! No!'

With Evan in its thrall, I will myself to move, grab the gun I took from the zoo out of my backpack.

'What's that?' he sneers, the force ebbing, his focus back on me as I raise the weapon. 'A nerf gun?'

I squeeze the trigger. There's a little *pffft* and Evan's eyes go wide.

'Ahhh.' He grabs the feathers of the tranquilizer dart stuck in his neck and pulls it free. 'That stings.'

The instructions for loading the dart with Telazol indicated one millilitre per five kilograms of body weight for spider monkeys. I've just hit Evan with four millilitres. It might not be enough. Or it might kill him.

There's the crack-crack-crack of gunfire and a return burst of machine gun clatter. Out there, Nathan's taking on the choppers. In here, Tregan raises the AR-15 at my little brother.

'Don't!' I say, but I'm too far away to get between them.

'That's the way, Tre—' Evan says and slumps back in the sofa with his eyes closed.

Tregan looks at me.

'Get down!' I scream at her. 'Get him down!'

I grab the hissing lantern. Switch it off. Plunge the cottage into darkness. Scramble to the laundry. Through its window, I see two choppers hovering above the Maritime Museum, chewing up the building with streaks of minigun fire.

If Nathan's in there he's not shooting back. I hope that means he's not giving away his position rather than something worse. I lob a smoke grenade across the lawn and it sputters and billows as I fire a full clip at the closest chopper to light up its cabin and engines with a shower of sparks. It spins away crazily. The other chopper swivels my way. Opens fire as I dive back into the house and walls explode behind me.

Gotta-help-gotta-help, Tregan thinks, feeling that Evan has a pulse as she drags him to the floor. *Gotta-help-Danby-or-we're-dead.*

I scrabble to a bathroom. Reload and pop up at the corner of a window. My burst of bullets doesn't kill the chopper but it does set the curtain ablaze. I dive away from the window behind a cast-iron tub as return spray of fire shatters glass and weatherboard.

Have-to-help-Kill-these—

'What can I do?' Tregan screams.

'Stay where you are!' I shout.

If she knows where I am she'll give me away to them.

There's a thumping through the side door. I crawl to the hallway and see a shadow creeping towards me. I'm about to fire—

'Danby?'

'Nathan!'

While the Jacks and I have been trading fire, he's made it under the cover of the smoke.

We huddle as bullets sizzle through the roof and punch through floorboards. It's only seconds before they hit us or Tregan or Evan. The bathroom's ablaze and smoke's pouring into the rest of the house.

'Next bedroom,' I say.

I scramble along the hallway, over plaster and woodchips and glass, and take a position beside a shattered bay window with Nathan on the other side. Through the smoke, Jacks with rifles are closing in for the kill from beside the Maritime Museum while the chopper pours its firepower into making sure we don't escape out the front door.

Getting out of here means taking out the chopper. I look at Nathan. He knows it's probably impossible. No choice but to try. We nod and swing our AK-47s and our muzzles flare and my ears shriek with the thunder of our combined guns. The chopper takes our hits unharmed and its pilot turns his bird our way so the miniguns are aimed right at us. There's a blur behind the chopper. At first I think it's a giant bat. Then I see Stannis under the wings of his ultralight. He's holding out a clenched fist.

Whoompa!

The ultralight goes into the rotors as his grenade explodes and the chopper becomes a cloud of fire. Nathan and I drop behind the wall a moment before it's peppered with hot shrapnel.

I don't wait to recover. Fresh clip in, I jump up and fire at the stunned shadows out in the haze, hear screams, see a few drop, the others dive for cover.

'Go!' I say to Nathan and we charge into the lounge room where Tregan's protecting Evan with Damon's AR-15.

I run past them and throw open the windows that look out over the road and sea path.

'Flynn's Beach,' I yell, knowing the ruse won't hold up as soon as she's running with us the other way. 'They're coming!'

'Sorry. For everything.' Tregan shakes her head. 'You go!'

Not-going-anywhere-You-want-to-know-what-I-think-Jack-Here's-what-I-think.

Tregan runs to the side door and fires the AR-15 wildly. There's no time to speak or think. I haul Evan up over my shoulder, jump from the couch to the window ledge and drop us onto the soft grass below. Nathan lands beside me and for a moment the fire and smoke and noise are behind us and there's only the dark bush and sea ahead.

FORTY-THREE

I don't even feel Evan's weight as we tear across the coast road and down the sea path. Nathan pants after me and we hide in banksias with the surf below us catching the flicker of the fires. But what I see for a moment is Tregan, stumbling across the lawn, the weatherboard cottage engulfed in flames behind her and muttering shadows looming all around.

You - all - die - like - Gary - you - die, Tregan's mind shouts as she fires the rifle until it clicks empty. She doesn't know if she's hit anyone but the air is as filled with screams as it is with smoke. Fireworks go off beside her face and the world shunts and she feels blades of wet grass against her cheek. There's no pain. Just that force. Stronger. Closer. Then nothing.

'Jesus,' Nathan says. 'She didn't deserve that.'

'I know.'

Above us, on the road, Jacks speak in a crowded whisper as they try to get their collective shit together.

'Can't Flynns Beach not house who else up coast road apartments into rainforest true-true could be diversion diverting nothing everything go there go here go everywhere get get—'

The craziness of three or four Jacks chattering is lost in the rumble of vehicles. Cars pull away. Headlights slash through the trees. Weapons clack as they're reloaded. Boots scuff on the path above us but there are no torch beams. They're coming this way with night vision. Will be on top of us in a minute.

I point. 'Down there.'

I feel Nathan's surprise that the jet ski really is on the trailer behind the car on the ramp like I said. 'Seriously?'

I know what he means. The sea out there is just black. There's no sign of the Chinese junk. The *Fu Hao* might never have made it out of the marina. And if it did get down the river and through the breakwater, I don't know how we'd ever find it on the vast darkness of the ocean. But I'd rather drown myself than die at Jack's hands.

'Take Evan,' I say, shifting my little brother so Nathan's got him. 'I'm right behind you.'

While Nathan slings his AK-47 and drags Evan onto the sea path, I bend a young tree to thread a thin branch through the metal ring of my last grenade. I arch the sapling down across the path, use my razor and its pearl handle to spike it to a tree trunk and sprint down the path to the beach.

Nathan has laid Evan between rocks on the sand and is beside the car pulling a partial skeleton in board shorts out of the driver's door.

'Reverse,' I say. 'Reverse it.'

Nathan starts the engine and the car and trailer roll backwards towards the surf as the bluff above us lights up with muzzle flashes. Bullets zing off rocks, clink through panels and thud into the sand. I drop behind the ramp, fire quick bursts at their flashes and duck again. There's a *shush* in the foliage and when I look up I see my branch whip back to its original position.

I empty a clip at the shadows on the sea path and send them into the banksias as the canopy above them erupts, leaves and branches igniting with a whoosh. My grenade's catapulted up and created an instant bushfire over and around the Jacks.

'Get Evan,' I yell.

Nathan stumbles away towards the rocks as I dive on the corpse and see what Stannis told me to look for—a rubber loop with a jet ski key hanging around the dead guy's wrist. I wade into the water around the trailer, unclip the straps so the jet ski floats free and struggle onto its front seat. With a silent prayer, I slide the key on my wrist home and stab my fingers at the green button like Stannis said.

The jet ski engine sputters then roars beneath me. Just like the quad: that's what I hope. I turn the throttle and the machine thrusts away from the trailer before I turn it parallel with the beach so Nathan can drape Evan between the seats and haul himself aboard.

I twist to face the ocean. Now we're on the water the presence feels tangible. It's like I should be able to touch it. At least see it like a wall of cloud, wind and lightning, stretching from sea to space, horizon to horizon. Whatever it is, it's nearly on us. All I can do is wrench the throttle and thrust the jet ski up and over the next wave before it breaks. Behind us the air and water whizz and fizz with bullets.

FORTY-FOUR

Ahead of us, above us, below us is only infinite blackness. We're out of range and sight of the Jacks, churning our way through dark water, Nathan holding onto me and squeezing Evan between our bodies. It's like we're tiny creatures on the back of something huge, barely visible mites on a vast black beast that might flick us off at any moment. It's enough to make me ease back on the throttle.

'All around us,' Nathan says in my ear. 'It's here.'

I glance over my shoulder. There's enough firelight from Port Macquarie to see his expression. He looks how I feel. What we're sharing is beyond words. Not telepathy. Common awe and terror.

'Shit,' he says.

I see why.

Boats with searchlights are thumping out of the river. Even this cosmic immensity can't stop Jack from coming after us.

I turn the throttle and the jet ski roars and sputters and dies. I try it again. The engine catches, I crank it and we shoot forward across the water for a few seconds before it conks out. Months out in the elements, exposed to sand and salt and rain, it's a wonder it started in the first place.

'Goddamnit,' I say.

I can't even swing it around so we can shoot at them. Not that we'd have a chance of hitting anything from a bobbing jet ski with guns filled with sea water. We're sitting ducks.

Speedboats churn towards us, spotlights streaming closer across the waves. Behind them, there's that last chopper, wounded but not destroyed, sweeping in just above the waves.

FORTY-FIVE

Beneath the jet ski, the ocean bulges and we hydroplane down a watery slope before settling in the trough of a wave, wash all around us.

Something's in the deep and deep inside us. That presence. The storm in our souls and minds. But it's not here for us. Doesn't even see us. It's here for *them*.

'No! No! No!' I hear the Jacks yell in unison from across the water. Like Evan did. Only now it's not denial. It's terror.

A humpback whale explodes from the water, tossing speedboats like driftwood, becomes a mountain momentarily hanging in the air, and then slams back on more flailing Jacks, as inevitable as a landslide. There's splintering and crunching and screaming. Searchlights are snuffed and the bright beams that remain skew in all directions. Another whale rockets from the water and more enemies are thrown and crushed and plunged into the depths. A third leviathan breaches, a monstrous eruption of barnacles and flippers, capsizing and crushing the remaining boats. I see Jacks clinging to wreckage. Another whale towers up and they're all lost in its shadow.

But the chopper keeps coming, spotlight panning across wreckage and corpses for a moment before it zeroes in on us out on the dark sea. Its guns flare. Bullets boil towards us in the water as it races closer. I turn the throttle. The jet ski coughs, gets a burst of power, but I've got the handles turned so all I succeed in doing is turning us side on so Nathan and I present a bigger target. Then the chopper's searchlight is eclipsed and its bullets are stopped by a monolith launching from the sea. We scream—and the sea and air and earth and universe seem to scream with us—as the aircraft plunges into the whale's head and explodes with a muffled *thwump*.

There's a terrible moment where machine and mammal are fused like a mutated statue before they subside together beneath the surface.

Evan between us, Nathan and I cling to each other on the jet ski, rolling with the waves, eyes aimed back into the searchlight glare from the remaining boats back at the mouth of the river.

'They're not coming,' Nathan says.

'The whales,' I say.

I can feel them beneath us. The sensation's not like I had with the dolphins. There's no insight into their consciousness. They're in their waters early because of the new winter. Ready to do whatever they can to keep Jacks out of their world. The whales aren't here to spirit us to safety. I'm not even sure they care we exist.

We're dead in the water. Rolling with waves that'll push us to shore. And even if the currents take us north or south as soon as Evan comes around he'll lead the Jacks straight to us.

I try the jet ski's throttle again and again. The engine coughs and farts but won't catch.

'Ssssh,' Nathan hisses. 'What's that?'

Over the waves lapping us, there's mechanical rumbling. A Jack boat's eluded the whales, is bearing down on us, smart enough not to use its searchlight. But I can't see it silhouetted against the blazes back on land. The engine shifts down. It's not approaching from the shore, it's—

Dazzling light hits us from behind. We turn into the blinding glare of a boat's searchlight.

'Danby?' comes a voice. 'Nathan?'

Johnno.

FORTY-SIX

Will gets the *Fu Hao* in close and throws us ropes so we can come alongside and hand Evan up to Johnno and HB before we haul aboard.

'Whales,' Will says, shaking his head. 'Whales.'

My eyes go back to shore. No boats are coming for us. But they've seen the searchlight. They know we've been picked up by someone.

'Go north, with the light on for a bit,' I say.

Will turns the wheel, opens up the engine and thrusts the junk parallel to the coast. Then he kills the light, turns us east and we speed away from land in total darkness.

Down below, the porthole blacked out, we're met by teary faces. Lottie, Gail, Liam, Amber, Rachel, Hal and Milly—they're all fine in their life jackets. And the *Fu Hao* looks completely undamaged.

'They didn't see you?' Nathan says.

'The noise and fire and smoke you guys made,' Amber says. 'We could see them on shore, all racing around after you. It was pretty dicey but we were out on the ocean in five minutes.'

'When we got a kilometre off shore,' Gail pipes, 'that's when we voted to wait. Didn't want you to have to go too far on the jet ski.'

I smile. I'm not sure whether they believed we were coming or just wanted to give us a chance.

'We saw what Stannis did from out here,' HB says. 'That was so brave.'

I nod. 'Without him we wouldn't have made it.'

Johnno comes down the stairs. 'What on earth was that music?'

'Music chosen by a guy named Mac.' I feel like he needs acknowledgment. If he hadn't been crazy we wouldn't be alive. 'Pretty noisy, huh?'

I want to grin but I grimace because something's not right. My thoughts spiral away from me.

'Danby, you're hurt,' Lottie says.

I feel the burning ache in my side. See where blood's turned my camo black. I don't know when I got hit or by what as I go down dizzy onto the bench opposite where we've laid out Evan.

'Check Evan,' I say. 'Is he all right?'

'I will,' Nathan says. 'But you first. Guys, get the kids upstairs for some fresh air?'

He lifts my shirt. I want to make a joke he's taking things a bit fast given we've only just become friends again. But laughing would hurt way too much. Faces hover over his shoulder.

They wince when they see my wound. That can't be good. Then I pass out.

'It's gonna be all right,' Nathan says when I come around. 'You've got a piece of house in you.'

'Like the Wicked Witch?'

'Not quite that big,' Nathan smiles.

I stare at the ceiling and try not to watch as Nathan splashes his hands with antiseptic and injects me with a needle that makes me numb and then goes to work with forceps. When the sea gets rougher, Johnno holds me down across the shoulders and Rachel does the same for my legs while Gail and HB keep Nathan as steady as they can. It seems like an eternity before he pulls a shard of weatherboard out of me the size of an ice-cream stick.

'That it?' I say.

'I'm gonna have to clamp this,' Nathan says as blood squirts up his shoulder. 'Someone shine the torch in there.'

The world fades from me again.

The boat rocks and I swirl and the lights in the cabin flicker as Nathan stitches. Then he's wiping my side and telling me I won't be able to play the piano again.

'Evan,' I say.

Nathan nods.

I watch as he checks my little brother, the bad news writing itself across his features.

'What did you use and how much?' he said.

'Animal tranquiliser,' I say. 'Telazol I think. Four mils.'

Nathan picks his watch off a side table, runs a bloody hand through his hair.

'Shallow respiration. Weak pulse. It's been ninety minutes since you dosed him,' he says. 'He should be coming around by now.'

Panicked faces loom. I'm not going to cry. 'What can you do?'

'Epinephrine,' says Nathan. 'An EpiPen? Have you got any in the first-aid kit? For allergic reactions?'

I shake my head. The backpack I assembled was for the battlefield, not for bee stings.

Nathan looks around at Amber and HB and the others. 'This was a restaurant, right? They're out on the river. Someone has a bad reaction to a prawn. They've got to have an EpiPen. Find it!'

I want to get up but Rachel puts a firm hand on my shoulder and holds me down as Johnno and HB throw open cupboards of lifejackets and fire extinguishers, search in drawers of napkins and menus.

'Lottie found it!' shouts Amber, bounding down the stairs from the deck. 'In a wooden box by the wheel.'

She unzips the first-aid kit, holds it out to Nathan and he pulls out an EpiPen.

'Will this work?' I say, sitting up now, not caring about my wound.

When Nathan goes to speak, all we hear is Will yelling we have to come up on deck.

'Do it,' I say and Nathan injects Evan before I scramble up after everyone else.

FORTY-SEVEN

The Australian mainland's lost in the darkness west, apart from the blazes in Port Macquarie and the bushfires up the coast. But a star races across the water at us, a bright white searchlight flanked by red wing-lights and followed by the burning roar of its afterburners.

I raise the binoculars. Fighter jet. Wings embedded with cannons. Undercarriage bulging with missiles. Nathan races up the steps with the hunting rifle and takes a shooting stance beside HB and Johnno who have their AK-47s aimed out over our wake at the screaming jet.

Blowing choppers out of the sky's one thing but I've never read about small arms fire destroying an FA/18-Hornet in attack mode at close to the speed of sound.

Our end will be fast. Missiles and miniguns. Shot to pieces and blown apart.

There's not even time to get back below and die beside Evan.

The fighter's spotlight hits us, freezes everyone against the boat and the sea.

It's like we're outside time in the heart of the sun.

The plane shrieks wide past the *Fu Hao*, corkscrewing wildly out of control before it slams into the waves in a geyser of fire and steam.

No one moves or says anything.

What's left of the jet is swallowed up by the ocean.

Nathan and HB and Johnno stare at each other. Shake their heads. No one fired. Will and Amber look at me. My gaze goes to Liam. The kid stands wide eyed at the top of the cabin stairs.

'He's awake,' he says. 'The boy.'

FORTY-EIGHT

I weep as I hold Evan to me. Nathan encircles us in his arms.

'Danby?' my little brother says. 'Ferry to Luna?'

Going to Luna Park. It's what he thought we were doing on Christmas Day.

Evan is like Lottie—he doesn't remember a thing, has been spared everything we've seen.

'Not Luna,' I say. 'The beach.'

Evan squirms free and blinks at me. I don't regret not being able to read his mind. I'm just glad he's free of Jack and himself again.

'Beach?' Evan says. His eyes light up but then he frowns and looks around. I hope he's not going to ask about Dad or Stephanie. I just don't know what to say.

'Big bear?' he asks.

The absence of his soft toy—lost long ago—might send Evan into a spin.

But Liam steps forward and holds out his teddy.

'Blue bear,' he says. 'Name is Diggity.

Evan considers the offering.

'Diggity.' My little brother turns the word. 'Diggity.'

He takes the bear and hugs it with a smile. But Evan still has a frown for me.

'Chocopops?' he says.

Everything else on board and I forgot to pack them.

I laugh so hard I actually split my side.

FORTY-NINE

'We were here when the plane went down,' Will says, pointing to the map. 'Thirty-seven or so kilometres from shore.'

With Evan unconscious, the pilot was alone at the edge of the Radius. I hate to think what it was like for him when he crossed the threshold. Suddenly released from Jack's control and wondering where the hell he was before crashing into the ocean.

That was ten hours ago.

Since then Nathan's restitched my wound. I dozed a while with Evan and when I woke up I took my plastic-wrapped letter from the pocket of my camo pants. Going up on deck, I threw it into the sea, a message in a bottle that might still wash up and strike fear into the Jacks. That's if there are any left. My hope is that the knowledge they've been beaten by us and that the natural world is against them will see them weaken and die. Maybe the process will be hurried along by the crocs I set free or the bushfire marching down from the north. Maybe their craziness will mean they self-destruct before any of that happens.

With the kids and Amber and Gail sleeping below, Johnno, HB and Rachel sit behind us in leather seats and slowly drink the beers Stannis smuggled on board even though he knew he'd probably never get to enjoy them. Nathan and I sit nestled together on a bench seat beside Will as he takes us east a while longer before it's Amber's turn to take the wheel.

The breeze is gentle and the water looks calm as the grey morning brightens around us. I know this is the treacherous Tasman Sea and it could all turn terrible in the time it takes to blink but I'm happy to go with how it is right now. Happy to believe that Lord Howe is . . . whatever it is.

'Are we there yet?' Nathan asks.

I try not to laugh. Don't want him to have to play doctor again.

'You wanna take the wheel while I go to the bathroom?' Will says.

I look at Nathan and we both nod.

'Just keep it on this heading,' Will says, pointing at the compass that shows we're sailing due east. 'Back in a sec.'

Will ducks into the cabin and Nathan and I stand at the helm, each with a hand on the wheel, holding the *Fu Hao* steady.

We look at each other. Trade a smile. But mine fades when I see the glow of fire on his cheek.

My heart thuds in my chest and Nathan frowns.

Slowly, we turn towards what's ahead, see we're following a golden ladder across the sea, sailing for the orange sun that's rising in a pale stretch of blue sky.

ACKNOWLEDGMENTS

Clare and Ava—who are always there, fun and supportive, when I blink my way out of the study after a long writing session.

My dad Noel, for his unwavering support and interest. Thanks also for the love from David and Tina, Ray and Denzil, the Lanes and Joyce Thompsons.

Melanie Ostell—for being a great friend, constructive critic and agent extraordinaire. Cat McCredie—for unfailingly awesome copyedits over the whole trilogy. A&U—Anna McFarlane, Jennifer Dougherty, Rachael Donovan, Angela Namoi, Clare Keighery—for believing in me and Danby. Melanie Fedderson and Marika Jarv—for wonderful cover and interior page designs.

Lachie Huddy—for early reads and tireless work on yet another top book trailer. (Check it out at michaeladamswrites.com). Karen Richards—for avid reading and the use of a jaw-droppingly beautiful Port Macquarie lair: sorry for re-imagining it in such grim fashion! Jenny Kerr—for the tour of PMQ's Aussie Disposals and info on what Danby might find and use in such a cool store. Mic Looby and Rachel Carbonell—for fun times, ever-loving friendship and editorial ideas. Same goes for you Mr Chris Murray. Michelle Newton—Danby's got nothing on your bravery: thanks for being such an enthusiastic reader. Cheers also: Daz, Dan and Charlotte, POF and Leonie, Huw, Linda, Matt, Eva, Bec and Klete, and Angela. Shout out to you good things: Roddizzle D-Mu, G-Mo and Alicia, Cibot and Emma V., Chris and Hali, Emma H. and Richard, Oscar and Sha-Sha, Sabina, Sophie, Liz and Muuuultaaaari (just read 'em already, goddamnit). Erin T., Mel W., Vanessa L., Mick C. and Claire S.— your enthusiasm for the books helped me maintain mine. Matilda, Ella, Mia, Eric, Ivy—thanks for making our house a lot of fun. You can read these books when you're older.

Author mates Kirsten Krauth and Ellie Marney—knowing you're out there slogging the same slog is invaluable. YA blogging community—cheers for putting in so much effort to help our books get read and discussed.

Reader of The Last Trilogy—thanks for following Danby's journey. Hope you enjoyed it.